Dear Mystery Reader:

Computer wiz Anneke H̶a̶... ...lber's latest mystery set amid the comings and goings of coeds at the University of Michigan. Holtzer, winner of the St. Martin's Malice Domestic Contest, is known for spinning tales of intrigue in and around the usually pristine town of Ann Arbor, Michigan. Even if you're not a Midwesterner, you'll still want to check out *Black Diamond*, her latest and greatest DEAD LETTER title.

Here's the situation: University of Michigan student Claire Swann finds a corpse in her dorm room. Allegations are flying all over campus as folks feel the death has some connection to the Swann family's long history in the harsh Michigan lumber camps. With murder lurking around every corner, Anneke and Claire have got to find the killer before they end up taking a swan dive. Incorporating a modern crime with 19th century Michigan history, *Black Diamond* is a family saga that is Holtzer's most gripping work to date.

After you hit the books with Anneke, you'll be hungry for more of her University of Michigan adventures.

Yours in crime,

Joe Veltre
Associate Editor
St. Martin's Press DEAD LETTER Paperback Mysteries

BLACK
DIAMOND

A Mystery at the University of Michigan

SUSAN HOLTZER

St. Martin's Paperbacks

BLACK DIAMOND

Copyright © 1997 by Susan Holtzer.

Excerpt from *The Silly Season* © 1998 by Susan Holtzer.

Library of Congress Catalog Card Number: 97-16101

ISBN: 0-312-96629-6

Printed in the United States of America

St. Martin's Press hardcover edition/October 1997
St Martin's Paperbacks edition/September 1998

10 9 8 7 6 5 4 3 2 1

Although this novel is, of course, fiction, Cora Brown and John Smalley were real people, and many of the details of the Black Diamond legend are true, derived from the actual history of the old, lawless days of the northern Michigan logging frontier. While I have used literary license to invent much of their story, the basic events of August 25, 1895, are similarly drawn from historical fact.

On the other hand, the twentieth-century characters in this novel are all entirely fictional, and no resemblance of any kind is intended to any real persons, living or dead.

Maybe, like they say, no one can teach you how to write; but they can sure teach you how to be a writer. This book is dedicated to the people who taught me: Ruth Cavin; Vicky Bijur; and especially Janet Dawson, without whom I would quite simply have sunk without a trace.

BLACK
DIAMOND

ONE

By the time Zoe and Clare arrived, the argument, like the weather outside, was in full flood. Zoe stood dripping in the entrance hall wondering what the hell she was doing here.

There were two men and two women in the big, over-furnished living room. Zoe, who was given to making snap judgments about people even though she knew she shouldn't, liked both of the men and disliked both of the women at once, possibly because it was the women who were doing the arguing, faced off on opposite ends of a big Persian rug like opposing gunslingers. They argued almost comfortably, like old enemies, as much from habit as from animosity. It was clear that they disliked each other, but they seemed so accustomed to both the dislike and the argument, that the ex-change was stylized somehow, a choreography of antipathy.

"Helena, you can't be serious." The petite, dark-haired woman in the camel-colored skirt and matching cashmere sweater spoke didactically. "What would Clare, of all people, do with sixty-five pieces of Spode dinnerware?"

"What's that supposed to mean, Olivia?" The woman called Helena was one of those faded blondes who might have been a pretty girl once. She could be an attractive woman, Zoe thought, if she weren't still trying to be a pretty girl. Her soft, puffy body, encased in a too-tight dress of an unbecoming bright blue, made an unfortunate contrast to Olivia's sleek sophistication. Once upon a time, Zoe guessed, somebody must have told her that blue brought out the color of her eyes. But now her eyes were pale and surrounded by pads of flesh, and a coating of thick pink lipstick did nothing to soften her tight, discontented mouth. "Are you saying they're too good for Clare?"

"All I'm saying," Olivia replied, "is that the Spode is far too elaborate for Clare's . . . lifestyle." She spread her hands. "Now, if you think she'd want the Franciscan . . ."

"In other words, you want the Spode for yourself," Helena accused her angrily.

"No, Helena," Olivia said loftily. "But you want it for *your-self.*"

Clare had better have meant it when she said this would only take a few minutes, Zoe thought. If I wanted a good old knockdown family squabble, I could've gone to my cousin Sheila's wedding. Although it wasn't as if she hadn't expected it, even though Clare had insisted otherwise. After all, splitting up an inheritance, even if everyone was well intentioned, couldn't help but bring out the worst in people. And she was already pretty sure that *well intentioned* wasn't the term she'd apply to this crowd.

Clare had explained it in the car on the way over, after Zoe had come upon her standing in the doorway of the dorm, staring out at the downpour with an expression of mixed frustration and anxiety.

Clare Swann was a small, dumpy girl dressed in normal East Quad grunge—blue jeans, dark blue sweater over white

T-shirt, and olive-drab parka. But for Clare, grunge seemed more a default choice than a fashion statement. Her brown hair hung long and limp down her back, and her brown eyes were half-hidden behind defiantly ugly glasses with black plastic rims. Zoe knew her only casually, but this morning she'd been relieved to come across her.

"Oh, good, I'm glad I caught up with you," Zoe greeted her. "Can I borrow your notes for American lit?" Like all *Michigan Daily* staffers, Zoe missed more classes than she attended, and was constantly dependent on the kindness of other students.

"Sure, I guess," Clare replied grumpily. "Hey." She turned to face Zoe. "Don't you have a car this week?"

"Yeah. My mother's in D.C. on a lobbying junket, so I've got hers for a few days." Knowing what was coming, Zoe accepted the inevitable, figuring a quick ride was a fair exchange for the best notes in the class. "Where do you need to go?"

"It's . . . kind of complicated." Clare was uncharacteristically hesitant. "Look, were you planning to go to class this morning?"

"For a change, yes."

"Well, would you mind driving me somewhere and hanging around for a little while? Then we could go on to class together."

Oh jeez, what've I gotten myself into? Zoe wondered. But there was an undercurrent of entreaty in Clare's voice, and she knew the favor hadn't been asked lightly.

"Sure," she said cheerfully, her mother having taught her that a favor done grudgingly was worse than no favor at all.

"Thanks," Clare said gruffly.

"No biggie." Zoe rummaged in her bookbag for keys, pulled the hood of her slicker tightly around her head, and dashed with Clare across the street to the small white Buick.

When they were inside the car, she asked, "Where exactly are we going?"

"It's my great-aunt Julia's house, way out on Geddes. She died last month, and this week they're dividing up all her stuff."

"Do you get to take whatever you want?" Zoe asked. "Cool."

"Well, not exactly. See, she had no children of her own, so she left everything to her three nephews—my father and his two brothers. Since my father's dead, I get his share."

"Wow. So you're an heiress."

"Yes." There was a note of harsh satisfaction in Clare's voice, and after a moment she laughed. "It sounds real Jamesian, doesn't it? But y'know something? James was right—money matters. Anyway," she went on as if changing the subject, "most of the stuff'll be sold and the money divided, but today we're all supposed to go through the house and take any of the things we want. Then their value will be deducted from our shares. There's another house up north, too, that they're going to go through this weekend, but I've already told them I don't want anything from there."

"What're you going to take today?" Envious visions of emerald brooches and diamond necklaces went spinning through Zoe's mind.

"Nothing." Clare spoke sharply. "Wait'll you see this place—the whole house is crammed with this awful old crap that makes me feel like a refugee from the Castle of Otranto. But I still have to be there; it's just, like, a formality. Besides, if I'm not there, my dear mother will probably try to land me with a silver tea service or something."

"Isn't there even any jewelry you want?" Zoe asked, disappointed.

"Nah. The jewelry's just as ugly as everything else. There's even a pin made from some dead person's hair. Besides, even if there were something good, I'd still rather have the cash."

"Yeah, I guess that would be more practical." Zoe gave up her visions of glittering gems and concentrated on steering her mother's Buick through the rain-drenched streets. As usual, spring in Ann Arbor meant the monsoon season; so far, it had rained every day for the entire month of April.

Now she stood uncomfortably in her wet slicker, waiting for Clare to make some sort of move. Only Clare didn't seem anxious to get involved either; she lingered in the doorway, and Zoe of necessity remained next to her, examining the room.

Big it might be, but it still managed to feel claustrophobic, even under its twelve-foot ceilings. No one had bothered to open the dark green velvet drapes, and the elaborate chandelier overhead lighted only the center of the room, leaving most of it in gloomy shadow. No one had bothered to turn on the heat, either, and everything felt damp and chilly. Dank, Zoe thought; that was the word.

It was also one of those overstuffed rooms that old people seemed to like, and Clare hadn't been kidding about the stuff in it. The room was crammed full of the ugliest furniture Zoe had ever seen. There was wood tortured into repulsive shapes, there was upholstery in dark, mottled prints, there was wallpaper with enormous flowers crawling toward the ceiling—what it looked like most was a stage set for a road-company *Rocky Horror Picture Show*.

The two women were arguing toward a crescendo, and they still hadn't even bothered to say hello to Clare. It was one of the men—the older one, in a dark business suit and conventional striped tie—who finally acknowledged Clare's existence.

"Come on in, Clare." He motioned impatiently at her. "They're arguing about your choice, after all."

The two women swiveled toward the doorway. "Yes, for

heaven's sake stop *hovering*, Clare," Helena said. "And why haven't you hung up your coat? You're dripping all over Julia's floors."

"Shouldn't you introduce us to your friend, Clare?" Olivia asked.

"Clare, you're practically standing in a puddle," Helena complained.

"Oh, Christ," Clare muttered. She snatched Zoe's coat from her hands and turned toward the coat rack next to the door. It was one of those big oak things with a hinged seat beneath a beveled mirror surrounded by coat hooks. All the hooks were already filled. Clare, holding her own coat in one hand and Zoe's in the other, hesitated.

"Clare? Introductions, please?" Olivia said.

"Okay, okay." Clare turned awkwardly, still looking at the coat rack, and Zoe's slicker slipped from her grasp and landed on the polished floor in a puddle.

Helena made a *tsk!* of annoyance and darted forward to pick it up. "Honestly, Clare!" She rolled her eyes upward. "Why are you always so clumsy?"

"Clare, for heaven's sake, will you *please* introduce your friend," Olivia said with exaggerated patience.

Zoe wanted to protest this verbal whipsawing, but she couldn't figure out any way to do it. It was the younger man who finally interrupted.

"Come on, you two, cut the kid some slack." Grad student, Zoe categorized him immediately, taking in the blue jeans and faded Crash Worship T-shirt, the dark blond hair falling over his forehead, and the air of self-confidence just short of arrogance. "Hi." He took three steps forward, grabbed both coats and dropped them on the seat of the coat rack. Then he grinned and held out his hand to Zoe. "I'm Patrick Swann, Clare's cousin. This is her mother, Helena Swann," he indicated the faded blonde with a sweep of his other hand, "and this is her uncle Dwight and aunt Olivia." He moved closer to Zoe, his back to the others, and gave her a broad wink. "And you are . . . ?"

"Zoe Kaplan." With everyone's eyes on her, she didn't dare return his wink, but she grinned with what she hoped was a conspiratorial air. The looks on the faces of both women asked, as clearly as words: What is she doing here? "I live across the hall from Clare in East Quad. We have a class together at ten, and since it's pouring out and Clare doesn't have a car, I offered to drive her over here and hang around till she's done."

Clearly it hadn't occurred to anyone in her own family to call and offer her a ride. "Ouch," Patrick said, looking legitimately guilty. "I guess we all just forgot about you. Sorry, Clare."

"It doesn't matter." Clare's voice was sullen. "I managed."

"Honestly, Clare, if you'd only *called*," Olivia said, "of course we'd have given you a ride."

"And after all, this is strictly family business," Helena said.

"I can wait out in the car," Zoe interjected sweetly. "It's not *too* cold out."

"Don't be silly," Dwight said shortly. "There's nothing secret going on. Let's get on with this, shall we? Clare, you don't want those damn dishes, do you?"

"God, no." She screwed up her face.

"Yes, she *does*," Helena insisted. She darted over to a huge, heavily carved breakfront and yanked open one of the leaded glass doors. "They're beautiful," she said triumphantly, holding up a large plate entirely encrusted with multicolored flowers.

"They're ugly as shit," Clare said flatly, "and I wouldn't have them if they came with a genie and three wishes."

"Don't be offensive, Clare," Olivia said sharply. "Helena, I don't know why you can't do something about your daughter's language."

"Clare, why do you have to be so hateful?" Helena asked

tearfully. Her face seemed to droop. "You know I only want what's best for you, and you're so . . . well, you know how you are."

"No, mother. Tell me—how am I?"

"Stop it!" Dwight roared. Helena flinched, but Clare only glared at him. "If you people can possibly forego the pleasures of argumentation for just a *little* while, I'd like to get this done and get out of here. Helena, why don't we find out what they cost before you squabble about this any further."

"What do you mean, cost?" Helena challenged. "They're part of the estate, aren't they? Clare can take anything she wants."

"Yes, she can." Dwight sighed. "But, as I've already explained, the value of everything she selects is deducted from her share of the total estate."

"Well, but not the retail value," Helena protested stubbornly.

"The appraisal will be based on fair market value," Dwight said. "That's why I asked Michael Rappoport to be here. Why don't we get his valuation before we go any further?"

Zoe hadn't realized there was another person in the room. She stared at the figure that stepped forward out of the shadowy corner, and only after several seconds did she become aware that her mouth was hanging open.

The man was tall and slim and dark and elegant and absolutely gorgeous. He wore a black suit with a black silk shirt, a diamond-encrusted wristwatch, and a large antique gold pin shaped like a spray of leaves on the lapel of his jacket. He was, Zoe concluded, either the most secure man she'd ever seen, or gay. She prayed for the former.

"Holy shit," she mouthed under her breath.

"Damn. I knew once you saw him you'd never look at me again," Patrick whispered in her ear. Zoe snorted with suppressed laughter, but she couldn't take her eyes off the other man, who had moved to the breakfront and was examining the ugly dishes with every appearance of appreciation.

"Mm-hmm. Yes. Spode, approximately 1887," he murmured, more or less to himself. "Service for eight. Not absolutely spectacular, but very nice. Estimate . . . three thousand, four hundred."

"Dollars?" Clare blurted.

"Dollars." Rappoport nodded politely.

"So you see," Dwight said, "Clare would actually be paying more than three thousand dollars for those dishes. May I assume," he turned to Clare, "that you don't want them at that price?"

"You got that right," she snapped. "I don't want them at any price."

"I didn't think so," Dwight said. "And neither," he said pointedly to Olivia, "do I."

"Good heavens, of course not." Olivia looked at him as if he'd lost his mind. "We already have the Wedgwood, Dwight."

"All right, then," Dwight said. "Now, Clare, is there anything here you really do want?"

"Julia's pearl teardrop earrings," Helena said at once, sounding sulky. "They'll look wonderful on her."

"Helena, for heaven's sake, let the girl speak for herself," Dwight said. "Clare, is there anything *you* want?"

"I guess I wouldn't mind the earrings." She sounded like the words were being dragged out of her.

"Michael?" Dwight said.

The gorgeous man consulted a sheet of paper. "Six hundred fifty."

"Oh, shit, that's too much," Clare protested.

"Clare, I've asked you to control your language," Olivia said frostily. "We'd rather not hear that kind of thing in Julia's house."

"Julia's house," Clare muttered. "A lot you ever knew about Julia." She turned to Rappoport. "Are you sure they're worth that much?"

"They're worth it. Put them on," he ordered, and when she had slipped the wires into her ears he stood for a moment with his head tilted, looking at her appraisingly. "Yes, very nice."

"You'd look beautiful in them," Helena said, "if you'd just do something with your hair." She stared at Clare with an expression of dissatisfaction. "And those clothes. Honestly, Clare."

"Yes, I know, Mother. I'm a great trial to you. But I guess I'll take the earrings anyway, even if I can't live up to them."

TWO

"All right then. Now, what about the rest of this stuff?" Dwight's voice was brisk with the customary male relief over avoiding a scene.

"I'd like the gold bracelet," Olivia said, picking it up from the dining table. "How much is the appraisal on it?" she asked Rappoport.

"I have it listed at three fifty," he said. He had returned quietly to the darkened corner, where he consulted a sheaf of papers lying on a marble-topped table. "It's approximately 1875."

"Fine." Olivia clicked the bracelet onto her wrist and wandered over to the window, pulling the heavy drape aside to look out at the soaking rain.

"My father asked me to get him the desk," Patrick said.

"The rolltop?" Dwight looked stricken.

"Yeah. Is that a problem?"

"In a way," Dwight said ruefully. "I wanted that myself." He shrugged. "Never mind. There's another one in the Missaukee house. I'll get that when we go up there on Sunday. I assume Christopher doesn't want it as well?" His voice was mildly acidic.

"He told me he didn't want anything from up there," Patrick said. "I'm not even going to bother going with you."

"Fine. Now, does anyone want anything else?" Dwight asked the group at large.

"I wanted the books, remember," Patrick said.

"That's right. Well, that's a question mark, I'm afraid." Dwight ran one hand through his thinning brown hair.

"What do you mean?" Patrick asked sharply.

"Well, Julia's will specified that all her papers should go to the Bentley," Dwight replied. "In fact, there's a curator in the den right now boxing everything up."

"Not the books, he isn't," Patrick snapped. "The word 'papers' doesn't include books, Dwight. I'd better go stop him." Before Dwight could reply, Patrick disappeared through a door in a far corner of the room.

I wonder what's in the papers that would interest the Bentley, Zoe thought. The University of Michigan's Bentley Historical Library was a repository of documents dealing with Michigan history; there might be a *Daily* story in it somewhere. Not for her, of course; she was a sportswriter, not a feature writer. But she made a mental note to pass it on to the features editor.

Dwight again ran his hand through his hair distractedly. "The Bentley could lay claim to the books," he said. "They could even sue."

"Oh, for heaven's sake, Dwight." Olivia swung away from the window. "The University of Michigan is hardly going to sue a high-profile alumnus over a batch of moldy books."

"It's not a problem, Mr. Swann." The voice from the doorway was low and throaty, the sort of sexy voice Zoe wished she had. But when she turned toward it, she saw a small woman of indeterminate age in indeterminate Ann Arbor clothes—blue jeans, nondescript shirt, denim jacket, black running shoes. "We don't consider the books to be part of Ms. Vanderlaan's bequest."

"Oh. Well, good." Dwight looked relieved. "How are you coming, Ms. Pryor?"

"I've got nearly all of it packed up. It's a terrific collection." The woman's face shone. "And I'm really looking forward to seeing what else is in the house up north."

"I wouldn't expect much," Dwight warned her. "I think Julia . . . oh, good." He turned at the sound of the doorbell. "That must be John Singleton."

Sheesh, what now? Zoe looked at her watch. It was already pushing nine-thirty, and she hated to miss a class for something like this—she missed enough of them because of the *Daily*. Besides, it was nearly finals. She glanced toward Clare, but the other girl was facing the door, with a look of fierce expectation on her face.

"John, come on in." Dwight stepped forward to shake hands with the newcomer, a short, pudgy man of middle age in a conventional business suit similar to Dwight's own. The man stood still for a moment, the focus of all their eyes. There was an air of expectancy in the big room, a kind of suppressed excitement at odds with the wholly ordinary appearance of John Singleton.

"Have you got the numbers?" Olivia asked.

"Yes, I've got them." Singleton, for some reason, didn't look happy.

"Well?" Helena prodded.

Singleton didn't seem in a hurry to respond. He walked over to the table behind the sofa, cleared a space for his briefcase, set it down, opened it, and withdrew a sheet of paper. He looked at the paper, cleared his throat, looked up at the assembled gathering.

"For heaven's sake, John, get on with it," Olivia snapped tensely.

"Yes. Well." He sighed, cleared his throat again. "As you know, our bank was Mrs. Vanderlaan's trustee for more than thirty years. I have here an accounting of her estate, as requested by the executor, Dwight Swann." He nodded toward Dwight. "The cash value of the estate of Julia Swann Vanderlaan, including bank accounts, bonds, and other fiduciary holdings, and excluding real and personal property and other properties otherwise provided for, is twenty-three thousand, four hundred sixty-two dollars and seventeen cents."

"What? *How* much?" Olivia sounded stunned.

"A little over twenty-three thousand dollars." Singleton shoved the sheet of paper back into his briefcase and turned to Dwight. "I'm sorry."

"But that's impossible," Olivia said angrily.

"I'm sorry. Believe me, I'm as sorry as you are." Dwight's grim expression emphasized his words. "But that's all there is."

"But that's only . . . what? A little over seventy-five hundred dollars apiece." Zoe, trying to work out the math in her head, was impressed with Olivia's instant calculation.

"But she was rich!" Helena's voice shook. "I mean, she was putting Clare through school—tuition, room and board, everything. How could she do that if she only had a few thousand dollars?"

"She probably spent it all before she died," Patrick suggested. "Good for her."

"That's easy for you to say." Olivia shot him a glance full of loathing.

"It's not like you and Dwight need the money," Patrick replied with a shrug. His eyes narrowed suddenly. "Or do you?"

"Don't be absurd," Olivia replied sharply, but Zoe thought she detected an uneasy note in the woman's voice.

"Besides, what about Clare?" Helena's face was blotchy with what Zoe thought was fear. "There isn't even enough for Clare to finish school."

"With the sale of the house, there will be," Dwight reassured her. "She's only got one year to go, and if the sale is held up, Christopher or I will advance her tuition money."

"Even so, what about afterward?" Helena's hands were tight fists at her sides. "I mean, Clare is . . . who's going to look after her? How will she manage?" Her voice shook. "No husband, and even if she does finish school, I mean, a degree in English . . ."

"You're forgetting the French and the Japanese, Mother," Clare interrupted. "I can actually be useless in *three* languages." She spoke caustically, but Zoe thought she looked sick; her face was pale, and there was something immobile and expressionless in it that Zoe found disturbing.

"She *was* rich, Dwight," Olivia was insisting. "You know she was. What happened to it all?" She whirled on Singleton. "Where is the rest of it?"

"Is that it? Did you do something with Julia's money?" Helena flung the accusation at the banker, her face contorted.

"Helena. Olivia. Stop it." Dwight's expression was grim. "I apologize, John. I should have warned them."

"You knew about this?" Olivia asked, her eyes glittering dangerously.

Dwight shrugged and spread his hands. "I knew it wasn't going to be a great deal. I went over all of Julia's holdings myself."

"What about her safe-deposit box?" Helena demanded.

"It was opened, as required by law," Singleton replied pointedly, "in the presence of Dwight Swann as executor, myself representing the bank, and a representative of the Internal Revenue Service."

"And I assume it didn't contain a mysterious key to an unknown chest?" Patrick said with a grin. "Or a hand-drawn map? You know—walk eighteen paces from the big rock, turn right, walk twenty-three paces, and dig under the dead elm tree?"

Nobody laughed. "No," Singleton said, as if the question had been entirely serious. "It contained only what you would expect—insurance policies, car title, things like that."

"Helena, you're welcome to hire your own accountant to do an independent audit," Dwight said tiredly.

"Oh, sure," Helena muttered. She lowered herself onto the sofa and stared at the floor, her rage apparently turned to despair.

"So this is it?" Olivia looked around the crowded room.

"I'm afraid so," Dwight replied. "Of course, the house is worth about two hundred fifty thousand, and the contents should bring a good price at auction. But otherwise . . . yes, I'm afraid this is it." He turned to the banker. "Thank you, John."

Singleton looked around the room, and his eyes lighted on Clare. "You are Clare Swann?" he asked.

"Yes." She looked surprised and a little wary.

"Good." Singleton reached into his briefcase once more and extracted a large, flat object. "I have the Black Diamond box for you."

"The what?"

"The Black Diamond box," he repeated impatiently. He thrust the object at her. It was about the size and shape of a laptop computer, covered in some sort of reedy material woven into a diamond pattern. It took Zoe a minute to recognize the material as porcupine quills.

"What is it?" Clare asked.

"But surely . . ." He peered at her. "You mean Julia never told you about it?"

"No, but . . ." Clare's brown eyes seemed to blaze, but she

held out her hands for the box slowly, almost hesitantly. "What's in it?" she asked.

Singleton shook his own head in turn. "I have no idea."

"Oh, Clare, how nice!" Helena, her expression unpleasantly eager, stood up quickly and reached for the box, but Singleton yanked it away.

"This is for Clare Swann."

"But . . . oh, well, of course." Helena made a sound that Zoe thought was intended to be girlish laughter, but emerged as a kind of whimper. "Go ahead, Clare. Open it."

Clare took the box from Singleton's hand but only stood and stared at it, licking her lips.

"Yes, Clare, please do open it." Olivia spoke with poisonous sweetness. "Let us all see what sort of windfall dear Aunt Julia left just for you."

Under the gaze of seven pairs of eyes—angry, suspicious, greedy, impatient—Clare fumbled with the latch of the box. There were *tsks* of annoyance. Zoe, too, felt her curiosity stretched to the breaking point. She held her breath as Clare lifted the lid, her imagination filled once more with visions of glittering gems.

"Oh." Clare's voice was curiously flat, her expression even more rigid than before as she stared into the open box.

"Clare? What is it?" Helena craned over Singleton's shoulder.

"It's just . . . I guess they're old letters. And photographs, things like that." Clare stirred the contents of the box with a forefinger, the sick look back on her face. "It's just a batch of old papers."

Zoe could almost feel the whoosh of air as held breaths were released, and the electric tension in the room collapsed like a punctured basketball.

"How peculiar," Olivia said softly. "But then Julia always was a trifle *odd*." The others all seemed to shrug and turn away; only Patrick, Zoe noted, maintained an air of interest.

"But what *is* it?" Clare addressed Singleton, who shook his head.

"I told you, I have no idea." He was shoving papers back into his briefcase as though anxious to leave, which Zoe imagined he was—probably as much as she was. "I assumed you'd know—Mrs. Vanderlaan told me you'd be expecting it."

Once again seven pairs of eyes swiveled suspiciously. "But I wasn't." Clare shook her head. "I didn't know anything about it."

"Well, probably she was going to talk to you about it and never got around to it." Singleton closed his briefcase with an audible snap. "And now, if you will excuse me . . ." With a brief nod, he strode to the door and out into the rain. The Swann family watched him go, silent and deflated.

It was Helena who broke the silence. "What about those papers, Clare? Maybe there's something valuable about them. Let me look at them."

"No," she said quickly, taking a step backward. "They're just old family things, mementos, stuff like that."

"You can't be sure." Helena wasn't giving up without a struggle. "Let me look through them." She reached for the box again.

"I *can* read, Mother. Believe me, if there's anything valuable in here, I want to find it a lot more than you do."

"All right. I can see you don't want me to look at them." Helena's voice was a martyred whine. "I just don't know why you have to be so *difficult* all the time."

"Oh, shit, what's the use?" Clare turned her back on the others. "Let's go, Zoe."

THREE

• • • • • •

"Wow." Zoe peeled rubber down the driveway, seeking as much distance from the house as quickly as she could manage. She was half-afraid that someone would come charging outside after them. "That wasn't more than semi-brutal." Zoe kept her tone light.

"Yeah. The dysfunctional family circus, that's us."

"Well, one thing you learn in a dorm is that all families are a little weird."

"I suppose." Clare sounded tired. "Aunt Julia was okay, though. You could really talk to her." She stared down at the box on her lap.

The sky overhead was black with thunderclouds, and dripping trees overhung the narrow road. Zoe flicked on her headlights. "She never told you anything about that box?" She turned the Buick onto Geddes, keeping the main part of her attention on the rain-slick streets.

"No, never. I suppose she just never got around to it. I mean, she didn't know she was going to die."

"I thought she was real old."

"Well, yeah, she was in her sixties or something. But she was perfectly healthy."

"How'd she die?" Zoe asked curiously.

"Auto accident. She hit a patch of ice on Twenty-three coming back from Lansing after speaking at a public hearing of the State Historical Commission. The state police said she was doing eighty-five at the time."

"Not bad for an old broad," Zoe said respectfully.

"I think she'd have been more upset about totalling the car than about dying. She loved that car."

"What'd she have?" Zoe was always interested in people's cars.

"A first edition fifty-seven Thunderbird. She was the original owner," Clare said with a note of pride in her voice.

"You must have been pretty close for her to be laying out Michigan tuition and room and board for you."

"I thought we were." Clare sounded near tears. "She was the only one . . . ah, shit."

"If she felt that way, you'd think she'd at least leave a small trust fund to make sure you could finish school." Zoe took her eyes briefly off the wet road for a glance at the box. "So maybe there really is something valuable in there."

"Nah, that's too stupid." Clare shook her head. "I mean, Julia had a sense of humor, but she'd never do a stupid stunt like that."

"Then what *is* the story with the box, do you think? I mean, she did want you to have it. And there *is* supposed to be more money around than they found in her bank accounts and stuff."

"That's true." Clare leaned back against the car's headrest, her gaze on the ceiling. "Look," she said finally, "how bad do you want to go to that class?"

"*Moi?*" Zoe laughed. "When have I ever been anxious to go to class?" She swung the car left instead of right on Forest. Aunt Julia had sure known what she was doing, getting Clare into the dorm and away from that god-awful family. And that being the case, Zoe refused to believe she'd have left the girl high and dry when she died.

"Y'know," she said thoughtfully as she circled East Quad in search of a parking space, "it's not really Jamesian. It's more like Dickens, y'know? Like you're this secret heiress, only nobody knows it, including you. Only, in Dickens there'd be some bad guy who knew all about it and was trying to steal your inheritance."

"How about a TV movie?" Clare retorted. "Then someone would know about it and would be trying to kill me for it."

"Well, either way," Zoe said, zipping the Buick into a parking space seconds ahead of an angry Honda, "the first step is solving the Riddle of the Black Box."

East Quad is one of the oldest of the Michigan dorms, a huge, rambling pile of brick and concrete and oak fronting directly onto the sidewalk of East University Avenue. It is flanked by pizza mills, copy shops, drugstores, and the usual commercial slurb that surrounds any campus area. It is also only half a block from the Diag. Not for East Quaddies an idyllic expanse of lawn or woods or lake; not for them, either, the mile-long trek to classes through icy winters or sodden springs that residents of the more scenic dorms enjoyed. Zoe, who could take trees or leave them, figured she definitely had the better of the deal.

East Quad also boasts another unique amenity absent in the newer, more "cost-efficient" dorms—single rooms. At the January semester break, Zoe had miraculously scored one of them, to the vast relief of both herself and her former roommate. Paula had wanted a confidante, a best friend, a soulmate. Zoe, whose every free moment was spent at the *Daily*, simply wanted a place to crash between stories or classes.

Clare's room was also a single. Zoe dropped her coat and bookbag on the floor and plopped down next to them on the blue-and-white striped cotton rug that was nearly the only ornamentation in the room. There was something almost monastic about its plain beige curtains, neatly arranged books, and the single poster on the wall, a sepia-toned print of a Rembrandt etching.

"Okay, haul it out and let's see what you've inherited," Zoe said impatiently.

"Okay." Clare hung her wet coat carefully on a hook over the door before sitting down opposite Zoe on the rug and placing the porcupine-quill box between them. She opened the box and withdrew a piece of paper at random. "Here—this one's an old photograph of two women from about the eighteen-nineties. And here." She pulled out another piece of paper. "An old map of Missaukee County."

"A map? Let me see." Zoe reached for the map eagerly.

"No, there's no big 'X marks the spot.'"

"But why would she have a map of Missaukee County?" Zoe examined the map, reluctant to relinquish her treasure-map fantasy.

"Because that's where our family is from." Clare shrugged. "We still have the old house up there."

"Oh, that's right. Well, what else is there?" Zoe asked stubbornly.

"Look, why don't we sort through everything first, put things into categories and then see what we have?" Clare suggested. Zoe grumbled—her instinct was always to dive into things headfirst—but had to agree that the proposal made sense.

Fifteen minutes later they had four neat piles between them. The piles were neat because Clare had straightened each one as she went along. The contents of the box really did seem to be, as Clare had conjectured, just a collection of keepsakes.

"So much for the fortune," Clare said gloomily. "There isn't even a year's tuition here."

"No, I suppose not." Zoe glared at the piles; the stuff sure didn't look like anyone's idea of secret treasure.

The first pile contained what they'd classified as "printed matter." Besides the Missaukee County map, there was a Michigan League Life Member card, dated 1942 and made out in the name of Julia Louise Swann. There were three photographs—one of two women standing stiffly next to each other, one of the same two women in front of a large Victorian house, and a third of an old wooden building. There was an old land deed, for the purchase of property in Lake Township, Missaukee County by "Walter Swann and Henrietta Marbury Swann, his wife." There were two newspaper clippings, one from the August 23, 1895 *Grand Rapids Herald* detailing a daring train robbery, and the other announcing the birth of Cornal Arthur Swann on May 23, 1896 in Detroit.

The second pile was handwritten materials. These included about half a dozen old letters, an unsigned picture postcard of a large public building, postmarked Grand Rapids and bearing the message "I got here all rite, will see you in a few months," and a handwritten recipe for Huckleberry Fool.

And finally, occupying pride of place in the center of the rug, was the pitifully small collection identified as "valuables"—two ladies' gold wedding rings, unmatched, and money—three old twenty-dollar bills, an 1881 half dollar, four old dimes, and a single gold ten-dollar coin.

After a moment, Zoe reached into the first pile, extracted the three brownish photographs, and moved them to the pile in the center.

"What are you doing?" Clare asked.

"Sometimes old photographs are valuable."

"Only if they're of someone important, I think."

"Well, it's worth checking. And y'know, the box itself could be valuable." Porcupine-quill boxes weren't uncommon in Michigan, but this one was far larger than most, and the pattern of dark-colored diamonds was beautifully woven.

"Not the kind of valuable we're looking for." Clare shook her head decisively. "Quill boxes are collectible, but they're not that big a deal."

"Still, you ought to have it appraised also," Zoe insisted. "This one is pretty special." She swept the small pile of semi-treasures into the box and snapped the lid shut. "Now, what about the letters and stuff?"

"What about them? Oh, come on, Zoe." She snorted. "You don't really think there's going to be some sort of clue to a secret treasure, do you?"

"Of course not." Although she still harbored the sneaking hope they'd find exactly that, she poured disdain into her voice. "But maybe there's something about the letters themselves that's valuable."

"I doubt it."

"Well, at least they might tell you why your aunt left you this mess in the first place," Zoe persisted. Without waiting for Clare to reply, she plucked one of the letters off the stack and unfolded it carefully. Clare, with a shrug, did the same.

The paper was thin and brittle. It had been folded in half, and it cracked slightly when Zoe unfolded it. "Oh, jeez." She glared at the lines of beautiful, precise handwriting, elegant and curlicued and very, very tiny, crammed onto both sides of the paper with hardly any space at all between words or lines. The ink was badly faded. And if all that weren't enough, the paper was so thin that the writing on the reverse was faintly visible behind the words she was trying to read.

". . . 'express my feelings' . . ." Zoe read aloud. ". . . 'pot trivet' . . . no, 'pot trinket' . . . oh, shit." She broke off. "I can't make out the words. Here—this says 'you may quail at the depth'—no, 'you may guess'—oh, crap." She slapped the letter down on the rug in front of her and rocked back on her tailbone. "This isn't going to get us anywhere."

"No." Clare set her letter down. "I suppose someone at the Bentley might be able to work it out, but I don't know why they'd bother."

"Besides," Zoe said, "if your aunt Julia had wanted these to go to the Bentley she'd have included them in the rest of her papers."

"That's true." Clare looked thoughtful. "I wonder why she didn't. Well," she said with a shrug, "I haven't got time for this now. I need to get to the library."

"There is one other thing we could try," Zoe suggested. "How about if we Xerox the letters?"

"What good would that do?"

"We'd get a darker print, and the stuff on the back probably wouldn't show through. It should come out clearer than the originals, at least."

"That's not a bad idea," Clare said grudgingly.

"Come on, we've gone to this much trouble already," Zoe cajoled. "Let's give it one more shot."

"What the hell, why not." Clare stood and gathered up the letters.

"And not that crummy machine in the lounge, either." Zoe jumped to her feet and grabbed her slicker. "We'll take it to the place on Forest."

The place on Forest, barely a month before finals, had been a freaking circus—undergraduates copying chunks out of library books, grad students copying dissertation proposals, faculty copying last-minute lecture notes, locals copying whatever it was that locals copied. It was nearly lunchtime when Zoe and Clare finally tumbled back into East Quad and trotted up the dark back staircase to Clare's room. Zoe hopped back and forth impatiently as Clare inserted her key into the lock.

"That's funny." Clare stopped with her hand on the door-knob.

"What is?"

"It isn't locked."

"That's not good." Zoe knew at least three people whose rooms had been ripped off. "You'd better be more careful."

"But I am." Clare took a step backward and stared at the door as if it had suddenly become an entry to the twilight zone. "I know I locked it when we left."

"Yeah, that's right, you did. I remember seeing you do it." Clare wasn't the type to leave her room unlocked anyway. "Shit." Zoe shook her head. "Well, cross your fingers and open it."

Clare nodded, turned the knob, and pushed the door open gingerly with an outstretched forefinger. Then she made a weird noise, like a teakettle with something stuck in its spout. Zoe craned over her shoulder to see into the room.

"Holy shit."

The room had been trashed. Totally. Closet, desk, and bureau had been emptied of their contents, which were strewn ankle-deep across the small space: a blizzard of clothes and papers and food and books and pieces of small appliances and towels and makeup and computer disks. The mattress had been pulled from the bed, and it listed against the dresser, which lay on its side under the window. Curtains and curtain rod had been yanked down, the brackets pulled out of the wall. The Rembrandt print had been pulled from the wall and torn out of its frame, adding a layer of broken glass to the general carnage.

None of which was the focus of Zoe's attention. Instead, she stared at the man in the center of the chaos. He looked about sixty years old. He wore cheap and none-too-clean khaki pants and a plaid shirt. His hair was long, gray, and greasy, and his face was shadowed by a three- or four-day stubble.

He was very, very dead.

He lay with his head thrown back against the upturned desk chair, so that Zoe could see the great, ugly gash in his neck. There was blood everywhere, great gouts of it pooling on and under and around Clare's belongings. Mostly under and around, actually; Zoe realized suddenly that a lot of the stuff thrown around the room was on top of the dead guy.

Clare was still making that weird noise. Zoe grabbed her by the shoulders and shook her, none too gently.

"Hey." She shook harder. "Hey, Clare, get a grip." Clare's black eyes snapped into focus. Zoe jerked her head at the bloody figure. "You have any idea who he is?"

"Any idea . . . ?" Clare giggled; the question seemed to strike her as uproariously funny. "Oh, yes, I have an idea." She choked on giggles, an ugly sound. "I have an *idea*," she said harshly, "that he's my father."

Oh, jeez, she was really wacked out. "Clare, come on, bite the bullet for shit's sake. Your father's dead, remember?"

"N-no." Clare shook her head rapidly back and forth. Her gaze was fixed on the bloody corpse. "No, see that's the thing. He isn't. Only—" she laughed loudly once again "—now he really is. Now he really is. He really . . ."

"Come on." Zoe grabbed the other girl and jerked her toward the door, hard, backing them both out into the hall. She snapped the latch and slammed Clare's door shut. Two steps took them across the hall to Zoe's own room, where she breathed a sigh of relief when she finally got Clare inside.

"Here, sit down." She swept a sweater and two notebooks off her desk chair, and Clare obediently did as she was told. Thank God for that, anyway. Zoe unearthed the telephone from beneath a pile of bluebooks, and dragged the phone book out from behind the computer. She crossed her fingers and dialed.

"Lieutenant Karl Genesko, please," she said to the dispatcher. "Please tell him it's Zoe Kaplan, and that it's a double-digit emergency."

She thanked three or four gods that he was there, described the scene in Clare's room, and promised to stay where she was. Then she hung up and looked at Clare. The girl was still sitting where she'd been put, her face a blank, white and still and somehow not all there. It occurred to Zoe that maybe she should call someone to help. Clare's mother? Shit, no; Zoe discarded the idea immediately. The Resident Advisor? She didn't think it was such a good idea to alert the dorm authorities until the cops got there. She thought about her own mother with a gust of affection that surprised her. Unfortunately Berniece Kaplan, Activist Mom—who could manage a petition drive with one hand and a fund-raiser with the other, and who could have handled this situation and three or four more like it without blinking an eye—was five hundred miles away.

Finally Zoe picked up the phone and dialed again.

"Anneke? Thank God you're there. It's Zoe. Look, could you by any chance come over to East Quad? Yeah, see, I've got a kind of a situation here."

FOUR

· · · · · ·

The voice was young and female, and for half a second Anneke thought . . .

"Oh, Zoe. Sorry, I thought you were my daughter Emma."

"Something wrong?" Zoe must have picked up the disappointment in her voice.

"No, not really." Anneke sighed. "Never mind. You said something about a situation?"

"Yeah. If that's the right word for a bloody corpse and a freaked-out dormmate."

"A what?" Anneke listened with horror as Zoe outlined the situation in quick, terse sentences.

"The cops are on their way," she said finally, her voice tight with anxiety, "but I don't know what to do about Clare."

"Zoe, if she's really disturbed, the police will have people who can help." Anneke tried to soothe her.

"No, she doesn't need that kind of help. At least, I don't think she does. It's just . . . I'm not real big on maternal skills, you know? I was hoping you could come over and help."

"Oh, Zoe." Anneke swallowed the bitter words on the tip of her tongue. "That's not a good idea. Unless she's from out of state, you really need to call her own mother."

"No. Not an option." Zoe's response was absolute and somehow grim. "Trust me on that one, please."

"Zoe . . ."

"Anneke, please?" There was urgent appeal in the girl's voice. Anneke reminded herself that, despite the wide difference in their ages, Zoe was a good friend who didn't often ask a favor. Well, what the hell? If her current relationship with her own daughter was a disaster, maybe she could store up karma by helping someone else's.

"All right. I'm on my way." She hung up the phone and looked longingly at her computer screen. Ever since that last, bitter conversation with Emma she'd done what she'd always done in times of emotional stress—escaped into her work, into the cool logic of algorithms. On the screen, soothing lines of code beckoned, her latest attempt at bringing her long-planned game to life. With a sigh, she saved her work, started a backup, and picked up her briefcase.

She locked her private office and stepped across the wood-paneled hall of the Nickels Arcade, through the old oak door that used to read A/H, INC., COMPUTER SOLUTIONS. Now the shiny gilt letters on the frosted glass panel said HAAGEN/SCHEEDE, INC. Inside the big main office, Ken Scheede, once a student intern and now her new partner, was sitting cross-legged on the floor surrounded by electronic flotsam.

"If we ever buy another motherboard from Selmon, I quit," he said.

Despite her concern for Zoe and her friend, Ken's young, cheerful Howdy Doody face made her smile. "You can't quit," she reminded him. "You're a partner now, remember?"

"Well, then I'll sue." He scrambled to his feet, knees poking through worn jeans. "You leaving?"

"Yes. I've got a personal errand. I may be gone most of the

afternoon. Is there anything I need to know before I leave?"

Carol Rosenthal, now the senior of Haagen/Scheede's all-student staff, looked up from her terminal, knocked her mouse onto the floor, and hit her head on the desktop as she bent to retrieve it. "What about that search request?" she asked.

"Oh, right. Marisol Electric called a little while ago," Ken said to Anneke. "They want us to do an Internet search for all Web sites dealing with building construction. They want to contact all of them and ask them to link in the Marisol site." His blue eyes were bright.

"Hmm. That's a pretty clever idea," she said. "But it would be a whole new direction for us. We're set up for programming and installation, you know, not Internet research." She smiled at Ken's eager face. "I guess I don't have to ask what you think. Who would you put on it? Calvin?"

"Uh-uh. He's busy doing graphics for that Antique Co-op Web site. He's turning out to be pretty good at graphics, by the way. I thought Max could do this one."

"Okay, I'm game. So long as they know we probably can't get to it until after finals."

"Sure." Ken wrinkled his snub nose at the nearly empty office. The one downside of hiring only part-time student programmers was the necessities of the academic schedule.

From her office in the Arcade to East Quad was only five blocks, but Anneke took one look at the downpour outside the arch and headed for her car. As she steered the black Firebird down the ramp of the Maynard parking structure, she wondered what Zoe had gotten herself into.

It was odd, at the age of fifty, to number a nineteen-year-old undergraduate among your best friends, but Anneke realized it was true. At least it meant her trouble with Emma wasn't simply a generation problem. Not that she'd ever thought it was—the reasons were both simpler and more complex than that. Dismally she peered through the windshield at the sheeting rain and mentally replayed her last telephone conversation with her daughter, nearly a month ago.

"You're *marrying* him?"

"Yes, in the fall." Anneke had utterly failed to recognize the anger behind Emma's shock. "And then we'll probably have a quick honeymoon in San Francisco, right near you."

"You must be joking." This time there was no mistaking the ugliness in her tone.

"Emma? I thought . . . I mean, you've known about Karl and me for months."

"Yeah, sure. I knew you were screwing the guy." The contempt in Emma's voice crackled down the phone line. "But I figured that was just recreation. I never thought you'd try to present me with a dumb jock *cop* for a stepfather." She endowed the word "cop" with loathing. "What's the matter, were all the ski instructors taken?"

That was when Anneke had gently replaced the receiver, knowing that if she said a single word in response the damage would have been irreparable.

The worst of it was that Emma's reaction had been so unexpected. She'd known about Anneke's involvement with Karl Genesko almost from the beginning, of course— Anneke had made sure both her daughters did. And, she realized now, each girl had reacted entirely in character.

Rachel, busy in Boulder with her husband and small daughter, had asked merely: "Is this one a good guy?" And when assured that Karl was a very good guy indeed, had said, with every evidence of satisfaction, "Well, it's about time."

Emma's first words, on the other hand, had been: "A cop? And a *football* player?" giving it the sort of intonation with which one usually pronounces the word "cockroach." But her next words were: "Oh well. I guess you have a right to enjoy yourself." And she'd gone on to talk about her new jewelry designs, the weather in Santa Cruz, and the latest outrage of California's notorious right-wing governor.

They did each react characteristically, Anneke saw now, as she circled the East Quad block in search of a parking space. Rachel thought automatically in terms of relationship, Emma in terms of sex. We totally misunderstood each other, Anneke admitted. If I'd realized what Emma had been thinking, I could have . . . well, what? She saw a flash of red taillight at the curb and gunned the Firebird forward to the space about to open.

She'd been so preoccupied that she hadn't really noticed the activity around East Quad. Only when she trotted up the wide steps, umbrella held low over her head, did she register the police cars and emergency vehicles, and the uniformed police guarding the door.

"Sorry, ma'am." The fresh-faced young patrolman held up a hand as she approached, his black rain gear glistening with water. "Residents only."

"I'm Anneke Haagen." She shifted her grip on the umbrella and held out her hand. "I'm here to meet Lieutenant Genesko."

The patrolman looked at her hand for a minute in confusion, then accepted the handshake. Anneke took a step forward. "Second floor of Cooley House, I think he said?" She waited for the patrolman's nod before saying, "Thank you," and stepping past him into the building.

She let herself enjoy mild amusement as she headed up the stairs. Another case of experience and treachery overcoming youth and enthusiasm. But at the second-floor landing she was stopped by another uniform, a beefy middle-aged cop without a trace of either youth or enthusiasm on his face. Behind him, the narrow corridor seemed full of people.

"Sorry, ma'am, residents only." He ran the words together in a single bored slur.

"I'm expected." She slipped the now-furled umbrella into her briefcase. "Would you please tell Lieutenant Genesko that Anneke Haagen is here to see Zoe Kaplan." She mentally crossed her fingers. Zoe would have told Karl she'd called, but only if she'd gotten the chance.

The cop, still looking bored, turned and motioned, said something in an undertone to a man in jeans and a brown windbreaker, and in a moment Karl's huge form filled the hallway, dwarfing everyone else in view. Anneke felt warmth flow through her at the sight of him, coupled with a sense of relief when he nodded as though he'd been expecting her.

"Zoe told me she'd called you." He led her down the corridor, steering through knots of people who Anneke knew were police personnel.

"Is she all right?"

"Oh, *Zoe's* fine." Karl looked briefly amused. "I doubt she'd come unstuck at a nuclear blast. It's the other girl."

"Zoe told me it was her father who was killed. And in her own dorm room—no wonder she's in shock." They had made their way nearly halfway down the corridor, to where the crush of people was thickest. To the left, the door to Zoe's room was shut. Across the hall to the right, an open doorway was clogged with police functionaries. Anneke kept her face turned firmly to the left. "Have you called the girl's mother?" she asked.

"Not yet. That's one of the problems. She gets very disturbed when we mention her mother. And Zoe," he added pointedly, "is backing her up."

"Yes. She said the same thing to me." Anneke gazed at the closed door. "Does she say why?"

"Only that it would 'make things worse.' " He put verbal quotation marks around the phrase.

"I think," Anneke said slowly, "that I'd be inclined to take Zoe's word for that."

"By and large, I suppose I would, too," Karl agreed. "But the victim is the girl's father."

He didn't need to explain further. The mother wasn't a

side issue, but an integral part of the investigation. The police would *have* to call her, and fairly quickly.

"All right," she said at last. "Let me talk to them." She knocked firmly on the closed door. "Zoe? It's Anneke."

"Thank God." The door was flung open, and Zoe all but pulled Anneke into the room before slamming it shut behind her.

The room was a shambles, but Anneke knew that had nothing to do with the murder—Zoe's room was always a shambles. She looked past the clothes-strewn bed and the paper-strewn desk to the room's other occupant, sitting ramrod-straight in the only available chair.

Anneke's first thought was that she didn't appear to be all that upset. Then she noticed the twitch at the corner of the wide mouth, and the unblinking stare of brown eyes large behind ugly, black-framed glasses. She was expressionless and rigid, like a robot that had shut down.

"Anneke, this is Clare Swann. Clare, Anneke Haagen, a friend of mine." Zoe made the introductions with quick impatience, but then stopped. She seemed unsure of where to go from there.

"How do you do." Clare spoke formally, in a clear, emotionless voice. Zoe looked at Anneke and shrugged in a silent *See?*

"I'm sorry about your trouble." Anneke stepped forward, hand outstretched, meeting Clare's formality with her own. The girl accepted the handshake in polite response, and Anneke held the small, surprisingly delicate fingers for a moment longer than necessary. Cold, but not damp or clammy; and her eyes looked perfectly normal. Anyway, if she were in clinical shock Karl would have known it and called a doctor. As far as Anneke could tell, Clare had simply . . . shut down.

A sudden, fugitive memory struck her—Emma, age twelve, coming home from school one day with that same blank, strained look, refusing to say what had happened, refusing even to admit anything *had* happened. It had taken Anneke three days to discover that Emma had accidentally killed a squirrel with her bicycle, and two more to get her to talk about it.

In this case, of course, she already knew what had happened. She shoved a pile of newspapers aside and sat down on the bed.

"All right, Clare." She dropped into the calm, authoritative tone she always thought of as the mother-voice. "Tell me about it, please."

"My father was killed." Clare's voice remained polite and self-contained.

"And?"

"And?" Clare repeated, confused.

"What else?" Anneke prompted. She was forcing the girl to think, forcing her to get her mind working again. She hoped.

"They're all going to be really, really pissed off at me again."

"Why?" Anneke asked quietly, keeping surprise out of her voice. In the back of her mind, she made a mental note of the word "again."

"Because he's supposed to be dead. I mean, he *was* supposed to be dead. When I was little. Only he wasn't, he just left. I was seven years old. I was *always* a difficult kid." She stared at Anneke. "And now, of course, not only will everyone know that my mother was an abandoned wife, they'll also know that my whole family's been lying about it all these years." She blinked rapidly and seemed to focus on Anneke for the first time. "They're really going to be furious at me."

"Why at you?"

"Because." Clare looked at her in surprise. "I mean, he was killed in my room."

"Did you—" Anneke choked back the question. That was

for the police to ask, preferably in the presence of an attorney.

"No, she didn't." It was Zoe who answered the unasked question. "She's been with me all morning, every minute of it," she said firmly.

"All right, then." Anneke looked at Clare carefully. There was a bit of color in her face, and her eyes had lost their blank, unfocused look. "Clare, do you think you're ready to talk to the police now?"

"Yeah, I guess. Can you and Zoe stay?"

"I don't know, but there's no harm in asking."

FIVE

• • • • • •

"This is all just preliminary, Ms. Swann, so don't worry too much about it." Karl had arrived bearing a tray which held a Thermos and four thick china dorm mugs, and the process of providing everyone with coffee had taken the edge off his entrance. After a quick look around the cramped, messy room he had taken up a position near the door; still, his sheer size seemed to fill the room, and Clare darted a nervous glance at him over her mug.

"N-no," she stuttered. "I mean, yes. Okay."

"Don't worry," Zoe said cheerfully. "He's big, but he's a teddy bear."

"Zoe, if you please. I assume," Karl said to Clare, "that you would like Ms. Kaplan and Ms. Haagen to remain?"

"Yeah," Clare muttered. "I guess."

"All right. Please note, Zoe," he directed a stern look her way, "that everything said in here—and I mean *everything*— is entirely off the record."

"Not an issue," Zoe said immediately. "I'm not covering this anyway."

"Good. Now, Ms. Swann, why don't you start by telling me when you last saw your father."

"I guess . . . when I was seven."

"Seven years old?" Karl asked sharply.

"I think so." Clare furrowed her brow. "It might have been when I was eight."

"If you haven't seen him for more than ten years, how did you recognize him so quickly?"

"He's my father. Granted, he wasn't much of one, but what the hell." Clare reached for her purse on the desk behind her, and drew out her wallet. "Here's his picture."

Karl took the wallet and examined the picture carefully. "I see. I'd like to make a copy of this, if I may. We'll return it to you when we're done." He slipped the photograph out of its plastic sleeve before handing Clare's wallet back to her.

"Can I see it?" Zoe asked. "Just in case I might have seen him around," she explained. She took the small picture from his hand and peered at it. Anneke, sitting next to her on the unmade bed, looked over her shoulder curiously. A beautiful, youthful-looking man with delicate features and a shock of light brown hair stood in front of a huge rock laughing into the camera; one hand held something aloft that Anneke thought might be some kind of musical instrument. "He looks kind of like a younger brother of the guy across the hall." She returned the picture to Karl.

"What about other kinds of contact?" Karl asked Clare. "Have you had any letters or telephone calls from him since you last saw him?"

"Not a chance." Clare shrugged. "He didn't want anything to do with me."

"What a schmuck," Zoe muttered under her breath.

"All right," Karl continued, "do you have any idea why he came to see you today?"

"No, I don't." For the first time, Clare's voice wobbled. "Maybe he . . . No. I don't know."

"You've known all along, I take it, that your father was living?"

"I guess so. At least, I knew he didn't die when I was seven, like we pretended."

"But you had no idea where he was, or what he was doing."

"No."

"Do you know if your mother knew? Did she have any contact with him?"

"No. She wouldn't have. She hated him. She would never even talk about him."

"All right. Let me ask you about something else," Karl said. "Do you have any idea what someone might have been searching for in your room?"

"Searching for?" Clare's eyes widened. "No. What could anyone . . ."

"Searching!" Zoe interrupted, slapping her forehead with the heel of her hand. "Oh, shit, of course! I thought the room'd just been trashed, but it wasn't, was it?"

"No," Karl replied. "It was fairly methodically, if messily, searched. Do *you* have any idea what the object of the search was?"

"Maybe." Zoe bounced up and down on the bed. "Did you happen to find a Black Diamond box in that mess?"

"A what?"

"A box. About yea big." Zoe measured air with her hands. "Covered with porcupine quills woven into a diamond-shaped pattern."

"I don't know if it's there or not yet," Karl replied. "The crime scene people have only begun working on the room. Why don't you tell me," he said to Zoe, "what was in this box and why you think someone might have wanted it."

"They wouldn't," Clare insisted. "Zoe, that's dumb."

"Just let me tell him, okay? He can make up his own mind." Zoe described the events of the morning quickly and economically. When she was finished, Karl stood thoughtfully for a few moments.

"Ms. Swann," he said at last, "when you went out to the copy shop, where did you put this box?"

"On my desk."

"In plain sight?"

"Yes. It was just sitting there."

"Shit," Zoe said. "So it couldn't've been the box itself they were searching for. But still," she continued stubbornly, "what if they were looking for the letters?" She scrabbled on the floor for her bookbag and withdrew a large plastic zipper-locked bag within which Anneke could see a mass of papers. "Maybe there's something in the letters that someone didn't want anyone to know. Like some sort of family secret or something?"

"Zoe, my father *was* the family secret," Clare blurted, with the first trace of humor Anneke had seen her display.

"Yeah, well maybe, but there's still your aunt Julia's missing fortune."

"Oh, hell, there is no missing fortune," Clare said tiredly. "I expect she just spent it all, like Patrick said."

"May I have the letters, please, Zoe?" Karl held out his hand. Zoe unzipped the plastic bag and withdrew a collection of stiff, yellowed pages, but Karl shook his head. "I'd better have the copies as well."

"No." Clare snatched at the bag. "Those are mine."

"We'll return them when we're finished," Karl promised.

"Yes, but Clare's got a better shot at figuring them out than some clueless cop," Zoe pointed out, then looked mildly abashed. "No offense."

"None taken," Karl replied, smiling slightly.

"She's right, though," Clare said. "Aunt Julia wanted me to

have them, so if there is anything important in them, she must have thought I'd understand it."

"All right, you have a point," Karl conceded. "But I don't want to leave copies unsecured. What I will do is keep the copies in my office, and you can have access to them there."

"I have a better idea." Zoe turned to Anneke. "How about keeping the copies in *your* office? Anneke's got a computer business in the Arcade," she explained to Clare. "You have a safe, don't you? That way," she said to Karl, "we won't have to keep bothering you, and no one else will know where they are."

"And Anneke could help you decipher them," Karl said thoughtfully. "Well?" he asked Anneke.

"Yes of course, if you think it's a good idea." She was both surprised and amused; Karl couldn't think the letters were really relevant to the murder if he were so casually willing to involve the two girls. And of course, the letters did sound interesting.

"Ms. Swann? Is that satisfactory?"

"It'll have to be, won't it?" Clare looked at Anneke with suspicion.

"Ms. Swann," Karl continued, "you say you knew nothing about this 'Black Diamond' box?"

"No, I didn't." Karl's question had been matter-of-fact, but Clare spoke as though denying an accusation.

"Did anyone else in your family know about it before today?"

"Not that I know of. Not that they said, anyway."

"All right. Who was there when you received the box this morning?"

"Well, my mother . . ."

"Her name, please?"

"Helena Swann. And my uncle, Dwight Swann, and his wife Olivia, and my cousin Patrick."

"And the banker himself," Karl reminded her. "Do you know his name?"

"Yes, it's John Singleton, from Mackinac State Bank."

"Don't forget the hunk," Zoe interjected.

"Who?" Karl asked.

"Some antique dealer who was doing the appraisal." Zoe grinned. "The most gorgeous stud I've ever seen."

"Michael?" Anneke blurted, and felt her face redden as Karl laughed.

"You know him?" Zoe demanded.

"If it's Michael Rappoport, then yes, I know him." Anneke grinned in her turn. "But don't get your hopes up."

"Shit, I knew it." Zoe threw herself back against the wall. "He's gay."

"No, he's perfectly straight." Anneke laughed at the eagerness on Zoe's face. "But, aside from the fact that he's more than twice your age, Michael runs like a rabbit at the slightest hint of strong emotion."

"He just hasn't met the right woman yet," Zoe grumbled, but to Anneke's relief the broad grin was still on her face. Michael was an old and valued friend, but, as he would be the first to admit, he was the worst relationship material imaginable.

"If you ladies are quite finished?" Karl asked with the hint of a smile.

"Not quite." Zoe leaned her head to one side, her eyes turned to the ceiling and a beatific expression on her face. She held the pose for a count of three. "Okay, now I'm finished."

Anneke broke up. She noted that Karl was holding back laughter, and that even Clare allowed herself a smile. Zoe wore an expression of bright self-satisfaction.

"Shall we move on, Ms. Kaplan?" Karl said finally.

"Oops." Zoe sat up straight and arranged her face into an

expression of solemnity. "When he starts calling me 'Ms. Kaplan'," she said to Clare, "I know I'm in trouble."

"That's enough, I think, Zoe," Karl said quietly, and the girl had the grace to look abashed.

"Sorry," she said, once more serious. "Didn't mean to get carried away."

"Now, Ms. Swann—" Karl stopped as the telephone shrilled. Zoe scrambled to her knees on the bed, reached over the headboard to the floor, and shoved papers aside until she unearthed the instrument. Then she stopped with her hand on the receiver and looked a question at Karl. When he nodded, she picked it up.

"Yeah," she said into the mouthpiece. Then: "No chance, sorry." She listened for a while, shaking her head continuously, then said: "Sorry, but I just can't. I'll explain later, but take my word for it. Faye, I said *no*." She slammed down the receiver and glared at them all impartially. "That was the *Daily*. The city editor wants me to cover the murder."

"Oh, shit, I forgot about the wonderful American free press." Clare made a face. "Well, I guess better you than most of the others."

"What? Are you nuts?" Zoe looked amazed. "No way."

Clare shook her head. "Sorry, I wasn't thinking." She seemed to have pulled herself together, Anneke noted with relief. "Seeing that . . . " Clare gestured in the general direction of the hall. "I guess it grossed you out, too."

"It's not that." Anneke thought Zoe looked guilty, probably because she *wasn't* upset. "I just can't cover a story that a friend's involved in, that's all. It'd just fuck things up."

"Not necessarily." Clare spoke slowly, staring down at the floor. "Look, from your side, you get an exclusive with the daughter of the victim. From my side, I know all that stuff—about my father and all that—is going to come out anyway. And at least if you write it, it'll be—I don't know—not sympathetic, maybe, but at least straightforward. But the big thing," she added, as if she'd just thought of it, "is that it's not like it's going to go away. I mean, all the papers are going to be covering it, and they're probably all going to be hassling me. If you do it for the *Daily*, I can just tell all the other reporters to bag it. That way, maybe they'll leave me alone."

A pretty good point, Anneke thought; she might actually save herself some grief this way. Zoe apparently thought so, too. Her mouth was tight, but she looked uncomfortable.

"The trouble is, I know *too* much," she muttered almost to herself. "For instance," she looked directly at Karl, "do I print anything about the Black Diamond box?"

"No," Karl replied at once. "You print the basic facts of the murder, you print background, and you print official police statements. That's all."

"I don't know if I can work this way," Zoe said, shaking her head. "Look." She turned to Clare. "Let me talk to the city editor. I'll write up today's story—just reporting the murder and the background, like he said—but then I'll have to see about the rest of it. Okay?"

"All right, yeah, I'll take what I can get." Clare shrugged ungraciously. "Thanks, I guess."

"Don't thank me yet," she said gloomily. "Any more questions?" she asked Karl.

"Just a few." He looked down at his notebook. "Dwight and Olivia Swann, Patrick Swann, Helena Swann, Michael Rappoport, and John Singleton. Are those all the people who were there when you received the box?"

"Yes," Clare said.

"The Bentley," Zoe said suddenly.

"What?"

"The woman from the Bentley who was going through Julia's papers. I didn't catch her name, but she was there, too."

"We'll check on her." Karl turned at a knock on the door. He opened it a few inches, engaged in a brief, muttered exchange with someone outside, then closed the door again.

"Ms. Swann?" He waited until he had the girl's full attention. "Your mother is here, and she's asking to see you."

"Oh, shit." Clare went white once again. "So you called my mother, you bastard."

"You *called* her?" Zoe, all her ebullience gone, glared at him with furious disgust. "You had *no right* to do that, it's an absolute violation of Clare's right to privacy and you know it! Clare's a legal adult. You can't drag her parents into this without her consent. And you didn't even have the decency to ask her before you. . . "

"Ms. Kaplan." Karl's voice, not a decibel louder than normal, whip-cracked through Zoe's tirade. The girl blinked at him, her face filled with anger, and with something else.

"I trusted you," she muttered.

"Zoe," Karl said quietly, "Helena Swann is the victim's wife." He waited until Zoe's expression changed, realization flowing in. "She is here because she is Gerald Swann's next of kin, not because she's Clare Swann's mother." He turned to Clare. "Ms. Swann, Zoe is quite correct. You're legally an adult, and you're not required in any way to see your mother. But you'll have to see her eventually," he added gently. "Whatever your concerns are, it might be better to get it over with now."

SIX

But before Clare had a chance to reply, sounds of commotion outside the door stopped her. Above the rumble of male voices, a woman shrilled: "You can't do that! She's my daughter!" Anneke saw Clare's whole body stiffen, her face turn blank and still.

"Oh, jeez," Zoe muttered.

"Ms. Swann." Karl remained quietly where he was, his back against the door, as if to guarantee Clare a barricade if she wanted one. "You don't need to see her if you'd rather not."

"But . . . " Clare's hands fluttered. "Oh, shit, I suppose . . ." She made a visible effort to compose herself. "Besides, it would only . . ." Her hands fluttered again, a complicated gesture that Anneke translated without difficulty to mean: I'll have to see her eventually. She wondered what on earth Clare's mother was like, to cause such a reaction.

"All right." Karl nodded, turned to open the door and said something to the uniformed policeman outside. Clare stood up and watched the door tensely, her back against the window.

"It's about time." A plump blond woman shoved her way roughly into the room, ignoring everyone but her daughter. "Oh, Clare." She wrapped her arms around the girl in a too-tight hug that made Clare wince. "Are you all right?" she demanded.

"Yeah, I'm okay." Clare twisted out of the hug.

"That terrible man! As if he hasn't done enough damage to this family. And what was he doing in your room?" She flung the question at Clare like an accusation.

"How the hell would I know?" Clare protested.

"You must know." The woman grasped Clare by the shoulders, her fingers tightening. "Oh, Clare, please don't lie to me—not about this. I can't help you if you don't tell me the truth."

"Excuse me." Karl stepped forward and laid a hand on her arm. "I take it you are Helena Swann?"

"Yes." She took a step backward and looked around, as if registering the other people in the room for the first time. "Who are you?"

"Lieutenant Karl Genesko, Ann Arbor police. And you are Helena Swann?"

"Police. Of course." Helena glared at Karl, ignoring his question. "I have something to say to you, too. How dare you question my child without my consent?"

"Mother, knock it off."

"Oh, Clare, *please* behave." Helena gave her daughter a beseeching glance before turning back to Karl. "There are laws protecting the rights of children, you know," she said to him angrily.

"Indeed there are, Ms. Swann," he replied quietly. "But your daughter is not a child; she's a twenty-year-old adult."

"Of course she's still a child," Helena snapped. "What did you tell him?" she demanded of Clare. "Never mind;

don't say another word until your uncle Dwight gets here."

"Uncle Dwight? What the hell did you call him for?"

"Who else would I call when you need a lawyer?" Helena sounded exasperated.

"Mother, I don't need a lawyer."

"Clare, even you should know better than that." She swiveled toward Karl once more. "Did you even warn her that she was a murder suspect?" she demanded.

"Mother, put a sock in it, will you?" Clare said wearily. "I am not a murder suspect."

"You *didn't* warn her, did you?" she said furiously. "Did you think because she's a child you could do anything you want?"

"Ms. Swann." Karl's calm voice overrode the woman's shrill voice. "I did not warn your daughter that she is a murder suspect, because as far as I know, she isn't." Helena started to interrupt, but Karl continued without giving her a chance. "Ms. Swann has been in the company of Ms. Kaplan—" he indicated Zoe with a glance "—continuously since before nine o'clock this morning."

Helena stared at him suspiciously, then swung on Zoe. "Is he telling the truth?" she demanded.

"He always does," Zoe said tightly.

"So Clare didn't do it?" Helena blurted.

"Apparently, she did not." Anneke heard the rigidly controlled distaste in Karl's voice, and hoped she had as much control over her own face. The notion that this woman automatically assumed her daughter had killed her father made her feel sick to her stomach.

"Well, then," Helena said uncomfortably. "Good. Come on, Clare, I'll take you home."

"Take me home? What do you mean?"

"Oh, Clare, please don't be difficult now, of all times. You must know you can't stay here. Sometimes I wonder what Julia could have been thinking anyway, encouraging you to live in a place like this." She looked at the pile of clothes under the desk and made a face. "Now you can live at home like a young girl should, with someone who'll take care of you."

"In your dreams," Clare snapped. "I'm staying here, thank you very much."

"Don't be silly, Clare. Of course you're coming home. You can't go back to your room, for heaven's sake." There was intense satisfaction in her voice.

"You can crash here with me," Zoe blurted.

"Can I?" Clare turned and stared at her.

"Sure. No problem," Zoe replied immediately.

"Here?" Helena looked around the small, messy room with an expression of utter revulsion. "You can't stay in this place."

"Yes, mother. In fact, I can. I can stay here, and study for exams, and finish classes. Remember, thanks to Aunt Julia I'm paid up for the rest of the semester. And there isn't a damn thing you or dear Uncle Dwight can do about it."

"Ms. Swann." Karl spoke to Helena quickly. "As Gerald Swann's next of kin, we need you to make a formal identification. And then I'll need to ask you some questions." He turned toward the open door, where Anneke saw a uniformed patrolman standing impassively. "If you'll just go along with Officer Marino, we'll try to get it all over with as quickly as possible."

Helena looked from Clare to Karl, started to speak, then nodded jerkily. With her lips tightly pressed together, she left the room.

"Now, Ms. Swann," Karl said to Clare when Helena was gone, "is there anything else you can add at the moment?"

"No." There were beads of perspiration on the girl's forehead. "I just . . . It doesn't make any sense."

"I know. Don't worry about it for the moment." There was a knock on the door. Karl opened it slightly, and Anneke heard a mutter of voices before the door opened fully.

"My God, this is a hell of a thing." The man who entered had a pleasant, undistinguished face that wore an expression of dismay mixed with caution. He shook drops of water off his black umbrella and set it carefully against the door before turning to Karl. "I'm Dwight Swann." He offered Karl a business card.

"Lieutenant Karl Genesko." Karl took the card and slipped it into his pocket. "You're Gerald Swann's brother?"

"Yes." Dwight Swann wiped his hand across his forehead. "What's happened? I got a hysterical call from my sister-in-law, but all she said was that Gerald had been killed."

"I'm sorry to have to tell you that your brother was murdered," Karl told him.

"Murdered! Are you sure? Sorry." He shook his head. "Stupid question. Can you tell me what happened, please?"

"All we can tell you so far is that he appears to have been stabbed to death in his daughter's dorm room."

"In Clare's room?" Dwight looked around for the first time, and when he saw Clare his lips tightened. "I see." He turned back to Karl. "I'm not a criminal attorney," he said, "but I'll arrange representation for her. In the meantime, Clare, do not answer any more questions."

"Isn't it a joy to have such a trusting and supportive family?" Clare asked the room at large. "Thanks a whole bunch for your touching faith in me, Uncle Dwight, but you're too late—I've already spilled my guts to the cops."

"Oh, Lord. I can't say I'm surprised. Never mind, Clare." Dwight turned to Karl, his face grim. "A confession under stress will never hold up, you know. Especially from a young girl devastated by the death of her father."

Clare laughed aloud, a harsh sound that made Anneke wince. Karl looked down at Dwight patiently. "Clare hasn't confessed, Mr. Swann. She isn't even a suspect. As I told your sister-in-law, Clare spent the entire morning in the company of a friend."

"Really?" Dwight sounded more surprised than relieved. "A friend?" That seemed to surprise him even more. "Well, good. But then . . ." He looked at Karl. "Who did kill my brother? Some vagrant who just wandered in here?"

"Your brother *was* the vagrant who wandered in here." Clare laughed again. "Sorry you couldn't pin it on me, Uncle Dwight. I know how convenient that would have been for the family." Sarcasm and bitterness poured from her voice.

"Don't be silly, Clare." Dwight dismissed his niece without a look. "I assume the coroner will take charge of the body," he said to Karl, who nodded briefly. "Good. Please keep me informed." He picked up his umbrella, but as he turned toward the door Karl stopped him.

"I'll need to speak to you, Mr. Swann. Would you please wait in the lounge at the end of the corridor? I won't be long."

"Now?" Dwight looked at him sharply. "I suppose you do have to question the family, don't you?" He made it sound like a mere formality. He must know that he and the rest of his family are suspects, Anneke thought, but he's chosen to pretend otherwise. "Unfortunately, I can't help you right at the moment," Dwight went on. "I'm due in court in half an hour." He withdrew a small leather-bound book from inside his jacket pocket and consulted its pages. "I can meet you in my office at five, if you like."

"Five o'clock will be fine," Karl said calmly, "but in my office, please."

"Yes, all right," Dwight replied after a brief hesitation. For the first time, he looked uneasy. "God, what a mess," he said once more, leaving the room without another word to Clare.

"Well, he didn't seem all that cut up about losing a brother, did he?" Clare said into the silence that followed Dwight's departure. "I wonder if everyone in the family is relieved that he's dead."

"Ms. Swann," Karl said, "I'm going to need you to do something distasteful, I'm afraid."

"What?" Clare looked at him tensely.

"Our crime scene people should be through with your room tonight. Tomorrow morning we'll need to ask you to go through your belongings and try to determine if anything is missing. It won't be pleasant, but it is necessary."

"All right," Clare agreed gruffly.

"I'll help out," Zoe volunteered.

"Yeah, okay. Thanks." Clare seemed to have trouble with gratitude. "And thanks for . . . you know." She jerked her head toward the door.

"No biggie," Zoe said, but Anneke thought the look on her face was one of uneasiness.

SEVEN

• • • • • •

The lounge was disgusting, sticky surfaces littered with empty Styrofoam cups and candy wrappers and bits of unidentifiable detritus. The whole dorm was disgusting, in fact. That girl's room—Helena Swann couldn't imagine what kind of mother would let her daughter live in such squalor.

Girls that age should be living at home, where they could be supervised, taken care of. Helena remembered what it had been like to be a girl that age. She wasn't about to let Clare make the same mistakes. In fact, she'd never have allowed Clare to live in this place at all if Julia hadn't insisted—made it a condition of paying Clare's way through Michigan.

Not that there was much point to a Michigan degree—certainly not for Clare, anyway. But there was no way to refuse Julia's offer, and anyway, Michigan had seemed the best place to find her the kind of husband she needed. Someone who could take care of her.

Helena loved Clare, but she didn't allow herself to be deluded by that love. She'd always admitted to herself that

Clare wasn't quite . . . well, she just wasn't quite, that's all. And after all, what could you expect, considering her father? Bloody Swanns. Helena tightened her lips unconsciously. Bloody geniuses, they thought they were. Well, everyone knew geniuses were all a little crazy; only, why did she have to go and marry the craziest of them?

Why had she married Gerald Swann, anyway? Helena couldn't remember anymore. Probably just hormones, she figured. Gerald had been so . . . intense, so exciting. Words seemed to explode from him, ideas filling him like strong drink, intoxicating both of them. Not that she'd understood half of what he talked about, of course; but then, she'd only been a nineteen-year-old clerk pushing papers around in the dean's office and thinking that there must be more to life than that. Like a fool, she'd thought that Gerald would give her that "more."

Why on earth, she wondered, had Gerald married her? Well, she'd been a pretty girl back then, pretty enough that the right clothes, and makeup and all that, didn't matter. Intelligence wouldn't have mattered, either; Gerald had probably enjoyed her uncritical adoration. In fact, just hormones on his side, too. Besides, she reminded herself, he'd already been crazy.

She wondered suddenly what he'd have thought of her now, when the right clothes, and makeup and all that, did matter. Not that she cared about her appearance in particular. At least, there wasn't much point in caring. She looked down at the blue dress, knowing it was all wrong for her but without having the least idea why that was so. Clothing was just another thing to cope with.

Clare didn't seem to care at all.

Clare had been a difficult child even before Gerald had gone out of his head. She was never pretty, not even as a baby; she'd been cranky and demanding, and then as she got older she just never seemed to care what people thought about her. She didn't even take her schoolwork seriously; she argued with her teachers even when she knew it would cost her a grade, she argued with the other kids, she argued, endlessly, with her mother.

What terrified Helena most was that Clare was her father's daughter.

"Ms. Swann?" Helena jerked her attention back to the dangerous present, looking up at the huge policeman who sat down behind a wobbly plastic table. Another man sat down beside him, holding a notebook on his lap. Helena tensed, feeling her hands tighten around the purse on her lap.

"Would you like some coffee?" Genesko asked.

"No, thank you." She tightened her lips, wishing he would just get on with it. Another thing to cope with. Helena felt her head begin to ache.

"All right." He inclined his head. "I just need to ask you some background questions, to get the best picture of Mr. Swann that I can." When she said nothing, he continued, "When did you see or speak to your husband last?"

"About twelve years ago." How odd, she thought, to hear the words "your husband" after all these years.

"What were the circumstances of your separation?"

"He left." She shrugged, letting the words hang.

"How long had you been married?"

"Nine years."

"Clare was seven at the time?"

"That's right."

"And you haven't seen him, or heard from him, even once in all that time?" The words, spoken in a perfectly neutral tone, had the force of an accusation.

"No! He walked out on us and never looked back, not even once. No visits, no letters, no phone calls, no birthday cards, nothing. He abandoned me, period. Is that what you want to hear?"

"In all that time," Genesko said calmly, "you never divorced him?"

"No," Helena said sullenly.

"Instead, you told people he was dead."

"Yes," she replied bitterly. "Call it wishful thinking." She hadn't meant to say that. She straightened in her chair and looked at him warily, but his face registered only a businesslike interest.

"Can you tell me, Ms. Swann," he asked gently, "why he left you and your daughter?"

"Because he was crazy!" Helena blurted. She glared at him, but his continuing expression of calm interest punctured her anger. "He *was* crazy," she dragged the words out painfully. "He was seeing a psychiatrist for a while, but it didn't do any good. He had these . . . brainstorms. And then finally, he just sort of went over the edge."

"I'm sorry. It must have been a very difficult time for you."

"A 'difficult time,' " she mocked. "A lot you know. Did you ever have a house filled with hundreds of rocks, that you weren't even allowed to clean because they were 'sacred'? Did you ever try to communicate with someone who invented his own language and insisted everyone around him speak it? Did you ever have to go drag someone out of a bar because he attacked the piano with wire cutters? And that doesn't even include things like the time he gave an entire class lecture in Iroquois, or the time he was thrown out of a faculty meeting for spiking the coffeepot with some sort of Indian drug."

She ran down finally, letting the anger drain away, anger she'd carefully kept alive, nurtured, for the last twelve years. The image of Gerald, brilliant, doomed, lunatic, was suddenly so unbearably vivid she felt her eyes burn. She blinked and glared at Genesko; she hadn't shed tears over the son of a bitch since he'd left, and she wasn't going to start now.

"What else do you want to know?" she demanded.

"What department was he in?" Genesko asked calmly.

"Anthropology. He was an assistant professor. He was denied tenure the year before he left. For obvious reasons."

"And do you have any idea where he went, or what he had been doing in the last twelve years?"

"No," she said shortly. "I figured he was in hell." And to her horror and disgust, she burst into tears.

EIGHT

· · · · · ·

Helena had gone. Dwight Swann had gone. Anneke had left, and Genesko was somewhere around the dorm doing cop things.

"What now?" Clare asked.

"I'm not sure." Now that the immediate crisis was over, or at least in abeyance, Zoe examined the other girl cautiously, wondering what she'd let herself in for. In truth, she'd only known Clare casually, she realized, the way she knew most people in the dorm; her close friendships were all with *Daily* people. She and Clare had one class together, had sat together in the dorm dining room occasionally, had chatted in the lounge about this and that. But today's events had shown her how superficial their acquaintance had been. Clare was too abrasive to be what you'd call cheerful company at the best of times; now, when she had a right to be uptight, there was no telling how much of a pain she was going to be.

"Well, what kinds of things do you need to know for your story?" To Zoe's relief, Clare seemed perfectly normal.

"Not much that I don't already have," Zoe said. "Are you sure you want to do this now?"

"Yeah, let's get it over with. Oh, wait."

"Trouble?" Zoe had a moment of renewed worry.

"Not really. It's just that I'd really like something to eat first."

"No problem," Zoe said. "In fact, I bet we can get the cops to provide us with room service."

She'd called the *Daily* to tell them that she'd do today's story, at least, not forgetting to let them know she had Clare Swann as an exclusive. When she dashed from the parking lot into the old brick building on Maynard Street, shedding water liberally over the slate floor, city editor Faye Leonard met her almost before she reached the top of the stairs.

"It's about time, Kaplan. What've you got?"

"Jeez, Faye, give me a break. At least let me dry off." She trotted into the cavernous city room and down the long aisle between battered oak cabinets until she reached the row of Macintosh terminals, with Faye at her heels. Snagging a vacant chair, she shrugged out of her slicker, settled herself at a terminal, and pulled her notebook out of her bookbag. "Okay." She flipped pages. "I've got information about the victim and his family. I've got statements from the police, plus I've arranged to get more from them later tonight. I've also got an interview with the victim's daughter, and some crap from the East Quad director—about what you'd expect." She wrinkled her nose.

"Okay, write up what you've got," Faye said. "I've got a couple of people working on sidebars you should talk to— Jan Wacker is doing a piece on dorm security, and Doug Billings is doing background on the Swann family, including a retrospective on Gerald Swann's crack-up and disappearance twelve years ago."

"Okay. Is Doug here?"

"In the library. Let me know when you've got something for me to look at." Faye left quickly, disappearing down the back stairs to the production room. Zoe powered up the Mac and opened a file to stake her claim to the machine. Then she trotted back down the length of the city room.

The library was a corner room lined with tiers of shelves holding bound volumes of past *Dailies*, filing cabinets of microfilm, two big oak tables, and the usual empty Coke cans, crumpled newspapers, pizza crusts, and random pieces of paper. Doug Billings, a short, perpetually grumpy junior with a narrow face dominated by a jutting nose, sat cross-legged on top of a table, paging through a huge, folio-sized bound volume. When Zoe entered he looked up, grunted, and returned his attention to the book.

"What's the story on the Swanns?" Zoe asked, unoffended.

He said nothing for a moment. Then he straightened up and stared out through the leaded glass windows at the pounding rain.

"Okay, here's what I've got so far. Walter Swann was a northern Michigan sawmill owner up in Missaukee County, back in the lumbering era. He died in 1895, but the family stayed up there until 1942, when Julia Swann enrolled at Michigan and subsequently married Henry Vanderlaan. Eventually her three nephews—her brother Neil's kids—all graduated from the U and stayed in Ann Arbor."

"Are there any Swanns still up in Missaukee?" Zoe asked.

"No. Brother and sister-in-law both deceased. Anyway," Doug went on, "the three boys were all apparently successful. Christopher, the eldest, turned out to be a financial genius, or a financial shark, depending on your viewpoint. He's one of the biggest venture capitalists in the midwest."

"*That* Christopher Swann?" Zoe gave a low whistle. "Damn, I should have made the connection. So Clare's family is really loaded, huh?"

"Well, Christopher is, at any rate." Doug looked sour.

"Now, Dwight Swann, the middle brother, got a UM law degree and landed with Carmichael, Stubbs and Swann—he made partner at the age of thirty."

"Hmm. Was he that good, or that lucky?"

"That well-connected. He brought most of brother Christopher's legal business with him, and that's a lot of billings."

"And the third brother?"

"Ah, yes. Now we come to the notorious Gerald Swann. The baby of the family." Doug nodded wisely. Then, instead of saying more, he turned the bound volume he'd been studying so that Zoe was staring at the front page.

It wasn't the lead story; that was given over to a graduate employees strike. Near the bottom of the page, in the anchor position, was a grainy photograph of the dead man, looking more like Clare's keepsake picture than the body on the dorm-room floor. He was standing behind a lectern, and his handsome face, even in the already yellowing newsprint, looked flushed and excited. Zoe checked the masthead for the date, which was February 17, 1985. The headline read: ANTHROPOLOGY PROF CLAIMS SHAMANIC POWERS.

"Jeez." Zoe whistled. She read through the rest of the story quickly. According to Gerald Swann, he had rediscovered a primitive technique of "mental enhancement" used by certain Native American tribes, which gave him the ability to "transcend linear reality." The technique, he insisted, was not only scientifically replicable, but financially valuable as well. The reporter, Zoe noted, had given the story a strong tongue-in-cheek slant.

"Holy shit." Zoe stared at the paper. "Talk about being a few bees short of a hive." No wonder the family was happier pretending he was dead. "What was he working on before he went off the rails?"

"Don't know. His dissertation was on transmission of healing techniques between primitive tribes. I have a feeling he must have tried every weirdo drug he came across. But I don't know what he moved on to after that."

"What've you got on Julia Swann Vanderlaan?" Zoe asked.

"Well, Henry Vanderlaan was in the history department. Julia herself was mostly involved in historic preservation. I know she was one of the founders of the State Preservation Alliance, which has been giving state politicians fits for the last ten years."

"Olivia Swann?"

"Dwight's wife?" He shuffled scraps of paper covered with illegible scrawls. "Nothing much. B.A. in English, on the League board, couple of kids—occupation housewife, as far as I can tell."

"One more—Patrick Swann. I think he's Christopher's son."

"Yeah, he is. Grad student in econ." Doug shook his head. "Must be hell to try to follow in those footsteps. If it were me, I think I'd become a plumber or something."

"Yeah, me, too," Zoe agreed. "Must be tough to be the latest wunderkind in that kind of high-octane family."

"Oh, I don't know," he contradicted. "I'm a second-generation faculty brat myself—grandfather in chemistry, father in zoology, mother in psych. Far as I can tell, they aren't any weirder than anyone else's family. For Ann Arbor, anyway." He grinned. "Besides, we don't know yet how I'm going to turn out."

"We don't know how I will, either." Zoe returned his grin. "And I come from a union family."

"Now that's weird." Doug turned back to his reading. "Anyway, that's what I have on the Swanns of Michigan so far."

"Thanks, Doug." She left him to his research and headed back to her terminal, stopping at the sports desk for a quick check of the assignment sheet taped to the tile surrounding the window. There wasn't much stuff going on this late in the year, and what there was went to juniors and seniors, not to nineteen-year-old sophomores. The spring football scrimmage belonged to the sports editor, of course, but maybe she could promote herself a sidebar feature that would at least get her on the field. She wrinkled her nose at the assignment sheet.

"Nothing there good enough for you, Kaplan?" Sports editor Gabriel Marcus, seated behind the sports desk, intercepted her look and smirked at her.

"That's because you take all the good stuff for yourself," she retorted.

"Damn right. Rank hath its privileges, and all that." He leaned back in his chair. "Anyway, you seem to've landed yourself a biggie on your own."

"I think it landed on me." She grimaced.

"I heard the victim's daughter's a friend of yours?" When she nodded, he said, "You sure you should be covering this?"

"I'm pretty sure I shouldn't be." She sank down on the oak bench under the bay window behind the desk, and Gabriel swiveled to face her.

"Then why are you?" he asked.

"Because she more or less begged me to."

"Not much of a reason," he said severely. "If a friend begged you *not* to cover a story, would you drop it?"

"Oh, come on. That's not the same thing, and you know it."

"Isn't it? Seems to me, in both cases you're letting someone else override your own journalistic judgment."

"Oh shit, Gabriel." She stood up abruptly. "Don't you ever get tired of being so fucking *right* all the time?"

"Not me. I figure it's a dirty job but somebody's got to do it."

She made a face at him and stalked back to her terminal, where she sat down and spread her notes out around her.

She'd write it up strictly as breaking news, then turn it over to city side. She riffled through her notes in disgust, uncomfortably aware that what she was chiefly disgusted with was herself.

NINE

Anneke knew Karl would be home late, which meant she might as well dig in for a long work session. But instead, after a quick lunch in a State Street sandwich shop, she found that the mermaid in Whitehart Station had Clare Swann's face, and General Porteus had unaccountably become Michael Rappoport. Swearing, she powered down. The hell with it; she might as well spend the rest of the day doing something frivolous, like wandering through Briarwood Mall. It might not be the most enthralling place in the world, but at least it would be bright. And dry.

She was driving out of Washington when she saw the Chihuly.

It occupied pride of place in the window of Artful Exchange, a small art resale shop. And even through the driving rain, even through the dark gloom and the streaming windshield, it sang aloud, an aria in glass.

She circled the block twice before she found a parking spot, grabbed her umbrella, and slogged to the shop. She pushed open the door with the sense of breathless anticipation she hadn't felt since her entire Art Deco collection—along with her house and everything she owned—had gone up in flames.

The small shop was bright with paintings and prints and high-quality crafts, but Anneke ignored them. She turned directly to the Chihuly and simply stood and gazed at it, drinking it in as though she could somehow absorb its essence into her soul.

She'd seen the works of Dale Chihuly before, of course, but only in museums or in extravagantly upmarket galleries. To see a piece by the world's premier artist in glass, here in a local resale shop, was astounding.

It was classic Chihuly, an installation of two irregular, bowl-shaped seaforms, like impossibly delicate sea anemones. It wasn't huge, of course; the main piece was perhaps eighteen inches across, in glowing and shifting tones of orange, the mouth of its opening rimmed in a narrow band of pure aquamarine. The smaller piece nestled inside it, echoing its color and form without in any way mimicking it. Looking at it was like looking into the heart of a living organism.

"Amazing, isn't it?" a voice murmured.

"Michael! I didn't see you." She turned toward Michael Rappoport, tearing her eyes from the Chihuly with difficulty. "Has Karl talked to you yet?"

"Karl? No. Was he supposed to?"

"Yes, I think so. About the murder."

"Murder?" Michael's cobalt-blue eyes widened. "What murder?"

"Oh, Lord, of course, you wouldn't know." She shook her head; the spell of the Chihuly was affecting her thought processes. "It's connected with an appraisal job you did this morning." Quickly she sketched the events in East Quad; when she was finished, Michael looked somber.

"Poor little misfit," he said.

"Misfit?"

"Clare Swann. She's like a . . . no, that's not it."

"What are you talking about?"

"I was going to say she was like an ant in a family of butterflies, but that doesn't really describe it." Michael pondered briefly. "Say instead that she's a parrot in a family of swans." He gave a brief, unamused smile at the aptness of the metaphor. "Both beautiful birds, but try to put them together and they'll tear each other to shreds. And unfortunately, in this case the swans have the numbers against her."

"So the poor parrot doesn't have a chance."

"Oh, it has one chance," Michael said grimly. "It can fly the hell out of there as fast as its bright little wings can carry it." His brilliant blue eyes were dark with memory. "But first it has to understand that it *is* a parrot. If it continues to believe that it's really a maladjusted swan, then it is, indeed, well and truly doomed."

He was talking about himself as much as Clare, Anneke understood. Michael's apparently complacent flamboyance hadn't come without cost; she knew he had barely spoken to his own mother in the years before she died.

"God, the things families do to each other." She shook her head in angry frustration. "Michael, will you call Karl? I know he'll want to talk to you."

"Yes, of course, as soon as I get home. Now," he said, "what about the Chihuly?"

"What about it?"

"You are going to buy it, aren't you?"

"Michael, don't be silly. I can't afford a Chihuly." But even as she spoke she was leaning forward to read the price tag. When she saw it she gulped. "Nineteen hundred dollars."

"Well, to start with, knock off ten percent—remember, it's on consignment, and I've never known a consignment contract that didn't allow the dealer to cut ten percent off the price."

"That's still over seventeen hundred."

"Which, as you well know, is an absolute steal for an original Chihuly, even a small one. When will you ever get another opportunity like this?"

"Michael, I can't," she protested. "With all the work we still have to do on the house, how can I justify such an insane extravagance?" She heard the plaintive note in her own voice, and realized she wasn't asking the question rhetorically but seriously—help me justify this mad purchase, she pleaded silently, yearning toward the glowing, living glass.

"Anneke," Michael said quietly, "when was the last time you wanted anything this badly? Or at all?"

He was right, of course. After the fire, she had discovered that the collector's passion, or whatever you wanted to call it, was gone. Oh, she could still appreciate beautiful things, but for a long time now, nothing had *moved* her. Until today.

"My God, I must be out of my mind. All right, yes, I'll buy the damn thing." She laughed aloud. "Find someone to take my money, quick, before I lose my nerve."

Karl arrived home shortly before eight o'clock, looking tired but not entirely dissatisfied.

"You look like you've made some progress," she said to him, standing in the wide hallway as he shed his raincoat.

"Possibly." He kissed her, then stepped back. "And you look like you just won a trip to the Super Bowl."

"Does it show?" She laughed. "Come look." She grabbed his hand and led him through the wide arched doorway into the living room.

It was a huge room, running the full length of the house from front to back. The furniture was almost entirely Karl's, of course—after the fire, she'd had nothing to contribute—but, after some hesitation, Anneke had begun to put something of herself into the room.

The long brown velvet sofa remained, as did most of Karl's fine antique wooden furniture. But the dark green drapes had been replaced by pale beige in a light, open weave; the Persian rugs were gone, in their place a huge, nearly room-sized sweep of beige Berber carpet; and instead of the dark wood coffee table, there was a long slab of glass in front of the sofa.

At the far end of the room, the Queen Anne dining table and chairs were still in place. But now, instead of the large ceramic bowl that had served as a centerpiece, the chandelier overhead glowed on pale, brilliant, shimmering orange glass.

Karl stood in the doorway and looked at it silently for a moment. Then he moved to the table and gazed down at the glass for a long time before turning back to Anneke.

"Amazing," he said at last. "I take it this didn't come from the supermarket with a half-off coupon?"

"Uh, not exactly. It's a Dale Chihuly. Let's just say I'd better be happy with my summer wardrobe, because I'm not going to be able to afford any new clothes for the foreseeable future."

He stepped back from the table and gazed at the Chihuly. "I wouldn't have thought," he said, "that it would look so good on this table."

"I know. That's one of the wonderful things about it." The round table, with its gracefully curved legs, seemed to embrace the delicate glass forms. "Michael always says that anything supremely beautiful is incapable of being wrong. Oh, by the way." She remembered suddenly. "Did he call you?"

"Yes, he did. Thanks for alerting him." He went to the antique sideboard and opened the upper doors. "Brandy?"

"Sherry, I think." When they were seated on the big sofa

with their drinks, she said, "You've made some progress on the case?"

"Possibly," he repeated his earlier cautious response. "We have an APB out for Patrick Swann."

"Patrick?" She was momentarily lost. "Which one is he?"

"Clare's cousin. He's the son of Christopher Swann."

"*The* Christopher Swann? Resident financial genius?" Anneke asked, surprised. "I didn't realize he was connected to this."

"Well, he himself isn't, at least not directly. Christopher and his wife are in Japan. We're still trying to get hold of them, in fact."

"Christopher Swann's son—hard to believe, somehow."

"Do you know Christopher?"

"Not to know, really, but I've met him a couple of times." Anneke leaned back, recalling a huge man—tall, broad-shouldered, big-bellied, with a shock of white hair and enough pure charm to light up Angell Hall. When Christopher Swann entered a room, everyone else seemed to fade into the woodwork. "Why on earth would Christopher's son kill his uncle?"

"I've no idea," Karl replied, sipping brandy.

"Then why the APB?"

"Two reasons. First, because we can't locate him. And second, because his fingerprints were found in Clare's room."

"Well, but she was his cousin. Mightn't he have visited her at some time?"

"He might have, but she says he didn't."

"Oh." She thought for a moment. "How old is Patrick?"

"Twenty-five. Why?" he asked curiously.

"So he was, what, thirteen when Gerald Swann disappeared?"

"About that." He waited for her to continue.

"It doesn't make sense," Anneke said slowly. "The other

family members had possible reasons to want Gerald dead, but Patrick? I mean, he wouldn't have cared about possible scandal, surely. And he was too young when Gerald left to have had any real history with him."

"Not necessarily." Karl's expression was sober. "I can think of a number of connections between an adult male and a thirteen-year-old boy that could result in murder."

"But. . . oh, God." As she absorbed the implication of his words, Anneke felt sick. "Sexual abuse, you mean? Do you know that for a fact?"

"Not at all. I'm not even conjecturing it; it's just one among several possibilities, that's all. It's equally possible that Gerald knew something about Patrick that the boy didn't want revealed. Or that Gerald had something Patrick wanted. Or half a dozen other motives we can't even guess at."

"In other words," she said rather acidly, "motive isn't your job."

"Given both physical evidence and flight, not really. At least, not at this stage of the investigation." His words were positive enough, but Anneke thought she heard an undercurrent of dissatisfaction in his voice.

"There's something about it you don't like, though, isn't there?" she asked.

"Not exactly." He pursed his lips. "Just some loose ends."

"Such as?"

"To begin with, there should have been more fingerprints." He took another sip of brandy and leaned back, thinking out loud. "Patrick's prints were on the door, on Clare's desk, and on the window frame, but nowhere else. Yet the room had been torn apart."

"Mm." Anneke considered the point. "I can think of scenarios to explain it, but they all depend on his making silly mistakes. Still," she went on, "most criminals do make stupid mistakes, don't they? Especially amateurs, and especially in an unplanned crime." She turned to look at him. "It was unplanned, wasn't it?"

"Probably. At least, that's what we're hypothesizing at the moment. Although," he added, "that's only because it doesn't seem to make sense as a premeditated murder, not because there's any evidence either way."

"No, it wouldn't make much sense as a planned murder, would it? Unless he set it up to throw suspicion on Clare?" she suggested. "He couldn't know she'd have an airtight alibi."

"Perhaps." He sounded dubious.

"Too convoluted?"

"I've no idea. Amateurs do get convoluted brainstorms like that occasionally." He sipped brandy, staring into space.

"What else?" she asked, knowing him.

"That porcupine-quill box," he said reluctantly. "The one Zoe described? It wasn't there."

"You're joking." Anneke sat up straight and stared at him. "You mean all this lost-treasure business is *real?*"

"I don't know." He threw up his hands, his expression halfway between grimace and grin. "In this town, I suppose anything's possible. But all it does is add another motive, not another suspect."

"I guess that's true. I take it," Anneke pursued a new train of thought, "that nobody saw any of the Swanns arrive at or leave the dorm?"

"Well, nobody noticed, at least. Two residents said they recalled seeing 'an old guy,' which from their descriptions seems to refer to Gerald. But if anyone did see Patrick, he'd just register as another student and they wouldn't notice him."

"But they probably would have noticed the older members of the family, wouldn't they? I can't imagine Clare's mother, for instance, passing through an undergraduate dorm unnoticed."

"Not necessarily." It was Karl's turn to play devil's advocate. "In the right clothes, with the right attitude, any one of them might have slipped in unnoticed."

"Do any of the others in the family besides Clare have alibis?"

"Not really, no. And none of them admits to having had any contact with Gerald since he left Ann Arbor, although Dwight did say he knew he'd been seen up north."

"Oh?"

"The family has a house in Missaukee County, and Dwight said he was in occasional touch with the sheriff up there. Apparently the sheriff mentioned seeing Gerald in the area once or twice."

"You said something about Patrick's fingerprints on the window," she recalled. "Could anyone have come in that way? No, of course not," she answered her own question. "It's on the second floor."

"Actually, that's not the problem," he said. "Clare's window opens out onto the roof of the lobby below."

"So anyone could have gotten in that way," Anneke said eagerly.

"No." He shook his head positively. "Remember the rain. There was hardly a trace of water under the window, no damp spots, nothing."

"Damn, that's right."

"Our best guess, in fact, is that he got in through the door and *left* through the window."

"Patrick, you mean." When he nodded, she said: "How did he get in? Wasn't the room locked?"

"We're not sure. There was no sign of forced entry, so we assume a key was used. Whether it was a duplicate of Clare's key, or one of the master keys, or an old key from a previous resident, we won't know until we catch up with him. But there are so many keys floating around any dorm that it's not hard to get into a room if you want to badly enough.

And by the way," he added, "Patrick was an RA in East Quad three years ago."

"Was he." It did seem to be falling together, Anneke thought, and wondered why she was discontented with the easy solution. "You're assuming," she said, "that Patrick got there first, and Gerald walked in on him?"

"As a working hypothesis, yes. Gerald's fingerprints were on the door but nowhere else."

"I wonder why," she pondered. "No, not why he was killed. Why was he *there*, after all these years?"

"Given what we know so far about Gerald Swann, I wouldn't even want to hazard a guess."

"What do you mean?"

"I mean that Gerald Swann was crazy." He smiled grimly at her quizzical expression. "It may not be politically correct, but 'crazy' is the best word I can come up with at the moment." He recounted the interview with Helena. "Once we get hold of Gerald's psychiatrist, we'll probably find a diagnosis of schizophrenia, possibly drug-induced. But for now, 'crazy' will have to cover it."

"That poor woman." Anneke tried to rearrange her attitude toward Helena, but found her sympathies still engaged by the daughter rather than the mother. "Poor Clare."

"Poor Gerald," Karl added.

"Yes. What a mess." She sighed. "Do you have any idea what he'd been doing since he disappeared?"

"Not precisely. We're assuming he was living somewhere up north, because of Dwight's report from the Missaukee County sheriff. And the label on his shirt is from a store in Petoskey. We've got a call in to the sheriff's office, but they haven't replied yet."

"He was in anthropology, wasn't he?" Anneke recalled. "He could have been involved in some sort of conservation group up there."

"From what I've gathered so far about Gerald Swann,"

Karl said, "he could equally have been trying to exhume Hiawatha."

"Wrong peninsula." Anneke laughed slightly. "Gitchie Gumee is Lake Superior, remember?"

"Oh, I remember." Karl sounded gloomy. "I'm just not sure Gerald would have."

TEN

· · · · · ·

The blue and white rug was gone. So were the mattress and sheets, and the majority of Clare's clothing, all of it blood-splattered or blood-soaked and removed by either the police or the dorm maintenance workers. With the furniture up-right and back in place, the floor scrubbed, and the curtain rod rehung, Clare's room looked more or less normal.

So did Clare, Zoe concluded; in fact, she looked almost too normal. She should have been more upset about the de-struction of her room, shouldn't she? Instead, she'd gone ahead with the straightening-up process with an icy calm that made Zoe nervous. She wondered if last night had helped at all.

The dorm had provided some semiofficial crisis counsel-ing, but to Zoe's total lack of surprise, it had been less useful than the bull session that followed it. By the time she finished up at the *Daily* and got back to her room, the counseling was over; she found Clare next door, in a room shared by two guys that was even messier than her own. Half a dozen people lounged on the bed or the floor, passing a joint around the circle and solemnly discussing love and death and the meaning of life.

They were particularly interested in the fact that Clare hadn't talked about her father at all since he'd left.

"What do you remember about him?" someone asked.

"He was. . . exciting," Clare said slowly, thinking seriously about the question. "He was so intense, so. . . I don't know, *passionate* about everything. And happy. He always seemed so happy." She paused. "My mother was *never* happy." There was a hard note in her voice that made Zoe look at her sharply. Clare herself seemed to hear it, too. "Well, she wasn't," she said defensively. "She was always complaining, all the time."

"What about?" The quietly probing question came from Ben MacDonald, a senior in physics.

"Oh, everything." Clare waved a hand. "About his specimens, and about his music—he used to play this old flute kind of thing, and my mother hated it. She complained that he was never home, and then when he was home she spent the whole time bitching at him. No wonder—" she stopped abruptly.

"You blame your mother for driving him away, don't you." It was a statement, not a question, from a tall, athletic girl named Pamela Grant.

"Not particularly," Clare said. "In his own way, he was as much of a schmuck as she was." She leaned back in a posture of nonchalance. "I always figured they deserved each other. Besides, he probably only showed up here today because he found out I was going to inherit some money."

"Y'know," Pamela said, taking a puff of the diminishing joint, "it's pretty common for kids to blame themselves when a parent bails." She stared thoughtfully at the ceiling. "And of course, that gets pretty heavy, so the kid displaces all that guilt onto the remaining parent." She passed the joint to

Zoe, who took a puff and handed it on. Clare took it from her, watching the smoke curl upward.

"Spare me the pop psychology, okay?" Clare took a puff of the joint. "Next thing, you're going to be talking about incest fantasies and accusing me of being anal-retentive."

"Hey, that's how these things work." Ben laughed as he took the joint from Clare's fingers. "If you leave, we accuse you of being in denial."

"Oh, I won't leave." Clare reached for the bag of chips on the floor. "And miss all this good dope?"

"I had a friend back home," Gracie Bonilla recounted, "whose father ran off with his dental assistant—talk about your clichés." She laughed scornfully. "Anyway, this girl kept insisting that if her mother had only taken better care of herself, he wouldn't've left. Like it was her mother's fault that she wasn't twenty-one anymore."

"Men." Zoe tossed a pillow at Ben, who grinned good-naturedly.

The conversation, like the smoke, drifted, became more general, less personal. They didn't try to probe Clare's psyche, or convince her of anything; they just talked, weaving together personal anecdotes, bits from remembered psych classes, their own thoughts. At two A.M. or so, they drifted back to their own rooms. When Clare crawled into her borrowed sleeping bag on Zoe's floor, she looked more thoughtful than angry.

It was the *Daily* story the next morning that seemed to shake her most. They grabbed papers out of the box on their way to the cafeteria, where they picked up coffee and doughnuts and sat together in a corner, trying not to notice the curious stares directed their way. Clare hunched over the newspaper for a long time, and looked up finally with narrowed eyes.

"Did I screw up?" Zoe asked anxiously.

"No, it's not yours. It's this other thing." Clare jabbed a

finger at Doug Billings's sidebar, which ran under a headline reading THE STRANGE, SAD SAGA OF GERALD SWANN. "He was really nutsoid, wasn't he?" she said.

"Oh, shit. I'm sorry, but there wasn't anything I could do to stop it."

"No, that's not it." Clare shook her head as though confused. "See, the point is, he really was crazy. I mean, like mentally ill, you know? So, in a way, it wasn't really his fault, was it?"

"No, I suppose not." Zoe still wasn't exactly sure what wasn't really Gerald Swann's fault, but Clare was obviously taken with the idea, so she let it lie.

Now Zoe retrieved one last sheet of notebook paper that had escaped notice, added it to the stack on the desk, and flopped down on the chair. "Well, it's a start." She plugged the keyboard into the Mac on Clare's desk. "Want me to power up the computer and see if it still works?"

"Thanks, but don't bother." Clare spoke from the depths of the closet, where she was arranging the few clothes that had escaped the general bloodbath.

"At least it's still here. So's your stereo. Have you figured out if anything's missing?"

"Not that I know of." Clare's voice was muffled. "Everything I can think of is either still here, or was taken away."

"Everything but the Black Diamond box," Zoe pointed out. "Still, at least he didn't get the letters—I can't wait to get at them."

"Yeah, me, too." For the first time there was a spark of emotion on Clare's face. "If there is anything in them, I promise you I'm gonna find it."

"You sound like you really think there may be," Zoe said hopefully.

"Not exactly." Clare hung the last of her shirts on the closet rod and shut the door. "But the more I've thought about it, the more I can't believe Aunt Julia would leave me high and dry like this. I mean, it's not just next year—there'll probably be enough for that. But she knew I was planning to go to grad school, and I *thought* she believed in me. Or maybe," she said with a grimace, "it was all just wishful thinking."

"I don't think so," Zoe said slowly, meaning it. "I never figured you for the self-deluding type. I think, if you got those kinds of vibes from your aunt, then the odds are they were real."

"I hope you're right." Clare gave her a glance of odd gratitude. "How soon can we get started on them?"

Before Zoe could reply, there was a knock on the door.

"Hi, Lieutenant," she greeted Genesko. "Any word on Patrick?" The news that Patrick was being sought as the primary suspect had been a late-night coup, giving her the break over every other paper in the area. It had also surprised her; she found she could easily picture Patrick as a charming con man, but she had trouble seeing him as a murderer.

"No, nothing yet." The look on Genesko's face, and the morning edition of the *Daily* in his hand, made her stomach flutter suddenly.

"Uh-oh. Did I get something wrong?"

"No, unfortunately the reverse." Worse and worse, although Zoe couldn't figure out what he was talking about.

"What did I do?" she asked soberly.

Silently he handed her the newspaper, open to the breakover of her story on page four. He had circled a paragraph near the bottom in heavy black marking pen:

Clare Swann herself was not in East Quad at the time of the murder. She was at a local copy shop making copies of some family papers.

Zoe read the graf twice before looking up at Genesko in confusion. "Didn't you want anyone to know that Clare had an alibi?"

"That's not the relevant point." He retrieved the newspaper from her. "It's the fact that you've revealed the existence of copies of those letters."

"But . . . I don't get it. I mean, you've got both the originals and the copies."

"Yes. But the murderer doesn't know that."

Comprehension flooded her. "Oh, shit. So he might think that Clare has the copies. Which means he might come after her to get them?"

"Come after me?" Clare asked. "What do you mean?"

"If Patrick killed your father for those letters," Zoe said rapidly, "he may come back for them. And because I'm an idiot, he's going to think you have copies of them."

"That's silly." Clare appeared unconcerned. "Patrick would never hurt me."

"Maybe not. But you don't want to stake your life on it." Zoe, whose childhood had been filled with politicians seeking her mother's support, distrusted charm on principle. And Patrick Swann not only had it, she had the idea that he knew how to use it.

She was struck by another thought. "Does this mean," she asked Genesko, "that you think the letters really *were* the motive for the murder?" The idea surprised her; for all her romanticizing, she really hadn't, apparently, bought into the hidden-treasure notion.

"I have no idea." Genesko sounded irritated, although it didn't seem to be at her. "We have to cover all the bases, that's all."

"You're not going to do anything like lock us in our rooms, are you?" Zoe asked anxiously.

"A tempting suggestion." She was relieved to see a slight smile on his face. "What are your plans for the day?"

"Lunch, then Anneke's office to take a crack at those letters," Zoe replied promptly.

"All right." Genesko nodded. "Can I depend on you to stay together at all times?"

"Absolutely," Zoe said, seriously enough so he'd know she meant it. "We'll even go to the john together."

"Ms. Swann?"

"Yeah, I suppose." She sounded resistant.

"Do I have your word?" Genesko pressed her.

"Yeah, okay." She shrugged with annoyance. "If I have to."

"Good. Now, Ms. Swann, have you been able to determine if anything is missing besides the porcupine-quill box?"

"As far as I can tell, everything's here."

"I'm not surprised." He nodded to himself. "All right. Then if you're through here, I'm going to have to ask you to spend at least one more night in Ms. Kaplan's room."

"Why?" Clare asked irritably.

"Because we'll be posting an officer in this room, at least for the rest of today and through tonight."

"A stakeout? Cool," Zoe said.

"Will I at least be able to get in and out and get my stuff?" Clare asked.

"Yes, if you're fairly quick about it."

"Shit, all right." Clare grumbled but acquiesced.

"Good. That's settled, then." Genesko opened the door and stepped outside; almost immediately he returned with a young woman behind him. "This is Officer Eleanor Albertson," he said. "She'll be staying here until later this evening. Eleanor," he said to the officer, "this is Clare Swann and Zoe Kaplan."

Zoe nodded, her eyes widening at the sight of Eleanor Albertson. She wasn't much taller than Zoe's own five foot two, with finely chiseled features under a cloudy halo of blond hair. One of those petite, beautiful blondes whom Zoe loathed on sight.

"This is the room to be staked out?" the woman asked.

"Yes. Ms. Swann will be staying in Ms. Kaplan's room, across the hall, but her things are still in here. She can be allowed in and out briefly, but no one else is to come in."

"Right. Drapes drawn, lights off?"

"Yes. We may flush someone, but I don't really expect anything to happen before evening. If then."

"Yes, sir." She kept her eyes fixed on Genesko a little too long, Zoe thought, sensing Eleanor Albertson's more than professional interest in her boss. She wondered if Anneke knew that one of Genesko's subordinates had a major-league crush on him. Well, shit, probably half a dozen of them do, she told herself; if I were ten years older and Anneke wasn't a friend of mine, I probably would too.

"Okay then." She gave Eleanor Albertson a brilliant smile. "Remember, we'll be right across the hall. Come on, Clare, let's roll."

ELEVEN

Captain Westron was beginning to take shape. Anneke stared at the lines of code creeping down the monitor screen and saw in her mind a slim, wiry woman in a futuristic jump-suit reaching for the control panel that would open the underwater airlock. . . .

The knock on the office door startled her unwillingly backward to the twentieth century.

"Anneke? You in there?"

"Zoe? Yes, come in."

"Hey, cool digs." Zoe, with Clare behind her, stepped across the threshold and looked around. "About time the boss had her own private office."

"I suppose it is." Anneke tried to put enthusiasm into her voice. The new Haagen/Scheede partnership had expanded into an additional suite of offices in the old warren of the Nickels Arcade, giving both Anneke and Ken offices of their own. Now she had a modern, white workstation, neat shelves and file cabinets, cool gray carpet, and a pair of gray wool visitor's chairs. Most of all, she had a workplace free of the clutter that students—especially student programmers—seemed to produce by spontaneous generation.

So why did she so often find herself contemplating the fine line between privacy and isolation?

"We're ready to work on those letters, if it's okay with you." Zoe dropped into one of the chairs and leaned forward to peer at the monitor. "Weird. I don't know how you make any sense out of that stuff."

"Sometimes I don't." Anneke made a face at the screen. "This morning I discovered I'd told a database program to count each sales tax payment as a discount percentage."

"Like saying *rokumai* instead of *roppon*," Clare said. She had seated herself in the other chair, and was looking at the screen with apparent fascination.

"What do you mean?" Anneke asked.

"In Japanese, quantity numbers are linked to the shape of the object. If you're talking about six pieces of paper, it would be a different word than if you were talking about six pencils," Clare explained. "And numbers for the days of the month are different, too."

"Wow. Too strange," Zoe said.

"It's only strange to Anglocentrics," Clare retorted. She kept her eyes fixed on the monitor. "I've heard the term 'computer language,' but I never realized before—it really is just a language, isn't it?"

"That's right." Anneke registered the word "just." "What's more, it's a fairly simple language, in linguistic terms, because it's absolutely logical. Although 'simple' isn't a synonym for 'easy,' as I'm sure you know."

"Yes, but . . ." Clare continued to stare at the screen. "What language is that?"

"It's called Visual C Plus Plus." Anneke could almost see gears turning behind Clare's dark eyes, but after a few moments she turned away from the screen, in what seemed almost a gesture of self-denial.

"Can we look at those letters now?" she asked.

"Yes, of course." Anneke noted Clare's tight expression, as if she had carefully walled off any emotion behind a hard, blank surface. "This must be a very difficult time for you," she said gently.

"You mean because of my father?" Clare's lips pressed together tightly. "Not really." She shrugged. "Now that the shock is over, it's over. After all, he's been dead to me since I was seven."

"But still, he was your father," Zoe said.

"You're another fucking romantic," Clare said nastily. "You really believe this crap about undying love between parents and kids, don't you? Look, when he walked out, he quit being my father. So I figure I lost my father when I was seven. The guy who bought it yesterday was just some guy, okay? Now, can we move on?"

The anger was revealing, Anneke thought. Hostility seemed to be Clare's way of coping, of convincing herself how tough she was. Anger was a nice, strong emotion, strong enough to drive other feelings safely underground. The trouble was, as Anneke knew too well, all those other emotions wouldn't stay buried forever.

"Besides," Clare added, "it's not like I needed him. Aunt Julia was a lot more of a parent to me than either my father or my mother. At least I always thought she was. That's why . . . " She stopped abruptly.

"That's why you think there may be something valuable about these letters." Anneke finished the sentence for her.

"Or something else in the box." Clare made an angry face. "How's that for dumb?"

"What else was there?" Anneke asked curiously.

"Just a bunch of old papers." Clare shook her head. "An old deed to the house in Missaukee, some newspaper clippings, photographs, that sort of thing. No, if there's anything there, it has to be in the letters. Which you have to admit is pretty unlikely."

"Let's see what we can find out," Anneke said mildly. She got up from her desk and crossed to the small safe, where she'd put the Xeroxed sheets a policeman had delivered earlier in the day. "Here they are."

"Are they in order?" Clare asked.

"No," Anneke said. "Not all of them are dated, and even the ones that are have only month and day, not year."

"Terrific," Clare said sarcastically. "All right, I guess we just take it from the top." She reached for the stack of papers, but Anneke put out a forestalling hand.

"There is one thing I noticed," she said. "They seem to be from two different people."

"Yeah? Different handwritings?"

"Right."

"Maybe they're a set of love letters," Zoe suggested.

"They're from two women," Anneke said, smiling. "Here, take a look." She selected two sheets of paper and laid them on the desk. "This one is from someone named Henrietta Swann." She pointed to one of the pages, covered with fine, spidery writing in tight, neat lines. "And this one is from a woman named Cora Brown." The writing on the second sheet was more ragged, the letters larger and less well formed, half-printed, half-cursive. The lines straggled upward on the page. "I think what we have is two very different women," she said. "Henrietta is clearly well educated and upper-class, while Cora has very little formal education—possibly just enough to read and write."

"Henrietta Swann was my great-great, I think, grandmother," Clare said. "But I've never heard of Cora Brown."

"Any ideas how to start?" Zoe asked.

"I think we need to take it a step at a time." Anneke reached for her loathed reading glasses and shoved them onto her nose. "There are seven letters altogether, three from Henrietta and four from Cora. Let's number them for reference—H for Henrietta, C for Cora—and open a file for each one. Then we can type in the words we're sure of, leave marked spaces for the ones we can't decipher, and when we're done we'll see what we've got."

"That'll at least give us some contextual clues." Clare nodded. "Okay."

"Okay," Zoe said impatiently when the pages were all sorted and numbered, "where do we start reading?"

"Why don't we start with the Cora letters?" Anneke suggested. "They look like they'll be somewhat easier to read."

"No, they won't," Clare said sharply. "The individual letters may be easier to recognize, but the spelling is totally nonstandard."

Anneke looked at one of the Cora letters and sighed. "You're right. Well, just pick a letter at random, then, and let's find out how bad this is going to be."

They were still at it at five o'clock when Karl called to tell her he'd be home late.

"I assumed as much," she said. "I'm starting to learn that being a policeman's wife isn't always a whole lot of fun."

"But think how much fun it is when it *is* fun." The wicked note in his voice made her face grow warm.

"Just hold that thought, Lieutenant."

"And what thought is that?"

"Yes, Zoe and Clare are here." She stifled a laugh.

"Ah, well. We'll be businesslike if you prefer." His voice turned brisk. "Have you made any progress with those letters?"

"Some. It's a real bitch, though."

"I can imagine. How much longer are you planning to work?"

"I don't know. Why?"

"It occurred to me," he said, "that it would be helpful if

you could keep those two away from East Quad for the evening." He told her about the stakeout. "Actually, I don't expect anything to happen until after midnight—if anything happens at all, of course, which admittedly is very unlikely. But even so, I'd rather not have them roaming the halls all evening talking to people, if we can avoid it."

"All right, I'll try to manage something," she said carefully, aware of Zoe's bright eyes on her. "At least for a while."

"Good, thanks. I'll see you later."

"All right, where were we?" she said when she hung up.

"Beats me." Zoe squirmed in her chair. "How much progress have we made?"

Anneke turned toward the computer, where the bar at the top of the WinWord screen read H1.DOC. She had typed the letters they were sure of in black; unrecognizable letters were indicated by @ symbols set in red. Against the white background, the screen seemed more than half red.

"Some." She sighed. "Not as much as I'd hoped." She switched windows, so that the file bar read C2.DOC. "I did have better hopes of the Cora letters." The screen seemed slightly more black than red, but for all Anneke could decipher, it was more than half gibberish. "Look at that." She pointed to a line on the screen:

al@ron@ but yunotha@

"One problem," Clare pointed out, "is that she ran words together. That last word could be two or three words— maybe the last word is 'that'."

"Or 'not' something," Zoe offered.

"What about using a spell checker on it?" Clare suggested.

"Hey, yeah, that's a great idea," Zoe said enthusiastically.

"You think so?" Anneke smiled grimly, from long experience with spell checkers. She highlighted the string "al@ron@" and clicked on the spell check icon.

"No suggestions," the spell checker returned. She tried "yuno."

"Yukon," replied the spell checker.

For the string "notha@" the spell checker suggested "Nathan."

"So we've got a Jewish Dan McGrew." Zoe erupted into giggles. "Yukon Nathan, the Gold Rush hot dog vendor."

Clare looked at her in disgust. "I'm glad you think this is fun and games."

"I don't know about you two," Anneke said hastily, "but I've just about had it." She stretched her arms out in front of her, easing stiff shoulder muscles.

"Yeah, okay," Clare said glumly.

"Don't get discouraged," Anneke reassured her. "We've only begun. Let's attack it again tomorrow, when we're fresh. Hang on while I secure all of this." She closed the files and set a password for them, then powered down the computer and stood up, feeling muscles creak. "Look, I'm on my own for the evening," she said. "Would you two join me for dinner and a movie? The Greenery, my treat."

"The lieutenant wanted you to keep us away from the dorm, didn't he?" Zoe asked shrewdly.

"You're too clever for your own good." Anneke laughed. "It's still a pretty good offer."

"Best one I've had all week," Zoe said. "Unfortunately. Clare?"

"If I can't go back to the dorm," she muttered, "I ought to at least log some library time."

"Tomorrow," Zoe said firmly. "There's that new Schwarzenegger flick at the State, and I think it would be real good for us to spend tonight watching a lot of things blow up."

"Yeah, all right. If you want." Clare nodded jerkily, an ungracious response that Zoe, to Anneke's surprise, accepted without comment.

McBain, Michigan: June 15, 1895

It was real late in the spring for full-scale gang riots, Cora Brown knew, but it'd been a long winter and the shanty boys from Windy Camp, up near Petoskey, had broke camp late. Word was there was even still some ice in the Jordan River. Twelve of the Windy Camp boys had got their Tickets to Hell punched for McBain, and when they got off the train they were already drunk and looking for action. A little less booze—or a little more—and they'd of been looking for the kind of action Cora offered, but right now they were just enough likkered up to be spoiling for a fight. They didn't much care who the opposition was, neither.

Cora sized them up from the wooden walkway outside the front door of Tommy Kelly's saloon as they roared down the middle of Water Street, their caulked lumberjack boots spitting geysers of mud out behind them. The street was lined solid with ramshackle wooden buildings housing saloons and brothels, but that wasn't what the Windy Camp boys were after. They wanted to fight.

A month earlier, and there'd've been half a dozen gangs from other lumber camps ready and eager to oblige. But this late into the spring, most of the lumber camp gangs had already been and gone, leaving their pay—and a lot of the time, their teeth—behind. The Windy Camp boys were coming up empty, and they were getting right testy about it.

"We're the meanest, toughest camp in these north woods!" the Windy Camp leader bellowed. He was a huge man with a wild mop of reddish hair and a tangled beard stained with tobacco juice. Spit dribbled out of his mouth as he yelled. "We can lick any camp in this shithole town. Come on, you yella dogs, ain't there nobody round here with the guts to take us on?" Behind and beside him, his pals from Windy Camp shouted challenges to passersby, most of whom stepped aside or slipped into one of the saloons to let them past.

Not Johnny Bullwhip, though. Johnny was plain crazy, of course, everyone around knew that, but he was near as big as the Windy Camp leader and he purely loved to fight. Johnny popped out of Tommy Kelly's and skidded across the muddy street in his haste to confront the Windy Camp boys.

"I'll fight you, I'll fight you," he called out, his falsetto voice cracking with excitement. "I'll fight any three of you together, or all of you at once. Any way you want."

"Yah, you and what army?" the Windy Camp leader sneered. Still, he stumbled to a halt and glared boozily around. "This the best this shithole town has to offer?" he challenged the world in general.

"You guys are makin' a hell of a racket for a buncha shanty trash." Mo Danton rumbled out of Tommy Kelly's and stood on the edge of the wooden walk. Behind him, Cora saw half a dozen faces peering around the door of the saloon. Mo stepped off the walk into the mud and approached the Windy Camp boys.

"Attaway, Mo." Johnny Bullwhip danced up and down. "Let's get 'em." He turned to face Tommy Kelly's saloon. "Come on, boys!" he shouted. "Let's show 'em what we're made of!" Tommy Kelly's door was flung wide and half a dozen men came charging out, whooping and hollering.

Cora had already stepped aside. Now she leaned against the building and watched the battle commence, hoping that the Windy Camp contingent would be the big winners. They were the ones with money in their pockets, after all, and so long as they didn't get too banged up, they'd be ready to spend some of it for Cora's services once the fighting was over.

Mo Danton had gone straight after the Windy Camp leader, and the two of them were slugging it out in the middle of the melee. Billy Campbell was rolling around on the ground with a guy the size of a draft ox, both of them so covered with mud she could hardly recognize Billy's toothless grin. Johnny Bullwhip had pulled his namesake whip out of his jacket and was rolling about him, grinning and cackling madly. Cora watched the Windy Camp leader go down, and Mo Danton stomp down hard with his caulked boots; when Mo picked up his foot, she could see the neat rows of bloody holes in the man's hand. He leapt up, bellowing with rage and pain, and kicked Mo square in the balls.

It was going to go on for a while, Cora decided, having seen dozens of similar gang battles in the last few years. Even though this area was mostly lumbered out, they still got a fair number of shanty gangs coming through in the spring. She turned back toward Tommy Kelly's door, figuring to sit inside until it was over, when a flash of color caught her eye.

Around the corner, stepping carefully on the rough boards of the walk, came a dainty lady in apple-green skirt and jacket, with a pale green shirtwaist underneath and a tiny feathered hat on her blond curls. She was concentrating on her steps, looking down as she placed each foot, so she didn't see the melee until it was too late. Didn't see it, in fact, until they saw her.

"Oi, looka there now!" One of the Windy City boys looked up, blood streaming down the side of his neck—another one who'd had his ear bit off.

"Hey, I wouldn't mind gettin' myself some of that," Hank Marble said, laughing from between swollen lips.

"Hey, pretty lady, how'd you like to try a real man for a change?"

"Yeah, blossom, c'mon over and we'll show you what a good blow really feels like."

The battle slowed as the lady's presence penetrated. A couple of dozen pairs of eyes swiveled toward her, battle-hot eyes that were maybe not quite all there. Under normal circumstances, Cora knew they wouldn't lay a hand on a lady like this one—there wasn't any question she belonged to someone important—but right now they were so fight-mad, she wasn't sure what they'd do.

The lady herself had frozen in place when she realized where she was, just stopped dead and stood there like a wooden Indian, her face white and scared. The mob had gotten ominously quiet, smelling fear. Oh shit, Cora thought.

A dozen long strides brought her to the lady. Cora stepped in front of her and held her arms out wide.

"All right, fellas," she shouted. "I'm givin' it away free this afternoon, upstairs over Tommy Kelly's." She waited for the raucous hoots to subside before adding, "But *only* to the winners, y'hear? So let's see what you guys are *really* made of." There were roars of defiance. The mob, reminded of its original purpose, turned on itself once more.

"C'mon." Cora grabbed the lady's arm and hustled her around the corner, away from Water Street. Not till they were a full block away did she stop.

"What the hell were you doin' in Water Street?"

"I—I got lost—made a wrong turn. You s-saved my . . . " The lady's voice broke. "They were—they would have—"

"Prob'ly wouldn't've done nothin', actually," Cora said roughly. Once away from Water Street, she was painfully aware of the contrast between this little flower and her own rough, grubby condition—the ugly, plain black dress, brown hair scraped back from her face in a tight bun, her face itself, with its hard, emotionless expression, already turning brown from the sun.

The lady was shaking like a dray with a loose wheel. Cora dug into the pocket of her coat and pulled out a bottle.

"Here. Take a slug of this."

"What is it? Oh, no. Th-thank you, but. . . I don't d-drink alcohol."

"You got a choice between drinkin' alcohol or fallin' down in the middle of the street," Cora said gruffly. "Up to you." The lady took the bottle then and managed a small sip, choking and making a face.

"Thank you." She looked some better, with a little color returned to her cheeks. "I'm Henrietta Swann." She held out her hand in its lacy black glove.

Cora looked at the hand a minute before taking it. "Cora Brown. You're Walter Swann's new wife, ain't you?"

"Yes." Henrietta nodded. "Do you know Walter?"

"Everyone in McBain knows the mill owner," Cora said, purposely ambiguous.

"Thank you for what you did for me."

"Didn't do it for you. If those boys had laid a hand on you, they'd be dead meat."

"I see." Henrietta's face had gone white again. Good, Cora thought savagely; sooner she learns her place around here, the better. "Then I owe you a debt of gratitude for preventing me from causing trouble for them," Henrietta said soberly. "Whatever you promised them, I'd be grateful if you'd let me provide it."

"What?" Cora let out a shout of laughter, but at the same time she felt a grudging respect for this downy chick. "Look, sister, I don't think you're up to spendin' a couple hours with your legs spread for those boys." She was deliberately coarse, and she was rewarded by seeing Henrietta's delicate face turn scarlet.

"Is that what—oh." Henrietta squirmed and looked down at her feet, but then looked up again directly into Cora's eyes. "In that case," she said, still blushing furiously but speaking with determination, "you must allow me to reimburse you for your. . . services."

"Ain't necessary." Now why the hell did I say that? Cora wondered. She owes me, for Pete's sake, and she can sure as hell afford it. "Won't be more'n three or four of 'em left standing anyway, by the time they're done fightin'." She glared at the beautiful, richly dressed lady. "You just stay off Water Street, you hear? We don't need no trouble."

"I will." Henrietta nodded seriously. "I promise you." She held out her hand again. "Thank you for your assistance, Miss Brown. I hope we may meet again."

> *My Dear Miss Brown:*
> *I am writing to thank you for your invaluable assistance over that unpleasantness last week. Please be aware that you have my very deepest gratitude, and that you will be in my prayers. I want you to know that if there is any favor I may do for you in return, you have only to ask.*
> *With my very best wishes, I am*
> *Yours truly, Henrietta Swann*

TWELVE

· · · · · ·

She'd selected the Greenery purposely, because it offered a "dining experience" that took a long time to finish. That brought them to the nine o'clock show, and it was nearing midnight by the time Anneke pulled her Firebird up in front of East Quad.

"You think the lieutenant'll let us back in our room now?" Zoe asked.

"Probably." Anneke smiled in the darkness. "As long as you *stay* in—"

That was when they heard the gunshots.

"Don't shoot! Jesus, are you crazy?" Patrick Swann felt his sphincter muscles loosen with fear. "He's getting away!"

"Stay where you are!" a voice boomed out of the darkness. "Put your hands on top of your head!"

"But he's getting away!" Patrick, hands clasped tightly on his head, wanted to weep with frustration.

"Check the courtyard," another voice ordered. Patrick

heard the clatter of footsteps. He stood perfectly still on the low rooftop above the East Quad cafeteria, peering into the black night for a glimpse of the figure that he knew was no longer there.

They would never believe him now. And what would he tell his father?

Patrick wasn't sure which was going to be worse—being arrested for murder, or telling his father that he had been arrested for murder. No—actually, worst of all would be explaining why he had been arrested for murder while standing on a rooftop in the middle of the night.

"Another one of your daft schemes," Christopher would call it. Or: "I'd ask what you were thinking, but you obviously weren't." And, undoubtedly: "It's a good thing you're planning an academic career. You certainly have no idea of how to cope in the real world."

His father's contempt for academe was one reason Patrick had chosen it, of course. It was the one area, he told himself, in which he wouldn't have to compete with his father's reputation, where the shadow of the giant wouldn't eclipse his own accomplishments. A Ph.D. in economics from the University of Michigan would start him on his own path, to his own kind of glory. Especially if his dissertation was . . . well, no time to think about that now.

Not that his father would be impressed. Patrick knew that nothing he ever did in the academic world would impress the man for whom genius was a commodity like any other, to be bought and sold but never respected for anything but its monetary value. He believed he'd long ago given up trying to impress Christopher.

As a child, he'd learned quickly that temper tantrums merely got him banished to the care of one of the succession of au pairs or housekeepers. Whereas humor, or cleverness, or charm might occasionally result in attention, even if the attention was no more than a vague smile or a pat on the head. Christopher and Vivian Swann made it very clear that they were only interested in people who could offer them either profit or amusement.

Patrick set out to charm his parents.

By the time he reached Huron High, he'd discovered the power—and the limits—of charm. It would earn him friends, but only so long as he remained cheerful and amusing. It would get him dates with pretty girls, but not relationships of any depth. It would dig him out of holes with his teachers if he forgot to do his homework, but the homework had to be done eventually, and in the end the cold numbers on the test papers were impervious to a ready grin. He was bright enough to recognize that charm was essentially manipulative, and sufficiently self-aware to realize that he instantly lost all respect for those he was able to manipulate.

But worst of all was the discovery that the charm his father had found appealing in the small boy, he now found superficial in the young man. Christopher, after years of being hustled by experts seeking his financial support, believed that charm was the last refuge of the lightweight.

Patrick discovered that charm was a quality his father enjoyed, but did not respect.

By the time he found this out, of course, it was too late; he knew better than to try to remake his whole personality. This is who I am, he told himself at last; and thought with bravado: Fuck 'em if they can't take a joke. The only respect I need, he reminded himself, is from myself.

They were suddenly all around him. A young guy in a police uniform, younger-looking than Patrick himself, grabbed his hands and shoved them behind his back. Patrick felt the chill of handcuffs, felt hands patting none too gently at his clothes, was spun around and dragged away from the edge of the roof, toward an open window.

"Inside," someone ordered.

* * *

"Did you get him?" Zoe shouted breathlessly.

Anneke wouldn't have thought anyone could make it up the stairs faster than she did, but Zoe was ahead of her when they reached the second floor. A small crowd was gathered in the corridor, Karl among them. Anneke let out the breath she hadn't realized she was holding and gasped for air, so shaken that for a moment nothing registered but Karl's presence, alive and unharmed.

"You idiots! You let him get away." The young man spit the words at Karl. His hands were behind his back, and his curly dark hair shadowed a face creased with rage.

"Let who get away?" Zoe called, pushing as close to the circle of police as she dared.

"Patrick!" Clare shoved roughly past Anneke and confronted the young man. "Did you have to kill him in my room?" she demanded harshly.

"But I didn't kill him!" Patrick all but howled in protest. "The killer just got away. Clare, I'd never kill your father!"

Along the corridor, doors were flung open and students stood staring and chattering, their faces avid with curiosity. Other students peered around the corner of the adjoining corridor, and behind her, Anneke could sense noise and movement as still more students cantered up the stairs, drawn by the promise of drama.

"Mr. Swann, come with me, please." Karl took Patrick's arm and tried to lead him toward the stairs, but Patrick squirmed and tried to pull away.

"No, wait," Patrick said desperately. "You've got to listen to me. Clare, please. And Zoe—it's Zoe, isn't it? Make them listen." His face was shiny with sweat; he jerked against Karl's restraining hand, trying to pull back into Clare's room. Around them, the crush of students continued to grow; the chatter was beginning to turn to mutters of protest. Karl bent down and spoke into Eleanor Albertson's ear, his eyes on the mass of students. Then he turned back, with Patrick, toward the room, bringing Brad Weinmann, his sergeant, with him.

"Them, too," Patrick insisted. "Please, Clare?"

Somehow Anneke found herself carried along into the room—not that she'd tried to avoid it, she admitted to herself. She backed into the narrow space between the closet and the bed, trying to remain inconspicuous. Zoe and Clare, as though by common consent, sat down side by side on the newly made-up bed. Brad took the desk chair, pulling out a notebook and sitting with it on his lap, pen poised above it.

Patrick and Karl remained standing, facing each other.

"Mr. Swann, I have no intention of allowing you to start a riot in a dormitory," Karl warned him.

"Oh, God, you still don't understand." Patrick shook his head jerkily, his hands still cuffed behind his back. "I don't suppose there's any chance you could take these off, is there?"

"I'm afraid not," Karl said. "Now, Mr. Swann, before you go any further, I want to inform you that you are under arrest for the murder of Gerald Swann. Anything you say can and will—"

"Wait a minute. Please," Patrick interrupted.

"—be used against you in a court of—"

"Dammit, you've got to listen to me."

"Mr. Swann." Karl's voice crackled. "Do not say one more single word until I have finished." He completed the Miranda warning. "Now, do you understand what I've just told you?"

"Yes!" Patrick hurled the word at him. "And do *you* understand that you caught the wrong person on that roof tonight?"

"Do you want an attorney, Mr. Swann?"

"No! Look, let me just tell you what happened, okay?" He turned to face the bed. "Clare, I'm the one who broke into your room. But that's *all* I did."

"You son of a bitch." Clare spoke in a flat monotone. "He might not have been much, but did you have to kill him?"

"But I didn't! See, that's the thing." He spoke quickly, eagerly. "I came by to ask you if I could take a look at the stuff in that box. I knocked, but there was no answer, so—" he looked embarrassed for the first time "—I sort of let myself in." He turned back to Karl. "I was an RA here a couple of years ago. I still had my keys.

"Anyway," he hurried on, "I came in, and there was the box in the middle of your desk. I was looking through the stuff in it when I heard a noise at the door. I thought it was you coming back, and I. . . I sort of panicked, I guess. I just dropped the box and split out the window."

He shrugged awkwardly. "That's all."

"An interesting story, Mr. Swann." Karl broke the silence.

"It's not a story, it's the truth."

"Then you didn't trash my room?" Clare demanded.

"Why would I? The box was right there in plain sight. And anyway," he said earnestly, "why on earth would I want to kill old Gerald?"

"Maybe because he caught you searching my room."

"That's silly. For one thing, I *didn't* search it. But even if I had—what's the worst that would've happened? You'd have been furious at me? There'd have been an unholy family row? So what? Isn't there always, about one thing or another? Clare, it's just not the sort of thing anyone would *murder* over."

"No, but maybe the contents of the box *are*." Clare continued to stare at him, unyielding.

"You mean, because there may be some sort of clue to hidden treasure? Honey, I'd dance a jig if you found Aunt Julia's fabled fortune—you deserve it. But why the hell would I kill someone for *money?*" He sounded honestly outraged. "Dad's got more money than God, and I've got a three-million-dollar trust fund of my own."

"That's right, you do." There was surprise in Clare's voice. "You know, I keep forgetting that you're rich."

"That's probably the nicest thing you could have said to me." Patrick grinned at her. "Except maybe that you believe I didn't kill your father."

"I think, you know, that I do," Clare said slowly. "The Swanns have other ways of destroying each other."

"Poor Clare," Patrick said with genuine sympathy. "You've taken even more of a reaming than I have, haven't you? But, y'know, you're tougher than you think you are."

"I'm as tough as I have to be, don't worry." Clare's face tightened again.

"If you didn't kill him," Zoe spoke suddenly, "why were you on the run?"

"I wasn't 'on the run,'" Patrick said. "After I ducked out of the dorm, I spent the rest of the day doing research. I was up at the computing center for a while, and then I was at a couple of libraries, and then I hit a bar downtown for a quick dinner, and *then* I went to a movie. That's it, I swear."

"But you didn't go back to your apartment," Karl pointed out.

"No." Patrick looked irritated. "I guess this is where I started to come a little unstuck." He paused. "See, I was driving home from the movie when I heard a news report of the murder. Well, hell, I'd been in the room, and I figured my fingerprints would be all over it, so I was pretty sure I'd be Suspect Number One." He shifted uneasily and stepped backward, leaning against the wall.

"I drove around for a while trying to think what to do, and I finally decided I was too tired—I'd had a few beers with dinner—so I drove out Huron River Drive a ways, found a spot in the woods, crawled into the back of my car, and sacked out till morning."

"And then?" Karl asked conversationally.

"Then I saw the story in the *Daily.*" His face became more

animated. "Once I hypothesized that those papers they'd been Xeroxing were the object of the search, I hoped that the killer would make another try for them. I spent five hours behind a bush outside this place," he said, glaring at Karl, "and when the guy finally shows, you let him get away."

"It didn't occur to you to come forward?" Karl asked.

"Shit, no. If I had, you'd've figured you had your man and not even bothered to look for anyone else."

"When was the last time you had any contact with Gerald Swann?"

"God, I don't remember." Patrick stared into space, thinking. "I don't think I've even heard his name mentioned since I was, what, thirteen or something."

"Did you think he was dead?"

"I didn't think anything. I guess I knew he wasn't really dead, but mostly he just sort of didn't exist for me, you know? Don't you have cousins or uncles somewhere, that you kind of know about, but you haven't thought about in years and years?" It was a shrewd comment, Anneke realized; the name Margot popped into her head suddenly, a cousin she hadn't heard from, or of, in at least ten years.

"Poor old Gerald." Patrick shook his head sadly. "He should have stayed on the reservation. I'm sorry, Clare. This must be hell for you," he said to her, and then to Karl: "Could we go now?"

"Yes." Karl turned, his eyes sweeping the room. "Ms. Kaplan."

"Don't even bother to say it," she interrupted him. "I'm not on this. I do not intend to write another word about this. I'm not even *here*. And besides, there's no *Daily* until Monday anyway."

"Good." He nodded, directed at brief smile at Anneke, and they were gone.

THIRTEEN

· · · · · ·

When the girls were little, Saturday mornings had been special. Tim, of course, went off with his male friends for games of golf or racquetball—the accepted ritual of the male breadwinner. For Anneke and Rachel and Emma, Saturday was a day for elaborate brunches, for visits to museums, for excursions into the countryside. For talking and laughing and bonding.

Rachel used to order the most outlandish omelettes on the menu, Anneke recalled, and never finished them. Both girls loved the Dexter cider mill. Both hated shopping for clothes. Emma would stand in front of the museum dioramas and demand to know how the stuffed animals had died. Emma, small and curly-haired and determined, serious from birth.

Karl was still asleep, one arm flung over the side of the king-size bed. She hadn't heard him come in last night, but she knew he must have been late. She propped herself up on an elbow and looked down at him; his face, under the dark, curly hair, had a contemplative look, as if he were dreaming about some deep philosophical conundrum. She watched him for a long time before she finally slipped out of bed as gently as possible, picked up her robe from the chair, and padded barefoot out of the bedroom, closing the door quietly behind her.

She was on her third cup of coffee and her second muffin, with a mystery novel propped in front of her, when he finally appeared, dressed for the office in his customary dark suit.

"You look nice and comfortable." He leaned down and kissed her lightly in greeting, then put his hand on the back of her neck and held her for a longer, deeper kiss. "Mm. Very comfortable." His hands moved from her neck down along the silk of her robe.

"Watch it, Lieutenant. Don't start something you can't finish. All right, let me rephrase that." She laughed as he arched an eyebrow at her. "Don't start something you don't have time to finish."

"Well, not to finish satisfactorily, at least." He sat down and poured himself a cup of coffee, dropping a small book in front of him. "Are you going in to the office today?"

"Yes. That's the one thing that police and programmers have in common—the concept of weekends is meaningless. We're interviewing some possible new hires—two of our people are graduating this year. And Zoe and Clare are planning to come in later and work on those letters."

"How far have you gotten?" He reached for a raspberry muffin.

"Not far enough to be useful to you, I'm afraid. But we may get more done today." She watched him peel the paper frill off his muffin. "I take it you don't really think those letters are relevant to the murder?"

"I can't say until I've seen their contents." The words were neutral, but Anneke thought he looked skeptical.

"You think Patrick Swann was lying, don't you?" she said.

"Well, he did spend part of the afternoon in the Bus Ad library. And he apparently did sleep in his car that night. We found evidence of his tire tracks and a small campfire out along the river."

"Well, that's some corroboration, isn't it?"

"Yes, but where he spent the night isn't relevant to guilt or innocence. He'd have to sleep somewhere, regardless."

"Ouch. Stupid of me. Is he in jail?"

"In fact, no. It was decided," Karl phrased the statement carefully, "not to charge him at this time."

"Oh, hell." Anneke knew what that kind of careful phrasing meant. "This is going to be one of those political ones, isn't it?"

"Christopher Swann is a very wealthy, and very well-connected, man in Washtenaw County," he said obliquely. "Besides. . . " He shrugged, the irritated look back on his face.

"Something's bothering you, isn't it?" she said.

"Let's just say there are a couple of things I'd like to account for," he said, sipping coffee. "For one thing, I'm fairly sure there were two people in that room the morning Gerald was killed. And since Patrick claims he can't remember whether he left the door to the room locked or not before he went out the window, there's every chance someone else could just have walked in. Before we can legitimately tie this one up, we really need to find out who that second person was."

"You said 'a couple of things,' " she pressed when he didn't continue.

"Yes, there is something else." He paused. "I'm also fairly sure there was another person in the East Quad courtyard last night."

"You're joking." She stared at him.

"I wish I were. Oh, you might want to see this." He handed her the small book, and she saw that it was actually an academic journal, titled *Historical Economics*. She opened it to the contents page and Patrick Swann's name jumped out at her, under an article titled "Analysis of the Trade Value of Ceremonial Objects Among a Chippewa Sub-Tribe."

"So Patrick's already been published," she said. "Not bad for someone still working on his dissertation."

"No. Apparently he really does have an extraordinarily bright academic future, at least according to his committee chair."

"Well, then."

"We also got in touch with the psychiatrist who treated Gerald before he left Ann Arbor," he said, changing the subject. "His diagnosis, as I suspected, was drug-induced schizophrenia, with a fair number of other polysyllabic words thrown in." He drained his coffee cup and stood. "Assuming I get finished at a decent hour today, why don't we try that new Indian restaurant for dinner tonight?"

"It's a date." She stood also and began collecting plates and cups. "And remember, Lieutenant, I don't take kindly to being stood up."

"If I do, I promise to make it up to you," he said with a grin.

"I understand you hold a contract with LifeSites?" The young woman crossed one nylon-sheathed leg over the other and leaned forward, the short black skirt of her power suit riding even further up her thighs. "Are they your biggest client? In terms of billings, I mean."

"No, they're not." Anneke didn't elaborate, having no intention of discussing Haagen/Scheede's finances with a job applicant.

"Do you market your applications to the public?" she asked. "Or through any of the larger software houses?"

"No, we don't." For a while, Anneke had been fascinated by the girl's arrogance; now she was merely bored. She stood up. "Thank you for your time, Ms. Archer. We'll be in touch." Ken, on the other side of the desk, gave her a surreptitious grin.

"My God, what *are* they thinking?" she said in exasperation when the girl had left.

"Well, the in-your-face attitude was for you, the skirt was for me." Ken laughed. "Unfortunately for her, she was rattling the wrong cage today. But someday she'll find a personnel director who'll buy into her act, and ten years from now she may be able to buy Haagen/Scheede and fire both of us."

"No, she won't," Anneke snapped. "It won't be for sale."

FOURTEEN

• • • • • •

"What's not for sale?" Zoe poked her head through the doorway.

"Damn few things, nowadays," Anneke muttered. "Sorry, don't mind me. Time to get back to work on those letters?"

"Yeah, if this isn't a bad time."

"No, I was expecting you. Is Clare with you?"

"I'm right here." She stepped out from behind Zoe, looking scruffier than ever in baggy jeans and a stretched and shrunken sweatshirt with a faded blue T-shirt hanging below it. Her hair was shoved back behind her ears, secured haphazardly with large black bobby pins. Only her eyes looked alive with intensity. "I had an idea," she said.

"About the letters?"

"Well, yeah, what else? See, I was thinking about syntactic drift."

"What do you mean?" Anneke blinked at her rudeness, making allowances for stress.

"Okay, look. Those letters were written, like, a hundred

years ago, right? Well, language changes over time. Words and syntax both. I think we've been getting too hung up on our own concepts of contemporary American speech."

"Possibly." Anneke considered. "But what else do we have to work with?"

"With our ears, of course," Clare said impatiently.

"You mean, you think we can *hear* meaning better than we can see it."

"Sure. Language was meant to be spoken long before it was written."

"Interesting. Worth a try, certainly." Anneke led them briskly to her own office, removed the Xeroxed letters from the safe, and spread them on the desk once more.

Zoe picked up one of the letters, coded H1, and peered at it dubiously. "What are we supposed to do?"

"Just read something out loud," Clare commanded.

"If you say so. How's this? 'Wonight moatagon.'" She burst into giggles.

"Could you bother to take this seriously?" Clare glowered at her. "Try it again," she ordered. "Say it faster this time, and try to slur the words together slightly. Especially the consonants."

"Wunite mutagin,'" Zoe said obediently.

"Again." Clare leaned back and closed her eyes. Zoe repeated the words, then repeated them once more.

"Wait." Clare sat up straight, her eyes flashing behind the round glasses. "Try this for that last part: 'meet again.'"

Zoe peered down at the letter more closely, and when she looked up her eyes were wide. "I think that's it."

"May I?" Anneke took the letter from her hand. "Yes, I think you're right," she said after a moment's perusal. "What's more, look at the *g* in 'again'—see the short descender? That seems to be a constant—I think we've been missing them in other letterforms. That's one of the elements that's been confusing us."

"Right." Clare leaned forward. "So now we can work back and forth between aural and orthographic clues." Her pale face held an expression of savage eagerness. "Zoe, read another sentence."

They were on the third letter when Zoe uttered a startled: "Hey, listen to this."

"What?" Clare asked.

"Here—I think this says, 'Black Diamond or any something something of something something blood money.'"

"Get out." Clare, who had been slouched back in her chair, jerked erect. "Whose letter?"

"One of Henrietta's."

"Are you sure you got it right?" Clare snatched the paper from Zoe's hand and stared at it intently before finally looking up. "Yeah, that's what it looks like, all right." Her eyes blazed.

"Black Diamond?" Zoe seemed to taste the words. "I figured that just meant the design on the box. Clare, this has to be it!"

"Maybe." Clare's voice was taut. "But we still don't know what it is. Or *where* it is." Her hands were tight fists, clenched in her lap; now she loosened them and leaned back once again. "Let's get all the way through this crap before we get too excited."

They worked furiously after that, driven by Clare's demanding urgency. The clues became certainties; the scribbles became words. As they filled in more of the blanks, the task became easier. It was a few minutes after noon when Anneke looked at her monitor and realized that the major proportion of red @s were gone.

Even without the impetus of possible hidden treasure, the letters themselves were fascinating. They chronicled the burgeoning friendship between two totally disparate women, in a time and in circumstances that Anneke could barely imagine. She wanted to sit down and read them through, more leisurely, to try to comprehend the lives behind the faded handwriting.

"I think we're as done as we're going to be," she said. "The Henrietta letters are pretty clear—I think the only gaps left are places where the letters themselves are stained or too worn to read. We haven't got all of the Cora letters clear, but I don't know what else we can do with them."

"So what've we got?" Zoe stretched widely. "We've been working on them in such bits and pieces that I never really got a sense of what they're about."

"We've got fucking a, is all." Clare's face was a mask of frustrated anger.

"From what I can gather," Anneke said, "they were helping each other out in some way—Cora even says that Henrietta saved her life. There's a lot of talk about gratitude, and about fear," she added soberly, "but I have to admit I don't see any key to a hidden treasure."

"What about the Black Diamond stuff?" Zoe protested.

"Garbage." Clare glared into space. "Doesn't say what, doesn't say where. Garbage."

"Jeez, you give up easy." Zoe turned to Anneke. "Can you print out all the Black Diamond references?"

"Sure." There had been, she recalled, four instances of the words *Black Diamond*. She ran a "Find," located them, and dumped them to a new file. Then she looked at the screen:

C2: The Blak Dimond stuf sur maks me mad but thers Nuthin I can do about it.

C3: If you hear about Blak Dimon @@@@@@ hoodlums but you be carful.

C4: At least he @@ Blak Dimond and all that and dont Care.

H3: neither Black Diamond nor any other sources of what must @@@@@@@@@ blood money are necessary for either of us.

"There's no way to figure out those words in C3?" Zoe asked, looking over Anneke's shoulder.

"No." She shook her head. "It was written in pencil, and the letters have simply rubbed off." She looked at the screen thoughtfully. "You know, there are a couple of things that strike me about this. First, the words *Black Diamond* are always capitalized—like a title of some sort."

"That doesn't mean squat," Clare said. "Old-style orthography sometimes used uppercase for important nouns, and Cora mixed her cases pretty much whenever she wanted to."

"Cora does," Anneke agreed. "But Henrietta doesn't. She doesn't uppercase any other words except the normal ones—names, and the first words of sentences. There's something else odd, too—the lack of an article. It's never 'the' Black Diamond; it's always just—" The muted trill of the telephone stopped her. "Excuse me." She punched the button for her private line and picked up the phone. "Hello?"

"Mom?"

"Emma?" Anneke felt her chest constrict. "I'm so glad—"

"No, Mom, sorry. It's me, Rachel."

"Oh, Rachel." The wave of sick disappointment left her almost dizzy.

"You haven't heard from Emma recently, I gather?" Rachel asked.

"Not recently, no. Why? Is something wrong?" Surely Emma would at least let her know if she were sick, or. . .

"Only with her mental capacities," Rachel said acidly. "She called me last night—went on for ten minutes about how we had to stop you from marrying, quote, a fascist side of beef, unquote. I finally hung up on her."

"Oh, shit," Anneke said quietly.

"What the hell is her problem, anyway? Has she even met Karl?"

"No. She was supposed to come in at Christmas, remember, when you were here, but she was invited on a ski trip."

"Then I don't get it—why is she coming unglued over this?"

"As near as I can tell," Anneke said tiredly, "she hates cops, and she hates football players."

"Ah, shit." Rachel's voice was scornful. "In other words, he's not politically correct enough for her."

"Look, Rachel, I don't want my problems to affect your relationship with your sister. Believe me, that would make me feel even worse."

"You're not having second thoughts, are you?" Rachel sounded alarmed. "I mean, you *are* going to marry him?"

"Yes, of course." Anneke was surprised by the question; in fact, she realized, it had never occurred to her. "Emma will come around once she actually gets the wedding invitation," she said with more confidence than she felt.

"She will if I have to tie her to the back of my car and drag her to the wedding."

"Rachel, please don't get in the middle of this."

"Don't worry, Mom. And give Karl my best, okay? Make sure he knows that not everyone in your family is a jerk."

Anneke hung up the phone and swiveled back to her monitor. "All right, where were we?" she said briskly, aware of Zoe's eyes on her.

"Talking about the Black Diamond," Zoe said, looking at Anneke thoughtfully. "What d'you think it is? Is it an actual diamond?"

"There's no such thing as a black diamond," Clare said irritably.

"Yes there is." Zoe snapped her fingers. "Coal. Diamonds come from coal, don't they? So maybe Black Diamond is the name of a coal mine."

"Yeah, right." Clare looked scornful. "The closest thing you'll find to a coal mine in that part of Michigan is a gravel pit."

"Oil?" Zoe asked, apparently unoffended. "I know they pump oil up around Mount Pleasant. Black Diamond could be the name of an oil well."

"If so, it's either played out by now or it never brought in anything," Clare pointed out.

"I suppose." Zoe subsided.

"But there were some mines up there," Anneke said. "I know they found at least small deposits of gold and silver, and I think amethysts as well."

"The amethyst mines, such as they were, were almost all in the Upper Peninsula. The gold mines were barely streaks of ore, and none of them ever produced anything but mythology."

"Well," Anneke struggled to overlook Clare's hostility, "what *was* up there?"

"Peat bogs." Clare laughed without humor. "Mosquitoes. Tree stumps, after the lumber barons got through with it. Wild huckleberries. Hoodlums, drunks, and murderers. Leon Czolgosz worked in the lumber camps for a while before he assassinated President McKinley."

"Did he really?" Zoe asked with interest.

"Yeah, but I don't think he left a big diamond to one of my ancestors." Clare slouched back in her chair. "This isn't going anywhere. We might as well be on a snipe hunt." She sat and stared at the ground.

"There's one other possibility," Anneke suggested. "What about the rest of your aunt's papers? Is there any reference to a Black Diamond in them?"

"I don't know." Clare looked up. "Everything but the box went to the Bentley."

"Well, why don't we go on up there and take a look?" Zoe bounced out of her chair.

"You don't have to do all this, you know." Clare looked at Zoe suspiciously.

"I know," Zoe said cheerfully. "C'mon, let's go."

When they were gone, Anneke sat for a while and thought about Henrietta Swann and Cora Brown, about the life they might have lived isolated on the northern frontier. Finally she turned to her computer and logged on to the Internet.

She went first to Alta Vista and ran a search for the keyword "logging," then laughed when it turned up responses in the thousands, most of them references to logging onto the Internet. She tried "lumbering," and found multiple references to "lumbering dinosaurs" but nothing about northern Michigan. And the first three responses to a search for the keywords "Michigan history" brought up the University's Exhibit Museum of Natural History, *Michigan History* magazine, and, utterly inexplicable even for imbecile computers, Access Statistics for Baylor University.

Jumping to Yahoo, she went to Regional/U.S. States/Michigan, and surfed a dozen or more sites dealing with northern Michigan until she found the Hartwick Pines Lumbering Museum. This was more promising, but when she jumped to it, she found that the exhibits all seemed to deal with technology rather than people.

She was excited at first when she came across a huge treasure trove at the Library of Congress site—nearly 25,000 pre–World War I photographs from the old Detroit Publishing Company. The digitized collection was magnificent, and she wasted more than half an hour browsing through images of railroad stations and old hotels and unspoiled scenery. But only a few of the photographs specifically represented the lumbering era, and like the museum, most of these showed men standing in front of huge pieces of machinery.

From Yahoo/Arts/Humanities/History/19th Century/U.S. History she found the Gallery of the Open Frontier, from the University of Nebraska Press, with more wonderful images but still nothing about Michigan. Likewise the WPA Folklore

Project at the Library of Congress site. After that, for a while she simply surfed, clicking on links almost at random, finding skiing information from Cadillac and real estate sales pitches from Traverse City and the National Women's History Project.

She found the plat maps by accident, via a route so circuitous that only a trail of bread crumbs could have led her back. She felt a thrill of discovery when the map of Missaukee County unreeled on her monitor and she spotted the name SWANN in printed capital letters. But all it told her was that someone named Swann owned a parcel of land in Lake Township at Sec. 19, T22N R8W, information she already knew. Henrietta Swann and Cora Brown remained buried in the past.

With a sigh she closed Netscape and started to log off, but instead clicked on Telnet even as she told herself not to. In a moment, she saw the "Welcome" screen of On-Line Santa Cruz. Emma, of course, considered the big national on-line services to be an offense against freedom of information.

She found her daughter's uid—JewelArt—in a fierce discussion of "Art for Art's Sake," and was amused to discover Emma defending herself against the accusation that the jewelry she designed and created contributed to social dissonance and politically incorrect self-aggrandizement.

"Jewelry, done properly," Emma had posted, "is art that the wearer can carry along, to enjoy and appreciate all the time. It beats hell out of bloated canvases by dead white men hanging in museums you have to pay to get into."

"Except women don't buy expensive jewelry to feed their souls," posted someone with the uid BlueDog. "They buy it to impress other people. If you were doing jewelry from found materials, I might buy the 'Art for Art's Sake' business, but you're working in gold and silver and 'precious' stones that are all produced by exploited workers, because your customers insist on it. They're not buying art, they're buying status."

Anneke's fingers itched to defend her daughter's work. Instead, she logged off and returned to perusing résumés.

FIFTEEN

* * * * * *

"Maybe you'd better just drop me off." Clare shifted uneasily in the passenger seat of the Buick. "I can get the shuttle back to the dorm."

"That's okay." Zoe steered the car through the multiple intersection behind the medical center and headed out Fuller.

"What are you getting out of this, anyway?" Clare twisted around toward Zoe, her eyes narrow with suspicion. "You're not going to write about this, are you?"

"Hey, you *asked* me to write up the murder, remember?"

"Yeah, well, I was upset," Clare mumbled. "But I don't want to see any of this Black Diamond stuff spread all over the *Daily*."

"Oh, come on. I don't rat out my friends."

Clare didn't reply, only slumped back in her seat and stared out through the windshield. Overhead, the gray sky seemed to press down on them, dark and glowering. "Look," she said finally, "if we actually find Aunt Julia's money, or whatever it is, you get a ten percent finder's fee. Okay?"

Zoe started to refuse, then stopped. This was Clare's way of staying in control, she guessed; her way of avoiding the need for gratitude. Maybe she really couldn't figure out any other reason but self-interest for Zoe to be involved.

And why *was* she involved in Clare Swann's problems? Zoe asked herself the question for the first time. Well, because it was an interesting puzzle, with a whiff of intrigue to it; because she'd already gotten involved and just wanted to see how it played out. It wasn't like Clare was her best friend or anything; Zoe wasn't even sure she liked her. Not that Clare would care if she did or not—and maybe that's what I do like about her, Zoe thought. She shrugged; she never wasted much time contemplating her own motives.

"Okay," she said finally, turning into North Campus. "Thanks." She grinned. "I'll just keep that new 'Vette in my mind for incentive."

The main campus of the University of Michigan meanders in bits and pieces throughout central Ann Arbor. Over the years, the U has gobbled up as much city property as it could get away with. When major expansion was deemed necessary in the late 1950s, North Campus was the answer. It is a huge, sprawling tract of land, with rolling hills and parklike settings and sleek, contemporary brick buildings, and even enough space for parking lots.

Zoe, who had grown up in the Detroit suburb of Birmingham, thought it looked like an outsized industrial park—a piece of Southfield dumped in Ann Arbor. She pulled into the parking lot beside the Bentley and got out of the car, feeling the dark sky like a weight above her. Too damn much sky out here, she decided, without enough surrounding buildings to anchor it. She hurried toward the glass entry, with Clare behind her.

She'd never been in the Bentley before; she stopped for a moment to get her bearings. There was one large main room, with library tables, a reception desk, and a small card catalog, but only a few shelves of material. At the moment, late on a Saturday afternoon, the only occupant of the room was a middle-aged woman behind the reception desk. She had short, tightly curled brown hair and eyeglasses in bright red frames that obscured much of her doughy face. The gaiety of the glasses contrasted sharply with the dour suspicion with which she glared at them.

"Do you girls want something here?" she asked, in the tone of voice usually reserved for stray dogs. Undergraduates, she communicated with raised eyebrows, especially a pair as scruffy as these, did not customarily sully these premises.

"Yes, thank you." Clare coolly took the lead. "I'd like to examine the Julia Swann Vanderlaan papers. They were—"

"Just a moment." The woman's mouth closed with a snap. She punched keys on her computer terminal, then looked up triumphantly. "We have nothing under that name in the catalog."

"If you'd let me finish, I could've told you that," Clare rapped out. "They were just brought in yesterday."

"Nothing's available to the public until it's been catalogued." The woman ostentatiously turned her attention back to her computer.

"Excuse me," Clare said, her voice sharpening with anger, "those papers came from my family. I think that gives me the right to see them."

"The rules apply to everyone," the woman said, keeping her eyes fixed on her screen.

"Then you better find someone who can bend them." Clare's voice was harsh and loud. "Because I'm not about to be blown off by some fat bitch who throws her weight around just to make herself feel important."

"Don't you dare talk to me like that!" the woman shouted. "Both of you, get out of here right this minute, or I'll call Security and have you thrown out!" Zoe, who generally figured that it was easier to manipulate people with a cute-little-girl routine, was nevertheless impressed with Clare's performance. It wasn't easy to bring someone to a state of gibbering rage in under a minute.

"Jeannette, what on earth is going on here?" Zoe turned at the sound of the low, throaty voice. The woman emerging from a corridor on their left was the same one who'd been at Julia's house two days before.

"These two *students*—" Jeannette spat the word like an obscenity.

"I'm Zoe Kaplan." Zoe spoke quickly, raising her voice. "And this is Clare Swann. We met Thursday at Julia Swann's house. Clare was hoping to take a quick look at the papers you got there." It wouldn't be quick, of course, but Zoe knew it sounded better that way.

"I told them they hadn't been catalogued yet," Jeannette said spitefully, "but they seem to think they're better than everyone else."

"Never mind, Jeannette. I'll take care of it," the woman replied. To Zoe and Clare, she said, "Come with me, please." Without waiting for them to respond, she turned and strode back down the corridor. Zoe and Clare trotted along in her wake. At the end of the corridor, she ushered them into a large, windowless room lined with shelves and long tables, all of them covered with cardboard cartons and file boxes and papers that seemed to spill out of every corner. Only when she had shut the door firmly behind them did she turn back toward them.

Kate Pryor examined Clare covertly, seeing no resemblance whatsoever to the elegant, quick-witted elderly woman who had been her great-aunt. For one thing, Julia Vanderlaan had had manners, the kind of cultivated politeness that came from another era. And had apparently gone with it, too, if this girl were any indication. Well, she'd better mend whatever fences she could. Clare Swann could very possibly be important to her.

"I apologize for Jeannette," she said gravely, speaking adult to adult. "She's a temp—our regular receptionist is on maternity leave. Jeannette's one of those people who can't stand undergraduates. I think she took this job because we get so few of them in here."

"Right. We're the lowest form of life on campus." Clare was obviously still simmering.

"I know, isn't it awful?" Kate allowed herself rueful laughter. "You have no idea how many faculty members I've heard say what a great place this would be if it weren't for the students. Anyway, I'm Katherine Pryor—call me Kate. As you know, I'm the one who collected Julia Vanderlaan's papers."

"I know. Can I see them?"

"Yes, of course. But I'd better warn you that what we have right now is just cartons and cartons of *stuff*, all jumbled together. Are you looking for something in particular?"

The two girls looked at each other hesitantly. They're not very good at being secretive, are they? Kate laughed to herself.

"Not really." Clare shrugged with overstated casualness. "Mostly I want to look for historical stuff—not so much Aunt Julia's own papers as old family things she might have saved. I kind of want to do a family history," she said in a burst. "I mean, the Swanns go back to the old lumbering days in northern Michigan."

"Yes, I know." Kate nodded enthusiastically at the patent lie. "That's one of the reasons the Bentley was so interested— it was a fascinating historical period. It's amazing, really—we had our own Wild West here in Michigan, but almost nobody knows about it. I'm hoping for some really exciting material from your aunt."

"So can I see them?" Clare asked again.

"Of course." Kate nodded, carefully ignoring Clare's abruptness. There was, after all, no earthly reason why Clare shouldn't look through her aunt's papers; in fact, her search might even be a help to Kate herself. Still, she felt a possessive pang as she pointed to the big table.

Not that the papers were "hers," in any way whatsoever. As an assistant curator in the Michigan Historical Collections, her job was to harvest original source material, organize it, catalogue it, and make it available for other people's research. Other people's, not her own. Yet, from the first moment she'd met Julia Vanderlaan, Kate had had the sense that she'd come across something special.

Katherine Pryor was that most pathetic of all academic creatures, the ABD. The initials stand for All But Dissertation, indicating the completion of coursework only for a Ph.D. They could, of course, apply to someone in the final throes of thesis completion, but they are rarely used that way. Mostly, the initials are used to indicate a permanent status, someone who is no longer actively working toward a degree.

Mostly, in the upper academic reaches of places like Michigan, the initials indicate failure.

Kate Pryor refused to think of herself as a failure. A failure, she told herself, was someone who'd given up on herself. Kate hadn't given up; she'd just gotten sidetracked for a while, that's all.

She could blame Jake, of course, but what would be the point? Kate, who prided herself on her lack of self-deception, understood that she, not her ex-husband, was the one who'd put things off—while Jake was finishing his own Ph.D., while he worked his way through a series of affairs, while he plunged into the academic job market. When he'd finally gotten an offer, from the University of Nevada, Kate discovered she was positively relieved when he told her he didn't want her to go with him. Now, she had told herself, she could finally get on with her own career. She still wasn't quite sure why she hadn't.

"Don't say I didn't warn you." She laughed at the looks on their faces. "There they are."

"Oh, jeez—all of them?" Zoe asked in dismay.

"I'm afraid so." She continued to smile. "I know it looks like a worthless jumble to you, but it's a treasure trove to us. Paper trail, paper chase—it's always about papers in Ann Arbor, isn't it? But you know, papers aren't just dry documents—they're living, breathing history."

"Are they in any sort of order?" Clare asked, clearly uninterested in the metaphysics of academic papers.

"Well, not what you'd call order. But I boxed them up as I came to them, so they more or less reflect the way Mrs. Vanderlaan had them organized. And I do seem to remember," Kate said slowly, "that there was a file drawer of things that looked particularly old. Let me see if I can find the box I put them in."

They attacked the vast pile of boxes, shuffling them from table to floor and back again as Kate opened each one, peered inside, and closed it back up. Both girls, Kate noted with scorn, were puffing with exertion by the time she said, "Aha. Here it is."

The contents of the box consisted almost entirely of a series of age-spotted file folders. "These are old newspaper clippings." Kate pointed to one folder. "And there are a few photographs in this one. The rest of it seems to be business material—old bank drafts, ledgers, payroll lists, inventories, that sort of thing. Probably not very interesting to you, but the sort of thing researchers would sell their firstborn for. We were ecstatic when we saw what was in here."

Clare picked up a file folder at random and opened it. Kate

saw that it contained sheets of yellow paper marked off in a blue grid. "No personal papers?" Clare asked. "Like letters, or diaries, or something?"

"Not that I recall," Kate replied. "But I think you'll find a good deal of family history in the file of newspaper articles. Some of them go back to the eighteen-seventies. Why don't you go through what's here, and I'll check some of these other cartons."

As she went through the cartons, she wondered once more what the girls were really after. Not a family history, that was for sure. They were looking for something specific, not merely random historical material. Not the kind of thing you drew deep historical truths from.

She could still finish her Ph.D. in history, Kate thought to herself, fully aware that the academic clock was every bit as inevitable as any biological one. But increasingly, a doctorate seemed more and more irrelevant. It was hard to become motivated, yet harder still to accept this job as the ultimate fulfillment of her life. Sometimes she felt suspended, waiting for something, without the smallest idea what it was she was waiting for. Her greatest fear was that she wouldn't recognize it when it arrived.

Zoe squirmed impatiently, but Clare stubbornly saved the newspaper articles for last. Only after they had plowed fruitlessly through folder after folder of boring financial stuff did they turn to the clippings. They were a mix of new and old, all of them detailing Swann family milestones. There was a page from the *Ann Arbor News*, dated June 17, 1945, that carried the wedding photo of Julia Swann and Henry Vanderlaan, and another that contained Henry's obituary. There was a yellowed cutting from the *Lake City Plain Dealer* announcing the appointment of Walter Swann to the Missaukee County Chamber of Commerce in 1892.

"Hey, look at this." Zoe held up a front page from the

Plain Dealer. It was dated September 12, 1895, and the screamer headline read:

WALTER SWANN BURNED TO DEATH;
CONFLAGRATION DEMOLISHES MILL OWNER'S MANSION IN MINUTES WHILE HIS WIFE WATCHES HELPLESSLY.

In the manner of old-style newspapers, the story was told in diminishing subheads and florid prose. The distraught young widow described her terrified awakening to the smell of smoke; her desperate but futile attempts to wake her beloved husband; her despairing flight from the burning house.

"The guy was probably bombed out of his skull," Zoe said. "That's why she couldn't wake him up."

"Do you know where she moved after the fire?" Kate asked, reading over their shoulders.

"She didn't really move," Clare replied. "She must have re-built the house—at least, I know the family lived there right up until after World War II. It's certainly no mansion, though; just a big old house."

"And Mrs. Vanderlaan kept it all these years?" Kate asked. "I'm surprised, considering how long she lived in Ann Arbor."

"She used to go up there a couple of times a year. I guess she used it as sort of a summer cottage." Clare stared down at the clipping. "Can I make copies of some of these?" she asked. "Just the ones from up north."

"Yes, of course." Kate pointed to a large copier in a corner of the room. Clare and Zoe sorted through the clippings and ran the copies.

"I guess that's about it." Clare sounded glum.

"There's another approach you could take," Kate suggested. "That's to go through other collections of papers from the same general locale and period, looking for references to the Swann family. And you could also do a search of old newspapers for other mentions—your aunt might not have gotten them all."

"Maybe later." Clare shrugged. "I guess I'd better let it slide until after finals. Anyway, thanks."

"You're welcome." Kate smiled cheerfully at them. "Any time you want to go further, just give me a call. And of course, if I come across anything as I catalog things, I'll let you know."

Outside, the lowering sky was, if anything, even blacker than before. Zoe checked her watch and glanced nervously to the southwest. Quarter after four—tornado time. She had been assured by a number of people that no funnel cloud had ever touched down inside the city of Ann Arbor, but that information failed to comfort her. Especially out here, surrounded by all this nothingness. She hustled Clare into the car and tromped hard on the accelerator, heading for the relative safety of the dorm.

"Hey, easy," Clare protested as she swung a hard right onto Huron River Drive.

"Sorry." Zoe slowed the car with an effort.

"What's your problem?"

"Nothing." Zoe gritted her teeth. "Sorry," she repeated. "I'm terrified of tornadoes, that's all."

"Tornadoes never touch down inside the city," Clare stated.

"I wish people would stop telling me that," Zoe said acidly. She cast about for something to take her mind off the weather. "What about a search of old newspapers, like Kate suggested?" she asked. "Julia didn't necessarily have everything that mentions the Swanns."

"So?" Clare said. "I mean, it's not like I really *am* doing a history of my disgusting family. We were looking for references to Black Diamond, remember? And that's not going to turn up in some moldy old newspaper."

"I suppose not." It began to rain, fat drops splatting against the windshield. Zoe could feel the small Buick buck against the increasing wind. Her fingers tightened on the steering wheel. "God, I hate spring in Michigan," she said.

McBain, Michigan: June 29, 1895

"So you're back." Cora Brown looked up from the stocking she was darning. The two-room log cabin on the edge of McBain was warm with the heat of the leaky old stove and chilly from the wind whistling through the cracks between the badly caulked logs. Once this had been deep woods, but now no trees remained to serve as windbreak.

"Yeah, I'm back." John Smalley dropped his wide-brimmed hat on the stool next to the scarred table, shrugged out of his long black duster, and hung it on a nail by the cabin door. Guns glinted dully at his sides.

"How'd it go?" Cora asked carefully.

"Never mind that." Smalley took a withered apple from a bowl on the table and crunched it between his teeth. "How come you ain't out workin'?"

"End of the month." She knew there was nothing he could say to that; if nobody had any pay left, she couldn't be expected to do much business.

"Cora got a letter, Cora got a letter." Her mother sang out the words, her voice raspy with alcohol. "Wha'd you bring?" Ella Brown asked Smalley. "I bet you got a bottle on you."

Smalley ignored her. "What letter?" he asked Cora.

"Nothin'. Just a letter."

"Perfumed, it was," Ella sang. "Real pretty."

"Ma, stuff it, okay?" Calvin Brown said. Cora gave her

brother a look of gratitude; he rarely spoke in Smalley's presence.

Smalley ignored him too. "Lemme see the letter."

"I tossed it out," Cora lied. "Why'd I want to keep somethin' like that?"

"Who was it from?"

"Just a woman in town."

"What woman?" He was getting impatient; his hand dug into her shoulder.

"Henrietta Swann," she muttered.

"Walter Swann's wife? What's the mill owner's wife doin' writin' to you?"

Shit, he'd find out anyway; best get by it as quick as possible. "She was just thankin' me for doin' her a favor. She got onto Water Street by mistake in the middle of a gang bustup, and I got her clear, that's all."

"And how'd you manage that?" His voice was cold and clear.

"Promised the winners free doin's." She went on quickly, feeling his hand tighten painfully. "If they'd've touched her, we'd've had coppers all over the place, and that would've been a lot worse for business than a few giveaways."

"Yeah, maybe." His grip on her shoulder loosened fractionally. "What've you got to eat around here?"

"Stew's on the stove." She stood up, glad for the excuse to remove herself from his grasp, and ladled food into an earthenware bowl. He ate lumberjack-style, quickly and in silence, bent low over the bowl and shoveling food into his mouth. She filled another bowl and handed it to Cal, who took it from her with the shamefaced air he always wore when Smalley was in the house. She patted his shoulder, careful not to look at the arm attached to it, the arm that ended in a stump where a saw blade had cut it off clean, just below the elbow.

Smalley finished his food and stood up. "Let's go," he said, jerking his thumb toward the ladder that led up to the sleeping loft.

She nodded and went up the ladder ahead of him, hoisting her skirt to keep from stepping on it. He followed behind, one hand on her buttocks, pushing and kneading at the same time. When she reached the top she lay down wordlessly on the blanket-covered pallet, lifting her skirts carefully to avoid getting his stuff on them. Smalley dropped his pants to his ankles and climbed on top of her, fumbling at her crotch with one hand before managing to shove himself inside her.

Lying there waiting for him to finish, she wondered as she often did what men got out of it. Something worth paying for, at least, although she couldn't imagine what. Well, every now and then she thought maybe she'd felt something kind of okay—usually with Pete Slocum, she recalled suddenly. Pete wasn't bad; he took longer than most of the boys, but he also made it kind of fun. At least he seemed to know she was there, an actual person instead of just something to shove himself into.

Smalley came with a grunt of something she assumed was pleasure, and rolled off of her. She wiped herself off with a corner of the coarse blanket and got to her feet, rearranging her skirts. Smalley was already backing down the ladder, and she followed him with an inward sigh.

"Wait up," she said at the bottom. "I'll get my things."

"Where d'you think you're goin'?"

"I figured to go to your place with you." She glanced at her mother, who was lolling back in her chair, her mouth hanging open in sleep. A string of saliva drooled down her chin. When Smalley was away on business, his big log house was off limits to her, but she looked forward to the space and privacy of it when she had the chance.

"What's the good of that?" he demanded. "Ain't no customers for you way the hell over to Clare County. You get yourself into town tonight and do some business, you hear?"

She ducked her head in disappointment, and he grabbed her by the chin and forced her head back. "I said, you hear?"

"Yeah, I hear you."

"You better had. And I better not hear a you givin' it away again." He twisted her head viciously sideways before releasing her. "I'll be back in a couple of days."

SIXTEEN

• • • • • •

"We probably shouldn't have ordered the samosas." Anneke looked dubiously at the heaping platters of chicken tikka masala, lamb vindaloo, and biryani rice, flotillas of food surrounded by outriders of naan, papadum, and raita.

"What we don't eat, we'll take home and have tomorrow night." Karl spooned rice and chicken onto his plate.

"True." Anneke tore off a chunk of naan and dipped it into the masala on her plate. "I'm glad you got through in time for dinner," she said around mouthfuls of the chewy bread. "This is wonderful."

"I didn't think I was going to make it," he said. "The Missaukee County sheriff didn't return my call until nearly six o'clock."

"And then I'll bet it wasn't worth waiting for." She had become aware, in the year she and Karl had been together, how often police work consisted of following promising leads down dead-end canyons.

"Actually, for a change it was."

"Did he have real information about Gerald Swann?"

"A fair amount, surprisingly. The Swanns grew up there, of course, so he's known Gerald since they were both kids. And since his breakdown, it seems Gerald's showed up a number of times. The sheriff referred to him as 'one of our less troublesome crazies.'"

"What was he doing up there?" Anneke reached for the lamb vindaloo.

"The sheriff wasn't really sure what he did when he wasn't in town. Are you all right?" he broke off.

"Barely," she choked, grabbing for water. "My God, does this stuff come with a fire extinguisher?" She gulped water for several seconds. "Thanks for the sympathy," she said, grinning in response to Karl's laughter.

"That's authentic vindaloo." He helped himself to a serving. "You wouldn't want them to water it down for midwest sensibilities, would you?"

"Damn right I would." She took another gulp of water and applied herself to the biryani.

"Anyway," Karl continued his report, "according to the sheriff, Gerald Swann would show up in the area occasionally and just hang around for a few days—buy some supplies, have a few drinks in a bar somewhere, walk around muttering, and then disappear again. The sheriff said he never bothered anyone, except now and then when he'd start haranguing them on the streets, and even then no one really complained." He took a bite of vindaloo and ate it, to Anneke's amazement, with no evidence of distress. "He was a local boy, after all. And besides that, I got the idea that people up there thought of him more as free entertainment than as a problem."

"But couldn't they see he was mentally ill?" Anneke protested. "Why didn't they try to help him?"

"You have to understand, that's just not the way they do things up there. Remember, you're talking about an area with its roots firmly set in the old lumber town days. There's still a certain amount of frontier mentality left over from that period—as long as you're not hurting anyone, they'll most likely leave you alone."

"Which is one reason," Anneke said acidly, "why right-wing lunatics like the Michigan Militia seem to thrive in northern Michigan."

"Actually, the Michigan Militia is headquartered mostly on the other side of the state. But the sheriff sounds like he's trying hard to keep it that way. One reason he said he didn't bother Gerald is because he's too busy keeping an eye on what he called 'the *real* crazies.' "

"Where did Gerald live between forays into town?" she asked.

"The sheriff didn't know, but he said he'd try to find out. He did say some people referred to Gerald as the Mad Prospector."

"As in prospecting for gold?" Anneke looked up from her plate with interest. "Could that possibly tie into this Black Diamond business?" She'd filled him in on their findings from the letters during the ride to the restaurant, feeling somewhat deflated when he'd shown only a mild interest. Now, once again, he shrugged.

"I really don't know," he said.

"But there were gold mines in northern Michigan," she persisted.

"One or two," he agreed, "but none that was ever put into any kind of ongoing production."

"Still, it's a possible tie-in. And money is always a motive. Speaking of which, what about the Swanns' financial situation?"

"From what we've gathered so far, there aren't any surprises there. Patrick really does have a three-million-dollar trust fund. And as he said, it's largely untouched. Christopher and Vivian Swann are apparently as wealthy as they appear, although in his business it would take a full audit to be really sure. Dwight draws a comfortable salary, but he's not truly rich, at least not in the same way Christopher is. Helena, of course, has only her clerical salary from the University. It's all pretty much as it appears on the surface, as far as we can tell."

A thought struck her. "Karl, what did Julia's will actually say?"

"What do you mean?"

"Well, as I understand it, her estate was split three ways, among the families of her three nephews—Christopher, Dwight, and Gerald. But was Gerald's share left to 'Gerald Swann or his heirs,' or was it left to Clare by name?"

"It was left specifically to Clare Swann. Remember," he pointed out, "the family knew that Gerald had left rather than died, even if they didn't know where he was. If the will had specified Gerald, they'd have had to spend a great deal of effort trying to locate him."

"Which probably none of them would have wanted to do anyway." Anneke ate a forkful of biryani thoughtfully. "So it doesn't sound like the will itself could have been the motive for his murder," she said. "Doesn't that seem to focus attention on his activities up north?"

"Not necessarily. Not any more than on his activities in Ann Arbor, at least. Both before he left, and after he came back."

"I never thought of that. Why *did* he show up in Ann Arbor at this particular moment?"

"And also," he said, "when did he actually arrive in town, and what was he doing before he wound up in Clare's room?"

"I never thought of that either," she admitted. "In fact, I haven't really been thinking about Gerald at all. I guess I still assume that he was murdered simply because he was in the wrong place at the wrong time." She looked at him quizzically, awaiting his opinion, but he just shrugged.

"The truth is," he said, "we still know practically nothing about Gerald Swann. Even the people in his department could hardly tell us anything."

"He was in anthro, wasn't he?"

"Yes. As near as I can tell, he started out in ethnobotany, then got involved in something to do with Native American resource usage. But I haven't been able to get any details about precisely what he was working on."

"Didn't any of his former colleagues know?"

"They say not. They're more than happy to gossip about him—" Karl made a face "—in fact, I got the distinct impression that anthropologists consider lunacy to be a departmental status symbol. But no one admits to having any idea what he was researching, and they didn't seem to care much, either. One of them said he was, and I quote, 'such a fruit loop that he could have discovered the Cosmic Egg and no one would have believed him.' "

"Well, what about his papers?"

"Missing, presumed destroyed. There's nothing of his in the department office, at least."

"You mean they just tossed them?" Anneke asked in surprise. "That doesn't sound like the academic mind-set."

"No, it doesn't, does it?" He nibbled a corner of papadum. "And no one admitted to being the one who did it. On the other hand, there's a fair amount of turnover in any department over twelve years, especially if you factor in the various teaching fellows and graduate assistants. They're on their fourth department secretary since Gerald left, too."

"Even so—" Anneke was interrupted by a sharp buzzing sound.

"Damn." Karl reached into his jacket pocket for his beeper. "I'd better call in." He was gone for no more than two or three minutes; when he returned to the table he remained standing instead of sitting down again.

"Something serious?" she asked, responding to the look on his face.

"Something odd." The look resolved itself into a mixture of irritation and curiosity.

"Do you want me to get a cab home?" she offered.

"I don't think that's necessary." He shook his head. "You can come along—it shouldn't take much time. Assuming you're finished eating?"

"God, yes." She looked at the nearly empty platters with mild dismay. "There isn't even enough left to take home."

"Where are we going?" she asked when they had splashed the half block to Karl's Land Rover.

"Out to Julia Vanderlaan's house." He swung the car onto Geddes, windshield wipers on high. "There's been a report of vandalism."

"Serious?"

"I don't know." He accelerated on the rain-slick blacktop, and Anneke withheld further questions. Karl drove fast and well through the black tunnel of road whose widely spaced streetlights were only glints in the encompassing dark. There was a kind of exhilaration to the ride, the speed combined with the sense of isolation making her feel that she and Karl were alone in the universe. She put her hand on his knee, and he turned his head slightly so that she saw the flicker of a grin, and a look in his eye that said he was aware of her thoughts. She felt warmth flow between them, leaned toward him, then was abruptly pressed back against the seat as the car swung a hard left into a driveway.

"Damn." Her voice was slightly breathless.

"Don't fret." His grin was wide as he braked the car to a stop. "When I'm through here, I know a spot up on Cedar Bend Drive."

"And wouldn't that make a great headline?" she retorted, laughing. "Top cop caught in lover's lane bust?"

"Besides," he said, "the fun went out of parking once cars had bucket seats."

There was already a car in the driveway in front of them, a Taurus station wagon that gleamed white through the rain. Anneke pulled the hood of her raincoat tightly over her head as she descended from the Land Rover and hurried behind Karl to the relative shelter of the small front porch.

The door was thrown open almost before Karl removed his finger from the doorbell. Dwight Swann confronted them with an apologetic expression.

"Lieutenant Genesko, come in, come in. Thank you for coming." He stepped back from the door and waved them into a small vestibule, accepting Anneke's presence without comment. "I appreciate your coming yourself," he said to Karl. "I realize you don't usually investigate a simple vandalism, but under the circumstances. . . " He waved a hand. Beneath his rather pedantic manner, Anneke thought he was badly rattled.

"Dwight?" a woman's voice called from beyond the doorway. "If that's the police, for heaven's sake bring them in and let's get this over with."

"Please, through here." There was a flash of irritation on Dwight Swann's face, instantly shuttered, as he ushered them through a wide doorway into the kind of room Anneke knew would haunt her dreams if she ever had to spend a night in it, dark and gloomy and crammed to overflowing with furniture and knickknacks and *things*. This must be the room Zoe had described; it was as bad as the girl had said, but so far, Anneke had seen no evidence of vandalism.

"Olivia," Dwight said, "this is Lieutenant Karl Genesko, and Anneke. . . Haagen, wasn't it? My wife, Olivia."

SEVENTEEN

* * * * * *

"Thank goodness." Olivia Swann darted a look at Anneke, still wrapped in her dripping raincoat. "Dwight, please show him the damage so we can get out of here." She heard the sharpness in her voice, and carefully modulated it to a more polite tone. "I don't mean to make difficulties for you, but the boys are getting quite restless."

As if in counterpoint to her words, a dull, rhythmic thud caused all their heads to turn. Tyler—of course it would be Tyler—was sitting on an ugly carved chair next to an ugly carved table which he was kicking, at a rate of approximately once every two seconds, with the regularity of a metronome. He looked the way he usually did, bored and sullen and near revolt.

"Tyler, please stop that," Olivia said with a sigh.

"Yeah, Tyler, you better stop that." Jeremy crawled out from beneath a large dining table, his customary smile on his face. "You're gonna get it."

"Leave me alone, Jeremy," Tyler said, giving him a look full of loathing. He drew his knees up to his chin.

"Ty-ty-ty-ty-TY. . . ler," Jeremy taunted. "Ty-ler's gon-na get it."

"Tyler, take your feet off Aunt Julia's chair," Olivia said sharply, unable to control her irritation at the boy. "For heaven's sake, you're old enough to know better. Dwight, please? Even Jeremy is beginning to get cranky."

Tyler, of course, was always cranky; Olivia didn't even bother to voice the thought. Tyler was the "difficult child," difficult from the day he was born ten years before—eight pounds, ten ounces of screaming, demanding, unlovable infant whose painful birth had turned her well-ordered life into unspeakable chaos.

Thank God, Jeremy was different. With Jeremy there'd been no disgusting morning sickness, no endless hours of agonizing labor, no months of sleeplessness. Jeremy had slept through the night at three months; Jeremy had smiled at her from the first, and held out his chubby arms to be hugged. Jeremy loved her.

She'd do anything in the world for Jeremy.

"Yes, all *right*, Olivia." Dwight dragged his hand across his forehead. "Sorry."

"Why don't you show me what happened, Mr. Swann," Genesko said. "You said there was vandalism?"

"Yes. It's . . . peculiar. That's why I called you directly, instead of just going through the police switchboard. It's. . . oh, hell, I'm babbling, aren't I?" He pressed his lips together tightly. "Here, see for yourself." He strode across the room, grabbed hold of one of the heavy velvet drapes, and yanked it aside. "There."

Genesko stood for a moment, his face immobile, looking at the spot where the windowsill should have been but wasn't, staring at the perfectly ordinary slab of golden oak that lay directly beneath the window. The woman next to him seemed to be choking back laughter. Then Genesko crossed to the window, dropped down on one knee, and examined the window and its sill gravely, careful not to touch anything.

"Pried off with a crowbar, at a guess." He stood up and turned back toward them, brushing off his trousers. "Carelessly but not viciously—whoever did it didn't care about scarring the woodwork, but didn't make a point of causing unnecessary damage, either." His face was blandly polite. "Is this the extent of the damage?"

"Good God, no." Dwight flushed. "What do you take me for? Look." He pulled back the drape on the other side of the window, where another oak windowsill lay on the floor. "Every single windowsill in the house," he announced, "has been ripped off just like these."

"I see." Genesko gazed around the room. "Did you note any sign of forced entry?"

"The kitchen door." Dwight jerked his head toward a passageway on his left. "A pane of glass in the door was broken."

Genesko nodded. "Can you tell me if anything has been taken?"

"Not without re-inventorying everything," Dwight said grimly.

"I'll go through it tomorrow," Olivia volunteered crisply. "I can check on the most valuable things, anyway. I can tell you, at least, that all the jewelry seems to be here." It was the first thing she'd checked when they'd discovered the break-in. It made the whole event even more preposterous.

"Then it wasn't a random burglary, at any rate." Dwight appealed to Genesko. "What the hell is it all about?"

"Mo-om, I'm hungry," Jeremy complained.

"We'll be leaving soon, Jeremy," Olivia said. "You can have some ice cream when we get home."

"Tyler's got his feet on the chair again," the boy said.

"Tyler, what did I tell you?"

"Tyler's gonna get it," Jeremy sang again.

"Olivia, can't you control those children?" Dwight snapped.

"Mr. Swann, just one more question," Genesko said. "How did you happen to discover the damage?"

"Olivia decided she wanted the opal earrings." He sighed audibly.

"Dwight, you have to admit Rappoport's appraisal is far too high," Olivia said. "Seven hundred fifty dollars is ridiculous for opals," she said to Genesko, "but I finally decided that, after all, family jewelry and all that." She waved a hand.

"Anyway," Dwight moved his shoulders slightly in irritation, "I went to the window to see if the rain had stopped, and that's when I saw it."

"When was the last time you were in the house?" Genesko asked him.

"Yesterday. God, was it only yesterday? When we were sorting out things."

"And the room looks the same as it did then?"

"Yes." Dwight spoke automatically, then stopped and looked around. "You mean, has anything been moved? Good Lord, look at the place." He waved an arm. "How would I know?"

"Ms. Swann?" Karl addressed Olivia.

"No, nothing's been moved." She spoke with conviction; this was her territory, the sort of thing she knew automatically. The sort of thing she'd learned to know automatically.

Olivia was perfectly well aware that she was shrewd rather than particularly intelligent. In fact, she had a mild contempt for the sort of intellectualism that seemed to impress most Ann Arborites. Look where it had gotten Gerald, for instance—first that impossible wife, then a psychotic breakdown, and finally getting himself murdered. Or perhaps the insanity first, *then* the wife—Olivia couldn't imagine any other reason why someone would have married Helena.

At the thought of Helena, Olivia straightened her spine

slightly and surreptitiously smoothed the back of her skirt. Helena was her personal Dire Warning—what you could become if you let yourself relax, stopped taking pains. Even for an instant. Because people like her, people who weren't born to it, could never take it for granted. It was something she had to work at, consciously, every single day of her life. She'd never bothered to define "it," of course; she knew what she meant.

That one, now—she was one of those who was born with it, Olivia thought, looking at Anneke. She could always tell. Even standing there quietly next to the huge policeman, wrapped in a damp raincoat, the woman exuded the kind of understated elegance Olivia had to struggle endlessly to achieve.

Well, she had achieved it. Olivia reminded herself of her status as the wife of a successful attorney, vice chair of the museum board, member of the Republican County Committee. Both she and Dwight were positioned for the next move upward, as long as nothing interfered.

Like murder in the family. She made a face. Well, even murder was better than Gerald Swann alive and insane, wandering around Ann Arbor. A dead brother-in-law, managed properly, evoked sympathy. A lunatic brother-in-law—Olivia shuddered inwardly. No, murder was vastly preferable.

"Are you sure the room is the same?" Genesko asked.

"Reasonably so, yes," Olivia said with conviction. "I'm quite certain there's been no major disturbance, at any rate." She turned to her husband. "Dwight, we really do need to go."

"All right." He dragged his hand across his forehead again, looking even more disturbed. "I guess I'd better take my family home," he told Genesko.

"I'd like to run a full investigation on this, if you don't mind," Genesko said.

"Of course. If you'll just lock up when you're done? Or did you want me to come back?" Dwight asked.

"That won't be necessary." Genesko shook his head. "I'll be in touch with you tomorrow."

"Do you think it's connected to the murder?" Dwight asked nervously.

"Mr. Swann," Genesko said, looking at him, "I wish I knew."

"Windowsills," Anneke said over a thick slice of raisin toast, feeling a twitch of intellectual annoyance. "Windowsills?"

"Windowsills," Karl said gravely, sipping coffee.

She had spent two hours the night before tucked into a corner of Julia Swann Vanderlaan's sofa, keeping out of the way of a small bevy of police experts. Once or twice she intercepted a sour look—highly skilled crime scene personnel weren't accustomed to being called out for cases of minor vandalism. She would have been amazed at Olivia's assessment of her—her father had been a car salesman in Grand Rapids—especially since, by the end of the evening, she felt damp and uncomfortable and wanted home and a hot shower more than anything else.

Now, at nine-thirty Sunday morning, Anneke sat at a table at Zingerman's and glared at her toast.

"*Window*sills," she repeated.

"That's all of it." Karl smiled slightly. "As far as we can tell, there doesn't appear to have been any other damage at all. Just the windowsills."

"Could they have been looking for something hidden under the sills?"

"Possibly. But then why didn't they ransack the whole house? Why *just* the windowsills?"

The word itself was beginning to sound ridiculous, from mere repetition. To avoid saying it yet again, Anneke asked, "Did the crime scene people turn up anything?"

"No. It was a very clean job. Break one windowpane in the

back door, reach in and turn the latch, go through the house, pry off all the windowsills, and leave."

"And *nothing* else was touched?"

"Not as far as we can tell. There isn't even any evidence that the place was searched."

"*Do* you think it has anything to do with the murder?"

"I don't know." He threw up his hands in a rare gesture of frustration. "Hell, for all I know, it could be a religious cult that thinks windowsills are the Antichrist." He picked up his bagel, then stopped at the sound of muted buzzing. "Damn, what now?" He reached into the pocket of his leather jacket and withdrew the beeper. "I'll go call in."

This time he was gone long enough for Anneke to finish her toast and start on her second cup of coffee. When he returned, his face wore a complicated expression she couldn't immediately identify.

"What is it?" she asked.

"That was Dwight Swann—this time they patched him through to me directly." He sat down, picked up his bagel, then set it back down in its basket. "This morning, he received a call from the Missaukee County sheriff. It seems," he said, "that the Swanns' house up north has also been vandalized."

"Not—" Anneke stared at him.

"Yes." He nodded, picked up his bagel again, took a savage bite, and chewed silently for a while. "Every single windowsill in the place has been pried off. What would you think," he asked, "about taking a quick trip up north?"

McBain, Michigan: August 3, 1895

Henrietta Swann sat quietly in the wagon, keeping her eyes down, just the way Walter had told her to sit. He would be inside the feed store for only a few minutes, he'd said; she was not to speak to anyone until he came out.

He'd heard about the trouble in Water Street, of course; it hadn't occurred to her that the mill owner's wife's activities would be grist for such furious gossip in the small mill town. Walter had been enraged, not only at her stupidity for getting herself into such a situation, but even more, it seemed, for allowing a common harlot to rescue her. She flinched at the memory of her punishment, keeping her eyes fixed firmly on her lap in stringent obedience.

Not that there was anything much to look at anyway. Henrietta had been surprised and disheartened by the ugliness of the town. Entranced by Walter's descriptions of the great north woods, she'd expected wide expanses of towering pine. But Missaukee County had been lumbered out years ago, and McBain and its surroundings seemed as barren as the fabled deserts she'd read about. The town itself was composed of muddy streets and plain board structures without the slightest attempt at beauty, and where there had once been woods, there were now acres and acres of unsightly, stump-filled plains.

Walter had met Henrietta's father on a business trip to Detroit. Franklin Marbury had brought the well-spoken young man home to dinner one evening, and Walter had declared himself instantly smitten with the delicate Henrietta. Her father had been delighted when he asked for her hand, even though Walter insisted politely on a speedy wedding. He had a mill to run, he explained, waxing nearly poetic over the beauties—and the opportunities—of the great north woods.

To Henrietta, whose world was bounded by the Detroit River and Gratiot Avenue, it had been an impossibly romantic whirl-wind, made even more exciting by her picturesque visions of the great north woods. Only when she and Walter were at last in their private compartment on the Ann Arbor Railroad train heading north, did she come bruisingly to reality.

"Afternoon, Miz Swann."

Henrietta jumped with surprise and squeezed her hands to-gether, as if she could choke off the voice. She mustn't speak to anyone, she reminded herself.

"Miz Swann? You okay?" It was a pleasant male voice, une-ducated but polite. Henrietta squeezed harder, willing the man to go away.

"Henrietta, what in the world's the matter with you?" The new voice, crackling with irritation, belonged to Walter. "Can't you see Mr. Slocum's speaking to you?"

She looked up, into Pete Slocum's puzzled blue eyes and Walter's implacable brown ones. She should have recognized Mr. Slocum, one of the mill's best workers, but she'd been afraid to look up.

"You said—" She stopped at the expression on Walter's face. She'd already learned, in two long months of marriage, that trying to defend herself only made the punishments worse. "I do beg your pardon, Mr. Slocum." She smiled brightly at him. "I must have been woolgathering in the worst way. I'm most pleased to see you again."

"Likewise, ma'am." Pete Slocum inclined his head gravely before turning to Walter. "Need to find out whether you want to go ahead and widen that booming pond, Mr. Swann."

"Yes, of course." Walter took Slocum by the arm and turned away to talk business, but not before Henrietta saw the flash of satisfaction in his eyes, satisfaction that now he had something to punish her for.

She shivered and looked around, and her eyes fell on the woman in the stiff black dress, coming out of the mercantile with a woven basket on her arm. She recognized Cora Brown with surprise; in the plain, high-necked dress she didn't look at all like a—like one of those women. She looked ordinary and pleasant, like someone who could be a friend. Henrietta desperately wanted a friend.

The motion of her hand, raised in a gesture of greeting which she instantly aborted, was altogether involuntary; Henrietta knew better than to admit acquaintance with one of those women. It was sheer bad luck, Henrietta's luck, that made Walter turn back toward her just in time to see her small movement.

"Mrs. Swann, I am surprised." Walter's voice oozed sadness. "I see I must teach you proper decorum," he said softly, too softly. His eyes flicked from Henrietta to Cora Brown. Cora stared boldly at him, in a way no lady would ever look at a man. Pete Slocum, Henrietta noticed with a corner of her mind, was grinning at Cora with a familiarity that hinted of—no, she wouldn't think about that. It was enough that she'd have to deal with—with that, tonight.

She shut down her mind then, but not before seeing Walter dart another glance at Cora, and then at her, licking his lips.

Dear Mis Swann, I am sending this letter by Pete to tell you that you best be Carful I dont want no trubel with yur Husband I am going away if you hear about Blak Dimon otherwiz Id hav to deal with the hoodlums but you be carful too its not only water Street thats danjers.
Yours, Cora Brown

EIGHTEEN

• • • • • •

Zoe dragged herself awake from a dream in which two giant squirrels were cracking football-shaped walnuts by pounding them with an uprooted goalpost while shouting choruses of "The Victors." She opened one eye. The squirrels were gone, but the pounding continued.

"Clare!" a voice called. "Clare, let me in." Zoe untangled herself from the blanket, untwisted her pajama pants, got herself erect, and staggered to the door, still disoriented. She threw open the door, and jumped back as Helena Swann pushed past her into the room.

"Mrs. Swann?" Zoe blinked, clearing sleep from her fogged brain. "What time is it? What's the matter?"

"Where's Clare?" Helena barked at her.

"Across the hall. She moved back to her own room last night. What—"

"She what?" Helena turned, ignoring Zoe, and crossed the hall in two steps. "Clare!" she shouted, pounding now on the other door.

Zoe checked the time. Jeez, it wasn't even ten o'clock. Across the hall, Clare's door finally opened.

"Mother? What the hell's going on?" Clare, in a long blue Michigan T-shirt, looked as sleep-muzzy as Zoe felt, but when Helena tried to push past her she held her ground. "Christ, you're waking up half the dorm."

"Never mind them." Helena shrugged one shoulder, jerkily. "Get your things together—now you *can't* stay in this place."

"What's happened now?" Clare tensed but didn't move.

"I'll tell you what's happened. Your uncle Dwight called this morning. Someone broke into Julia's house last night and vandalized it, and did the same thing to the house up north."

"How much damage did they do?" Clare asked quickly. "Bad enough to affect the sale price?"

"That's not the point." Helena shook off the question. "I'm not going to lie awake nights anymore worrying about you here alone while some maniac is stalking the whole family. For that matter, I can hardly believe that you're able to sleep in the room your father died in." Her voice dropped tearfully. "How can you *be* so insensitive?"

"How come you didn't tell me about him?" Clare spoke abruptly, her eyes fixed on Helena's face.

"Tell you what? What are you talking about?"

"Why didn't you ever tell me that he had a breakdown? That he left because he was nuts? All you ever said was that he was a bastard who bugged out and left us. You made it sound like he just didn't want us anymore, instead of admitting that he did it because he freaked out." Clare's voice remained flat and emotionless, but her breathing came quickly, in shallow gasps. "Why didn't you ever tell me the truth, Mother?"

"Because I didn't want you to know your father was crazy," Helena said shakily. "God knows it was bad enough just explaining to you that he wasn't coming home. Did you really want to know that there was a strain of insanity in your family?"

"You think I inherited his insanity, don't you?" Clare spoke quietly, with a kind of wonder in her voice. "That's what it's all been about, all these years, hasn't it?"

"Don't be ridiculous." Helena sounded uncomfortable. "Of course I don't think any such thing." Zoe thought she heard fear in Helena's voice that belied her words. "Now please get your things and come with me. You can come up to Missaukee with us today, and move back home when we get back."

"Oh, bag it, Mother." Clare was suddenly back to her normal acid self. "I don't have any interest whatsoever in anything in the Missaukee house—and don't you dare take anything and say it's for me, because I'll only dump it back into the estate. And there's no way I'm moving back in with you. I'm staying right here in the dorm, in my own room. I'm not leaving just because some old guy happened to croak in here."

Helena winced at the brutality in Clare's voice. "All right, then, I'll go up to Missaukee without you," she said. "And let's hope there's something up there worth the trip. Remember, Clare, I won't be around forever to take care of you." She stared pointedly at Clare's ragged T-shirt and matted hair. "And it's not as though you're even *trying* to attract a husband."

She turned and stalked away down the corridor. Clare slumped against the door, looking more shaky than triumphant.

"Want some coffee?" Zoe offered.

"Yeah, sure. I guess." Clare reached behind her and picked up a key ring, closed her door, and tested the lock carefully before crossing to Zoe's room. She sank to the floor, sitting cross-legged and staring at nothing, while Zoe trotted down the hall, filled the coffeepot with water, and returned.

"I wonder," Zoe said, as she spooned coffee into the filter, "what kind of vandalism was it, do you think? Was somebody searching for something?"

"I don't know." Clare was grim. "I guess I'd better call Dwight and find out. God, I'm still half-asleep. Where's your phone?"

Zoe flicked the switch on the coffeepot and dug the phone out from under a pile of clothing, then listened as Clare spoke to her uncle. Clare's face became increasingly puzzled; when she finally hung up, she turned to Zoe and said, "Windowsills."

"Windowsills? What do you mean?" She listened to Clare's description of the vandalism with disbelief. "Bizarro. What the hell is *that* about?"

"Beats me." Clare took a mug of coffee from Zoe's hand. "But Dwight said the house hadn't been trashed, or searched, or anything."

"But they did the same thing to the house up north." Zoe sipped coffee thoughtfully. "Y'know, maybe Missaukee really is the starting point of this whole business."

"The Black Diamond stuff, you mean? Well, it would have to be, wouldn't it? After all, Henrietta Swann and Cora Brown, whoever the hell she was, lived up there. But so what? The starting point may be up there, but Aunt Julia was down here."

"But until we find out what Black Diamond is, we don't know what to do next," Zoe said, the idea striking her suddenly. "So why don't we go on up to Missaukee ourselves and see what we can find out?"

"What, now?"

"Why not?" Zoe bounced off the bed, sloshing hot coffee on her wrist. "Ouch. I've got a car available, remember? We ought to take advantage of it while I've got it."

"There's probably a county historical society," Clare said, half to herself. "And county land records, deeds, that sort of thing. But the rest of it . . . " She snapped her fingers. "Patrick."

"What about him?"

"He's done a lot of his dissertation research up north—something about microeconomic patterns, I think. Anyway, he knows his way around up there. He wasn't planning to go up this weekend, but I think I'll ask him to go along."

"Is that such a good idea?" Zoe asked dubiously.

"Zoe, Patrick did not kill my father," Clare said positively. "I mean, why would he?"

"Well, if he's been doing research up there . . ." Zoe was struck by the connection. "Maybe he already knew something about the Black Diamond," she said excitedly. "Maybe he thought those letters would lead him to it."

"It wouldn't matter to him if he knew the location of the Hope Diamond." Clare shook her head impatiently. "Trust me on this—money just isn't Patrick's thing, that's all. He's got a three-million-dollar trust fund he's never even touched." She sipped coffee. "Patrick's got a whole different kind of obsession."

"Oh?"

"Yeah. See, Patrick's super-genius father made so much money that Patrick will never, ever be able to match him, no matter what he does. So Patrick's smart enough not to try—in fact, he very ostentatiously blows off money completely."

"Because it's so important to his father, you mean."

"Right. If it's Daddy's value system, it isn't going to be mine, you see?" Clare uttered a harsh laugh. "If we're not the most fucked-up family in town, we're sure as hell in the top ten." She reached for the phone once more. "I'll give Patrick a call."

NINETEEN

· · · · · ·

They were past Flint, heading north on US 23, by the time Clare finished explaining it all to Patrick.

"What an absolutely fantastic story." In her rearview mirror, Zoe could see Patrick's eyes snapping with excitement as he leaned forward, his arms crossed on the back of the front seat.

"So you think this Black Diamond really is some sort of valuable treasure?" Clare sat stiffly in the passenger seat, her thin fingers with their bitten nails gripping the door handle with a tension that had nothing to do with Zoe's driving.

"That depends on what you mean by 'treasure.'" Patrick pursed his lips. "Don't let tunnel vision lock you in to a single way of seeing."

"What's that supposed to mean?" Clare demanded.

"It means that there's treasure, and there's treasure. There's more than one kind of 'valuable,' you know." To Clare's snort, he went on, "There's intrinsic value, sure, but there's also historic value, and artistic value, and lots of other kinds."

"Oh, please, give me a break. As far as I'm concerned, if I can't turn it into hard cash, you can flush it down the nearest porcelain receptacle."

"See, that's what I mean about tunnel vision," Patrick said. "All those different kinds of value *can* be converted into cash, if you know how to go about it. For instance, those letters could lead to some major historical revelation even if they don't lead to a treasure, and that would increase their value."

"That's dumb," Clare said. "There's nothing all that exciting in them—they're just old letters from two women. Besides, there are only seven of them."

"But there's real excitement in them," Patrick insisted. "Think of the drama—two women, their lives intersecting in the wild, lawless days of the lumber camps. Their great differences, and their ultimate similarities, the parallelisms of two disparate women carving out lives on the Michigan frontier. And all of it playing out against the death throes of the great pine forests, now gone forever. And the best part of it is that we have their own words, pure and true, given to us by their own hands."

"Wow." Zoe could almost hear the rasp of the giant saw blades and the echoing crash of giant trees. In the mirror, Patrick's face was flushed with excitement.

"Yeah, right." Clare remained unimpressed. "Shit, that's a novel, not a batch of moldy old letters."

"Honey, novels and history are the same thing," Patrick said. "The only difference between them is that one of them's true."

"The difference is that someone puts a lot of creative energy into a novel. If I had the talent for that, I wouldn't need to be on this fucking treasure hunt in the first place. No way I can turn half a dozen letters into some fucking romantic adventure."

"I can," Patrick said, rather grandly, Zoe thought.

"Oh shit, here we go with the Swann arrogance again,"

Clare said bitterly. "Patrick, you're in econ, not history."

"Yes, I know. The dismal science," Patrick sneered. "Only it's *not* dismal if you approach it with the same sense of drama you grant to history. Economics is *life*, dammit. The day-to-day struggles of ordinary people are the fundamental building blocks of economics—and vice versa. When anthropologists describe the first groups of semicivilized *Homo sapiens* as 'hunter-gatherers,' they're defining them by their economic system." He stopped abruptly and uttered a small laugh. "Sorry. Didn't mean to get on my personal hobbyhorse."

"It's interesting, though," Zoe interjected. "Is that what your dissertation's about?"

"Not really. My dissertation is, well, let's say flashier. The working title is *The Economics of Magic: Magic, Technology, and the Invention of a Commodity*. The truth is," he said as though admitting to something shameful, "I'm doing the one thing every doctoral student is warned against—trying to write the Great American Dissertation."

"Why would anyone warn a student against trying to write a great dissertation?" Zoe asked.

"Because it's a waste of time and resources," Patrick replied promptly. "The secret of grad school is to get in and get out as fast as possible, and save your good stuff for *serious* publication, after you get your first job. Not many people have more than one truly brilliant idea in their lives, and if you waste it on your dissertation you're just throwing it away, because no one will ever read it."

"Then why are you doing it?"

"Risking it all on a single throw of the dice." The words sounded like a quotation, but Zoe couldn't identify it. "See, every now and then—maybe once or twice in a decade— someone writes a dissertation that's so awesome people *have* to pay attention to it. And if you can be one of those people, your career takes off like a rocket." In the mirror, Zoe saw

Patrick lick his lips. "After all," he said, "a degree is really only a ticket to ride. But one of the Great Dissertations is a ticket to ride first-class, probably for the rest of your life."

"So is a couple of million dollars," Clare pointed out acidly.

"Different train." Patrick pressed his lips together tightly. "That one doesn't go where I'm headed. Contrary to popular belief, it's economists who understand best about the things money can't buy."

"That's easy to say with a three-million-dollar trust fund," Clare muttered.

"Which I've never touched," Patrick said. "Clare, you know if you need tuition money, all you have to do is ask."

"That's not the problem." Clare shook her head. "There'll be enough from Aunt Julia's estate, even as it stands, to let me finish school. But then what?"

"Then you get a job."

"Yeah, right. Doing what?"

"Whatever you want. Clare, you're as bright as the rest of the family," Patrick said. "Hell, you've got a three six G.P.A., don't you?"

"A three seven, actually. Big, fat, hairy deal." Clare's voice sharpened. "The truth is, the only thing I *am* good at is going to school. I'm a fucking wizard with a test paper in front of me, but I don't think anyone in the outside world is going to pay me big bucks to ace exams. And God knows, as my mother so kindly points out to me on a regular basis, I'm not likely to find some guy who wants to take care of me for the rest of my life. Besides," she added, "this is a chance at *big* money—the kind you have. The kind that means never having to take any shit from other people ever again."

"Yeah, right. And don't I wish *that* were true." There was such a depth of bitterness in Patrick's voice that Zoe looked up sharply, but his face in the mirror looked perfectly composed. "Anyway," he said, "what about those letters? I'd like to look into them, see what sort of historical background I can turn up. If I can make any actual money on it, it's all yours—you'll get all the royalties, and you retain ownership of the letters themselves. Deal?"

"And all you get out of it is just your name on a book?" Clare looked at him suspiciously.

"Honey, you've been around Ann Arbor long enough to know that isn't a 'just,' " Patrick said with a laugh. "Names on books are the primary medium of exchange in the academic world. So how about it?"

"Yeah, sure, if that's what you want." Clare shrugged and turned her gaze to the road ahead. "But not until I find the Black Diamond. After that, you can set fire to the fucking letters for all I care."

They stopped for a bite to eat at Clare's namesake town, driving past signs that proclaimed Clare, Michigan, the GATEWAY TO THE NORTH. Patrick offered to drive for a while, but didn't press it when Zoe explained she'd promised her mother not to let anyone else drive her car. Not true, of course, but Zoe always felt better with her own hands on the wheel.

Northward on US 27, the scenery began to change. The pale green of budding deciduous trees gave way to the darker hues of conifers and white slashes of birch. DEER CROSSING signs became more numerous, and once Zoe thought she saw the flash of a white tail. Nothing else seemed to move in the wooded landscape that reeled past like a movie backdrop. Later in the year, of course, Highway 27 would be crowded with vacationers heading north, dragging boats and trailers and RVs behind them, but in early April only a few other cars shared the road. As mile after mile of empty blacktop unrolled beneath her wheels, Zoe began to feel the isolation as an almost physical weight, irritating her nerves. The temperature dipped as well, the north woods' cold seeping into the car. She cranked up the heater, wishing belatedly that she'd worn her heavy parka instead of the lighter wool jacket.

They had discussed the letters in as much detail as they could without having them there. Patrick had questioned Zoe and Clare closely, drawing from them as much detail as they could remember.

"Were specific locales mentioned?" he asked.

"McBain was, I know." Clare's brow furrowed with the effort of recall. "One of the letters was sent from Grand Rapids, and another from Detroit. Oh, and there was something about 'meeting in Ann Arbor,' but I don't think it gave a specific location."

"How about other people?"

"Let's see—there was someone named Pete mentioned a couple of times, and a 'Smalley,' and a reference to Henrietta's husband. I don't remember any other specific individuals. Cora wrote about shanty boys, and about hoodlums being a problem, I think."

"Hoodlums!" Patrick gave a shout of laughter.

"Why is that funny?" Clare asked.

"Because in the lumber towns, 'hoodlum' was another word for brothel." Patrick laughed again. "I wonder why a couple of nineteenth-century ladies were discussing whorehouses?"

"Me, too." Zoe searched her mind for the reference. "I think it was in one of Cora's letters. Something about staying away from them."

"Well, prostitution was one of the biggest industries in the lumber towns," Patrick said. "I imagine there were brothels all over the place."

The discussion wound down. When the silence began to get to her, Zoe tried the radio, but the only stations she could get carried either right-wing talk shows or country music. She was relieved when the M-55 exit finally appeared. Another thirty miles to civilization, she encouraged herself, accelerating toward Cadillac.

Her heart sank when Patrick ordered her to turn off well before Cadillac, and plummeted even further as the two-lane concrete road turned into a narrower graded dirt road that turned into a one-lane, rutted, dirt-and-mud track that sent the Buick's shocks into squawks of complaint.

"Jesus, you mean people really live out here?" She gripped the steering wheel tightly, wrenching the car out of one rut into another. Around them, trees seemed to press menacingly against the road, fighting to reclaim turf that was theirs. Only occasional shafts of sun broke through the branches overhead.

"The house is right around the bend." Patrick laughed at her.

"It better be," Zoe muttered. She eased her foot down on the accelerator, wondering what her mother would say if she returned the Buick with a cracked drive shaft. She steered around the bend, heard the rasping of tree branches that inevitably mean scratched paint, and swore under her breath.

"There it is." Patrick pointed past her cheek as the mass of looming trees suddenly ended in a wide, sunny vista that opened out in front of them. Zoe accelerated toward the sunlight. "Isn't it beautiful?" Patrick asked happily.

"Yeah, beautiful." Zoe jounced the car toward the house. "Now, if you'll kindly point me toward the nearest McDonald's, we'll all be happy."

"City girls." Patrick laughed and ruffled her hair. "Pull in over there, next to the station wagon." Zoe did as she was told, easing the Buick up onto a large concrete slab which already held a white Taurus station wagon and a small boat on a trailer.

"Hooray. Concrete." Now that she had pried her fingers from the steering wheel, Zoe laughed at herself, looking around the clearing. "Hey, that's a hell of a house."

"Isn't it?" Patrick beamed. "C'mon, let me show you around."

They got out of the car stiffly, stretching to unkink muscles, and Zoe took in the whole scene for the first time. To south and west, the wild forest had come back, pressing close against the cleared land. The eastern edge of the clearing was also wooded, but here the trees were deciduous rather than conifer, and somehow more orderly, neatly spaced. Directly in front of them to the north, a huge Victorian-style house loomed nearly as high as the trees, its white paint dirty and peeling. It looked as if it had been plucked from a Dickens novel and deposited here by a giant hand, as out of place as a football in a soup bowl. Behind it, Zoe could see the bright glint of water.

"Oh, cool. You've even got a lake."

"That's the Clam River," Patrick said. "Want to walk down and take a look?"

"Hey," Clare interrupted, "could we please put the travelogue on hold?" She stood next to the car, wound tight as a spring, Zoe thought. "We're not here on vacation, remember?"

"All right," Patrick said pacifically. He put his arm around Clare's shoulder and gave her a friendly squeeze, then reached out with his other arm and pulled Zoe toward him. "Come on," he said, drawing them along. "Let's go up to the house."

They started forward, three abreast with Patrick in the middle. Zoe giggled, and he looked down at her; he was taller than she'd realized at first, six feet at least, with the thin, wiry body of a distance runner. His arm around her shoulder was unexpectedly strong.

"Share the joke?" he asked.

"I feel like breaking into a chorus of 'Follow the Yellow Brick Road'." She giggled once more, and Patrick grinned.

"Well, Clare would be Dorothy Gale, because it's her

quest we're on," he said. "And I'm obviously Scarecrow." He wobbled his knees, his long legs jerking. "Which means you must be Tin Man."

"Now all we have to do is find the Black Diamond slippers, and we're home free."

"I'll say one thing," Clare said unexpectedly, looking toward the house. "We sure as hell have no shortage of witches."

McBain, Michigan: August 21, 1895

It'd been a good year for the huckleberry crop, and so a good season for Cora. There must have been nearly five hundred people at the pickers' camp on the shores of the Muskegon River, and like always, most of them were men up from Grand Rapids and other cities to the south, drawn by the prospect of summer wages. As usual, some of them worked alongside their wives and children, but most were on their own, lonesome and with their weekly pay in their overalls.

Her black canvas tent had attracted a nice steady business, to the disgust of the other whores working the camp, and she had a comfortable stash to go on into the winter with. Enough, in fact, to hold some back when Smalley demanded her take.

But now there wasn't much business in town. The shanty boys had exhausted their pay long ago, and either left for the cities or hung around McBain cadging drinks. So when One-Eye Joey Leiter dropped two dollars on the bar at Tommy Kelly's, Cora should've been pleased.

Most of the jacks, actually, were okay. For one thing, they were usually half-plastered by the time they staggered up the stairs with her. And they were mostly pretty simple types—all they wanted was a cunt and a kind word and they were satisfied.

One-Eye Joey was different. There was something about him that scared her shitless, a mad look in his one good eye and on his scarred face that hinted of appetites she didn't want nothing to do with. There'd been rumors, too, about that girl who'd come up north a couple of years ago—word was, when they put her on the train back to Grand Rapids, after a couple of hours with One-Eye Joey, she'd been bleeding so bad the conductor'd made her ride out on the platform. Cora didn't want anything to do with One-Eye Joey.

She was lucky to have the use of the room above the saloon, especially in the spring, when trainloads of whores descended on the town. Hell, it got so crowded then, some of them had to do business in the livery stable. Cora got the rights to the room because she was a local girl, so she was available to service Tommy Kelly's customers winter and summer both, and because she was available for Tommy Kelly himself, when the mood took him. But mostly, she got to use the room because Smalley said so. And Smalley wouldn't like it if he heard she'd been turning down business.

There weren't enough people around, was one problem. Only half a dozen men sat drinking, and most of them were skidders, too old for the rough life of the lumber camps, hanging around hoping to beg or con a free drink from someone. A couple of them snored gently, their heads on the table.

"Let's go." One-Eye picked up the two dollars, shoved it down the front of Cora's dress, and grabbed her wrist. She looked around the saloon, beginning to feel desperate. She breathed out a gust of relief when Pete Slocum came through the door.

"Sorry, One-Eye." She disengaged her wrist as calmly as she could and crossed the plank floor. Faced away from One-Eye, she looked at Pete and mouthed the word *Please?* "I promised to do Pete next."

"Yeah." Pete threw an arm around her shoulder. "I been waitin' all morning." His quiet face looked pretty good to her, even with the loggers' smallpox—the scarring from being stomped in the face by caulked boots.

"Well, you can wait some more." One-Eye came forward,

clamped a hand on Cora's arm, and yanked hard. She gave an involuntary squeak of pain and Pete's jaw tightened.

"Let her go, One-Eye. Like I said, it's my turn next."

"You can have her when I'm done with her. If there's anything left of 'er by then." One-Eye uttered a raucous laugh, and Cora heard a couple of the men behind her snicker in response.

"I *said* it was my turn." Pete smacked both his hands on One-Eye's arm, grabbed hold of his flannel sleeve, and jerked the other man around. One-Eye's good eye narrowed, although the glass eye did not; it gave him a weird expression that made Cora's flesh crawl.

"Get your hands off of me," One-Eye growled. Then without further warning, he swung a fist like a sledgehammer at Pete's head.

Pete roared with pain and rage, leaned over, and rammed his head into One-Eye's gut. As One-Eye grunted and doubled over, Pete brought his caulked boot down on One-Eye's instep. One-Eye snapped upright, bellowed, and hammered his fist straight down on top of Pete's head.

Cora, backed against the bar, saw Germany Heinz leap to Pete's aid, driving a punch into One-Eye's midsection. Big Mike Swenson grabbed Germany, swung him around, and slammed him on the side of the head with an axe handle. The front door banged open, and half a dozen more men, drawn by the sounds of fighting, tumbled into the saloon and began laying about them, more or less indiscriminately.

The sound of two quick gunshots rang through the racket like a flume-break. The combatants, now numbering nearly a dozen, turned in the direction of the unaccustomed sound.

"Okay, you boys take it outside." Smalley strode into the bar, gun held ready. "This is a place of business." He looked at Cora coldly.

"Hey, we was just havin' some fun," Germany Heinz rumbled, blood dripping from his nose. "Ain't no call to shoot up the place, Smalley."

"Yeah?" Smalley pointed the gun at him. "Like I said, have it outside."

"What the hell." Germany shrugged. "Come on, boys." Even if any of them carried a firearm, which would have been unlikely anyway, they wouldn't have wanted to take on Smalley.

Smalley turned his back on them before they had even left. "Gimme a shot," he said to Tommy Kelly.

"Sure, Smalley. Anything you want, on the house." There was a sheen of sweat on Tommy Kelly's face. "I was afraid they was gonna break up the place."

"Don't like them interferin' with business." He looked at Cora again.

"Yeah, an' I already paid her—two whole dollars." One-Eye hadn't been hurt much in the fight, and he hadn't been distracted, either, the way Cora had hoped. Now he brought his grievance to the bar and dumped it in Smalley's lap.

He ain't gonna want me damaged, Cora thought to herself with hope, but Smalley's face remained cold.

"Did he pay you?" he asked her.

"He stuffed a coupla bills down my dress." She pulled them out and flung them on the bar. "But I told him I'd promised Pete first."

"Pete Slocum?" Smalley's face got even colder.

"Yeah." Cora looked around the saloon, but Pete wasn't there. "He must be right outside."

"He ain't gonna want your services for a while." Smalley smiled, a mean twist of his lips. "He's out cold." He pointed, and Cora's stomach tied itself into a knot when she saw Pete sprawled unconscious under a table. Smalley picked up the two bills on the bar and carefully smoothed them out. "So you got time to go along and do One-Eye, you hear?" He wasn't even looking at her, Cora realized; he was looking at the money in his hand.

"Okay, One-Eye," she said abruptly. "Come on." She led him up the stairs to the door of the room.

"This it?" He threw open the door and shoved her roughly inside, where he stood and examined her. There was an ugly leer on his face that made her shiver. "You gonna be enough woman for a big man like me?"

"I ain't never had no complaints."

"Well, we're gonna make sure." He smirked at her and held up his hand, rounded into a fist. "First I shove this in, see? Then I dive in after it. Women don't never want no other man after they've had a taste of ol' One-Eye."

"Whatever you say, One-Eye." She dropped her shawl casually on the bed. "Only, I better go pee first. I'll be right back."

"Ain't there a pot in here?"

"Nah. Too many people in and out of here, if you know what I mean." She gave him a broad wink.

"In and out. Yeah, in and out." He roared with laughter and punched her on the shoulder. "Not bad. Okay, go ahead, but hurry on back."

"Sure." She walked to the door, keeping the smile on her face until she was out of the room. Three steps took her to the end of the hall, where the narrow window was thrown open to the August heat. Maybe ten feet down to the alley, with mud and trash at the bottom of it—she hesitated only for a moment before hoisting herself onto the windowsill, gripping her skirts in one hand, and letting herself drop.

She headed southwest for no particular reason except that it was the general direction of Cadillac, staying away from the roads, working her way through the scrub trees and scraggly underbrush that had grown up amid the stumps of pine. She put maybe a mile between her and Tommy Kelly's saloon—between her and Smalley—before she slowed, panting in the heat.

What now? She couldn't go home—that was the first place Smalley'd look. She had no money, Smalley saw to that, and the little she'd held out from the pickers' camp was under a loose floorboard in the McBain cabin. And she didn't have any friends.

Pete Slocum's face floated into her mind, but she shook her head. Even if he'd come to by now, he lived in a rooming house on Front Street, full of mill workers and other workingmen. No way could she hope to slip in and out of there unnoticed. Besides, she had a feeling Smalley'd check him out, too.

When she finally thought of Henrietta Swann she shook her head again. That one had troubles of her own, and Cora didn't want to mess with Walter Swann much more than she wanted to mess with One-Eye. Still, she could maybe sneak over there and wait for a moment when she knew Walter was gone, see if Henrietta could really come up with the money she'd offered. Enough for a train ticket to Muskegon, maybe.

She came to the Swann house from the rear—a big, fancy place half a mile or so from the Clam River. Cora had wondered sometimes what it would be like to live in a house like that, with servants, and fancy china, and big soft beds. Smalley could've had that kind of house if he'd wanted, but Smalley seemed to want money itself a lot more than he wanted the things money could buy.

The sun was beginning its downward path along the southern rim of the sky. Cora detoured to the river, keeping out of sight among the mixed willow and birch that lined the bank. She had to lean far over for a drink; the river was low and slow-moving this late in the summer. She turned to examine the house, and uttered an oath—Walter's trap stood next to the stables. He was home, then, probably for the night. She'd have to spend the night hiding out, wait until she saw him leave in the morning. At least it was warm, she thought, scrunching a hollow in the brush and resolutely not thinking about food.

TWENTY

"Honestly, Dwight, if that woman doesn't stop complaining about every single thing, I am absolutely going to throttle her." Olivia Swann paced the length of the living room, glaring up at the ceiling. Overhead, Helena's heavy footsteps made the ancient floorboards creak unpleasantly. "It's too cold, you're driving too fast, the road should be graded, the house is too dirty—as if I wanted to be here any more than she did." She glared around the shabby room, pulling her bouclé sweater around her more tightly against the chill. "Why on earth did you agree to let her come with us?"

"Do you think I wanted her along?" Dwight asked. "What could I do?"

"You could have told her there was no room in the car."

"Olivia, it's a nine-passenger station wagon. And after all, it's only for one night," Dwight said.

"I suppose so. And everyone will feel better once the house warms up." Olivia heard the clanking of the old-fashioned radiators with relief. Now that they were here, their comfort was her responsibility, of course. "I'm going to have to put the boys upstairs in that back room, you know," she warned him. "With Rappoport and that woman from the Bentley coming up, we won't have enough bedrooms otherwise."

"I know. But I thought we'd all be happier to get this whole estate settled at once. This way, we may not have to come back up here at all."

"Still, that's seven people." Olivia's voice took on a note of complaint. "I don't know how I'm going to feed that many. God knows Helena won't be any help."

"I'm sure you can cope. Look, Olivia, I know it's not necessarily going to be a pleasant weekend, but I really need to get this estate wound up. I do have other clients, you know." He turned away. "I'm going to start inventorying the dining room. Would you please make sure the boys stay out of there. Oh, and bring me some coffee as soon as it's made."

Why did women make such a fuss about everything? he wondered, as he dropped his briefcase on the dining room table. Not that Olivia didn't do her job properly; Dwight conceded that she ran their home and raised their children better than most women would these days. But why did she insist on constantly *talking* about it all the time? Why this endless litany of reporting and probing and analyzing? After all, he didn't expect her to involve herself in his law business; why did she expect him to involve himself in the details of her life? You'd think she'd want peace and quiet and restful evenings as much as he did, after days filled with responsibility.

Dwight looked out the window at the woods pressing against the clearing, woods that closed them in, that closed the world out. The house had belonged to Julia, but after Dwight's father's death she had let his family move in, an act of charity that, like most acts of charity in Dwight's estimation, had done more harm than good. His mother had used the woods to hide in, he understood now, unable to face the world once his father died. It was Julia who had dragged them out of their hidden clearing, Julia who had made them see the world beyond the trees. Julia had brought them all to Ann Arbor, sent them all to college. He felt a sudden gust of anguish at her passing, instantly suppressed.

Responsibility. He had always been the *responsible* one in the family, the middle child who accepted all the unwanted or unpleasant tasks the others couldn't be bothered with. While Christopher soared like a rocket, while Gerald wove brilliant, insane fantasies, Dwight plodded. He plodded through law school and into a job with a staid law firm, and dealt with all the plodding family details that the others were too busy, too important, too crazy to deal with. Whatever the problem, Dwight would take care of it.

He would, too. As far back as he could remember, he had always accepted his role as family caretaker. It was his job to solve the problems, to handle things so the others didn't have to. Sometimes, he reminded himself, he even had to solve problems the others didn't know existed.

"Here's your coffee." Olivia slipped the cup in front of him, pale with milk the way she knew he liked it. He took a sip and looked at her with respect and even a certain amount of affection. Yes, she might fuss a bit, but she did her job with laudable efficiency.

"What would you think of our buying this place from the estate?" he asked abruptly.

"What?" Olivia stared at him as though he'd lost his mind. "You must be joking. No one uses old summer houses like this anymore. If you want a place up north, we can get a condo in Cadillac or Traverse City."

"I suppose so." Dwight buried himself in the inventory papers once more.

Clare threw the front door open with enough force to slam it against the wall. Zoe and Patrick followed her through a large wood-paneled entryway with an elaborate staircase into a large living room to their left. The room was filled with what Zoe instantly classified as summer-cottage furniture, the kind that was too worn and tired to keep but too good to throw away.

"Clare?" Olivia Swann stood next to a small armchair whose cane seat was broken in three or four places. "And Patrick? What on earth are you doing here?" She looked surprised and not at all pleased to see them.

"We just came up to look around." Clare brushed past her to one of the tall windows running along the side of the room. Even from the doorway, Zoe could see the small slab of wood, presumably the vandalized windowsill, lying on the floor beneath it. Clare stood and looked down at it for a moment, then turned and threw herself onto a floral-patterned sofa, dropping her feet onto the coffee table with a thud.

"Clare, I do wish you'd checked with me first," Olivia said, her mouth compressed into a narrow line.

"Clare!" Helena rushed into the room, wearing a skirt in a peculiar tan color and what looked like three or four layers of sweaters. "Oh, I'm so glad you're here. Oh." Her smile wavered and disappeared as she caught sight of Zoe. "Well, at least you're here," Helena said, forcing the smile back on her face.

"Clare, I don't know where you and your . . . friend expect to stay," Olivia said frostily. "There simply isn't room for three extra people."

"Of course there is." Helena dove into argument. "Clare can stay in my room, and you can move your kids in with you so Patrick can have the sun room downstairs."

"Yes, but what about . . . I'm sorry," Olivia said to Zoe, in that fake-polite tone she recognized from some of her mother's political enemies. "I've forgotten your name."

"Zoe Kaplan," she reintroduced herself. "I'm sorry if we're causing problems."

"*We're* not causing problems," Clare said, "they are. Don't worry about it. The two of them would argue about the right color for life jackets if they were going down on the *Titanic*. Don't *trouble* yourself," she said sarcastically to Olivia. "We'll crash right here in the living room."

"Don't be absurd, Clare," Olivia said sharply. "I'm not going to have people sleeping all over the house."

"What do you mean, *you're* not going to have?" Clare said. "I own one-third of this house, remember? And tonight, this room is my one-third." She pried at the heel of one dirty white running shoe with the toe of the other, worked it loose, and shoved it to the floor, then did the same with the other. Her socks were grayish and drooping; she crossed one ankle over the other on the coffee table and smirked at Olivia.

"This is preposterous." Olivia threw up her hands angrily. "All right. Patrick, you can share the boys' room. Clare, you *and* Zoe can share your mother's room. We'll have to move some cots up from the basement. Patrick, will you do that, please?"

"Oy! Hey! As usual, you're not listening," Clare said loudly. "I *said*, we're staying right *here*."

"Actually, I think I have an even better idea," Patrick offered. "Clare, why don't we stay down at the lake?"

"What? You can't be serious," Helena protested. "You'll freeze to death—it's going down into the thirties tonight." She pulled the layers of sweaters around herself more tightly, mimicking a shiver.

"Besides, it's far too muddy this time of year," Olivia said.

"Not to mention that the mosquitoes will eat you alive," Helena added. "And you know how badly you react to insect bites, Clare. Believe me, you'll be a lot better off sharing the bed in my room. And I suppose we can find a cot for your friend."

"Thank heaven that's settled." Olivia sighed. "Now all I have to do is find blankets for three more people."

Clare ignored her. "I haven't been camping since I was a kid," she said slowly. "Is all the equipment still up in the attic?" she asked Patrick.

"It was the last time I was up here." He grinned at her. "I know there are at least three of those good L.L. Bean sub-zero bags, and a couple of North Face tents." Zoe realized suddenly, with dawning horror, that they were talking about sleeping bags, and tents, and actually *camping out*.

"Clare, you *can't*," Helena all but wailed. Zoe held her breath, hoping against hope that Clare would accept her mother's advice for once in her life, but expecting the usual bitter outburst. Instead, Clare surprised her by just shrugging.

"Zoe and I can share one tent, and you can use another," she said to Patrick, ignoring her mother and aunt entirely. "And let's hope the old Coleman still works." She looked almost cheerful.

"Sounds good," Patrick replied. "Don't worry, we'll be fine," he said to Helena soothingly. He looked like an eager little boy, one Zoe could cheerfully murder. "I'm sure there's still some mosquito repellent in the medicine cabinet from last year." Zoe shuddered; maybe she'd sleep in the car. With the windows rolled up. And the heater running—so what if she asphyxiated herself? "Come on," Patrick said, grabbing her hand and hauling her toward the stairs. "Let's go get the gear together."

She let him drag her upstairs, with Clare following along behind, down a narrow hall lined with dark wooden doors and covered by a threadbare runner. From behind one of the doors, Zoe heard childish voices and the unmistakable sounds of a video game. Maybe I could make a break for it and hide out with them, she thought. At the end of the hall, Patrick opened a door that led to a narrower staircase, so narrow that he was forced to let go of her hand and trot upward ahead of her.

"Yep, it's all still here," he called over his shoulder. "C'mon up."

Zoe crested the staircase, and stopped dead, gaping. The attic was enormous, virtually a full third floor, pierced with leaded glass windows that would have sparkled with sun if they hadn't been so grimy.

"Hey, move it." Clare jostled her impatiently from behind, and Zoe climbed the last few steps and moved aside. As far as contents went, it was your basic attic, full of broken furniture and boxes and plastic clothing bags on pipe rods attached to slanting beams. But it was so big that there was still plenty of vacant floor space.

"Y'know," she suggested hopefully, "there's enough room up here for us to crash. It's warm, too."

"Up here?" Clare wrinkled her nose. "Yuck. Why would anyone want to sleep in this filthy mess?"

"I have a feeling," Patrick said, grinning, "that Zoe isn't exactly the outdoor type."

"You got that right," she retorted. "My idea of roughing it is a car without a CD player."

"You mean you've never been camping?" Clare asked in surprise.

"I'm a nice Jewish girl from the burbs, remember?" Zoe laughed. "The only time I ever camped out in my life was waiting in line for Pearl Jam tickets."

"You'll love it, I promise." Patrick's eyes sparkled. "There's nothing in the world like sleeping under the stars, seeing the sky the way it was meant to be seen. Hey, look." He pulled a long pole out from under a pile of canvas. "My old trout rod. And they should be running by now, too."

Oh, great. If he expects me to put worms on a fishhook, Zoe thought, I really am out of here. She looked around the attic gloomily. She'd be a whole lot happier looking at the stars through nice, shiny panes of glass.

"Hey, look at that." She pointed toward the end of the

attic, at a diamond-shaped window set into the wall at just above eye level. She swiveled her head; no, the one on the opposite wall was different. "The window," she said when they looked at her blankly. "Look at the pattern in the glass."

Their gazes followed her pointing finger. The window's diamond shape was repeated by diamond-shaped pieces of glass set in lead. Most of the glass was clear, the kind of old wavy stuff that distorted and altered the view as you moved your head. But in two places, the glass diamonds were solid, opaque black.

"Black diamonds." Clare stared at the window, her eyes wide.

"And someone's vandalizing windowsills," Zoe said excitedly.

"But that window doesn't have a sill," Patrick pointed out. "None of the windows up here do."

He was right, Zoe realized. The Black Diamond window, and several of the others, didn't even open; they were simply flush with the plastered walls. Only three of the windows were made to open, all on the south side, and all of them were casement windows that opened out. None of them had an interior sill.

She went to one of the casement windows and tried to open it, but the handle refused to turn; probably just glommed stuck by a hundred years of dirt. She peered through the glass at the track leading out of the woods, where a car was just emerging into the clearing.

"Hey!" she said in surprise. "That's Genesko!"

TWENTY-ONE

* * * * * *

"My God, do people really live out here?" Anneke asked as the Land Rover jounced over the rutted road.

She'd had to scramble to get ready for the trip, and now she wondered if it had been worth it. There was a lot of work to do at the office, but then there always was, and as Ken had pointed out, there always would be. He had urged her to go, and in the end she'd agreed. She'd even managed to pack in fifteen minutes, a personal best that left her wondering what she'd forgotten to bring.

"City girl." Karl laughed as he reached forward and pushed a button below the dashboard. "Where I grew up, in the western Pennsylvania mountains, this would be positively suburban."

"Well, you've come a long way, baby. Thank God." She gripped the door handle. "The closest I want to get to a log cabin is a tour of Greenfield Village."

"You'd be surprised. They still build a lot of log cabins up here, you know—log houses, really. You can buy a prefab kit complete with modern kitchen, plumbing, even cathedral ceilings."

"If it doesn't come with sidewalks, I'll pass." She winced as the Land Rover negotiated a long series of bumps, then gasped as the car leaped forward finally into an open clearing. "Wow. That's no log cabin."

"It certainly isn't." They both stared at the big Victorian house that dominated the vista. "Not your average cottage in the woods, is it?"

"Not your average anything." Anneke gazed at the house and beyond. "What a gorgeous site. And river frontage, too. I have to admit," she said, "that sometimes when I see a spot like this I do get caught up in the romance of camping under the stars."

"Take it from someone who did a lot of camping as a kid—there's damn little romance in sleeping with a tree root poking you in the rear, or not showering for days at a time."

"I'll take your word for it." She laughed. "A four-star motel on the shore of Lake Mitchell is my idea of a romantic north-country adventure."

"Well, we'll see what we can do about the romance." He grinned at her. "But if you're counting on a moonlight stroll along the beach, I hope you stocked up on mosquito repellent."

"Ugh. How about room service and the Pistons game on television? Ouch." The Land Rover bumped onto a concrete slab and came to a halt next to a white Buick.

"Good timing." Karl checked his watch as they descended from the car. "I'm meeting the sheriff here at three o'clock. Meanwhile, I want to take a look at the damage."

Dwight was apparently expecting them; he threw the front door open and greeted them with bustling relief.

"Good, good, you're here. Come in. You can hang your coats there." He waited impatiently for them to remove their coats and hang them on the battered Victorian hall tree, then led them through the front hall into the typically shabby living room of a vacation home. "There." He pointed toward a set of wood-framed windows looking out toward the woods. Unlike the oak trim of the Ann Arbor house, the woodwork here was all dark stained pine, carved and decorated in a less elaborate manner. But just like the Ann Arbor house, a slab of wood lay on the floor beneath each window.

"I've left them in place," Dwight explained. "Otherwise we'll never be able to tell which sill goes where."

"Windowsills." Olivia Swann emerged from a doorway at the end of the room. She looked disturbed, but Anneke could see her assessing Karl's gray cotton sweater, and her own black denims and heavy silver jewelry. "Vandalism and muggings," she said angrily. "We might as well be living in Detroit."

"Muggings?" Karl repeated the word quickly.

"Yes. Our leaseholder," Dwight replied. "Didn't the sheriff tell you?"

"I haven't spoken to him directly yet. He was out when I called. The dispatcher arranged for us to meet here. I didn't realize you leased this place."

"Oh, not the house," Dwight corrected him. "The trees." Before he could explain further, footsteps pounded down the stairs. They turned toward the sound, and Anneke was surprised to see Zoe burst into the room.

"Hi, guys. What're you doing here?" Her mass of curly black hair was even wilder than usual.

"Why am I not surprised?" Karl murmured. "You have cobwebs in your hair," he said to Zoe.

"Yuck. I hope that's all they are." She swiped ineffectually at her head. "We've been up in the attic, getting camping gear."

"Camping gear?" Anneke asked.

"Don't ask." Zoe's voice was sardonic, but her copper eyes snapped with excitement. "Come on up and give us a hand."

Anneke glanced at Karl, communicating without words. "All right," she said to Zoe. "Glad to help if I can."

She followed Zoe silently up two flights of stairs, aware of the girl's suppressed excitement. Zoe crested the top of the attic stairs and pointed dramatically. "Look at that."

"At what?" Anneke took the last step and stopped to get her bearings.

"The window!" Zoe jabbed her finger in the air, and Anneke saw the pattern of glass set into the wall. "The Black Diamond window!"

"It's probably just a coincidence," Clare said. She was down on hands and knees rolling up a sleeping bag. Anneke saw with a start that Patrick was beside her, working on a tangle of rope.

"It's all right," he said. "I've been paroled to Zoe's custody." When Anneke didn't reply, he said, "Honestly, I'm here because I can help. I know this part of the world. What do you think about the window?"

Instead of answering, she walked over to the window and looked out through it. Trees. Well, trees and a glint of river. She tried to look through one of the black panes, but it was fully opaque. Finally she turned back to the threesome and shrugged.

"But it must mean something," Zoe protested as though Anneke had spoken.

"Zoe, sometimes a cigar is just a cigar." Clare had finished rolling up the sleeping bag and was now doing something with a fishing rod.

"Yes, but—" There was a muted thump from below. "That must be the sheriff," Zoe said. "Come on." Without waiting for the others, she pounded back down the stairs. Patrick and Clare met each other's eyes for a moment and remained where they were. Anneke took a last look around the attic, seeing nothing of note, and followed Zoe downstairs. She reached the front hall as Dwight was ushering a large, beefy man wearing sheriff's brown into the living room.

"Lieutenant Genesko." The sheriff strode forward and held out his hand. "I'm Marv Kettleman, Missaukee County sheriff."

"Glad to meet you, Sheriff." Karl shook the man's hand.

Kettleman tilted his head. "Ain't often I have to look up to make eye contact. Remember seein' you play. You were a real headhunter." He sounded appreciative. "Okay if we go sit around the table, Dwight?"

"Yes, of course." Dwight led them through the doorway at the end of the living room, and after a quick glance at Karl, Anneke followed along.

The big, battered table was covered with papers, which Dwight hastily gathered together. One of them Anneke recognized as a deed to the property; she saw once again the odd, old-fashioned designation, Sec. 19, T22N R8W. As they arranged themselves around the table, Anneke examined the sheriff, finding him both like and unlike the stereotype in her head. He had the expected paunch pushing against his brown uniform shirt, the expected red, beefy face and balding head, the expected rural-folksy manner. What was unexpected was the quiet voice and the sharp intelligence behind the brown eyes that gazed at her.

"Don't believe we've met," he said to her.

"Anneke Haagen." She was at the end of the table, too far away to shake hands. "I came up with Lieutenant Genesko."

"How do." He nodded. Anneke was sure he understood perfectly the ambiguity of her response. He turned to Karl. "I read through the stuff you faxed me. Nasty. And now windowsills." He leaned back and folded his hands over his ample stomach.

"And, I understand, a mugging as well?" Karl asked.

"Well, yeah. Mind you," Kettleman said judiciously, "I'm not sure there's a connection. There's some weird stuff goes on in these woods. Guy's name's Pete Carmichael—leases a couple of acres of trees from the Swanns."

"I didn't realize there was still lumbering going on around here," Karl commented.

"Not lumbering." Dwight sounded shocked. "Those are maples."

"Syrup rights," Kettleman explained. "Carmichael taps the trees every spring, sells maple syrup. He says he was out checkin' his taps late Friday afternoon, pretty near the house, when someone comes up behind him and knocks him cold. Comes to about ten minutes later, he says, picks himself up, and goes on home. Says he didn't hear nothin' before nor after."

"Anything stolen?"

"Nah. Didn't have nothin' *to* steal, so he says. Didn't even have his wallet on him."

"And what do you think, Sheriff?"

"Call me Marv," Kettleman said. "Well, now." He cocked his head. "Coulda been kids. Coulda been poachers, either animal or syrup. Oh, yeah," he said to Karl's surprised look. "People'll come through and empty the sap buckets. Thing is, it's a little too early in the season for that. Also, it coulda been some fool scouting war game locations—we get some of them around here, too. Or," he said, sitting up straighter, "it coulda been someone breakin' into the house who didn't want witnesses. And if that's it, I figure Pete's a damn sight luckier than poor old Gerald was."

"I take it he wasn't hit very hard."

"Nope. And just the once. Coulda been something like a car jack, or a good-size tree branch, somethin' like that— couldn't do anything with forensics, 'cause the damn fool went home and washed it off before he called us. Not that we'd've been likely to anyway," he admitted. "Prob'ly just written it off, if we hadn't heard from you about this other stuff."

"How did you come to discover the vandalism itself?" Karl asked.

"After Pete's call, I had someone check the house. Just sort of for the hell of it." Kettleman shrugged. "Back door was hangin' open." He turned to Dwight. "I had Jarman come out and fix the window," he said. "He'll send you the bill."

"Thanks, Marv," Dwight said gloomily.

"You gonna sell the place, now that Julia's gone?" Kettleman asked.

"Probably." Dwight looked around the big dining room, and glanced at his wife before shaking his head. "I guess so."

"Hate to see the Swanns disappear from around here for good," Kettleman said. "On the other hand, it'd be nice to have full-time folks livin' here."

"Olivia, everything downstairs—what's going on?" Helena appeared in the doorway that Anneke assumed led to the kitchen. Her face was flushed, and there were smears of dirt on her brown pants. "What are you all up to?" She darted looks of suspicion around the table.

"We're merely talking to the authorities about the vandalism," Olivia said with exaggerated patience. "What on earth have you been doing?" She wrinkled her nose at Helena's disheveled state.

"I've been in the basement, *trying* to salvage things," Helena replied angrily. "There are *mice* down there." She shuddered. "They've chewed through everything they could reach, and left their disgusting droppings all over the place. God knows what they've destroyed. I thought you were supposed to be taking care of the estate," she snapped at Dwight.

"Helena, there's nothing of any earthly value in that basement," Olivia said.

"Not anymore, there isn't," Helena said. "And who knows what those vandals took."

"Is there anything you know of that's missing, ma'am?" Kettleman asked.

"How would I know?" She swung toward him. "It's not like I'm really *family*, after all. I'm not the one who grew up here and knows all the hiding places." She directed a dark look at Dwight.

"Hiding places." Kettleman, to Anneke's surprise, repeated the words thoughtfully. "Y'know," he said slowly, as if thinking aloud, "if I didn't know any better, I'd think that someone was huntin' for old Smalley's mythical stash."

TWENTY-TWO

• • • • • •

The name didn't mean anything, and then suddenly it did. Anneke froze, swallowing hard to keep an exclamation from escaping her lips. The line from Clare's letters swam through her mind: "I know it may be Smalley's but I promise you" something or other. Smalley! Smalley's stash? She maintained what she hoped was a mildly interested gaze at Kettleman, waiting for someone else to ask the inevitable question.

"Smalley's stash?" Karl asked.

"Yeah." Kettleman grinned. "Old northwoods tall tale." He gazed at them. "You folks know anything about the old Ticket to Hell days?"

"Ticket to hell?" Karl asked.

"That's what they used to call it. See, you got to understand that the loggin' operation—actual cuttin' down of the trees—was mostly winter work." He smiled at their dubious looks. "This is how it worked. Lumber company'd set up a temporary camp in the middle of the area they wanted to

• 1 8 9 •

clear. They'd hire themselves however many shanty boys they needed an' settle 'em in the camps around the first snows. Those boys'd live out in the camp right through the winter, cuttin' timber."

"Why in the winter?" Karl asked.

"Because that way they could use skidding sleds to bring the logs down out of the woods," Kettleman explained. "It's a lot easier to slide things over ice than it is to haul them in wagons over dirt tracks. Anyway, like I said, the shanty boys would be out in the camps for the whole winter, while their pay was buildin' up. When the spring thaws came, some of 'em would get jobs as riverhogs, but most of 'em were paid off and cut loose. And a whole lot of 'em would use that fat pay envelope to buy a Ticket to Hell."

He chuckled at their quizzical looks. "Hell was any wide-open mill town where they could get all the booze they wanted, all the women they wanted, and all the fightin' they wanted—as long as their money held out. Some of those towns got real famous for it, in fact—there was one called Seney, in the UP, that was s'posed to've had a kind of slave stockade run by a local boss who finally got took down when he murdered one of the girls. None of the towns around here were that bad, but there was plenty of them set up to separate the shanty boys from their pay."

"And this Smalley goes back to that period?" Karl asked.

"Yeah. John Smalley was the wild north's answer to Jesse James—a train robber. Oh yeah, we had 'em up here." Kettleman chuckled. "Smalley was smarter'n most of them, too. Mostly worked the areas downstate and into Indiana, then he'd come up here to live between jobs. Legend is that he cleared over a million bucks, back when that was really worth something."

"Which, I take it, was never found." Karl grinned. "What happened to him?"

"Oh, they got 'im in the end. A real Butch Cassidy–style

shootout, too, by all accounts. 'Cept John Smalley wasn't no romantic charmer—not that I figure ol' Butch looked much like Paul Newman, either. The thing to know about Smalley," Kettleman said seriously, "is that he was one mean sumbitch—like most criminals." He looked suddenly very much what he was, a cop.

"Anyway, back in August of '95 he pulls a job on a Chicago and West Michigan freight, near Fennville, down past Grand Rapids. Nice clean job, an' he gets away with some thousands of dollars. But see, one of the differences between the wild north and the wild west is that instead of everyone being on horseback, most travel was done by train. So a couple of days later, Smalley's spotted on a train headin' north through Grand Rapids, and when the cops try to arrest him, he shoots one of 'em in the head and gets away. And a few days after *that*, he's spotted gettin' off a train at McBain, right here in Missaukee County."

Kettleman was a natural storyteller; none of them took their eyes off him as he paused, letting the drama build.

"The sheriff gets together a posse, and they go after him. Now, some folks knew he had a hideout somewhere in the area, but no one in the posse knows where it is. What they do know is that he has a woman, common-law wife, livin' in McBain with her mother and brother. They figured that's what he was doin' in McBain, and sure enough, that's where he was."

Kettleman paused a moment. "Another one of the things that was different up here from the old west is that most of our fightin' was done with fists and boots and loggin' hooks, instead of guns. Gangs of shanty boys used to pile off the trains and go stompin' through town lookin' for other gangs to fight. But Smalley was different. He was famous for the amount of hardware he carried—as many as six or eight guns at a time. Always wore a long coat, winter and summer, to hide them. So that sheriff wasn't about to take any chances.

Anyway, the posse surrounds the Brown house and yells for him to come out. Cora and her brother dive out the back door and take off. Smalley doesn't. Posse goes in shootin' and Smalley takes two bullets in the head.

"Wasn't a penny in his pockets, and they never found the money." Kettleman leaned back in his chair, chuckling.

Anneke barely heard his last sentence. The names "Brown" and "Cora" seemed to reverberate through her head. She gritted her teeth with the effort of keeping her face blank.

"Quite a story," Karl said, smiling appreciatively. "Did they ever find his hideout?"

"Oh, sure. Big, two-story log cabin over in Clare County, near the Roscommon County line. Might still be there, for all I know, but if it is, I'll guarantee there ain't no money there. See, once folks knew Smalley was dead, there was a small stampede—he'd done a fair bit of braggin' about the jobs he'd pulled, so people figured there had to be a big wad stashed somewhere. But as far as anyone knows, nothin' was ever found." His light brown eyes were fixed on Karl as though waiting for another question.

"And why," Karl asked, "do you connect the legend of John Smalley with what's been going on here?"

"Yep, that's the question, all right." Kettleman nodded happily. " 'Cause of the windowsills." He chuckled at their blank looks. "Turns out Smalley's cabin had a fake windowsill, with a space hollowed out of the log under it. Everyone figures that's where he hid his loot, but all the reports say it was empty."

"Well, they would, wouldn't they?" Karl said, grinning. "It sounds very much like his common-law wife became a very wealthy widow."

"Maybe." Kettleman pursed his lips. "We don't know much about what happened to her after Smalley bought it, not even if she went back to working the huckleberry fields."

"Huckleberry fields?"

"Yeah, the huckleberry fields." Kettleman gazed out the window. "That's what we got in exchange for a few millenia of virgin woodland. A hundred twenty years ago, this whole county was primeval forest. A hundred years ago it was barren, clear-cut desert. That's all it took 'em to destroy it—about twenty years." His eyes seemed to look into the distance of time, not space.

"Anyway," he went on, "once the forest was nothin' but stumps, and once the fires took care of the stumps, the wild huckleberry bushes moved in. We wound up with acres and acres of prime wild blueberries. In the summer, gangs of pickers used to come up from downstate to harvest the berries. There was one big tent city over by the Muskegon River, you can still see signs of it, supposed to've had more than five hundred people."

"And Smalley's wife was one of the pickers?"

"Nope. She was one of the whores."

"One of the—" Anneke blurted out the words, then stopped.

"Sorry, ma'am." Kettleman, thank God, misunderstood her reaction. "Cora Brown was one of the prostitutes who worked the picking camps in the summer, set up her own tent an' everything. Rest of the year, of course, she'd've worked the mill towns. She was supposed to've made a pretty good living at it, too," he said in a matter-of-fact way.

"Sheriff, if you don't mind." Olivia wrinkled her nose in a gesture of distaste.

"Sorry, ma'am," Kettleman said again, this time without much apology in his voice. "But you get groups of men without families, you're gonna have prostitutes."

"All the same—" Olivia was interrupted by a sharp buzzing sound. "Excuse me, that's the doorbell."

"I have one other question," Karl said to Kettleman as Olivia hurried out of the room. "Why 'if you didn't know any better'?"

"Yeah, I did say that, didn't I? Well, look at it this way." Kettleman held up his hand, index finger extended. "First, I don't personally believe there ever was any hidden treasure. In my experience, and prob'ly yours, crooks don't save for a rainy day." He held up another finger. "Second, if there really was any treasure, someone would've found it by now—folks hunted for that mythical stash for a couple decades after Smalley bought it." He held up a third finger. "Three, there's no reason I can imagine why anyone would connect the Swann family to John Smalley and Cora Brown. And finally, the most important reason—this particular house wasn't even built until two years *after* Smalley was blown away. So, yeah, it don't make a lot of sense to me to figure someone's hunting for Smalley's stash."

He shrugged. "Well, I don't know if this gets us any further on." He put his hands flat on the table and hoisted himself erect. "It sure don't seem to have anything to do with poor old Gerald."

"It also doesn't help us find out who's been vandalizing our house. Houses," Dwight said with annoyance.

"I told you," Helena said sharply, "there's a lunatic running loose." She stood up and stalked toward the kitchen.

"If so, he's a damn tidy one," Kettleman said under his breath, glancing at the pine sills lying neatly beneath each of the windows. He turned to Karl. "You want to take a look at where Carmichael was hit?"

"Yes, I would, thanks." Both men stood, and Anneke got to her feet as well.

"Please let me know if you find out anything, Marv," Dwight said fretfully. "Oh, good." He turned toward the living room, and Anneke followed his gaze and raised her eyebrows in surprise.

"Michael? What are you doing here?"

"I have been asking myself that for the last thirty miles," Michael Rappoport replied. He followed Olivia into the dining room, resplendent in a soft, loose-fitting maroon silk jacket over a black silk turtleneck and black trousers; even in the north woods, Michael dressed for effect. Anneke noted with amusement the curious look Kettleman gave him. Curious but not derisive, she conceded, giving the sheriff full marks for tolerance.

"Come in, Mr. Rappoport, please." Dwight bustled forward. "I'd like to get started, if we could. Unless you'd like my wife to show you your room first?"

"Thank you, but I've arranged to stay in a hotel." Michael's voice was so firm that no one pressed him on the issue. "Shall we begin in here?"

"Yes, that's fine." Dwight shuffled papers again.

"Where would you like me to start, Mr. Swann?" The low, throaty voice came from a small, nondescript woman in blue jeans and a khaki shirt who had gone unnoticed behind Michael's peacock splendor. Although, Anneke thought, she was the sort of woman who would usually go unnoticed.

"Oh, Ms. Pryor, good." Dwight looked around. "Most of the papers are either in the basement or the attic."

"I'll start in the basement, I think," the woman said. "But if you don't mind, I'd like to use your bathroom first." She smiled and turned back toward the front hall.

"Let me start with your inventory," Michael said. He strode to the table, then turned toward Anneke and mouthed "Woodlake." She grinned slightly and nodded before following Karl and the sheriff to the front hall. But as she reached for her coat she heard her name called.

"Anneke?" Zoe stood halfway up the staircase, trying unsuccessfully to look nonchalant. Her eyes blazed with excitement. "Can I talk to you before you go?"

"You'll be a while, won't you?" she asked Karl, who nodded with the flicker of a smile. "Then I'll meet you at the car." She turned toward the staircase, aware of Kettleman's thoughtful gaze on her.

"C'mon up to the attic." Once out of earshot, Zoe made no further attempt to hide her excitement. "We've got to tell Clare!"

"You heard all that, I assume?"

"Sure. I was standing in the living room, just around the edge of the doorway." She pounded up the last few steps to the attic, where Clare and Patrick looked up, startled. "We know what the treasure is!" she burst out.

"What? How?" "What are you talking about?" They spoke together, but Zoe's excited voice overrode them both.

"It's loot hidden by a train robber, back in the eighteen hundreds!"

"What? How do you know?" Clare's eyes were wide, hope mixed with disbelief.

"From the sheriff." As quickly as possible, Zoe sketched out the story of John Smalley and Cora Brown. When she was finished, even Clare had dawning hope in her eyes.

"Robbery loot," she said. "It makes sense, I guess, doesn't it?"

"Sure it does," Zoe said. "And think of this—we're talking about actual cash here. I'll bet your aunt Julia was just drawing from it as she needed it."

"So Cora Brown was a famous whore." Patrick's face wore a thoughtful expression. "And our sainted ancestor Henrietta, of course, would have been every inch a lady. Well, it explains some of the references in the letters, like the one about hoodlums." He grinned. "The question is, what possible connection could there have been between a nineteenth-century lady and a whore?" He stopped. "The Lady and the Whore—what a book title. But considering the social structure of the nineteenth century, it's legitimate to ask which one was the lady, which the whore?"

"What's that supposed to mean?" Zoe asked.

"Well, you're talking about an era when women made their living from men, one way or another." There was something mischievous in his expression. "What's the real difference between getting money from one man, or a whole group of them? After all, the whore at least could do what she wanted with the money she earned on her back."

"Hell, maybe a lot of the stash really belongs to Cora," Zoe said, laughing.

"Remember this, too," Patrick added. "This was in the eighteen-nineties, so a lot of the money could be in old coins."

"Wow, that's right." Zoe's eyes flashed. "And some of them are worth thousands of dollars."

In the face of their palpable excitement, Anneke held back her comment. But as she hesitated, she saw Clare's face dim.

"It sounds great," she said. "There's only one problem— where the shit is it?" They stared at each other, enthusiasm draining from them.

"Well," Zoe said with a small laugh, "at least we know it isn't inside the windowsills."

"Shit, we don't even know that," Clare pointed out. "Whoever trashed the windowsills could've found it." There was a long mournful silence.

"The hell with this," Zoe said firmly. "We're going to assume it's still there—wherever 'there' is. For one thing, if everyone around here knows the Smalley legend, I think your aunt would've been too shrewd to use the one hiding place that was positively famous."

"That's true," Patrick said encouragingly.

"Besides, I'm a big fan of Jamesian pragmatism," Zoe went on. "If it's already gone, we don't lose anything but time hunting for it. But if it's still there and we *don't* keep looking, think what we lose."

"Good. I like that." Patrick nodded with appreciation. "So

we keep looking. And at least now we know what we're looking for."

"Do you?" Anneke finally spoke. Their eyes turned to her, puzzled. "If the 'treasure' you're hunting for is really John Smalley's hidden money, then what," she asked, "is Black Diamond?"

McBain, Michigan: August 21, 1895

He'd built the house away from the river, he'd told her, because of the spring floods. But now he talked of a gazebo.

"A summer house." Walter eyed the riverbank with satisfaction, owner of all he surveyed. "We can entertain down here, maybe little dinner parties. If you can ever teach that girl to cook a proper dinner, that is."

Henrietta flinched at the criticism, and even more at the notion of playing hostess, smiling and chattering and pretending to be a perfect, loving wife while the wives of the few other men who were their social equals watched, and measured, and found her wanting. Dinner parties, social occasions of any sort, were merely opportunities for her to commit greater transgressions, and earn greater punishments.

"We'll put it right there." Walter waved expansively, for once in a good mood. "Right by those willows. What's that?" He peered into the twilight, and Henrietta saw a black shape under the trees. As she watched, the shape moved, resolving itself into a figure. "Well, well, well," Walter said softly.

He strode forward and grasped the figure by the arm, hauling it upright, and Henrietta gasped in frightened recognition. Walter turned at the sound of her gasp, and his eyes narrowed before he gazed at Cora Brown once more with a speculative look in his eye.

"Would you like to tell me what you're doing here?" he asked her.

"Sorry, Mr. Swann." Cora ducked her head. "I was cuttin' through on my way home, and I twisted my ankle real bad." She stood on one foot, holding the other slightly off the ground. "I was waitin' for it to ease up some. I'm sorry I was trespassin'— it won't happen again."

Walter raised his hand with an air of utter casualness and backhanded Cora viciously across the face. Henrietta whimpered at the sharp crack of sound from the blow, and Walter looked at her briefly. "Now," he repeated to Cora, "what are you doing here?"

"I'm gettin' the hell out of town." She stood straight now, both feet planted firmly on the soft ground of the riverbank, looking directly at Walter.

"Why here?" Walter sounded casually curious, and Henrietta shivered. She tried to send Cora a warning glance, but couldn't catch her eye.

"I helped out your wife a while back," Cora said. "I thought maybe you'd help me out in exchange—maybe give me enough of a stake for train fare to Muskegon."

"So you and that criminal you consort with have had a falling-out." Walter stepped back and seemed to examine her thoughtfully. "I imagine Smalley would be very interested in your whereabouts?"

"Nah. He don't want anything to do with me no more."

"In that case," Walter said, "it won't matter to you if I hold you in the stables and send a man to inform Smalley that you're here."

"He won't care." Cora shrugged, but her eyes darted back and forth, and Henrietta knew Walter saw their movement. He tightened his grip on her arm.

"Let's go, then." He started to drag her toward the stables, but she hung back, pulling against his grasp.

"Come on, Mr. Swann. There ain't no need, just let me go,

okay? I won't bother you again." Her voice was firm and clear, with only a hint of reasonable entreaty, but Henrietta's heightened senses felt rather than heard her fear. Walter, she knew, was attuned to fear.

"But you were trespassing on my property, weren't you? That is, as you know, a criminal offense. Surely you must expect to be ... punished." Walter looked at her expectantly, and after a moment Cora shrugged once more.

"Yeah, I'll take my punishment from you, Mr. Swann."

"Walter, please." Henrietta forced out the words through shaking lips, then shrank back as he turned and stared at her. "Miss Brown s-saved me from that m-mob," she stuttered past her terror. "I owe her a d-debt of gratitude."

His light brown eyes regarded her. "You still don't understand your place, I see," he replied softly. "Perhaps you feel some ... kinship to this whore?" He gazed from her to Cora and back. "How interesting. I think this evening we might amuse ourselves with a threesome."

A few months ago she would not have had the smallest idea what he meant. Now she did. He said something else, a smile on his lips, but she couldn't make out the words over the roaring in her ears. She felt the dizziness with gratitude, letting it overtake her so that she didn't have to think about . . . think about . . .

"What a useless encumbrance you are." Walter's hands, gripping her arms none too gently, kept her upright. His voice rasped in her ear.

"You'll have more fun without her tonight anyway," she heard Cora say. "She'd only cramp my style. Besides, there wouldn't be no fun in it if she keeps faintin' on us."

"I suppose you're right." Walter let go of Henrietta so abruptly that she staggered and went down on one knee, the dizziness now of sheer relief. "I'm sure she'll be even more grateful to you than she is now, for sparing her my attentions for one evening, at least," he said mockingly.

The greatest shame of all, Henrietta thought, is that he's right.

Dear Mis Swann, Im sorry about gettin you into trubel if you dont act afrad he wont bother you so much. I no you tryed to help it wasnt yur falt. Im okay Im gong to tak care of things so I wont hav to wory no mor. I only tuk some food nuthin els.

TWENTY-THREE

* * * * * *

"I suppose I should have expected to see Zoe up here." Karl smiled slightly as he backed the Land Rover off the concrete pad.

"She heard the sheriff's story, of course. They're convinced that Smalley's money is the point of those letters." Anneke buckled her seat belt with one hand and grabbed the door handle with the other as the car bounced into the rutted track heading away from the house.

"And what about you?" Karl asked.

"Well, actually I suppose I am, too," she said slowly. "I mean, given the connection to Cora Brown. And Smalley himself is actually referred to by name. I wish we had the letters with us—I can't remember enough of them." She shook her head. "Besides, there's too much coincidence otherwise. Look at what we've got." She turned in her seat. "For a hundred years after Smalley's death, nothing happens. Then the letters turn up, and immediately afterward a man is murdered, and someone pries off all the windowsills in both of

Julia Swann's houses. It *has* to be someone searching for Smalley's money. And why else would someone suddenly link Smalley to the Swann family, except through those letters?"

"Aren't you forgetting something?" Karl steered the Land Rover expertly between ruts. "Nobody *got* the letters, remember? You and Zoe and Clare are the only ones who've seen them."

"But—oh, hell. But then, how *did* anyone connect Smalley to the Swanns?"

"Well, assuming that's what the windowsill business really is about, it had to have been recent," Karl pointed out. "Otherwise they would have searched the windowsills long before now."

"Which means there's some other clue to Smalley that we haven't identified. It also suggests," she said thoughtfully, "that Gerald was killed because someone assumed the letters would tell them where the money *is.*"

"Isn't that something of a stretch?" Karl asked. "After all, no one knew the contents of the letters at all, at that point. You're suggesting that someone committed murder for something, without even knowing if the something actually existed."

"God, what a nasty thought." Anneke shuddered. "Taking life almost on a whim, just like stepping on a bug. Ouch!" She grabbed for the dashboard as the Land Rover swung off the rutted path onto a marginally better dirt road, jouncing over a particularly deep chuckhole in the process. "What did the sheriff have to say to you outside?" she asked when the bouncing subsided slightly. "Did he know any more about Smalley?"

"I don't think so. We were talking about Gerald."

"Gerald." Anneke pondered for a moment. "Karl, do you think *Gerald* knew anything about Smalley's money?"

"I have no idea." He sounded amused. "I'll know more about Gerald tomorrow. Kettleman knows someone who spent time with him, and he's arranging a meeting. Supposedly, this man and Gerald were involved in something to do with northern Michigan Indian burial grounds."

"That doesn't sound like it has any connection to a nineteenth-century outlaw." Anneke leaned back, looking out at the woods lining the road. "It really is beautiful up here, isn't it?"

"Yes. It took a hundred years, but it's good to see the forests beginning to return."

"I'd never want to live out here myself, but I think I can understand those who do." Through the trees, she could see a small cabin huddled among the pines. "It's amazing that there are still places as isolated as this in what we think of as such an industrialized state."

"There are still a lot of places to hide, up here."

"Or to hide things in." The car turned onto blacktop finally, and Anneke felt an odd sense of relief as the Land Rover headed toward Cadillac. They crossed into Wexford County, then through town along the south shore of Lake Cadillac, and on around to Lake Mitchell. The bigger of Cadillac's two lakes, it gleamed coldly in the pale late afternoon sun; on its surface, ducks floated peacefully, or foraged in the reeds edging the water. Anneke watched the sun's reflection ripple on the water and felt the day's tensions drain out of her.

The sun was setting by the time they checked into the Woodlake Inn, a long, sprawling building tucked into a clearing along Lake Mitchell. From the sliding glass door of their ground-floor room, a flagstone path angled between the trees to a small sandy beach.

"Oh, look." Anneke pointed to a bowl of popcorn on the white dresser, with a little sign attached that read FOR THE DUCKS. "Let's go feed them."

"All right," Karl agreed. "But I'd like to unpack first and check in with my office."

"You know," Anneke said, unzipping her suitcase and peering irritably at the contents, "I used to be able to pack for a weekend by tossing a toothbrush and change of underwear into my bag. Now look." She pulled her makeup kit and blow dryer from the suitcase. "The older I get, the more *stuff* I have to haul with me."

"Just think," he said, grinning, "by the time you're sixty you'll have to trade in your car for a forklift." She threw a piece of popcorn at him; he caught it neatly in midair, popped it into his mouth, and promptly spit it out into his hand. "Ugh."

"Well, it *says* it's for the ducks," she reminded him, laughing.

She finished unpacking while Karl sat at the small desk talking on the phone. "Anything new?" she asked when he hung up.

"In fact, yes. Brad finally got hold of Christopher Swann in Hokkaido."

"And?"

"It turns out he was the one who gathered up Gerald's papers from the anthropology department, after Gerald disappeared."

"Oh, good. I know you wanted to find out what Gerald was working on." She still wasn't sure why Karl was so anxious to know, but she assumed he had his reasons.

"Except," Karl grimaced, "Christopher doesn't think he has them anymore."

" 'Doesn't think'?"

"It seems that he and his wife bought a house out in Barton Hills three years ago. And he *thinks* Gerald's papers were tossed when they moved."

"But if he's not sure, can't you at least look for them?"

"Eventually. Christopher told Brad he'd be glad to search for the papers when he gets back into town—in about two weeks—but he balked at allowing a police search."

"Well, I suppose that's understandable. I wouldn't give permission for the police to search my home, either," Anneke said. "Could Christopher at least remember anything about the contents of the papers?" She knew Brad Weinmann well enough to be sure he'd asked.

"He says not," Karl said. "According to Brad, Christopher apparently looked over the papers, decided there was nothing of monetary value in them, and put them out of his mind."

"Had he had any contact with Gerald since he left Ann Arbor?"

"Again, he says not. Brad says he thinks Christopher was telling the truth, but it's hard to make that judgment from a phone conversation."

"So that's another dead end." From what she knew of Christopher Swann, Anneke concluded that if he said Gerald's papers were worthless, they were worthless. "You'd think he'd at least come home for his brother's funeral."

"I gather there isn't going to be a funeral. We released the body today, but Dwight had already arranged for cremation and disposal."

"Disposal." Anneke mouthed the word. "Poor Gerald. And even more, I think, poor Clare. Oh, hell."

"Yes." His face was somber.

"I'd better call my office, too," she said, feeling depressed. Karl stood up, and she took his place at the desk and pressed buttons on the phone. No, Ken told her, there were no crises needing her attention.

"You enjoy yourself," he directed her.

"All right, I think I will." Karl had stretched out on the bed and turned on the television, keeping the sound muted; on the screen, the Pistons were leading the Golden State Warriors, 62–41. She smiled at Karl and punched into her voice mail.

"Hi, Mom." This time she recognized the voice at once as

Rachel's. "Talked to Emma again for about an hour," her elder daughter's voice continued, "and I finally convinced her to at least meet Karl. She's doing some craft show in Chicago next month, and she said she'd talk to him if you two want to meet her there. It's a start, anyway. Give me a call, okay?"

"No!" Anneke blurted as the message ended with a click.

"No, what?" Karl looked up from the basketball game.

"My darling daughter is willing to *consider* the possibility that you *might* meet with her approval. We're to present ourselves to her next month for examination, time and place of her choosing, of course." She was coldly angry now, and miserable at the same time, with a sick feeling like a chunk of ice in the pit of her stomach.

"I'm perfectly willing, you know," Karl said quietly.

"Thank you for that. But I am *not* willing." She took a deep breath. "Dear, the thing is, this isn't about you. It's about me. Either I have Emma's respect or I don't." She felt tears burning behind her eyes and blinked them back angrily. "The fact that I love you has to be enough for her, or Emma and I have no relationship worth salvaging."

"If you can't work this out," he said steadily, "there's a very real risk you'll end up resenting me for the breach."

"No." She crossed to the bed and sat down next to him, reaching for his hand. "I worked that through when I first heard from Emma." He smiled slightly, and she managed a brief smile in response. "All right, yes, I'm cursed with a logical mind. But for once in my life, logic and emotion are both telling me the same thing. I love Emma," she said soberly, grasping his hand tightly, "but you're the one I plan to spend the rest of my life with."

"I'm exceedingly glad to hear it." He put his arm around her and drew her down next to him. She stayed there for a while, drawing comfort from him, feeling the pain and anger recede. His arm around her twitched slightly.

"What's the score?" she murmured.

"Pistons by twelve." They looked at each other and laughed aloud.

"You see?" She sat up. "We're too well matched to dare risk losing this. Oh for heaven's sake," she said to the TV screen, determinedly cheerful, "get under the boards."

TWENTY-FOUR

. . . . . .

Having watched the Pistons game, they decided to forego room service in favor of the hotel dining room. This time of year, midway between skiing season and swimming season, the Woodlake was half-deserted; they were shown to a table by the long window looking out onto the lake, where ducks drifted in the moonlight.

"It's gorgeous." Anneke sighed with pure pleasure. "We should do this more often."

"You're right, we should," Karl said seriously.

They were sipping wine and examining the menu when Anneke became aware of a small stir in the room. She followed the gaze of the dozen or so other diners to the front of the restaurant, where a tall, elegant figure stood waiting for the hostess. She chuckled as Karl raised a hand in invitation.

"My God." Michael Rappoport, trailing drama, threw himself into the offered chair. "Civilization at last. A Galliano on the rocks, please," he said to the awestruck waitress, "and consider it urgent."

"God, how can you drink that stuff?" Anneke wrinkled her nose. "It's like swigging pure syrup."

"I know, but it suits my image so well I can't resist." He looked out at the lake, then back at Anneke and Karl. "Are you sure I'm not intruding?"

"Not at all," Karl said at once.

"In fact," Anneke had a sudden thought, "I wanted to ask you something. Confidential, if you don't mind." When he nodded, she continued, "As you went through the things in the Swann house—in both houses, in fact—did you find anything with a Black Diamond on it?"

"A black diamond?"

"Anything with a black, diamond-shaped pattern on it."

He thought for a moment before shaking his head. "Nothing but that box, as far as I can recall. I'm not done yet, of course; if you like, I'll make a point of keeping my eyes open for it."

"If you would. Thanks, Michael."

"May one ask what this is about?"

"I'll explain later, I promise," she replied, feeling guilty. "It's not really my secret."

"Fair enough. Ah, thank you." The waitress set a glass of dark yellowish liquid in front of him. He took a sip. "Excellent. I might actually feel human any time now." The waitress, young and thin with bright yellow hair piled hugely atop her head, batted mascaraed eyelashes at him.

After they had ordered, and the waitress had simpered away toward the kitchen, Michael sighed dramatically. "Perhaps if I tell her you're a former football player," he said to Karl, "she'll transfer her attentions to you."

"Not necessarily," Anneke said gloomily, recalling Emma.

"Oh? Problems in paradise?" Michael spoke the flip words seriously.

"No, not between us," Anneke assured him. "It's my

daughter Emma. She's come unglued over the prospect of a 'dumb jock cop' as a stepfather."

"Oh dear, one of those." Michael looked at Karl. "I imagine that isn't a new problem for you, of course."

"No, although this is the first time I ever considered it worth concerning myself about. It more or less comes with the territory for football players—for all athletes, really." Karl shrugged. "When you earn your living through physical abilities, a certain proportion of people think you have no intellectual abilities."

"I suppose people like plumbers and carpenters have the same problem," Michael suggested.

"In a way. But because athletes can make a great deal of money, they're often the target for special resentment. And because their lives are so public, every negative is both magnified and generalized."

"There *is* something wrong with a culture that makes millionaires out of athletes and peons out of schoolteachers," Anneke pointed out.

"Oh, absolutely," Karl agreed. "But athletes aren't the ones who make the rules; they just play by them."

"Besides," Michael said shrewdly, "there's also the cop part of the equation."

"Yes." Anneke nodded unhappily. "With Emma, that's probably an even bigger problem."

"It usually is," Karl said. "For that matter," he looked at Anneke, "I think it bothered you, too, when we first met."

"Yes, it did," she admitted. "There was something . . . disturbing, I guess, about you being a cop. I found myself wondering if you lived in a state of perpetual suspicion of everyone, even me. It was unnerving for a while, until I got to know you better."

"Most people have very ambivalent attitudes toward the police." Karl sipped wine. "Even the most knee-jerk law-

and-order types are uneasy in the presence of a cop. That comes with the territory, too, I'm afraid."

"And the problem isn't helped by some of the scum walking around with badges," Anneke said.

"Of course it isn't." Karl accepted her statement as he knew she meant it. "I could protest that there are scum in every profession, and of course there are. But I know that would be specious. A rotten cop is a great deal more tragic than a rotten computer programmer, because we give the cop so much authority."

"And of course, my Emma was practically born opposing authority." Anneke laughed without much humor. "She was the kind of kid who had to have a reason for every single thing she did, from wearing clothes to reading *Huckleberry Finn.*"

"In other words, she has her mother's logical mind." Karl smiled at her. "In which case, why not give her a logical reason for marrying me?"

"Because I don't believe I should have to justify my actions to my daughter."

"I agree thoroughly." He nodded. "But there is a difference between justification and explanation. Why not try approaching Emma's objections as if they were logical rather than emotional, and see what happens?"

But is this sort of problem ever anything but emotional? Anneke thought. Besides, what would she say? That the only thing in common between Karl Genesko and Mark Fuhrman was the profession they listed on their income tax returns? No, that would be justification; the only thing Emma had a right to ask was why her mother was marrying this particular man.

The arrival of their food put an end to her speculation, and they spent the rest of the meal in companionable conversation about forest reclamation, the validity of psychohistorical analysis, and the scandal in the Ann Arbor city clerk's office. Anneke listened more than she spoke, drank wine, and watched wisps of cloud drift across the nearly full moon. Every now and then she reached over and touched Karl's hand.

"Thank you for the company," Michael said gravely when they had finished eating. "I'll leave you now. And I'll keep my eyes open for any black diamonds."

"Thank you, Michael." Anneke watched him stride toward the exit under the stare of every woman in the dining room. At the door the hostess, a well-groomed woman in her forties, stopped him on his way out. They spoke briefly, her hand on his arm; Michael smiled and shook his head. He turned back toward Anneke for a moment and rolled his eyes upward before finally making his escape.

"Poor Michael." Anneke giggled.

"Poor Michael, indeed." Karl grinned at her. "Although it's hard to feel sorry for a man just because women fall all over him."

"Oh, is that what you want?" she retorted. "Sorry I'm cramping your style, Lieutenant."

"Not interested. I told you—been there, done that."

"Yes, you did tell me. And you can stop bragging about it any time now."

They walked back to their room, and when they stepped inside Anneke's eye fell on the bowl of popcorn.

"We forgot to feed the ducks," she said. "Let's go do it now."

"In the dark? I don't know if there'll be any to feed. Why don't we wait till morning?"

"No, now," she insisted. She felt strangely manic, wanting to do something, to be outside in the moonlight. "It's not dark. See?" She pulled him toward the glass door. "The moon's so bright you can see shadows."

"All right." He smiled at her eagerness. They put their coats on and Anneke picked up the bowl of popcorn and slid the door open. It was cold, cold and exhilarating. They picked their way carefully down the flagstone path to the narrow strip of sand that ran the length of the inn but no further. Like most northern Michigan lakes, Lake Mitchell is rimmed by nature with trees and weedy marsh; the small beach was artificial, laid down by the inn for its guests.

"Damn, they're all over that way." Anneke pointed toward her right, where a small flotilla of ducks floated near the edge of the lake, just beyond the sand. She carried the bowl of popcorn to the end of the beach and threw a handful in the direction of the ducks, only to discover that popcorn is notoriously hard to throw. Most of it landed more or less directly at her feet. "Come help," she called to Karl. "You're the one who knows how to throw."

"Unfortunately, popcorn doesn't have the aerodynamic qualities of footballs." He caught up with her, took a handful of popcorn and heaved it toward the ducks. The popcorn landed in the water a foot or so from where they were standing. The ducks ignored them.

"Phooey." Anneke laughed at him. "What's the point of having a football player around if that's the best you can do?" She stepped off the sandy surface, working her way along the edge of the lake, feeling for solid footing as she went. Moonlight glittered off the water, drenching the world with brightness. The ducks were beginning to look interested; two or three of them began to drift in her direction. She took one more step, reaching with her foot for a rock at the edge of the water.

She knew instantly that she wasn't going to make it. She flung her arms wide, scattering popcorn, in a desperate effort to regain her balance, knowing it was a doomed effort even as she went face-first into the lake with a resounding splash.

"Oh, *shit.*" She scrambled onto hands and knees, sputtering and gasping. The lake at its edge was barely a foot deep, but the bottom was weeds and pebbles and thick, gooey muck.

"Are you all right?" Karl's hand was outstretched, pulling her to her feet.

"No, I'm not all right. Look at me!" She swiped futilely at the mud caking her sheepskin coat. "And stop laughing, you loon. I'm fr-freezing."

"At least you accomplished your purpose." He stopped laughing long enough to point out into the lake, where popcorn floated on the surface and a dozen ducks quacked and gobbled happily.

"I never knew you had such a w-warped sense of humor," she said between chattering teeth.

"Comes from all those years of locker-room practical jokes." He laughed again and reached for her hand.

The manic feeling was back. She took a step sideways, acting on pure impulse, turned slightly, and pushed as hard as she could, using her hip and shoulder, hoping that surprise, luck, and leverage would accomplish what physical force never could. And laughed with pure delight when Karl went down. His physical control was good enough to keep him from sprawling full-length into the lake, but he sat down, hard, in a foot of muddy, icy water.

"How's that for a locker-room practical joke?" She stood over him grinning, hands on hips, her own soggy condition forgotten. "Wow, wait'll I tell people that I blocked out the great Karl Genesko."

He got to his feet in a single smooth motion, his eyes glittering in the moonlight. She turned and ran, laughing, but instead of chasing her he walked casually toward the flagstone path. "You look worried," he said, the smallest flicker of a grin on his face.

"Take your best shot," she retorted.

"Oh, I will." He nodded amiably. "But right now, all I'm planning is a hot shower for both of us."

"Together?" She followed him up the path. "I like your idea of revenge, Lieutenant."

They took off their mud-soaked boots and coats, and left them outside on the patio before crossing quickly to the bathroom, where they turned on the shower full blast and shed their sodden clothes. Anneke felt the hot water like a benediction on her chilled skin; Karl's body, soap-slick, moved against hers as they stood under the steaming spray.

"Your hair is caked with mud," he said. "Turn around." She leaned back against him as his hands massaged her hair, then slid down her body in long, soapy strokes, fondling and caressing. The warmth of the water and the feel of his hands seeped beneath her skin into her veins. She turned toward him, eyes closed against the spray of the shower, reaching along his body by touch alone.

"Are you warm enough now?" he murmured in her ear, his hands moving over her body.

"Mm. What do you think?" She wrapped her arms around his neck, pressing her body to his, water coursing over them.

"Good." He stepped back and turned off the shower with a snap. "Time to get dried off," he said, patting her gently on the rear.

"Time—" She jerked her head back, every nerve in her body electrically charged.

"Was there something else?" He raised an eyebrow.

"You son of a bitch." She laughed up at him, hearing her voice shaky and breathless. "You would, wouldn't you?"

"Well, you could try saying please." He grinned slightly.

"In your dreams." She laughed again and took a step toward him, so that their bodies were touching once more, moving against him deliberately, feeling him hard against her stomach. "Just to remind you what you'll be missing."

He grasped her shoulders and kissed her, long and hard. "I think I can take that as a please," he said, grinning widely at her.

"I thought you might," she said.

McBain, Michigan: August 22, 1895

The early morning sun that broached the top of the stable door dragged Cora to wakefulness. She sat up and stretched, working her body experimentally, discovering that she was stiff and sore and bruised but otherwise not damaged. She'd managed to pour enough drink down Walter the night before to make him muzzy-drunk; he'd been about ready to pass out when he got to the point, so he didn't really hurt her as much as he thought he was.

She'd done Walter Swann a few times in the past, so she'd known what to expect. His big thing was pain, but Cora'd figured out that it wasn't the pain itself that got him going, it was the fear. Walter could only do it if the woman was terrified. Once she'd realized that, she'd stopped letting him see she was afraid, and after a while he'd moved on to other whores. She didn't think poor little Henrietta would ever stop being afraid.

She judged from the sun that it was barely daybreak, and she crossed the grass quietly to the kitchen door. Once inside, she found a pitcher of milk and drank a glassful, poured and drank another, broke off a chunk of ham and crammed it into her mouth. Then she stuffed her pockets with biscuits and apples and strips of dried beef. There was paper in the pantry, and she scribbled a note to Henrietta and shoved it into the flour bin before taking a loaf of bread to eat on the way.

The knowledge that she was finished with Smalley had come

neither suddenly nor slowly, but as an accepted fact. So did her plan. As she trudged eastward, she ran it through her mind. She knew that Smalley was supposed to leave town for a job yesterday, and knew also that he wouldn't bother to change his plans for her. Not when there was big money involved, and not when he figured he could take care of her when he got back.

If she was there when he returned, he'd beat her for sure. That she could put up with. But he'd also make her do One-Eye, and that she refused to do. She'd stayed with Smalley all this time because he'd been her protector—no one around here would mess with her if it meant answering to Smalley. But if he'd give her to One-Eye Joey, he wasn't no protector any more.

Out on the road, she hitched a ride on a hay wagon south to Marion, in Osceola County, where no one would know her, and more important, where she could hope no one would have heard of Smalley. She stood outside the telegraph office for a few minutes planning the message to Hank Beamer. Hank was a longtime customer who made a point of looking her up whenever he came through McBain selling logging equipment. But more important at the moment, Hank was a guy who was always looking for an easy score. She was sure he'd do it, for the reward if not for her.

SMALLEY GR & INDIANA TRAIN STOP FULLER STATION GR STOP TELL FOR REWARD.

She reread the message, hoping it was ambiguous enough not to attract the attention of a telegraph operator. It would take almost all the coins Walter had tossed contemptuously at her the night before. Well, that was okay. This was an all-or-nothing roll of the dice; she was about to make herself either very rich or very dead. She gave the slip of paper to the telegrapher, relieved to see that the message—and the name Smalley—didn't seem to mean anything to him.

Outside, she hung around town for a while until she saw a drayload of lumber heading in the right direction. She hitched a ride with the driver, a grizzled old-timer who talked her ear off for fifteen miles, but let her off near the Marion-Leota Road without curiosity. When he was out of sight she trudged the remaining half mile to Smalley's log cabin.

It was a pretty good-sized place, two stories with a sitting room and kitchen on the ground floor and a single large bedroom above, connected by a real staircase instead of a ladder. It was in good repair, too, the logs well-caulked and the plank floor neatly jointed and smooth. But it looked empty, almost abandoned, the way it always did even when Smalley was there. He had the bare minimum of furniture—a square oak table and two chairs, a couple of pine benches, a single kerosene lamp in each room. Upstairs, a bed, nightstand, and wardrobe.

Smalley didn't spend money on *things*.

Well, fewer places to look. She began upstairs, methodically searching the few clothes in the wardrobe, under and around the bed, even opening the stitches of the mattress and feeling around inside. When she was sure there was nothing hidden in the bedroom, she headed downstairs and gave the kitchen and sitting room the same careful search.

It was nearly two hours before she finally sank heavily into one of the chairs, gazing around the room and gnawing her lip. She knew it had to be here. She knew, from occasional newspaper accounts and one or two unguarded comments by Smalley himself, that he'd taken thousands and thousands of dollars from train robberies over the years—and he sure hadn't spent it on much.

He wouldn't've hid it anywhere else, either. He'd want to take it out often, count it, look at it, play with it. That was the whole point of money for him.

Okay, she hadn't expected it to be that easy. She eyed the floor, but when she examined the planks more carefully she could see no irregularities anywhere in their smoothly fitted expanse. She rapped on the stairs and ran her fingers over each tread, but they all seemed secure, and there were no traces of their having been pried up and renailed.

Baffled, she went to the front window and looked out at the gathering darkness. She only had a couple of days, she figured; once word of Smalley's capture got out, everyone who knew about this cabin would come haring out here to search for his stash. She pounded her fist on the windowsill in frustration.

Heard the scrape of wood on wood. Felt the pine sill move slightly. Caught her breath, yanked at the sill, dug her fingernails into the soft wood. When the sill came loose she tossed it aside and plunged her hands into the hollowed-out log beneath it, dragging out bills and coins and dropping them in a growing heap on the floor, laughing out loud all by herself in the empty log cabin.

She stopped counting at a hundred thousand and something, awed by the sheer volume of paper and metal. Her imagination choked at the amount—she couldn't comprehend the reality of so much money. How could you even spend that much in a lifetime?

The possibilities spread themselves in front of her like a tangle of huckleberry bushes, too many branches to think about. Stay or leave? Muskegon? Grand Rapids? Maybe even Chicago? And to do what—how to live? What to buy? Maybe go all the way out west to San Francisco—but why?

She'd never thought about the why of any of it before; it was the thorniest question. You couldn't answer the what or the where until you'd answered the why, but how even to begin? She slept finally, surrounded by money, worn out with the thinking about it all.

My dear Cora:

Coward that I am, I am sending this by way of Mr. Slocum, whose professions of friendship and loyalty to you are such that I am forced to believe them.

I have no words to express my feelings, but perhaps you may guess at their depths. Please believe me when I say that I understand fully the sacrifice you made, and that I believe you to be one of the bravest, and most decent—yes, decent— women it has ever been my privilege to know.

Out of my own poor cowardice, this is all I dare send you. It was my own before marriage, and therefore is unlikely to be missed, or to be recognized, should it be seen by another. I hope and pray that it is enough to start you on the path that you seek.

It would be my dearest wish that we might meet again, but I must put aside such selfishness and hope, instead, that this poor trinket assists you on your way. I promise you from my heart that you will always be in my prayers, and that I am, now and forever,

Faithfully yours,

Henrietta Swann

TWENTY-FIVE

. . . . . .

"How do you do it?" Clare asked curiously, holding her hands out to the campfire.

"Do what?" Zoe scooted forward, wrapping the blanket more tightly around her and contemplating the hitherto unappreciated joys of soft beds and hot showers. Beside her, two mushroom-shaped tents flanked the campfire, which blazed and crackled inside its circle of stones. A pot of hot water sat on the Coleman stove, along with a pot containing the remains of a couple of cans of corned beef hash. The frying pan that was to have cooked fresh brook trout lay abandoned next to the stove.

"This really isn't your thing, is it?" Clare waved an arm to encompass the campsite. "I mean, you really hate it. And yet you still seem to be having a good time. You're still *happy*. How the hell do you do it?" Clare asked the question seriously; she genuinely seemed to want an answer.

"Jeez, I don't know," Zoe said, embarrassed. "I guess I just . . . my mother has a thing she says, that most people are pretty much as happy as they make up their minds to be."

"Isn't that a lot like blaming the victim?" Clare retorted.

"I don't know. Maybe." Zoe spread her hands. "You asked."

"You make it sound so easy," Clare said morosely.

"Isn't that really another way of talking about empowerment?" Patrick offered.

"That's just redefining your terms," Clare pointed out. "It still doesn't explain how to do it."

"I think we're born with the ability to be happy," he said. "It's just that some of us forget how. Or let the bastards beat it out of us. Now, you did a pretty fair job of taking it back today."

"What do you mean?"

"You didn't even realize it, did you? The whole business about camping out—instead of getting into a screaming match about it, you just sort of ignored them. Went ahead and did what you wanted."

"I did, didn't I?" Clare seemed struck by the notion. "It just seemed like I didn't need to pay any attention to them, you know? I mean, with everything that's been going on lately, they just seemed so *silly*. It was like I suddenly realized I don't have to be angry anymore."

"Bingo," Patrick said softly.

"It can't be that easy," Clare said. "There's got to be a catch somewhere."

"There is. You have to refuse to let yourself be mind-fucked." Patrick spoke quietly and with enormous bitterness.

He had surprised Zoe, who had taken him for the comfort-loving type. Her respect for him had jumped a notch as she watched him set up the tents and build the fire. What's more, he'd cheerfully laughed at himself over his failure to catch anything from the river but an ancient tennis shoe. He was even the one who'd sneaked into the house and raided the larder for the cans of hash.

"It's easy to say just take control," Clare said. "It's not so easy to do, especially when they've *already* fucked with your head so badly you don't even know who you are half the time."

"Tell me about it." Patrick stared moodily into the fire. "Still, I think you've got a pretty good shot at pulling it off, Clarabelle." He reached over and ruffled Clare's hair.

"Stop that." She jerked away from him. "And don't call me Clarabelle."

"See what I mean?" He turned to face her. "You're a fighter. Once you learn to pick your battles, you're going to be okay." This time he sounded not so much bitter as sad.

"What are we going to do tomorrow?" he asked after a while.

"I'm going to search the house," Clare stated.

"Remember, it's not the original house," Patrick reminded her.

"I know, but Henrietta did live there. And there are a lot of hiding places besides windowsills. Maybe it's under something else, like the mantelpiece, or a loose stair."

"Or maybe a loose floorboard," Patrick offered.

"Hey, there could even be a secret passage," Zoe suggested, earning herself scornful looks from the other two. "All right, all right, it was just a thought. Anyway, I'd like to spend tomorrow finding out more about the whole Smalley–Cora Brown thing. I thought I'd go look up old local newspapers and check out the original stories."

"Sounds like a plan," Patrick said. "Why don't I go along with you and help out?"

Zoe thought about suggesting that he'd be far more useful helping Clare search the huge old house, but she discovered she rather liked the idea of Patrick's company. As she considered this, the crackling of footsteps approached.

"Hello?" The warm, rich voice of Kate Pryor floated on the night air. Zoe started, wondering how much of their conversation she'd overheard. "Am I intruding?" Kate emerged into the moonlight, stepping carefully on the spongy turf. "I needed to get outside for a while, just to clear my head."

"I can imagine," Patrick greeted her. "You never want to have more than a couple of Swanns in one pond at one time." He moved sideways on the blanket spread over the damp ground. "Have a seat. Want some coffee?"

"Thanks, yes."

He refilled his own mug and handed it to her. "Sorry, we only brought three mugs."

"That's okay." She took the mug from his hand and took a sip. "It's nice out here."

"Better than being in there, anyway," Patrick agreed. "How are you coming with Aunt Julia's papers?"

"I think I'm just about finished. There wasn't that much left up here. Julia told me she'd brought nearly everything down to Ann Arbor a long time ago."

"I didn't realize you'd discussed it with her personally," Clare said.

"Oh, yes. She knew how valuable her papers were. She wanted to make sure that they went to a place they'd be appreciated." She sipped coffee and looked up at the moon. "It must be nice to have a place like this—to have real roots somewhere."

"Roots. Gaah." Clare made a nasty sound.

"Clare and I were just wishing we'd been conceived in petri dishes." Patrick laughed without amusement.

"Oh, no," Kate said seriously. "Family connects you to the past, and to the future. Connection is important, even—" She stopped abruptly.

"Even when it's with a family like ours?" Clare finished her sentence for her.

Kate shrugged. "Why not? At least you feel connected to something." There was an odd intensity in her lovely voice. "Sorry." She scrambled to her feet. "I'd better get back inside."

"What was that all about?" Zoe wondered aloud when Kate had disappeared back into the trees.

"Beats me," Clare said. "I wonder how fucked-up you have to be to envy *our* family?" She giggled slightly, the first honest-to-God giggle Zoe had ever heard from her.

"Bedtime," Patrick said, yawning widely. "Two in the big tent, one in the smaller one. Want to draw straws for who sleeps where?" He grinned and winked at Zoe.

"In your dreams," she retorted with an answering grin. "And I do mean that literally."

She was dreaming that she was paddling a raft made of marshmallows down State Street. She broke off one of the marshmallows and put it in her mouth, and the sensation felt so real her eyes popped open. Patrick was leaning over her, his eyes looking into her own, his lips just brushing hers.

"Wha—" Zoe jerked backward in startled surprise and grabbed reflexively for the zipper of her sleeping bag.

Patrick jumped and turned red with embarrassment. "Hey, I'm sorry. I didn't mean to do that, honest. I just came in to wake you up, but you looked so . . . I don't know." He grinned suddenly. "I just couldn't resist."

"Well, try harder next time," Zoe said acidly, but she found herself grinning slightly in response. "What time is it?"

"Six-thirty."

"What!"

"Well, Clare and I have been up for a while, and she's antsy to get going," Patrick said apologetically. "I brought you some coffee," he offered, holding out a steaming mug.

"Well, that's something," Zoe grumped. She worked her arms free of the sleeping bag and reached for the mug. "Jeez, it's cold out."

"It's not so bad once you're dressed."

"Well, get out of here and let me do it, then. And no peeking."

"Now that wounds me." He put his hand over his heart. "I'm a romantic, not a Peeping Tom."

"You're a man," she retorted. "Out."

And not a half-bad one, she thought as she pulled on her jeans, shivering in the morning chill. Although there was something about him, a sometimes brooding quality, that bothered her. She'd always thought that *Wuthering Heights* was a really dumb-shit book. Well, see where it goes; she pulled a sweatshirt over her sweater and took another gulp of hot coffee.

When she stuck her head out of the tent, Clare and Patrick were burying the remains of last night's campfire. The smaller tent was already down, and the minute she appeared Patrick began to dismantle hers.

"I'm going to start on the house as soon as we're through here," Clare said. "How about you?"

"At seven o'clock in the morning?" Zoe poured herself more coffee from the pot on the Coleman stove. "Beats me. The library sure won't be open at this hour."

"Have you ever seen Hartwick Pines?" Patrick asked, dragging sleeping bags and blankets out of the tent. He looks a lot better than we do, Zoe thought, comparing his down-filled parka and L.L. Bean hiking boots to her own grubby clothes and Clare's ratty old khaki jacket and scuffed Doc Martens clones. He'd even managed to shave somewhere, which, if he had planned to kiss her, was the least he could do. She grinned to herself as she shook her head at him.

"Nope. I've only seen pictures of it."

"Pictures just look like a batch of trees, they don't give you the effect. Let's take a swing by there. It's only about fifty miles north, right on Seventy-five. If you let me drive," he grinned, "we can make it in less than half an hour. Besides, there's a great breakfast place right on the way."

"Now you're talking," she replied enthusiastically. "But if

you can make it in half an hour, I'll guarantee to do it in twenty minutes. And where do you brush your teeth around here?" she asked plaintively.

"Right over there." To her dismay, Patrick pointed toward the river, a big grin on his face. "And by the way, have you ever read a great little book titled *How to Shit in the Woods?*"

"Well, what do you think of camping, now that you've tried it?" Patrick asked.

The two of them were driving north on I-75 after a breakfast of bacon-cheese omelettes as good as promised. Yesterday's sunshine had been replaced by pale, pearl-gray skies, but the air was crisp and still, and Zoe drove with the window open and her elbow resting on the door. The wide interstate was nearly deserted, and she kept the speedometer hovering around the eighty to eighty-five mark.

"Let me put it this way," she said. "For a writer, no experience is ever completely wasted." Chuckling, she turned off 75 onto M-93, following the signs that read HARTWICK PINES STATE PARK.

They walked past the log buildings of the lumbering museum that wouldn't be open for another month, and followed the paved path through the trees for a few hundred yards; then Patrick led her away from the groomed area and deeper into the woods. Only when they were out of sight of the buildings did he stop.

"This is what it used to be like. Before the *capitalists* got here." He pronounced the word like an epithet, the pouring bitterness palpable once more. He must have heard it himself, because when he continued his voice was more matter-of-fact. "This is one of the last bits of primeval forest in the entire state."

"It's awesome." They were speaking in the sort of hushed tones usually reserved for cathedrals. It felt like a cathedral, in fact, Zoe thought; the towering pine spires, rising a hundred feet and more above their heads, must have the effect Gothic architects had striven for, with their soaring arches and flying buttresses. A thousand years' worth of drifting growth and decay carpeted the ground with a thick, soft covering that swallowed sound; the silence was so profound it seemed a physical presence. Gray light filtered through the branches overhead, dappling the scene. Once upon a time, she thought, you could walk from lake to lake, all the way across the state, and never come out from under these ancient trees.

"Awesome." He mouthed the word. "That's how we refer to a hamburger, these days. But this is what the word used to mean. Awesome—inspiring awe—the sense of something beyond one's own feeble little activities." He turned to look at her. "Would you mind if I kissed you?" he asked abruptly.

Zoe, who wouldn't have minded the kiss but did mind the question, took a step backward and shook her head lightly. "I don't think that's such a good idea right now," she said. The whole scene felt weird, she thought; she liked Patrick, but here under these looming trees he was beginning to creep her out. She smiled to take the edge off her rejection. "But check with me later, okay?"

"Okay. Sorry." To her relief, he didn't seem offended. He walked a few steps deeper into the woods, looking up at the trees.

"I think we'd better get going," Zoe called to him, her voice swallowed by the thick silence. The sense of isolation was beginning to make her feel edgy. "The library should be open by the time we get back."

"Right." Patrick seemed to snap himself back to reality with a click. He came back and took her arm. "Let's go see what we can find out about the legendary John Smalley."

Forests were all well and good, Zoe decided forty minutes later, but libraries were the really awesome things. She and

Patrick sat in front of the ungainly microfilm reader, spinning the handle and watching the past unfold in grainy splendor. She felt a small flicker of gratitude to the former Michigan Regent who'd invented this marvelous contraption.

They had started with the *Grand Rapids Herald*, the major area newspaper of the period. At first they had been slowed down by sheer fascination, their attention caught by references to Teddy Roosevelt, or by advertisements for "complete dinners, only Twenty Cents." But when they reached August of 1895, they scanned more quickly, impatient to find what they were seeking.

"There!" Zoe pointed to the screen.

"Yep, there he is, all right." Patrick leaned forward. "August 27, 1895." Zoe leaned forward as well, peering at the film, blinking slightly to focus on the old-fashioned typeface.

The words leapt out at her like a flashing neon sign. She gaped, blinked again, stared at the screen, then turned to Patrick. He stared back at her, his eyes as wide as she knew hers must be.

". . . his common-law wife Cora Brown," the newspaper story read, "known in these parts as Black Diamond . . ."

TWENTY-SIX

"What time is the sheriff picking you up?" Anneke asked. She took a last bite of her spinach omelette, leaving half of it on the plate along with a young mountain of fried potatoes, and put down her fork. Outside the Woodlake dining room, ducks still floated on the lake under pearl-gray morning skies.

"Any minute now." Karl poured them each more coffee from the white Thermos container on the table. "What are your plans?"

"I think, as long as I can have the car, that I'll go up to Lake City. The County Clerk's office has records that go back to the eighteen-seventies. I thought I'd look for references to Cora Brown."

"Mm. Might turn up something." He put down his coffee cup and raised his hand. Anneke turned to see Sheriff Kettleman approaching.

"Mornin'. Don't mind if I do," he said, sinking into a chair at Karl's gesture. He poured coffee from the Thermos into an empty cup and took a long gulp. "Anything new?"

"Not really." Karl shook his head. "Another dead end in the search for Gerald's academic papers. I'm still trying to find out what he was working on."

"Well, Red Joe might be able to help out—assuming he's still willin' to talk to you. Never know, with him."

"Red Joe?" Anneke repeated.

"Yes, ma'am. Friend of Gerald's, or at least someone who hung out with him now and then. Trouble is, he's as secretive an old cuss as Gerald was. Don't know how much he'll be willin' to tell us. Or how much of what he does tell us can be believed, come to that." He drained his coffee cup. "Ready to go?"

"Right." The two men stood. "I should be back early afternoon," Karl told Anneke.

"All right. I'll meet you back here then." When they were gone she lingered for a while over coffee and the *Free Press* sports section, marveling at Mitch Albom's glittering prose while disagreeing violently with him over Michigan's latest basketball recruiting class. Then she went back to the room and spent a relatively futile fifteen minutes brushing and scraping mud off her sheepskin coat, swearing the whole time. Finally she lifted the lid of her laptop for one last check of her notes before heading out.

The notes, file name BDNOTES, were sparser than she'd remembered. There was hardly anything relating to the Missaukee County end of things, she realized—in fact, nothing except that old plat map she'd downloaded. She looked at the area along the south bank of the Clam River, where the name SWANN was printed in block capitals. Under it was the legal description of the parcel, Sec. 19, T22N R8W.

She looked at it again. That wasn't right, was it? She had seen the legal description on one of the papers Dwight had been shuffling yesterday; she wracked her brain trying to remember the arcane designation, but she simply wasn't sure.

At last she powered down the laptop, grabbed her mud-spotted coat, and headed out to the car.

Driving the Land Rover was an unaccustomed pleasure—by common consent, she and Karl customarily drove their own cars—and she enjoyed the feel of the vehicle as she headed northeast toward Lake City, the Missaukee County seat. Once or twice, driving along the wooded roads, she spied a glint of water through the trees, and had to curb the impulse to take the Land Rover off-road to see what it could do.

She had parked the car and was on her way into the County Clerk's office when she spotted the antique shop across the street. She detoured toward it more by force of habit than anything else, reminding herself that the Chihuly had better be her purchase for the year.

She was more relieved than not to see that the shop windows were filled with junk—old kitchen implements, mismatched plates, depressed-looking teddy bears. But just as she was turning away she spied a small chunk of glass that drew her back for a second look.

It was about six inches high, thick and solid-looking, shaped roughly like a twisted, upside-down letter *U* in a rich shade of dark purplish-blue. On impulse, she pushed open the shop door and went inside.

"Well, well. What can I do for you, honey?" The man's voice was oily and unpleasant; so was the rest of him, Anneke realized as her eyes became accustomed to the gloomy interior of the shop. He was middle-aged, balding, and paunchy, in dirty, low-slung jeans and a short green Michigan State T-shirt that left a slice of hairy stomach exposed. "What's a city girl like you doin' around here?" he asked, leering.

"Business with Sheriff Kettleman," she said as crisply as possible, happy to see the expression on his face change instantly from avid to wary. "How much is that piece of glass in your window?"

"Which one? The purple one?" His little eyes narrowed in calculation. "I couldn't take less'n twenny dollars for it. It's signed, see?"

"May I see it?"

"Sure, sure. Anything for a pretty lady like you." He sauntered over to the window and plucked the glass from it. "Here y'are."

She took it from him without touching him and held the glass up to the dim light filtering through the dirty window, liking the color and feel of the piece in her hand. Then she turned it over and tilted it to make out the signature that read *Harvey K Littleton* in finely incised script.

"I'll give you ten," she said.

"Sorry." He shook his head. "Even for you, I can't go below fifteen."

"Sold." She whipped her wallet out of the briefcase slung over her shoulder and handed him a ten and a five, fairly sure that sales tax was something he bothered with only rarely. "Don't bother to wrap it," she said. "I'll just take it the way it is." She turned and left quickly, leaving him staring at her with a look of darkest suspicion on his face.

Harvey K. Littleton. She repeated the name to herself. Contemporary studio glass, but she couldn't come up with more than that at the moment. She nestled the glass into the bottom of her briefcase, dug around with her fingers until she found a purse-sized pack of Kleenex, and wadded tissues around it. She'd research it when she got back to Ann Arbor.

She was, she realized suddenly, beginning to feel like a collector again.

The County Clerk's office was empty except for a plump woman at a gray metal desk who looked at her with cheerful interest. She wore a flowered cotton dress with a heavy red cardigan buttoned over it, although the heat in the office was cranked up so high Anneke could feel perspiration begin to trickle down her sides.

"Can I help you?" the woman asked.

"I hope so." Anneke slipped out of her coat and dropped it on a chair near the door. Now that she was here, she wasn't sure exactly what to ask. "I want to research some property."

"Sure." The woman smiled amiably. "Description?"

"It's a tract of land out along the Clam River."

"No, I meant legal description."

"Oh, right. Well, that's the thing. I'm not sure." Damn, she thought, she should have worked this out more carefully before she came charging in here. She spotted a map on the wall, twin to the one she'd downloaded off the Internet. "There." She went to the map and pointed to the parcel. "That one."

"Oh, sure—Sec. 19, T22N R8W. That's the Swann property. Been in the family since 1898."

"Doesn't it go back even before that?" Anneke asked.

"Not that piece."

"That piece? Is there another one?"

"Sure—right there, see?" The woman pointed to an irregular rectangle adjoining the parcel labelled SWANN, with a pair of short lines on the boundary between them. "Those lines mean both parcels are owned by the same person. The legal on that one's Sec. 20, T22N R8W."

"I see," Anneke said slowly. "So the Swann family owned the parcel in Section 20, and then in 1898 they bought the one next to it in Section 19."

"Right. The original Swann house, from back in the old logging days, burned to the ground in 'ninety-five. Henrietta Swann didn't want to rebuild on the same spot, so she bought that second parcel and built that crazy old house there instead." She laughed at the look of surprise on Anneke's face.

"I'm sort of a local history buff—goes with being County Clerk, I guess. And the Swanns were an important part of the area back in the lumbering days."

"It must be a fascinating period," Anneke said.

"Oh, yeah, it is." The woman sighed with nostalgia. "Wide-open towns, lots of action, plenty of opportunities to get rich if you had the mind for it. Real exciting times around here." She spoke as though she were remembering her own youth.

"Tell me something," Anneke said, pursuing a sudden thought. "Do you happen to know if the Swanns owned any other property in the area?"

"They used to, sure. Old Walter Swann owned a couple miles of frontage along Lake Missaukee, and some commercial property in McBain, back when it was a mill town. That's mostly where the Swann money came from—he wasn't in lumbering per se, he owned one of the big sawmills, and then the family expanded into commercial real estate. But, of course, once the logging was finished there wasn't much commerce, either. Still isn't." She laughed slightly.

"I see." Anneke's mind was racing, but she kept her face carefully neutral. "Thanks very much for your time."

"Sure." The woman smiled at her. "Anything else I can help you with, you let me know."

Outside, Anneke stood for a moment with her coat slung over her arm, savoring the chill after the sweltering office. Then she climbed into the Land Rover and pointed it toward the Swann house. She wasn't as good with the Land Rover as Karl was, she conceded as she jounced over the rutted road; well, she didn't have much experience with it. She made the final turn in second gear, and emerged into the clearing just in time to see Zoe and Patrick leaping out of the white Buick.

Zoe was pulling on the door of the Land Rover almost before she brought it to a halt. "Anneke! Wait'll you hear!"

"What?"

"No, wait, we've gotta find Clare first. Come on." She raced toward the house. Patrick grinned at Anneke before following more sedately in Zoe's path.

By the time they reached the porch, Zoe was already half dragging Clare out the door. Olivia's voice floated out to them, didactic and severe. "Honestly, Clare, I can't understand why even you would—" The rest of her complaint was cut off as Clare quietly but firmly shut the door.

"How was that?" she asked Patrick.

"Perfect." He grinned and gave her a thumbs-up sign.

"Y'know, it feels pretty good at that," Clare said. "I'm practicing an old Latin form of self-discipline," she told Anneke, smiling. "Called *'illegitimi non carborundum.'* Now," she turned to Zoe, "what've you got?"

But Zoe dragged them all down from the porch and away from the house before she finally blurted, "We found out what Black Diamond is!"

"What?" Clare's face stiffened with tension.

"Not what," Zoe said. "Who. *Cora Brown* was Black Diamond."

"What?" Clare said again, her voice rising. "What do you mean?"

"That's what they called her," Zoe explained, laughing with excitement. "See, she really was kind of a famous local whore, just like the sheriff said. And she really did set up at the huckleberry pickers' camp. Only what she did was, she had this black tent, so all the guys would know which one was hers. So that's why they called her Black Diamond."

"You have got to be shitting me." Clare stared at her.

"My hand to God." Zoe raised her right hand, palm out. "Could I make it up?"

"It's true," Patrick confirmed. "It was in the newspapers after Smalley was killed. In fact, there's a story in the *Lake City Plain Dealer* that said she was threatening to sue the

Grand Rapids paper because they called her that in their stories about Smalley."

"So that's what Black Diamond is." Clare stared into the distance, pondering. "But what the hell did my sainted ancestor Henrietta have to do with it all? And *where*," she stamped her foot in frustration, "is Smalley's treasure?"

"I think I know," Anneke said.

McBain, Michigan: August 25, 1895

"Cora got a letter, Cora got a letter." The toothless old woman rocked back and forth in high glee.

"What's she on about now?" Cora shoved dirty plates off a chair and sat down, arranging her skirts carefully around the money sewn into hidden inner pockets. She'd spent two whole days and nights and half a day more at Smalley's cabin, savoring the luxury of being alone and safe, all the while carefully stitching long, narrow strips of fabric together, filling them with money, then stitching them down along the seams of her skirt. She'd also made herself a small bustle, filled with more money and added to the back; it felt odd, but she knew bustles were fashionable and it made a good place of concealment, especially for the heavier coins.

"Pete Slocum brought it by for you." Cal pulled a thick white packet from his shirt pocket. "There's somethin' in it."

She opened the letter and looked at the brooch, a circle of gold embossed in a leafy design, knowing its purpose at once and not sure whether to laugh or cry. She read the letter, working her way laboriously through the fine, spidery handwriting, hearing the fear and pain and unrecognized courage beneath the elaborate, carefully ambiguous sentences.

Was there anything she could do for Henrietta? Should she keep the brooch, or risk trying to return it? More choices added to the tangle.

"Is there anything to eat around here?" she asked.

"Not likely." Cal shrugged. "Prob'ly some apples in the bin." As she stood up to search for food, he asked: "Did'ja hear about Smalley?"

"What about him?" Cora waited for the expected news.

"They're sayin' he killed a cop on a train outside Grand Rapids."

"Shit, no kiddin'?" She stopped and stared at him. "They arrested him?"

"Uh-uh." Cal shook his head. "He got away clean."

"He—" She stopped, choking on the fear in her throat, her mind whirling in desperate circles. "When?"

"Yesterday. I don't figure he'll come back this way, though," Cal said sagely. "There's a full-scale manhunt out for him." His eyes flicked to his stump of arm, and Cora knew how bad he wanted to be part of the posse that must be gathering.

"Reckon you're right," she agreed, taking a stale biscuit from the breadbox and gnawing on it. She carefully avoided Cal's eyes as she forced her mind to function. Smalley would head for his own cabin first, of course. When he found the money gone, would he suspect her? Hell, he probably already figured she was the one who turned him in. No question, this would be his next stop.

"I'm goin' away for a while," she told Cal.

"Yeah?" He eyed her. "You plannin' to meet him?"

"Less you know, less you can tell," she said shortly, heading up the ladder.

In the loft she unearthed a worn travel bag and began tossing her belongings into it. Decision's made for her, she thought, almost with relief. First, put as much distance as possible between her and Smalley. The rest she could worry about later.

She was just snapping the bag shut when she heard the heavy footsteps below.

She shoved the bag into a corner behind the pallet, took a deep breath, and backed down the ladder, acutely conscious of the weight of her money-laden skirts. At the bottom, Smalley was standing watching her.

"I thought they'd got you this time," she said.

He grabbed her arm and swung her around. "Where is it?"

"Where's what?" she asked, and knew at once it was a mistake. She should have given him the money at once and said she'd thought he was dead.

For an answer, he backhanded her across the face, and she felt an explosion of pain in her cheek. Her head rocked backward, and she stumbled against the table.

"Hey!" She shook her head to clear the buzzing in her ears. "What's that for?" Committed now, she glared at him, brazening it out.

He hit her again, coldly and without apparent emotion. She tasted blood, felt it trickle down her chin. "Where is it?" he asked a second time, and without waiting for an answer hit her with his closed fist, the blow landing on her breast in a burst of pain like a Roman candle. He yanked her arm, twisted, and threw her to the ground, and as she landed his booted foot kicked her in the small of her back with sickening force. "Where is it?"

"Leave her alone, you'll kill her." Cal's voice was a distant sound; all Cora's senses were focused on the pain in her back. "What the hell are you on about?" Cal shouted.

Cal, don't mess with him, he'll kill you—she tried to squeeze the words out but only managed a mewling sound. She forced one eye open in time to see Smalley whirl and with the same booted foot kick Cal full in the crotch. Cal went down with a high scream and rolled on the floor retching.

"You bring me a bottle?" Ella Brown squawked suddenly, and Cora would have laughed if she'd had the breath for it. Smalley ignored her and Cal both, turned back to Cora and kicked her viciously in the side. She felt a screaming pain and knew a couple of ribs were broken.

Smalley's expression as he stared down at her was still coldly casual. It occurred to Cora that she was probably going to die.

TWENTY-SEVEN

· · · · · ·

"Where?" "What did you find out?" Three pairs of eyes blazed interrogation.

"Wait," Anneke said. "It's not that simple." She wished she'd been more equivocal. "You know this isn't the house Henrietta Swann was living in when John Smalley was killed."

"Yes, of course," Clare said impatiently. "The original burned down, and Henrietta rebuilt."

"Right." Anneke nodded. "But *not on the same site*. The original house was on a different piece of property, across the road."

"Holy shit," Zoe breathed. "What are we waiting for? Come on."

"Where to?" Anneke asked.

"To the—oh. But there isn't any house over there," she said plaintively. "There isn't even any burned-out shell. It's all just trees."

"If there really was a house over there," Patrick said, "it

should be possible to locate the site." They turned toward him. "Well, it's pretty basic stuff," he said. "For one thing, it would probably have been along the river. And assuming they just left the burned-out remains to disintegrate naturally, there ought to be indications from the terrain."

"You mean, like a barrow?" Zoe asked.

"Something like that," Patrick agreed.

"And you think you can find it?" Clare asked.

"Maybe."

"Then let's do it." Clare stood up, and the others followed suit.

"It'll be a fair hike," Patrick warned. "The road is really only a track between the two pieces of land. It dead-ends at the river. We'll need to go in at right angles to it if we want to follow the river."

"Maybe not," Zoe said, turning to Anneke. "Don't you have the Land Rover?"

"Yes." She was pleased at the opportunity to take the Land Rover off-road. "All right, I'll drive you all out there if you like."

They piled in, with Patrick in the front passenger seat giving directions. Anneke backed the car off the concrete pad and turned right, toward the trees.

Instantly the outside world disappeared. They moved through an alien landscape, inhabited entirely by the aloof trees through whose branches even light passed only on sufferance. It wasn't primeval forest, of course, but it was patient; in another century it would own this land.

She drove slowly, working her way between stands of trees, familiarizing herself with the vehicle and with the feel of off-road driving. When she reached the road, which was indeed barely a path between stands of forest, she turned left toward the glint of water. The path ended quietly at the river bank, and she stopped and cut the engine, the sound of lapping water suddenly loud in her ears.

"Now what?" she asked.

"I'm not sure." Patrick gnawed his lower lip. "The Clam River does a lot of meandering along here. I'd like to drive right along it, but the ground's awfully muddy this time of year."

"That's what four-wheel drive is all about," she replied confidently. She was really enjoying this, she realized, a whole new kind of driving that tested muscles and reflexes and analytic skills. She restarted the engine, released the clutch, and turned right, into the woods.

Fifteen minutes later, they were facing a low rock wall that marked the end of the Swann property.

"All right." Patrick appeared unfazed. "Drop south about a hundred yards and head back the other way." Anneke turned the Land Rover obediently, working her way around a clump of birch trees feathery in spring green. Back they went, bumping over the rough, spongy terrain.

They were, by Anneke's reckoning, about a quarter of a mile from the road when she heard the crack of sound. She slowed reflexively, looking around for its source, and as she did the sharp crack was repeated.

"Duck!" Patrick cried out. "Those are gunshots!"

"What?" Anneke brought the Land Rover to a shuddering halt. "Are you sure?"

"Yeah, I'm sure." Patrick, ignoring his own advice, was leaning out the window peering through the woods. "And I think maybe they were shooting at us."

"They came from over there." Zoe leaned forward from the back seat and pointed. "Over toward the road. Hurry— we may be able to spot them. Come on," she urged.

There hadn't been any more shots; probably whoever had been doing the shooting was gone. Still . . . Anneke considered for a few seconds, then shoved in the clutch and hit the accelerator, steering toward a natural break in the trees. She'd have to go around those three pine trees growing close together, and there was a downed log next to that one, take it carefully—good. The front wheels rolled over the log and bit into the soft ground. The back wheels rose, rolled, and hit the ground with a jounce. She fed more gas, shifted up, accelerated. . . .

Nothing happened.

She downshifted back into first and stepped on the accelerator again. The engine whined with effort. The Land Rover remained stationary.

"What's the matter?" Zoe asked anxiously. "Come on, they're getting away."

"I don't *know* what's the matter." Anneke eased off the accelerator. "It won't move—it's stuck."

"What do you mean, stuck?" Patrick asked. "A Land Rover? How?"

"I *don't know*," Anneke repeated, gritting her teeth. Well, whoever had been shooting, whether at them or at something else, they were probably in the next county by now. She cut the engine with an angry click and climbed out of the car, the others behind her.

It was Patrick who spotted it. "Anneke?" His voice, from behind the rear of the car, had an odd quality; it wasn't until she walked around to join him that she realized why.

He was pointing to a spot beneath the rear bumper, and his shoulders were shaking with suppressed laughter. "It's a st-stump," he said, breaking up totally.

"Where?" she snapped, too annoyed to be amused.

"There." He pointed again.

"Holy shit, you've been *impaled.*" Zoe, down on hands and knees, choked out the words between snorts of laughter.

"What are you talking about?" Anneke dropped to her knees and peered under the car. "Oh, *shit.*"

The Land Rover was equipped with a trailer hitch, a V-shaped bar of metal welded to the chassis. Sticking up through the hitch, wedged neatly into the crotch of the V, was a small but sturdy stump of white birch.

"When you went over that log, you must have dropped off right onto it." Patrick was still having trouble getting words out between laughs.

"Jesus," Clare said, "this is like being inside a fucking video game." She sounded both angry and amused.

Anneke couldn't decide whether to laugh or throw something. "What the hell do we do now?" she asked, feeling uncomfortably helpless.

"Is there an ax in the car?" Patrick asked. He wiped tears of laughter from his eyes, trying without much success to look serious.

"I don't know." She opened the back of the Land Rover and rummaged inside, finding a neat selection of implements, but no ax. "Not that I can see," she said.

"Well, I can hike back to the house and get one," Patrick offered. "Shouldn't take me more than a half hour or so."

"I don't think that's such a good idea." Now that the laughter had subsided, Anneke was struck by the deadening silence of the woods. They were probably less than two miles from the house, but the spot felt as isolated as a lunar crater. "Someone was just shooting at us," she pointed out.

"Oh, that." Patrick shrugged. "Probably a poacher. Anyway, they're long gone by now."

"Maybe not," Zoe chimed in. "There's been an awful lot of weird shit going on around here." She turned to Anneke. "Isn't there a police radio in there?"

"Yes, that's right." Her heart sank at the thought of having to inform Karl of this imbecilic mess.

"No!" Clare said sharply. "No police. I'm not going to have the cops getting in the way of finding the money."

"We have to," Zoe said reasonably. "We can just tell the sheriff that we were out here sightseeing, but after all,

Genesko'll know anyway. And it'd be stupid not to tell them about the shooting—they might be able to find out something from the bullets or tire tracks or something."

She was right, Anneke conceded, climbing into the Land Rover and fumbling with the radio. But dammit, she was *never* going to live this down.

TWENTY-EIGHT

· · · · · ·

"You're stuck? In the Land Rover?" Karl's voice crackled over the police radio.

"I wish everyone would stop saying it in that disbelieving tone of voice." Once she'd convinced the Missaukee dispatcher to patch her through to the sheriff, Anneke had explained the situation to Karl as economically as possible. "You'll understand when you see it."

"All right. If you can't get away from there, stay inside the car. Zoe and Clare are both with you?"

"Yes, and Patrick."

"Patrick! Never mind, we'll be there in—" he muttered something aside, presumably to Kettleman "—about fifteen minutes. *Stay in the car.*" She heard the rising whine of a siren as he clicked off.

They were there in twelve, bumping through the woods in the sheriff's big Ford Explorer. Kettleman opened his door and stood on the rim surveying the area with binoculars, while Karl climbed out and approached the Land Rover.

"I still don't understand why you're stuck," he said to Anneke as she and the others got out of the car.

"Under the rear bumper," she said. He walked around to the back of the car and bent down; when he stood, his mouth was twitching.

"Oh, go ahead and laugh." She forced an embarrassed grin. "Get it all out of your system now, Lieutenant, because once we're out of here, I don't *ever* want to hear another word about this."

"Can't see anyone still hangin' around." Kettleman approached and looked at the Land Rover. "What's the problem?" he asked quizzically, seeing the broad grin on Karl's face. Wordlessly, Karl pointed, and Kettleman, too, bent to view the obstruction. If he says one word about women drivers, Anneke decided, I will absolutely deck him.

"I'll be damned." Kettleman chuckled. "What you get for drivin' a foreign car." He threw back his head and laughed, the sound booming hollowly among the close-pressing trees. "Now," he said, "what's this about someone shootin' at you folks?"

"It sounded like a hunting rifle," Patrick spoke up. "Two shots, probably overhead."

"Were you right here at the time?"

"No." Patrick pointed. "We were about a hundred yards or so back that way. See that maple—the one with the dead branch? We were just the other side of it."

"Hmmph." Anneke was impressed with Patrick's woodslore, but Kettleman seemed to take it for granted. "Any idea where the shots came from?"

"Not for sure, but I think they came from the direction of the road."

"So you heard the shots, you figured someone was shooting at you, and you headed *toward* them?"

"Uh, yeah." Patrick looked sheepish. "Yeah, I guess we

were. Not too bright, was it? I guess we were just reacting in-stead of thinking."

Anneke kept her eyes fixed on Patrick, although she could almost feel Karl's gaze boring into her. For the first time she realized what she'd done, tearing after a sniper like someone in a bad Stallone movie—not that there was any other kind. Patrick was right; she hadn't been thinking at all, just fol-lowing Zoe's pointing finger.

Kettleman pointedly did not comment on their behavior. "Did any of you see anything?" he asked.

"I did," Clare said. "At least, I think I did. Nothing I could identify, but I'm pretty sure I saw a flash of something white out on the road. Or by the road, anyway."

"Hmmph. Coulda been a white car, coulda been a white-tail, coulda been a bird." Kettleman shrugged. "Not much to go on." He turned to Karl. "It's a long shot, but I'd like to see if we can find one of those bullets."

He herded them back toward the site of the shooting, and deployed them efficiently across the area. "Look for any kind of disturbance," he told them. "Fresh fallen leaves, fresh twigs, a chip off a rock, anything like that."

Anneke listened to his instructions dubiously, but obedi-ently began to scan the ground. To her city-bred eyes, there was nothing to see but a carpet of pine needles and rotting leaves, pebbles, and crawling things she'd just as soon not ex-amine too closely. She slapped at a mosquito, wishing she were at home in a hot bath. Just when she had concluded that the entire operation was an exercise in futility, Patrick called out from above: "Got it!"

She looked up. Patrick was perched about ten feet above the ground in a big maple tree, his legs straddling a thick branch. He leaned forward and dug at the trunk with a small penknife.

"Damn." He looked down. "This knife won't do it. Any-one got a better one?"

"You better let me take care of that, son," Kettleman said.

"Sure, if you want." Patrick shrugged and dropped to the ground. Kettleman pulled himself up with surprising ease, settling his bulk comfortably on the branch before pulling a wicked-looking knife from inside his heavy jacket. He applied the knife carefully to the tree, taking his time, before finally climbing back down and holding up a small object for all of them to see.

"That's it, all right. And definitely recent—nice, fresh edges to the hole."

"You mean it was way up there?" Zoe tilted her head back and looked up. "He wasn't much of a shot, was he?"

"Either that, or a real good one," Kettleman said.

"Yeah, that's what I thought," Patrick agreed. "The bullet was still rising when it hit—see the broken branch?" He pointed, and Anneke spotted a small branch hanging by a strip of bark below the level of the bullet. "That's what pointed me to it in the first place."

"He wasn't really shooting at us, then," Clare said. "The son of a bitch was shooting over our heads."

"Maybe." Kettleman was too wary a cop to state an opinion. "Tell me something." He turned to Patrick abruptly. "What were you folks doin' out here, anyway?"

There was the briefest possible pause before Patrick said, "Just sightseeing. Zoe hasn't been up here before, and we were showing her around." He laid an arm casually over her shoulders, and she snuggled against him, grinning up at him happily.

"That right, Miz Haagen?" Kettleman asked.

"Honestly, Sheriff, we were just out looking around." She heard the protest in her voice and knew it was unconvincing. Well, they *had* just been looking around; she simply wasn't specifying what they'd been looking *for*.

"Right," Kettleman shrugged. "Well, I'll check around,"

he said to Karl. He pointed to the Land Rover. "Need some help gettin' that little roller skate loose?"

"Actually, I don't think so." Karl smiled at him. "But why don't you stick around for a minute to be sure." He climbed into the driver's seat and turned the key, then pressed something below the dashboard. The engine growled deeply; there was a creaking sound; the Land Rover inched forward, and then suddenly lurched as the small stump was dragged free of the ground. Karl cut the engine and got out.

"Low-range differential," he said to Kettleman with a grin. "Pull limit is over seven thousand pounds."

"Hmmph. Not too shabby," Kettleman grunted. He stuck out his hand. "Good meetin' you, Lieutenant. We'll keep in touch."

When Kettleman had driven away, Anneke stood with her hands on her hips and glared at the Land Rover. "Do you mean to tell me," she demanded, "that all I needed to do was just *pull?*"

"Not exactly. Here, let me show you." He opened the driver's door and pointed to a small panel on the console behind the gear shift lever. "That lever locks the differential into low range," he said. "It increases engine torque." He stepped back so she could see more clearly. "If you plan to chase snipers through the woods," he said too calmly, "you'd better familiarize yourself with your vehicle."

"I didn't—" She stopped. "All right, I deserved that. I didn't stop to think, that's all."

"No, you didn't. The worst part of it is that you've put me in the position of lying to Marv Kettleman, at least by omission. And he doesn't deserve that."

"No, he doesn't," Anneke replied bleakly.

"Now, will you tell me please what you really are doing out here in the woods?"

"Looking for the site of the original Swann house." She

would have vastly preferred anger to this cold disapproval. Well, she had it coming. Quickly she filled him in on what she and Zoe had each found. When she was done, he nodded.

"All right. Let's go back to the others. I need to ask you all some questions."

Zoe and Clare stood a few feet away, looking upward at Patrick, who was about ten feet above their heads, clinging to handholds on a tall pine tree. As Anneke watched, he reached, found another handhold, and pulled himself higher.

"What's going on?" she asked.

"He's scanning for the site of the house," Clare replied, craning her neck upward. "He thinks if he can get high enough, he may be able to spot something in the terrain."

"Who besides you four knew you were out here?" Karl asked her.

"No one, as far as I know. Honestly, we were real careful," she protested when Karl looked skeptical. "We waited till we were a long way away from the house before we started talking."

"But I imagine it was fairly obvious that you were excited about something," Karl suggested.

"Well, yeah, I suppose." Zoe looked embarrassed. "You think someone followed us?"

"It's possible," he said. "Did you—"

"Hey!" Patrick called from overhead.

"What is it?" Clare yelled back.

"Hang on." He clambered down the tree, moving expertly, at least to Anneke's inexperienced eyes. "I think I spotted something," he said as he dropped the last six feet to the soft ground.

"What?" "What did you see?" Zoe and Clare spoke together.

"Over that way." He pointed in the general direction of

the road. "There's a big mass of wild huckleberry bushes." When they continued to look at him blankly, he said, "Ash. Huckleberries love ash. One of the reasons they grow so well in this part of the state is that the miles of stumps the loggers left behind tended to burn out."

"Well, what are we waiting for?" Clare said impatiently. "Let's go." She took a step toward the Land Rover, then stopped as if suddenly realizing that circumstances had changed.

"Lieutenant?" Zoe looked from Clare to the car. "Please?"

"All right." Karl nodded. Zoe grinned and raced for the car, with Clare and Patrick behind her.

With Karl at the wheel, Patrick directed them toward the road. They could see it as a break in the trees, a ribbon of clear light bisecting the shaded woods, when Patrick called a halt.

"There." He jumped from the car, and the others climbed out and clustered around him. "See? We were concentrating on the riverbank, but it actually makes just as much sense to figure that they'd build near the road."

The area they were standing in looked to Anneke like nothing more than a mass of anonymous vegetation, trees and shrubs and weeds and branches commingling in a tangle of foliage. But as she continued to examine it, she began to note subtle differences from the surrounding woods. The trees seemed more widely spaced, she thought, the weeds, or what looked like weeds, growing thicker and higher.

"These are wild huckleberry bushes." Patrick strode forward confidently and thrust his hand into the underbrush. He pulled, and a long, narrow length of branch unraveled itself from the mass. Along its length, small tips of green were just beginning to appear. "There's another mass of it over there." Patrick forced his way through the tangle of bushes, then stopped and bent down. "Hello."

"What is it?" Clare asked tensely.

"Come look." And Patrick abruptly disappeared from view.

"Hey!" Clare charged forward with Zoe at her heels, and stopped dead.

"Holy shit," Zoe said.

"It's—I think we found it." Clare looked up, eyes blazing.

"It's the basement." Patrick's head reemerged at knee-height. "What's left of it, anyway."

"What's down there?" Clare asked, shifting from foot to foot in an agony of impatience. "Could you see anything? Come out of there so I can look."

"Easy." Patrick emerged in full from the ground and brushed himself off. At his feet, Anneke saw the edge of a concrete slab, and a narrow opening where the tangled bushes had been broken or pulled aside. "It's one of those old-fashioned root cellars," Patrick said. "You know, the kind with the outside door like a trap door into the ground."

"But what's down there?" Clare repeated insistently.

"I don't know." Patrick shook his head. "It's pitch black in there. We'll need a flashlight before we can see what's in-side."

"You've got a flashlight in the car, don't you?" Zoe appealed to Karl.

"Yes." He nodded. "I'll get it." He walked back to the car, and returned moments later holding a square lantern. Patrick reached for it, but Clare stepped in front of him.

"No. I go first," she said.

"Actually, Ms. Swann, I'll go first," Karl said, drawing back the lantern. "I want to examine the area before it gets disturbed any further." He strode to the opening and flipped a switch on the lantern, aiming it so that a powerful beam of light shone downward. Then he slipped neatly through the narrow opening in the bushes. The others clustered around the opening, watching the flicker of moving light. He was down there for what seemed like a long time, Anneke thought, and must have seemed even longer to Clare. The girl's face was a mask of anguished tension by the time Karl reappeared.

"All right," he said. Clare snatched the lantern from his hand, barely waiting for him to step aside before she disappeared downward. Zoe and Patrick followed on her heels. Anneke hesitated briefly and looked at Karl; when he shrugged noncommittally, she followed the others, stepping carefully on the damp, lichen-coated concrete stairs.

It was, as advertised, a root cellar, surprisingly high and spacious. Anneke's eyes followed the moving lantern light—damp, dirt-covered concrete floor, the century-old dirt scuffed and roiled; cut stone foundation walls, greenish with lichen; the rotting remains of wooden shelves. Overhead, pinpricks of light filtered through the heavy bushes that now served as a roof.

"There!" Clare's voice rang out high and sharp, echoes bouncing off the stone walls. "There it is!" Anneke turned toward the voice; Clare stood, illuminated dimly at the edge of the lantern's light, pointing with a finger that shook with anticipation.

She was pointing at a metal bin, like an antique flour container. It had once been painted white, but age and damp and the natural forces of decay had turned it blackish and mottled with rust. But Anneke hardly noticed its condition; all her attention was focused on the diamond-shaped pattern scratched deeply into the metal. She held her breath as Clare reached out her hand and lifted the lid, craning forward with the others as the lantern shone down fully into the bin.

It was empty.

TWENTY-NINE

* * * * * *

They drove away from the old root cellar toward the house in dismal silence. Clare was white-faced and grim, and even Zoe's normal ebullience was damped. But when Karl pulled the Land Rover onto the concrete slab between the station wagon and Zoe's Buick, Clare was the first one out of the car.

"All right," she said, her voice harsh. "Let's go see which one of those sons of bitches stole my money."

Helena pounced on her the moment they walked in the door.

"There you are, Clare," she shrilled. "You could at least have let us know where you were. I've been worrying about you all day. Why do you *always* have to be so irresponsible?"

It was the "always" that did it, Anneke realized suddenly; it made irresponsibility not an action but a character trait, ineluctably attached to the person accused. Why even try to be responsible—or polite, or successful—when you've been convinced that all the negative traits are inescapable parts of your very being?

"Clare, for heaven's sake." Olivia hurried down the stairs, a suitcase in one hand, a child's decorated duffel bag in the other. "I hope you haven't been causing Lieutenant Genesko any trouble. Please excuse my niece, Lieutenant. She can be very difficult." She set the bags on the floor. "Do you have news for us?"

"I'd like to speak to all of you, if you don't mind," Karl said. "Is your husband here?"

"In the dining room." Olivia gestured, the first time Anneke had seen her look nervous. She wasn't quite her usual impeccable self, either; there were spots of mud on her brown walking shoes, and bits of her dark hair had come loose and trailed along the back of her neck. "Has something else happened?"

"Oh, Clare, what have you gotten yourself into now?" Helena asked anxiously.

"Nothing much. I just offed the sheriff and barbecued him," Clare said with sarcastic brightness. "He was delicious, too."

"Clare, that's disgusting," Olivia said angrily. From behind her, Anneke heard a muffled giggle that could only have come from Zoe. "Please remember there are children in this house." Olivia looked around uneasily, as if expecting the children to pop out of the air like genies.

"Please, may we talk in the dining room?" Karl said. Without waiting for agreement, he led them into that room, where Dwight was busily taking things from a drawer in the breakfront and stuffing them into a duffel bag.

"Lieutenant, I didn't know you were coming back. We're just about to leave." His face was flushed; he set the duffel on the floor and looked at Karl. "Have you found out anything?"

"Have you been here all morning, Mr. Swann?" Karl asked.

"Here? No." Dwight looked flustered. "I drove into Lake

City this morning to pick up some things for the trip home. Why?"

"Did you go with him?" Karl asked Olivia.

"No. I've been here all day. I took the boys for a hike this morning, and I spent the afternoon making one last search of the house, to make sure we didn't leave anything we wanted to keep." She looked at him. "Are you by any chance asking if I have an *alibi* for something?"

"Were you with her, Ms. Swann?" Karl focused on Helena, who bridled.

"I was in the house all day, if that's what you want to know," she said. "I have no idea where Olivia was." She seemed pleased not to corroborate Olivia's story, apparently unaware that it left her own actions unaccounted for as well.

"What about Mr. Rappoport and Ms. Pryor? Are they still here?"

"No." Dwight shook his head, the irritable motion of someone surrounded by a cloud of gnats. "Ms. Pryor left quite early this morning with her papers. Mr. Rappoport only finished up and left about half an hour ago; that's why we're getting out of here so late." He sounded harassed and sulky; he bent down and picked up the duffel bag, which he dumped on the table in front of him with a thud.

"Are there any guns in the house?" Karl asked.

"Guns!" Olivia darted a glance toward the kitchen door.

"Yes, there are a couple of hunting rifles." Dwight pressed his lips together. "They're kept in a cabinet in the kitchen, above the refrigerator—a locked cabinet, I might add."

"Would you show them to me, please?" Karl said.

"Yes, of course." He and Karl disappeared through the door. The others remained, listening to the muffled sounds. When the two men returned a few moments later, Karl was carrying a rifle in a leather case, and Dwight looked grimly concerned.

"One of the rifles is missing," he said.

"Yeah. Big surprise." Clare's voice was sarcastic, but her body seemed to tighten.

"What are you talking about, Clare?" Olivia said sharply. "Did you steal one of the rifles?"

"Oh, Clare," Helena wailed, "why would you want a gun?"

"Clare, I don't think you'd better say any more." Dwight sighed audibly. "Lieutenant, there's no proof that that rifle wasn't taken months ago."

"You motherfuckers." Clare snarled the word. "No matter what goes on around here, you're gonna try to make it my fault, aren't you?"

"Clare, I want you out of here." Olivia's face was white. "Now. Take your filthy language, and your friend, and leave before I do something you'll regret."

"Such as?" Clare asked mockingly. "What are you going to do, Auntie dearest? Maybe—oh, shit." She stopped abruptly, turned her back on Olivia, and faced Patrick. "It's not so easy, is it?" she asked him shakily.

"No, it isn't." Patrick came over to her and put both hands on her shoulders. "But recognizing it is a real start, truly it is." His hands tightened on her. "Hang in there, honey. After a while it'll become automatic, I promise you."

"What are you talking about?" Helena asked suspiciously.

"Nothing you'd understand, Mother." Clare managed a shaky shrug. "Let's go, Zoe. Time to get back to Ann Arbor."

"Okay. I left my bookbag in the living room. It's been there all day, with my car keys in it." She directed a pointed glance at Karl. "Hey!" She jumped back as two small bodies came hurtling into the room.

"You'll never catch me!" Jeremy Swann shouted, caroming off Zoe's leg and darting toward the kitchen door.

"Give me that! It's mine!" Tyler skidded behind him, twisting to avoid running into his mother. He raised his right hand threateningly, and Anneke saw there was a large bandage wrapped around two of his fingers.

"Tyler!" Olivia said sharply. "Don't you dare run in the house."

McBain, Michigan: August 25, 1895

"A local businessman spotted him getting off the train in McBain," Sheriff Dunham was explaining. "I don't expect you want to join up with the posse, Mr. Swann, but I was hopin' you'd see your way to loanin' us a few horses." The sheriff stood next to his own horse in a respectful posture. Behind him a dozen or so men milled in a nervous group, only a few of them with mounts.

"Of course, Sheriff. This Smalley isn't someone we want around here." Walter stood on the porch, looking down at the ragtag posse. Henrietta thought they looked more like schoolboys on an outing than serious adults on a manhunt. "I'm assuming," Walter said carefully, "that you'll take personal responsibility for their return in good condition?"

"The county'll be responsible, I promise," Dunham replied, and Walter frowned slightly, recognizing the ambiguity. Then he shrugged. "Very well, Sheriff. We all need to support the forces of law in our communities, after all. My stable man will show you which horses you may borrow, and good luck on your hunt."

"We'll need it, thanks." The sheriff sounded pessimistic. "There's a lot of miles to search around here."

They didn't know, Henrietta realized. Either they didn't know about Cora's relationship to Smalley, or they didn't know where she lived.

She didn't know exactly what was going on—Walter hadn't thought it suitable to discuss such things with her—but she knew that Smalley had killed a man, and that this posse was searching for him. And she knew that Cora was so frightened of him that she'd rather spend a night with Walter than be turned over to him.

Henrietta's imagination simply couldn't stretch to the possible depths that fact suggested. All she knew was that Cora must be in unspeakable danger.

"Cora Brown," she said aloud.

"Ma'am?" The sheriff looked at her quizzically.

"Cora B-brown." She could feel Walter's eyes boring into her, waves of his rage battering her. "His . . . Smalley is . . ." She halted, unable to find a word she was physically able to speak aloud.

"Yeah, Sheriff." A man in the posse spoke up. "I heard Smalley had himself a woman around McBain somewheres. Don't know where, though."

"Ma'am," Dunham asked carefully, "do you happen to know where this Cora Brown lives?"

"Sheriff, you are being unpardonably insulting." Walter answered for her, his face cold and tight, but red with the effort of holding back his fury. "Are you possibly suggesting that *my wife* would know anything about a common harlot?"

"I have to ask, Mr. Swann." The sheriff continued to gaze at Henrietta.

"Mrs. Swann." Walter grasped her arm, his fingernails digging into her skin. His voice dripped acid. "Please return to the house. I will deal with you later."

"Yes, Walter." She kept her eyes down as she turned toward the door. It was going to be bad, she knew, feeling the heat from his hand. It was going to be the worst ever. She didn't dare do anything else, she didn't dare.

"Pete Slocum," she blurted to the sheriff. "He works at the

Swann mill—he knows where she lives." She went inside quickly then, not looking back at Walter, knowing what she would see. It occurred to her that she was probably going to die at his hand one day, and probably soon.

THIRTY

. . . . . .

"I can't imagine Helena shooting at her own daughter," Anneke said.

They were heading south on 23, racing the twilight back to Ann Arbor. They had detoured from the Swann house through Lake City, where Karl left the rifle and a message for Sheriff Kettleman, out somewhere on patrol. Zoe, Clare, and Patrick were presumably somewhere on the road ahead of them, probably already home in fact, considering that Zoe drove nearly as fast as Anneke did.

Karl had asked a few more questions after the younger people left, but none of the answers struck Anneke as particularly useful. No one had an alibi—they knew Dwight had taken the station wagon out, and with Zoe's car standing outside, and the keys lying in the living room, neither Olivia nor Helena could be eliminated. None of them admitted to knowing the location of the old house site, or indeed, even that there was an old house site.

"I don't think anyone was shooting at Clare," Karl said.

"The shots were well over their heads—high enough that it doesn't seem likely it was simply bad aim."

"And Helena could want the money for herself, even though Clare is her daughter. Considering the hostility between them, she might believe Clare would take the money and leave." A thought struck her suddenly. "You know, with everything else, I forgot about this Red Joe you were talking to. What did he have to say? Is there any chance he knew anything about Smalley and Cora Brown? Or about the old house site?"

"I think Gerald was more interested in the existing house," Karl replied. "According to Red Joe, when Gerald found out about Julia's death, he decided that the Swann property should be turned into some sort of shamanic center—with himself as the shaman."

"What?"

"Apparently, Gerald believed that he had some sort of shamanic powers. He'd made a pest of himself bothering various Native American groups for a while, but they finally kicked him out." Karl shook his head. "Red Joe said Gerald insisted that he 'forgave' them because they had been 'sickened by civilization.' Red Joe himself," Karl grinned slightly, "believes that the disease is capitalism."

"Good Lord."

"He also said something else interesting," Karl added. "According to Red Joe, Gerald had been in contact with a member of his family."

"Really." Anneke turned to look at him. "Which one?"

"He didn't know." He steered around a car carrier and turned off 23 onto 14 for the loop into Ann Arbor. "By the way," he asked, "why didn't you tell me that Patrick was up there?"

"Didn't I?" The question surprised her. "Sorry; I guess it just never came up. Anyway," she went on, "since he was right there with us when we were shot at, at least now we know he's out of it. But dammit, *somebody* beat us to that cellar."

"We can't even be sure of that," Karl pointed out. "By the time I examined it, it was impossible to tell whether someone had been there before Patrick so thoroughly mucked up the scene."

"You can't think he stole anything before the rest of us got to it," she protested. "For one thing, he didn't have any light—he couldn't even have seen the bin itself without the lantern. And anyway, we'd have seen it."

"Quite true," he agreed. "But how do you know there ever *was* anything in that bin?" He glided off the expressway at North Main and headed south, while she chewed unhappily over his statement. "I need to go straight to the office," he said. "Why don't you drop me off there, drive home, and come back for me in a couple of hours?"

"All right." She still felt depressed over the failure of their treasure hunt, the understanding of Clare's need stabbing at her. Mothers and daughters. Parents and children. A hideous tangle of demanding emotion and grasping need. "There's one other thing," she said as Karl pulled the Land Rover up to the police entrance at City Hall.

"The child." He nodded, reading her mind. "Tyler. I'll see what I can set in motion. We can check up on him, anyway." He unbuckled his seat belt, leaned over and kissed her lightly. "Seven o'clock?"

"All right. We can get some dinner then." She got out and walked around to the driver's side, pulling her keys from her purse. The Land Rover was a fine vehicle, she decided, backing around and heading out onto Ann Street, but she'd be glad to get back behind the wheel of her own Firebird.

At home she unpacked and changed clothes, shedding her dusty and travel-worn denims for black wool pants and a long red silk tunic, hoping without much hope that the bright color would brighten her mood. She set out a pile of mud-covered clothes for the cleaners, smiling slightly at the memory they recalled. And she dug the Littleton glass sculpture out of her briefcase, and after consideration, took it into Karl's office and set it on his desk. There was something masculine about it that she thought he'd like.

Finally she went to her own room, where she booted up her computer and dialed into her office machine.

After two days away, her queue of e-mail nearly filled her mailbox; she plowed through it as fast as possible, drinking diet Coke and trying to shove Clare, and Tyler, and Emma, out of her mind, annoyed that they seemed to be tangled together in her brain somehow. She was relieved when six forty-five finally arrived and she could power down and head out to her car.

Brad Weinmann was in Karl's office when she arrived, the two of them contrasting oddly, Brad in his unremarkable dark suit next to Karl, still in his northwoods attire of jeans and heavy fisherman's sweater.

"Are you ready, or should I wait outside?" she asked.

"We're done, I think." Karl looked a question at Brad.

"Right." Brad nodded. "I'll get right on it." He gave Anneke a sketchy wave as he hurried out.

Karl picked up his briefcase and took his leather jacket from the coat rack. "Where would you like to have dinner?" he asked as they walked to the car.

"Somewhere easy," she said. "How about Berry's?"

"Fine." He paused at the car before going around and sliding into the passenger seat. My car, my hands on the wheel, Anneke chuckled to herself as she pulled out of the parking lot and turned right on Huron.

"Damn," she said as they crossed Main.

"Something the matter?"

"Nothing serious. I just should have stopped at the bathroom before we left."

"And you're usually so well organized," he said, grinning.

"Do you need to stop right away? Berry's is only a couple of miles out."

"No, I can wait. It's just that I should have known better." She sighed. "Too much Coke—the programmer's occupational hazard."

That was when it hit her. She slowed down unconsciously as she processed it, and barely heard an irritated honk from the car behind her. It had to be, she thought; at least, she could think of no other explanation. She accelerated slightly, continuing to head west by pure reflex.

"What is it?" Karl asked quietly.

"It's . . . I'm not sure. I just thought of something." Quickly she explained her frail deduction, waiting for him to shoot it down. But when she had finished he sat perfectly still for several seconds, until finally she said, "Does it make sense?"

"I'm afraid so. And if you're right, I think I'd like to get over there as quickly as possible."

"No problem." She swung a tight U across Jackson Road traffic, drawing angry honks from a red pickup truck, and headed back the way they'd come. She trod on the accelerator and roared across Maple on the yellow, enjoying the knowledge that, for once in her life, she actually wanted a cop to catch her speeding.

She drove east on Huron, racing yellow lights and veering in and out of slower-moving traffic. Karl pointedly tightened his seat belt but said nothing until they crossed Main.

"Turn on Fifth," he directed her, and she cut in front of a green Plymouth and hung a hard right. "Then left on William, and right on Hamilton."

"Now what?" She slowed and peered at the close-packed old houses lining the narrow street, finding it hard to make out details in the luminous half dark of twilight. She turned on her headlights and flicked the handle for the high beams.

"Over there, on the left," he said, pointing. "I'm going to

go knock on the door, but I want you to stay in the car. I don't expect any trouble, but I'd rather not take any chances."

"All right." She was suddenly nervous. She followed his finger toward a tall, narrow house with a wraparound porch and a sagging roof. At the curb was a small beige Toyota station wagon crammed full of someone's belongings. The figure in the driver's seat turned and blinked into the glare of the Firebird's headlights.

"It's her!" Anneke said. The Toyota sprang to life. And Kate Pryor fled out the other end of Hamilton.

THIRTY-ONE

. . . .

Anneke floored the accelerator without conscious thought and felt the Firebird leap under her. Kate Pryor had gotten away from her once before, but that was in a different place and a different car. Her car, her hands on the wheel this time. She roared after the Toyota, conscious that she was smiling broadly as she rocked into the turn onto Jefferson.

The Toyota turned left, and left again, heading north on Division, picking up the automated flow of the traffic lights. Anneke ducked around a huge old Mercury Cougar, cut to the left lane, then dodged back in front of an ancient Volkswagen beetle and roared through the yellow light at Washington.

Forever afterward, she would remember the chase of Kate Pryor as a kind of ultimate high, an adrenaline rush so pure it was like an out-of-body experience. All her reflexes, all her senses, were focused on the car ahead and the feel of wheel and engine. All her life, driving had meant freedom; now she added to it the thrill of the chase.

"She can't think she can outrun me in that thing," she said.

"She isn't trying to outrun you," Karl said quietly. "She's trying to lose you. Damn," he said. "I wish you had a cellular phone in here."

"What would I do with one?" she asked reasonably, using the center left turn lane to pass a slow-moving Volvo and another pickup. "Nearly all my driving is here in town, and when I do get out on the road, the last thing I want is phone calls reminding me of what it is I'm driving away from. Anyhow, no way is she going to lose me."

The Toyota crossed Huron and continued north—heading for Plymouth Road, Anneke thought. But at the last moment, it dove out of the center lane into a hard right on Lawrence. Anneke wrenched the wheel and felt the Firebird rock as she followed. The Toyota jogged across the offset intersection at State, turned back south on Ingalls, then left onto Ann, driving at speeds that drew outraged honks from other cars. She was running without lights, and the gathering dark was making her difficult to see on the narrow, badly lit streets. Anneke pushed harder on the accelerator, then slowed, swearing, as a metallic blue Cadillac blundered in front of her. When she blasted her horn and zoomed past, the Toyota was disappearing around the Observatory turn.

"Shit." She trod hard on the accelerator and the Firebird roared into the turn and almost plowed into the back of a Detroit Edison truck. She yanked the wheel to the left and dove past, closing on the Toyota.

"Anneke, ease up." Karl put a warning hand on her arm. "Crank it down a notch."

"What do you mean? We've got her."

"I don't mean the car," he said. "I mean you. You're in adrenaline overdrive."

The Toyota caught the light at Washtenaw and swung left on the yellow. Anneke brought her palm down on her horn, hard, and kept it there, the blaring scream accompanying her through the red light. She kept her eyes on the Toyota.

"But we'll lose her," she protested. "Besides—yes, all right." She took a deep breath; her hands were gripping the wheel so tightly that her fingernails dug into her palms. "I think she may be heading for the expressway," she said.

"I know." Karl's voice was tight. "It would be better if she didn't make it across the state line."

"Don't worry," Anneke said confidently. "There's no way she can outrun me." And then she turned her head briefly to look at Karl. Now that the adrenaline rush was over, the thought struck her for the first time. "But I can't make her stop, either, can I? I mean, I can't very well run her off the road, like a bad cop movie. Can I?" Well, could she? She found herself wondering how it might be done—a gentle sideswipe? It would take a good deal of control, but the Firebird handled so easily it shouldn't be all that difficult.

"No, you can't." For a moment, she thought he looked briefly worried. "We'd better leave that sort of maneuver to Bruce Willis." This time she saw the brief twitch of a smile on his face. Ahead, the Toyota once again caught the yellow at the Devonshire intersection, and again Anneke leaned on her horn and followed on the red, barely conscious of the Volvo that lurched sideways to avoid her. It lurched again as the wail of sirens rose behind them and the flashing blue lights came into view at last in the rearview mirror.

"Thank God." She started to ease back on the accelerator, and the Toyota immediately began to pull away. The police car pulled in behind the Firebird, siren keening.

"No, don't stop. Keep on her," Karl said sharply. Confused, she accelerated once more, watching out of the corner of her eye as he released his seat belt, reached into the pocket of his jacket, and withdrew his wallet. "I'm going to turn on the dome light," he warned her. "With luck, they'll recognize me." He flicked the switch, flooding the interior of the car with light. As Anneke blinked to adjust her vision, he raised both hands above his head, then turned his body slowly until he was kneeling on the seat facing the rear, arms stretched upward, his police shield flashing gold in his hand.

In the mirror, she saw the startled look on the face of the uniformed policeman behind the wheel of the police car; saw Karl motion deliberately at the Toyota ahead of them; saw the police car leap forward to overtake the Toyota. She eased off the accelerator again, and again Karl said, "No. Stay with her. This is a two-car operation."

"But I can't—" She sped up once more even as she spoke.

"Oh yes, you can." She flicked a glance at him and saw the feral grin on his face as he clicked his seat belt shut again. "You wanted to play cops and robbers. Now let's see how good you really are."

"Is that a challenge, Lieutenant?" She laughed aloud, shifting her hands slightly on the steering wheel, feeling the adrenaline start to flow again. "*My* car, this time." And no stumps to get stuck on, she thought. The Firebird leaped forward until it was barely inches from the Toyota's rear bumper. The police car pulled ahead of the Toyota, moved over, began to slow. Anneke released pressure infinitesimally from the accelerator, keeping pace with the Toyota as it slowed, swerved, sped up, and slowed again.

And finally braked, slowed, and turned quietly and sedately into the parking lot of a strip mall, where it coasted to a stop.

The police car whipped into the drive at the other end of the strip mall and squealed to a stop, angled across the Toyota's front bumper. Anneke pulled in behind the Toyota, suddenly shaky—from anticlimax more than from the chase itself. It felt, she realized, more like interrupted sex than anything else, and she had a sudden flash of understanding. This was one reason cops sometimes ran amok.

Driven by the adrenaline, she jumped out of the car and followed Karl as he ran toward the Toyota. The two uniformed policemen approached from their squad car, weapons drawn. And Kate Pryor, looking tired and ordinary, opened the door of the Toyota and stepped out, arms over her head.

"I'm sorry," she said, her rich voice carrying across the night air. "I didn't want anyone to get hurt."

After that, Anneke went back to the Firebird and sat for a long time, watching more police cars come and go; watching Karl talking into the police radio; watching finally as Kate Pryor was taken away and a tow truck came for the Toyota.

When Karl finally walked back to the Firebird, he was carrying a Hershey bar. "Here." He handed it to her through the car window. "This should help."

She hadn't realized she needed help, but the smell of the chocolate drew her like a pheromone. She gobbled half of it in two or three gulps before opening the car door and stepping out. Her legs were still wobbly, and the muscles in her arms were twitching.

"Are you done here?" she asked.

"Yes. We have to go back to the department, I'm afraid. You and I are going to have to collaborate on the formal statement of all this."

"Oh, God, I never thought of that." She sighed and took another bite of chocolate. "I guess I can manage. But would it be all right," she asked, "if I stopped at the bathroom first?"

By unspoken consent, Karl took the wheel for the drive back downtown. It wasn't until she had finished the last of the Hershey bar, and they were turning off Washtenaw onto Forest, that it occurred to her to ask: "You did find Smalley's money in her car, didn't you?"

"We found something that appears to be, yes," he said with innate police caution. "In a porcupine-quill box, if you can believe it."

"Clare's box?"

"Probably. There's a small collection of papers in it—old photographs, documents, and so on."

"How much money was there?"

"I don't know yet."

"For Clare's sake, I hope it's a lot." She sighed and leaned her head back against the headrest. "Poor Gerald. Getting murdered for something he didn't even know anything about."

"Oh, Kate Pryor didn't kill Gerald."

"What?" She turned in her seat to stare at him.

"Patrick Swann murdered his uncle," Karl said, turning the Firebird into the City Hall parking lot once again. "He was arrested about—" he checked his watch "—two hours ago."

McBain, Michigan: August 25, 1895

Cora was bracing for the next blow when she heard the shout.

"Come on out, Smalley!" the voice boomed from outside. "We've got the cabin surrounded." There was a minute or so of silence. "We know you're in there," the voice called out.

Cora heard Smalley's snarl of rage and looked up. He had stepped away from her and shed his black duster. Now he stood alongside the front window, a gun in each hand. She could see another gun tucked into the waistband of his pants, nestled against the small of his back; there was probably one in his boot, too, and who knew where else. She rolled sideways, pain knifing through her as she tried to get to her feet.

"No. Stay down." Cal was crouched next to her.

"But—" She didn't continue; instead, she flattened herself against the floor by sheer instinct as the first barrage of bullets tore at the cabin. She heard glass shatter and felt the whoosh of air as a bullet whizzed over her head.

"Can you crawl?" Cal's voice was firm and steady in her ear. She inched sideways, fighting the pain. "The back door. This way," Cal muttered. He used his good arm to support her, balancing himself on the stump of the other. She knew how bad that must hurt.

"I can do it," she muttered back to him, ducking as another bullet whined through the broken window. She glanced over

• 2 7 8 •

her shoulder; Smalley remained tucked against the wall next to the window, all his attention focused on the men outside. He'd told her once that he'd never be taken alive, and she'd believed him. She still did.

She blotted out Smalley, and the pain, and the sound of gunfire, fixing her mind entirely on the task of creeping across the endless floor. She couldn't remember exactly why she was doing this, nor what the goal of it was. She only knew that she had to crawl, or die.

"Here, give 'er to me." Somehow they were outside now, behind the cabin. She could feel the cooling night air on her face, and sense the presence of other men around her. The voice sounded familiar. She felt herself being lifted and carried; the man carrying her staggered, then righted himself. "Sorry, Cora," Pete Slocum said. "You okay? You're heavier than you look."

"Yeah, I'll live," she said from between teeth clenched against the pain. If she'd had the breath she would've laughed, feeling the cause of her extra weight still stitched securely along the seams of her skirt.

"Good thing you got here when you did," Cal said. They'd stopped moving finally, a ways from the combat zone of the cabin; Pete set her down on the damp ground as gently as possible, and she breathed a ragged sigh of relief. "I think he was fixing to kill her this time."

"Got here as fast as we could." Pete dropped to the ground next to her and patted her hair. It felt kind of nice, Cora thought. "You can thank Miz Swann that we got here at all."

"Henrietta Swann?" Cora blurted in surprise.

"Yeah." Pete nodded. "She's the one told the posse that I'd know where you lived. I take it that husband of hers wasn't none too pleased about her speakin' up, neither."

There really was some guts there, Cora mused. But if someone didn't do something to help her, that Walter'd probably kill her one of these days. She tried to sit up, and winced as the pain stabbed through her. She'd be all right in the end, though, she figured; she was going to live, at least. *I owe Henrietta Swann big,* she thought.

There was a sudden barrage of sound, a cacophony of gunfire. "I think we got 'im, Sheriff," a voice called out.

"Well, don't do nothin' dumb," another voice answered. "He's dangerous as the fires of hell—you make good an' sure he's dead, you hear?"

He's right, Cora thought; *dead is the only sure thing.* She was free herself now, but what about Henrietta Swann? Cora, lying quietly on the ground, considered the possibilities of the fires of hell.

Dear Miz Swann

Im riting to thank you and to let you no that Im heling okay and Im gonna be okay and its all thanks to you. Pete will bring yu this lettr he says yur the one who sent them otherwiz if you hadnt Id be ded now.

Yu no that what ther riting about me has got it all rong but yu no that anyways so it dont matter The Blak Dimond stuf sur maks me mad but thers nuthin I can do about it.

Saying thank yu isnt enuf thers more I can do to help you and I figur I owe it to you What you did for me I can do for you if you want.

Ill be by the river tomorow morning and we can talk about it you can mak up yur mind then I no that them kerosene lamps is dangerus thers lots of fires around this time of yer.

Yurs,

Cora Brown

THIRTY-TWO

· · · · · ·

"But he *can't* be the murderer," Zoe protested. "He was right there in the car with us when we were shot at."

She still couldn't quite believe the whole nonsensical thing. They'd dropped Patrick off at his apartment on Oakland and returned finally to the dorm, where she and Clare, talked out on the subject of John Smalley and his money, had parted company. Zoe was secretly relieved to be home, and she had the feeling Clare felt the same. She dug out her psych book and spent the next few hours pretending to study, on the unproven assumption that if she acted like a student some of it might take. She had no story due for Tuesday's paper, and for once she didn't feel like going to the *Daily*. She went down to the dining room for dinner, returned to her room, and was attacking her poli sci notes, feeling unbearably virtuous, when Clare burst into her room.

"My mother just called," she said. "They've arrested Patrick."

"What? That's impossible." Zoe turned from her desk. "He was with us when we were shot at."

"I know. What the hell's going on?"

"I don't know," Zoe said grimly, "but I know where to find out. Come on." She grabbed her jacket and bookbag and raced for the car.

Now she glared at Genesko, who regarded her calmly from behind his desk. Anneke sat off to the side, looking exhausted and somehow sad.

Instead of answering her, Genesko said to Clare: "I think we've found what you've been hunting for."

"You found Smalley's stash?" Clare leaned forward, her eyes blazing. "Where?"

"In the back of a car being driven by Katherine Pryor."

"Kate Pryor? You mean the Bentley woman?" Clare asked in dawning amazement. And then: "How much was it?"

"According to the evidence receipt," Genesko said, "four hundred forty-three thousand, three hundred twenty-one dollars."

"Four hundred—" Clare choked on the words. "And it's really mine?"

"Almost certainly, I should think." He smiled slightly at her. "Along with the money, there was a letter to you from your great-aunt. It's very likely that the courts would consider that letter to be a form of holographic will."

"Holy shit." Zoe looked at her, awestruck. "You really are an heiress."

"Yeah." Clare sat perfectly still, looking stunned. "Can I see the letter?" she asked finally.

"As soon as forensics is finished with it, yes. We'll have to keep it, and the money, as evidence until Ms. Pryor's trial, but then it will be returned to you."

"Kate Pryor." Zoe tested the name. "I never thought of her."

"Katherine Pryor was responsible for the search of Clare's

room, the vandalism, the assault on Pete Carmichael near the house up north, and the shooting in the woods." Genesko leaned back in his chair. "Katherine Pryor was the one who was desperately trying to find that money before you did. But it was Patrick who killed Gerald Swann."

"But—" Zoe sputtered.

"From the very beginning," Genesko overrode her, "there were two different trails. To begin with, we were fairly sure there were two people in Clare's room. One of them was Patrick, who left his fingerprints all over the desk and the door and window. But the room had been thoroughly searched, and there were no fingerprints on the dresser, or closet, or on any of the things strewn around the room."

"Well, that—"

"And there was also the nature of the various incidents," he went on. "First, you have a rather brutal murder. But you also have the attack on Carmichael, who was knocked on the head so gently that he came to only ten minutes later with nothing but a slight headache. And the shots in the woods, which were so far over your heads that there was never any question of risk to any of you. I couldn't reconcile those acts, but they made sense if you postulated one murderer and one . . . treasure hunter."

"So you're saying Kate Pryor was only after the money?"

"That's right."

"But how did you get on to her?"

"That was Anneke's deduction," he said, nodding in her direction. "If you recall, when Ms. Pryor arrived at the Missaukee house, she said she had to use the bathroom before she started working. She then went back through the living room, toward the bathroom in the hall under the front stairs. But how did she know where the bathroom was?"

"Because she'd been there before," Clare blurted, her eyes wide behind her glasses. "So she was the one who broke in and pried off all the windowsills?"

"It was a fairly frail chain of reasoning," he said, "but once we caught up with her and found the money, and the porcupine-quill box, that confirmed it. She was in the house when John Singleton handed Clare the box, and she was the one person there who recognized what the reference to Black Diamond was really about. Northern Michigan history was her field, of course. She thought at once about the possibility of John Smalley's treasure, but she didn't know where to start looking. When you opened the box and started talking about old papers, she became convinced there was a clue in it.

"She said she went to the dorm hoping to talk you into letting her see the papers. She knocked, and when there was no answer, she tried the door—that's who Patrick heard. He ducked out the window, leaving the door unlocked. And leaving Gerald's body on the floor."

"And Pryor just went ahead and searched the room with a body in the middle of the floor?"

"Yes. She was convinced she was on the track of a huge fortune. She grabbed the box, of course, but she realized at once that the letters had been removed, and that made her positive that there was a clue in one of them. She was furious when she couldn't find them."

"Yeah, y'know, I think she tore up the room more than she had to, just because she was angry," Clare said.

"Very possibly. In any case, the next day she read Zoe's story in the *Daily*, realized what had happened to the letters, and returned that night hoping to get another chance at them. She was cautious, though—more cautious than Patrick was."

"That's another thing—if Patrick wasn't interested in the letters, what was he doing hanging around the dorm that night?"

"Patrick knew he hadn't searched the room, so he knew someone else had been there. He thought if he could help capture that person, it would get him off the hook. When he shouted out in frustration that we were letting someone else get away, he was absolutely sincere.

"Ms. Pryor then took a guess that Julia Vanderlaan had followed the Smalley legend herself, so she searched all the windowsills in both of Mrs. Vanderlaan's houses, but of course came up empty. She was feeling utterly frantic when she overheard you talking about a previous house."

"So she was the one who shot at us? Except, wait a minute." Zoe concentrated. "She couldn't have followed us, because she was at the site *before* us. How did she know where it was?"

"From the copy of the old deed in that porcupine-quill box. It had the original legal description on it. She made the deduction when she saw the description on the deed Dwight had, but she was stuck working on the papers in the attic, so she couldn't get to it until the afternoon. Remember, too, she was as skilled at woodslore as Patrick was—she made the same deduction about the mound of wild huckleberries that he did."

"You said you found the money 'in a car being driven by' Kate," Zoe recalled. "You mean you caught up with her while she was trying to escape?"

"That's right." Genesko glanced at Anneke, and Zoe knew there was something there but she couldn't figure out what. "She was planning to disappear. She said she had nothing to keep her here."

"No, I suppose not." Zoe's mind went back to the conversation around the campfire. "She talked about 'connections' last night—shit, was that only last night? Anyway, I guess she didn't have any. Y'know," the thought struck her, "if that letter from Julia hadn't been with the money, would you have been able to prove it didn't belong to Kate?"

"Probably not." Genesko gave her one of his rare full

smiles. "But she was programmed to preserve historical papers. I don't think it ever occurred to her to throw it away. Or the things in the porcupine-quill box."

"Yeah. Jeez, Ann Arbor really is all about papers, isn't it? But I still don't see what any of this has to do with Patrick," she said stubbornly.

"It doesn't."

"But—" Zoe was beginning to feel like a broken record.

"Two different crimes," Genesko said. "Two criminals. Two entirely different motives."

"What motive could Patrick have for killing my father?" Clare demanded.

"The papers," Genesko said.

"But if he wasn't after the Smalley treasure," Zoe heard her voice rise in a squeak of frustration, *"why would he be after the papers?"*

"No, not those papers." Genesko smiled patiently. "Two crimes. Two criminals. *Two* sets of papers."

THIRTY-THREE

• • • • • •

"You mean Gerald's papers?" This time it was Anneke who blurted out the words.

"That's right. You were all so fixated on Julia's papers, you forgot about Gerald's."

"Are you trying to tell us," Zoe demanded, "that Patrick murdered his uncle over a batch of moldy old academic papers?"

"Why so surprised? This is Ann Arbor." She wasn't all that surprised, Zoe realized, bits and pieces falling into place in her head. "You were willing enough to believe someone murdered for a collection of letters they hadn't even seen," Genesko pointed out. "But in fact Patrick didn't kill Gerald to *get* his papers—he already had them. His father, Christopher, was the one who collected them from the anthropology department after Gerald left. Patrick came across them three years ago, when the family moved. And when Patrick himself was just starting graduate work."

"But then he already had the papers?" Zoe felt terminally confused. "I just don't get it."

"You have to understand one thing," Genesko said. "Gerald Swann really was a genius. If he hadn't drugged out, there's no telling what he might have accomplished. What Patrick found, three years ago, was a brilliant theoretical analysis of the fiduciary role of shamans and shamanism among Native American tribes."

"The Economics of Magic," Zoe whispered.

"Exactly." Genesko nodded. "Patrick's dissertation. And not only that." He reached into a wire basket on his desk and pulled out a small publication that Zoe saw was titled *Historical Economics.* He opened it and turned it toward them so they could see the table of contents. " 'Analysis of the Trade Value of Ceremonial Objects Among a Chippewa Sub-Tribe,' " Zoe read, "by Patrick Swann."

"Patrick didn't kill Gerald to get his papers," Genesko repeated. "He killed Gerald because he had already found the papers, *and used them.* Not only was his dissertation derived from Gerald's work, but he'd actually published a journal article based on his ideas. He killed to keep from being exposed as a plagiarist."

"The cardinal sin of academe," Anneke said. "It would have finished him totally."

"But that's silly," Zoe complained. "After all this time, all Patrick would've had to do was deny it. I mean, Gerald was so nutsoid who'd have believed him?"

"Christopher would," Clare said.

Of course, Zoe realized. It wasn't the academic status per se that drove Patrick; it was the value of that status in his ongoing struggle for his father's respect. Just one more battle in the War Between the Swanns. "When did you finally figure out that it was Patrick?" she asked sadly.

"Oh, I knew it was Patrick from the very beginning,"

Genesko said. "He insisted he hadn't heard anything about Gerald since he was a child, but then he said that 'poor old Gerald would have been better off staying on the reservation.' "

"And from that you deduced murder?" It was Anneke who asked the question.

"That, and the fact that his fingerprints were in the room, and one or two other things. Look," Genesko said, "most murders aren't complex puzzles. Most of the time, the obvious suspect is actually the perpetrator, and on those occasions good police work consists of nothing more glamorous than a slogging routine search for evidence, like piling up pebbles, usually focusing on the victim himself. This was one of those times."

"What evidence?" Clare asked sharply.

"To begin with, the testimony of a friend of Gerald's in Missaukee named Red Joe."

"Red Joe?" Zoe wrinkled her nose in disgust. "Isn't that kind of racist?"

"It would be, if he were Native American." Genesko chuckled. "But in fact he got the nickname because he's a loudly outspoken Communist. Anyway, Red Joe told us two things that were important. First, he told us that Gerald was going to bring a lot of money to the Native American groups in the area. Joe was happy about that, of course, because he views tribal economics as essentially communistic. He said Gerald had evidence that shamanism was the key to prosperity, and that spirituality, properly managed, was a financial gold mine."

"In other words," Zoe interrupted, "Gerald was still working on the same theory."

"Yes. That gave us an idea about Gerald's academic work, and it linked it to Patrick's. But Red Joe told us something else equally important—that Gerald had been in contact with someone in his family in the last couple of years."

"He told you Gerald had been in touch with Patrick?" Clare asked.

"No. He didn't know which member of the family. And I'll grant you, it could easily have been Dwight, who admitted maintaining contact with the sheriff, and did go up to Missaukee once or twice a year. It could also," he looked at her, "have been your mother." To Zoe's surprise, Clare didn't spring to deny the possibility, but seemed almost thoughtful. "Still," Genesko continued, "Patrick was the one who, by his own admission, spent a good deal of time up north doing research. Patrick was the one who was at home in the woods."

"I know," Zoe said. "I was impressed, in fact—he was real good at all that stuff."

"And well equipped," Genesko continued. "That was another thing—do you remember when he tried to dig that bullet out of the tree? He had to give up, because all he had was a little penknife. But he wore Timberland boots, carried a North Face pack—he had first-class professional equipment all the way. It seemed unlikely that he wouldn't have a high-quality hunting knife, but not so unlikely if you hypothesize that he'd used it to kill Gerald and then thrown it away."

"In which case, you'll never find it," Clare said.

"Oh, but I think we have. After Patrick told us where he'd spent the night after the murder, we did a ground search of the area, but after I saw that penknife I called the department and suggested that it would be worth searching back along the route he'd have taken out from town. They came up with a large Case hunting knife last night."

"Why now?" Clare asked suddenly.

"You mean, why did all of this happen at this time?" Genesko looked at her consideringly. "Because of you, I'm afraid. Or more accurately, because of your inheritance. Your great-aunt's death was written up in the Lake City newspaper, and Red Joe said your father became very excited when he saw it. He decided that you'd inherit the Missaukee property, and he wanted you to tear down the house and return the land to the Indians."

"So I was right," Clare said harshly. "He did show up only because he found out I was an heiress." She spit out the last word.

"Isn't it an awfully big coincidence?" Zoe asked. "I mean, all these people showing up in Clare's room at the same time?"

"That was one of my problems," Genesko conceded. "But in fact, the only true coincidence was the Black Diamond box appearing on the same day that Gerald arrived. As it turns out, Patrick and Gerald were both there because Gerald called Patrick and *told* him he'd be there. Patrick tried to talk him out of coming, but when he couldn't, he arranged to meet him there."

"But why kill him?" Zoe wasn't sure whether she now believed Patrick was guilty or not. "Why not just let him talk to Clare and then go back up north when he was done?"

"That's true," Clare said. "After all, Patrick knew I hadn't actually inherited the Missaukee property, and he had to be damn sure I wasn't going to give the son of a bitch anything."

"He didn't plan to kill him," Genesko explained. "He told us that he assumed he could talk Gerald down from whatever scheme he had in mind, and send him back to the woods. That's why he was so careless about fingerprints. Unfortunately, Gerald had even more grandiose plans in mind than Patrick had realized. He'd been 'refining' his research up there in the woods, he told Patrick, and now that he was going to have the Swann property, he was planning to publish."

"Oh, shit," Zoe said. "That would have torn it."

"Yes. That's why Patrick had to kill him. And then, of course, he got even more unlucky. He heard someone at the door, and he thought it was you coming back, so he fled out the window, just as he told us."

"He really was a schmuck, wasn't he?" Zoe said mournfully, remembering that she had liked him, even as she remembered thinking there was something creepy about him.

"No, just a Swann," Clare said bitterly. "Like my father—what did he want the property for, anyway?" she asked Genesko.

"According to Patrick," he said with a sigh, "Gerald believed it contained the source of something he called 'Gaia Prime,' the source of all spiritual life."

"God, he really was nuts, wasn't he?" Clare looked ill, and somehow frightened.

"Yes, he was." Zoe was grateful that Genesko didn't drag out platitudes. "But I would be, too, if I'd ingested as many different substances as your father did over the years. He spent half his life experimenting with every hallucinogenic drug he could lay his hands on. You haven't."

"His . . . psychosis really was drug-induced?" Clare asked, her voice wobbly.

"According to the psychiatrist who treated him in Ann Arbor, almost certainly—which is as positive a statement as you'll ever get from a medical expert. Your father got tangled up in his research on primitive magic—everything from shamanism to voodoo—and it just got away from him."

"God. Poor Daddy." There were tears running down Clare's face, the first tears that Zoe had ever seen her shed.

"Did Patrick actually confess?" Zoe asked.

"Yes. Once we found Gerald's papers, he didn't seem to care very much anymore."

"No, he wouldn't, would he?" Clare swiped at her eyes, knocking her glasses sideways. She didn't seem to notice. "Poor Patrick. Poor, dumb, fucking, broken-winged Swanns."

Zoe felt her own eyes burning. "How much of this is off the record?" she asked Genesko, to her own surprise.

"Most of what I've told you, I'm afraid." If he were surprised as well, he didn't show it. "In fact, if you're now planning to write this for the *Daily*, I'll have to ask you to let me read it first."

"All right." It was a request any reporter normally would have refused out of hand, but this wasn't a normal situation. "I'll call it in to you when I'm done. It may be late," she warned him.

"That's all right. I'll be here for several hours yet."

"I thought you weren't going to write about this," Clare said flatly.

"I wasn't planning to," Zoe said, feeling unaccustomed ambivalence. "It's just . . . writing is what I do, okay?" She wasn't sure how to make it any clearer than that, even to herself.

"All right." Clare nodded once and stood up stiffly, gripping the arm of her chair to steady herself. "Drop me off at the dorm on your way to the *Daily*, okay?"

"Yeah, sure," Zoe mumbled with embarrassment, looking down at the floor.

"It's okay, Zoe." Clare wiped her eyes once more and re-settled her glasses on her nose. "Really, it's okay."

THIRTY-FOUR

Zoe hadn't yet seen Monday morning's *Daily*, so she grabbed one out of the bin in the lobby on her way up the stairs. Doug Billings had done the murder follow-up; she skimmed his story quickly, seeing nothing new and wondering if he'd written anything for tomorrow's edition. He was probably going to be pissed when he found out she'd broken it open. For once, beating out another reporter gave her no pleasure.

She found Faye Leonard at the end of the huge city room, leaning back in a chair with her feet up on the night desk. Slow night, Zoe surmised, if the city editor was this relaxed at ten thirty.

"They've broken the East Quad murder," she told Faye without preamble. "I've got all of it."

"No shit?" Faye's feet hit the ground with a thud. "Who did it?"

"Christopher Swann's son. The great and powerful

Christopher Swann." She didn't even try to keep the bitterness out of her voice; she didn't plan to keep it out of her story, either.

"How much space do you need? Shit, forget that—how much space do you want?" As she spoke, Faye grabbed a dummy sheet and a pencil and began redrawing pages.

"Give me, say, twenty inches."

"You got it." Faye picked up the phone and spoke urgently to the production editor in the basement. "Yank the ISR story," she said into the phone. "Drop the school board piece below the fold, and you can use MSA for the anchor."

Zoe left her to it. Out of habit she turned to the sports desk, where Gabriel Marcus and Katie Sparrow broke off their discussion to eye her with undisguised interest.

"Christopher Swann's kid is the murderer?" Gabriel pursed his lips in a soundless whistle. "That's going to make this national news, you know."

"Yeah." Zoe dumped her coat and bookbag on a chair at the nearest computer terminal. Christopher's name was going into the lead, all right.

"Why'd the kid do it?" Katie asked, bright-eyed.

"Because his father is a slimebag, scum-sucking son of a bitch, that's why." Zoe turned her back on them, but not before seeing the glance that passed between them. The hell with them, she thought; they'll get it when they read my story.

She punched keys experimentally, waiting for her usual easy flow of words, but nothing came. All right, you start by getting the facts down, and the rest will come. Journalists didn't have the luxury of writer's block; if you were on deadline, you bloody well filled that white space one way or another. She began to type, slowly but steadily. Once, Faye came by and looked over her shoulder, but Zoe waved her away. It was after midnight when she finally stopped, taking her brain off autopilot and leaning back in her chair with a sigh.

She scrolled back to the top of the story and began to reread what she'd written, and as she did so, her eyes widened with surprise.

Patrick Swann, a graduate student in economics and the son of Ann Arbor millionaire Christopher Swann, last night confessed to the murder of his uncle, former anthropology professor Gerald Swann. Patrick admitted he had appropriated Gerald's research and passed it off as his own, and feared being exposed for plagiarism. If ideas are the coin of the realm in Ann Arbor, then Patrick Swann, the son of a fabulously wealthy father, had an empty purse.

She read all the way to the end, aware halfway through that Gabriel had come up behind her and was reading over her shoulder. When they were done, he dropped into the chair next to her and cocked his head.

"Patrick is the one who seems like the slimebag," he said.

"Yeah, I know." She leaned back in her chair, feeling tired and drained. "This wasn't what I started out to write."

She had meant to defend Patrick, because she'd liked him and because, she supposed, she automatically sided with her own generation. But her subconscious knew better; in the unhappy saga of the Swann family, the words "victim" and "villain" weren't that easy to assign. Christopher Swann might never make Father of the Year, but he wasn't the worst father she'd ever heard of, either. It was Patrick who'd murdered, not Christopher.

Patrick was charming, and her subconscious had reminded her why she distrusted charm. Because too often, it made everything too easy, so that the people who got by on charm alone came to believe that charm entitled them to whatever they wanted.

Clare, after all, had taken a far worse reaming at the hands of her family, but she'd turned out tough-minded and independent. Clare, in the end, would be okay.

"Writing can be a funny thing," Gabriel said. "Sometimes we write out feelings we didn't know we had."

"Yeah. And sometimes we'd be better off not knowing."

"It's a good story," he said, leaving her.

She called Genesko and read it to him over the phone, and when he approved its content she signaled to a relieved Faye Leonard that the story was ready to go. Then she sat for a while by herself, staring through the leaded glass windows into the black night outside. Finally she pulled over a telephone and punched buttons.

"Room fourteen eleven, please," and then, "Mom? Hi, it's me."

"Zoe? Is something wrong?" Berniece Kaplan's voice was sharp with concern.

"No, everything's okay. I'm sorry, I didn't realize how late it was. How's Washington?"

"As outlandish as ever." If she wondered at the late-night call, Bernie Kaplan kept it to herself. "The committee vote on the minimum wage is tomorrow. After that, thank God, I can get out of this hellhole." She laughed. "After a week in Washington, even the Michigan Legislature starts to look good to me. Can you still pick me up at the airport?"

"Sure," Zoe said. "And, Mom?"

"Yes?"

"I just . . . nothing. Love ya."

"Me, too," Bernie Kaplan said comfortably. "You can tell me about it when I get back."

Zoe hung up the phone, thought for a few minutes, then went hunting for a phone book. She checked area codes and punched in the number for directory assistance, feeling her anger grow.

"Information for Santa Cruz," she said. "I want the number for Emma Mortensen."

"I talked to Bill McHugh about doing a memorial service for my father at Huron House," Clare said. The bull session had reconvened in Clare's room when Zoe got back from the *Daily*.

"Very good." Ben McDonald nodded sagely. "Closure, and all that."

"I think it's going to take more than a memorial service." Clare took a puff of the joint and passed it to her right. She looked exhausted, Zoe thought, exhausted and sad but at least calm.

"How're you holding up?" Zoe asked, sinking to the floor and reaching for the joint.

"Not too bad." Clare cocked her head and considered. "I feel . . . sad, I guess," she echoed Zoe's thought.

"And angry," Pamela Grant suggested.

"Actually, no." Clare sounded surprised. "Maybe I'm just too tired to be angry. Besides . . ."

"What?" Gracie Bonilla asked.

"I don't know exactly." Clare shrugged. "I mean, what's the point? It wasn't his fault he went psychotic."

"In other words," Pamela said, "now that you know there was a *reason* why your father walked out on you, you can stop being mad at him."

"I guess so," Clare agreed. "Although that doesn't excuse the rest of my misbegotten family."

"Oh well, families." Pamela shrugged.

"Besides," Ben said, "the rest of your family, even your mother, isn't as integral to the self-image you've constructed for yourself. You've pretty much defined yourself as an abandoned child, haven't you?"

"Have I?" To Zoe's surprise, Clare took the suggestion seriously. "Yeah, well, maybe I have." She reclaimed the joint and puffed silently.

"Besides, now that you're going to be rich you can afford to blow them all off," Gracie said with cheerful envy. "How much was it, anyway—over half a mill?"

"Four hundred forty and change," Clare said. "That's face value—a lot of it is in old coins that're worth even more."

"All that money stuffed in a flour canister in a burned-out basement." Pamela shook her head. "How come your aunt didn't put it in the bank, or at least in a safe-deposit box?"

"She explained that in the letter—the one that was with the money," Clare said. "See, the money was a kind of extra, sort of a crisis stash, you know? Henrietta herself told Aunt Julia about it, just before she died—that it was supposed to be passed down to the next girl in the family, but only for a real emergency, so that it would be there for the next generation. And you can't keep something secret in a bank, even a safe-deposit box, because it all gets declared when you die. The trouble is," she said sadly, "Aunt Julia died before she could tell me about it."

"So now you have to figure out a way to hide all that loot for your own daughter," Gracie said, her eyes wide with fascination.

"Well, not all of it," Clare replied. "I'm not going to get to keep it all."

"Why not?" Zoe asked. "Genesko said that letter meant it was for you."

"Not exactly." Clare hauled herself into a sitting position. "He said it 'could be construed as a holographic will.' But my darling Uncle Dwight—egged on no doubt by his equally charming wife—has already informed me that he plans to claim it as part of Aunt Julia's estate, which means it gets split three ways." For a moment, Clare sounded like her old acid self.

"Well, maybe Christopher won't claim his third," Pamela said. "It's not like he needs the money."

"Oh, sure, that'll happen." Clare laughed aloud. "Money is Christopher's obsession, didn't you know that? He'd never give up a penny he thought was his."

"Well, if you need a good lawyer, I can put you in touch with one," Zoe volunteered.

"No thanks." Clare shook her head. "I'm not going down that road."

"You mean you're just going to let them have it?"

"I'm learning to pick my fights, remember?" Clare smiled briefly. "I don't want to spend the next five years of my life embroiled with those people. It's time for me to cut my losses and move on. There's still going to be enough money for me, even to stay in school a couple of extra years. I thought I'd try some computer courses."

"Bravo," Ben murmured.

"The only thing I'm sorry about," Clare said to Zoe, "is that it cuts down the amount of the finder's fee I promised you. And please don't try to refuse it."

"I wouldn't think of it," Zoe said, grinning happily and wondering how much a bright yellow used 'Vette would cost.

THIRTY-FIVE

· · · · · ·

The UPS card hanging from the doorknob read, "A package for you has been left at:" and gave the address next door. Anneke shifted the umbrella to her other hand, thought briefly of letting the package go until later, then sighed and trudged back down the walk, wishing that this year's April rains hadn't continued into May.

"Oh, hi." Peg Radnor answered the door in her usual dramatic disarray of multicolored clothing, with the usual smudges of ink on her face—Peg refused to write with anything but a fountain pen. "You came for your package, I assume—hang on a minute." She disappeared beyond the front hall, and returned a moment later holding out a package.

Anneke felt her breath catch painfully in her throat. The package was small, barely palm-size, wrapped in brown paper, its mailing label carefully covered with cellophane tape. The return address on the label, in an elegant script printed in dark blue ink, read: "emma mortensen, jewelry design."

"Thanks, Peg." She all but snatched the box from her

neighbor's hand. Peg waved negligently, her mind already back on her congressional election database, and Anneke turned and trotted back home, splashing through puddles without even seeing them.

But once inside, she carefully shook out the wet umbrella and hung her raincoat neatly on the hall coat rack before taking the package into her office and setting it down on her desk. Should she wait for Karl to get home before opening it? Ridiculous. She shook her head with irritation. She was acting like she was afraid it was a bomb. Quickly she tore off the wrapping paper and opened the white box inside.

Two gold rings, identical except for scale, nestled in white cotton, each of them set with a single, matching fire opal cut in a polyhedron. The gold curved and swirled around the stones, which flamed orange and red and gold even in the dim afternoon light. Wedding rings.

Next to the rings was a small, paper-wrapped object. Anneke removed the wrappings to discover another ring, this one a large, sculptured construction of brushed silver.

She'd left the note until last. She retrieved her reading glasses from her briefcase and opened the heavy folded notepaper, looking at Emma's tiny, almost calligraphic handwriting:

"You'll have to have the rings sized," she'd written abruptly. "Don't let them erase my ligature—it's useful for insurance purposes." No salutation, no introduction—typical Emma. Anneke's eyes filled, and she blinked down at the card. "Let me know when the wedding is. Don't expect me to wear pink." Anneke laughed shakily. No, Emma would refuse to come if she had to wear anything pastel—she'd probably wear black to the wedding and call it a celebration color.

So will I, Anneke thought.

She blinked down at the card again. There was a postscript.

"The silver ring is for Zoe," it said.

Grand Rapids/Detroit, Michigan: April, 1896

Dear Henrietta:

Everyon her are being real nise to me Grand Rapids is okay but I miss stuf at hom. They say my confinment will be over in a few weeks and well be redy to go. We will meet you in Ann Arbor like we planed and tak the train back to Mcbain I hop yur still sur about our arrangment.

I had a lettr from Pete Slocum he says the mill is doing good he a good man maybe when we get bak Ill see him sum mor. At least he nos about Blak Dimond and all that and dosnt care.

Yrs, Cora

My dearest Cora:

I urge you to put your concerns at rest. I know it may be Smalley's but I promise you that you need have no further concern about that, especially now that he is dead. Does that sound callous? If so, I am heartily sorry, but I find that the only thing that is important to me now is that it will be ours to cherish. Whatever its background, it will be a swan who will grow to a fine bird. I can find little or nothing to choose between the two men in any case, so what does it matter?

You were quite correct that selling the mill would have been a mistake. Cal and Pete between them are making a fine success of it. They have sent reports that show the mill is oper-

ating at a greater profit now than it did under Walter's management.

I have also discovered, rather to my surprise (I have been far too innocent for too long, my dear Cora) that I am now an extremely wealthy widow. I have even found that Walter had an insurance policy that will pay to rebuild the house. I have a fancy to live where we can watch the river flow by each morning, and enjoy the peace and harmony it must surely bring to us.

While this newfound wealth in no way makes up for the tragedies of recent months, it does mean that neither Black Diamond nor any other sources of what must be considered blood money are necessary for either of us. I am sure you must know that everything I now own is absolutely yours as much as it is mine.

I therefore do urge you, my dearest friend, to set all of that aside. Perhaps it may be needful in the future, or even for future generations, but I believe we will both be vastly happier and more content knowing we are not profiting from the grief of others.

Still, I wish you to know that I refuse to be ashamed of Black Diamond, for to me it will always stand for the utmost bravery, and for that I shall always cherish its symbolism. Indeed, far from avoiding mention of it, I believe we should embrace it for what we know it means, and use its symbol as our own.

I have been glad for the chance to visit with my family, all of whom have been most sympathetic, but I know they would not understand if they were to learn the facts, and I am growing weary of dissembling. To my own surprise, I shall be glad when it is time for me to leave Detroit.

I am counting the days until it is time to return north, the three of us together. Your most loving friend,

Henrietta

AUTHOR'S NOTE

· · · · · ·

Although the members of the Swann family, past and present, are my own totally fictional inventions, there really was a Cora Brown, who really was a northern Michigan whore known as Black Diamond for the color of her tent. (Throughout this book, by the way, I have used the word *whore* as a conscious preference, precisely because it is a more brutal and therefore, I believe, a more honest word than a euphemism would be.) And yes, there really was a John Smalley, train robber and cold-blooded murderer.

I first came across their story a number of years ago in a marvelous little book by Roy L. Dodge titled *Ticket to Hell: A Saga of Michigan's Bad Men.* I was delighted with the story; what a great McGuffin that never-found money would make, I thought. (A *McGuffin,* for anyone who doesn't know, is a term coined by Alfred Hitchcock to mean that thing—object or information—that jump-starts a story.)

I visualized Smalley's possibly mythical stash as the centerpiece of a treasure hunt, a cheerful romp in the north woods with, perhaps, the kind of romantic villain I love to read about.

It sounded good at the time. The literature and mythos of the American west, after all, frequently romanticizes the life of the frontier prostitute and her train-robbing lover. But the more I thought about it, the more Cora Brown—Black

Diamond herself—took on a hard reality. Try as I might, I couldn't manage that view of Cora Brown's life; I simply couldn't see her as the cheerful bar-girl of the average fictional western.

As for John Smalley, the situation was even worse. The sparse literature dealing with life in the northern Michigan lumber towns, almost all of it anecdotal, tends toward the "weren't they scamps" viewpoint even when describing the nastiest, most brutal events. But even using this romanticized tall-tale approach, Roy Dodge doesn't portray John Smalley as anything but a cold, murderous villain—a truly scary dude, as Zoe might say.

I struggled with these realities for a long time. Finally, I stuck the Black Diamond story into a file folder and told myself I just wasn't ready to write anything that complex yet.

In the interim, my husband and I moved halfway across the country, from Ann Arbor to San Francisco (with a pit stop in Davis that I'd just as soon not talk about). We started up our own business; we moved twice more (everyone in San Francisco seems to move at least once a year); I wrote and sold a couple more books. And all the while, Black Diamond kept nagging at me.

Then a plot I was working on fell apart in my hands, something that happens to all writers occasionally, so I've been told—which doesn't make the flop-sweat any less terrifying. So, with a deadline looming, I dug out the Black Diamond file and began on it in sheer authorial desperation. And it was only then that Cora began to come alive.

She still refused to become a kind of frontier party girl. But she didn't seem to want to be a victim, either. The Cora Brown who devised that famous black canvas tent had to be a fairly savvy businesswoman, in a time and place where prostitution was one of the few businesses available to women. Black Diamond, whoever or whatever she really was, had to be a woman who had at least learned how to make her own way in the world, even if whoring was the only way she could manage it.

A note about historical accuracy:
While I've tried to convey the Michigan logging era as correctly as possible, I can't claim total accuracy. For one thing, I'm aware that by 1895, the Cadillac/Missaukee area was pretty well logged out, and the action had by then mostly moved north to the Upper Peninsula. So the scenes of street fighting between lumber-camp gangs, while a fair representation of the kind of activities that did take place during the logging days, would probably no longer have been occurring in this area.

The last days of the real John Smalley, according to the historical record, were, in broad outline, as I've described them. His last train robbery, followed by the murder of a policeman, led to his death in a shoot-out by a sheriff's posse, at the Brown house in McBain and in the presence of Cora, her mother, and her brother.

And finally, searchers really did find a hollowed-out compartment under a windowsill in his cabin—empty, of course.

A note about the Internet:
It might interest Senator Exon to know that I spent countless hours on the Internet researching this book, without ever once being attacked by "feelthy peectures," or being electronically stalked, harassed, or having my morals (such as they are) imperiled.

With the exception of the Missaukee County plat map itself, which (so far) exists only in hard copy, every site visited by Anneke in her research is a real location on the Internet. There is a list of web sites on the next two pages for those interested in following her virtual trail, or in viewing some of the beauties of the area. I especially recommend the Hartwick Pines site for a small idea of what the Great Wild North once looked like.

Web sites for Michigan and the North:

http://lcweb2.loc.gov/ammem/detroit/dethome.html

Photographs from the Detroit Publishing Company, 1880–1920. Prints and Photographs Division, Library of Congress.

This collection of photographs from the Detroit Publishing Company includes over 25,000 glass negatives and transparencies, as well as about 300 color photolithograph prints, mostly of the eastern United States. The collection includes the work of a number of photographers, one of whom was the well-known photographer William Henry Jackson.

A small group within the larger collection includes about 900 mammoth plate images taken by William Henry Jackson along several railroad lines in the United States and Mexico in the 1880s and 1890s. The group also includes views of California, Wyoming, and the Canadian Rockies.

http://lcweb2.loc.gov/ammem/wpaintro/wpahome.html

Life History Manuscripts from the Folklore Project, WPA Writers Project, 1936–1940.

Oral history of recollections of pioneer men and women. Part of the Library of Congress American Memory Project.

http://www.unl.edu/UP/gof/home.htm

The Gallery of the Open Frontier, from the University of Nebraska Press and National Archives.

Wonderful photographs of people who don't look anything at all like Matt Dillon or Miss Kitty.

http://www.dnr.state.mi.us/
    Michigan Department of Natural Resources
        Links to campground maps and outdoor and recreation
    information.
http://www.exhibits.lsa.umich.edu/
    University of Michigan Exhibit Museum
http://www.sos.state.mi.us/history/mag/mag.html
    Michigan History magazine
http://www.sos.state.mi.us/history/museum/musehar.html
    Hartwick Pines Lumbering Museum, Grayling
http://www.sils.umich.edu/AnnArbor/
    Ann Arbor, MI—A Personal Perspective
        Superb views of campus and city from photographer
    Lee Lining. One of the best virtual tours I've seen any-
    where on the Internet.
http://www.michiweb.com/
    Northern Michigan Connection
        More than you'll probably ever want to know about the
    Northern Lower Peninsula.
http://www.nwhp.org/
    National Women's History Project.

**Here's a Preview
of Susan Holtzer's
Latest University of
Michigan Mystery,
THE SILLY SEASON
—Now in Hardcover from
St. Martin's Press**

•　•　•　•　•　•

"And it's not like he's really a dumb jock, you know." Jenna Lenski turned the topless '57 Thunderbird onto South U and proceeded slowly toward State Street and the promise of ice cream. "I mean, underneath all that silliness, he's got a first-class mind. He just won't—hey, what the hell is that?" She slowed the powerful car even further and pointed over the top of the windshield.

"What's what?" Zoe Kaplan peered upward into the blackness of the night sky. Overhead, stars blinked and glimmered, impossibly near.

"There." Jenna pointed again, toward the southwest. "Those lights."

"You mean those? Probably a plane."

"Uh-uh." Jenna, as always, spoke positively. "Can't be. They're not moving. See?"

"I guess. Must be stars, then." Zoe slumped, dropped her head back against the leather seat, somnolent with summer heat. One of those hot late-June nights, the air thick and still, sticky with humidity. She was more than ready for sleep, but East Quad was an oven after three straight days of ninety-degree temperatures. The stars seemed to shimmer in the saturated air.

No, they couldn't be stars. The lights—three of them?— swooped and whirled, then rose again to their previous position. At least, that's what it looked like. Zoe blinked and blinked again, finding it hard to focus. The night sky offered no point of reference, no perspective.

"That's weird." Zoe blinked once more, sitting up straighter. "They're out by the stadium, I think. Planes? Why would planes be doing maneuvers over the stadium in the middle of the night?"

"Beats me." Jenna shook her head. "Want to go see?"

"Yeah, I do." Zoe shook herself alert, feeling journalistic juices begin to flow. So far, summer school had been even more boring than she'd expected, especially with the *Michigan Daily* publishing only once a week.

"Okay." Jenna turned left on State, braking as the light at Hill turned yellow. Zoe's hands itched for the steering wheel; Jenna was the sort of careful, law-abiding driver who made her twitch. Why have a great car like this if you drove it like a Volvo?

"Are they still there?" Jenna kept her eyes on the road.

"Yeah. Just hanging there. No, there they go again. Sort of zipping toward the ground and then zipping back up again."

"Weird." Jenna accelerated fractionally.

"I don't suppose it's heat lightning? Uh-uh." Zoe answered her own question. "Balloons maybe?" She was getting really interested now. "Definitely somewhere over near the stadium. Can we go any faster? I'm afraid they'll be gone by the time we get there."

"Sure." To Zoe's surprise, Jenna took a firm grip on the wheel and picked up speed; the huge V-8 engine purred softly.

"Rebuilt engine?" Zoe asked.

"Partly. I had to replace the carburetor entirely."

"You did it yourself?"

"Yeah. I figure if you want a car like this you ought to be able to do the work yourself, y'know?"

"Right." Zoe, who loved cars but couldn't tell a carburetor from a carbuncle (and wondered what on earth a carbuncle was, exactly), was impressed. But then, Jenna was impressive all the way around. At least, when she wasn't talking about Ben Holmes. The trouble was, lately every conversation with Jenna ended up being about Ben Holmes, Michigan's great tight end.

Zoe had heard Jenna's litany half a dozen times since they'd met in East Quad at the beginning of summer school: Ben was irresponsible; Ben only wanted to have fun, "no matter what's going on in the world;" Ben never read anything more complex than the Michigan football playbook. Zoe forebore to point out that the Michigan playbook was probably as complex as a Derrida treatise—and a lot more useful besides.

She'd known Ben longer than she'd known Jenna, ever since she'd joined the *Daily* sports staff. She liked them both, but she thought that they were about the oddest couple imaginable. Jenna took everything seriously; Ben Holmes took nothing seriously. Zoe wondered why the smartest people seemed to make the dumbest relationship choices.

"There they are—over that way." As they neared the Stadium Boulevard overpass, Zoe pointed to the right, where the lights still hovered overhead.

"I see them." Jenna steered around to the Stadium intersection and accelerated to the top of the overpass, where she slowed to take in the panorama of the athletic campus below.

The huge bowl of Michigan Stadium filled the corner at Stadium and Main; Crisler Arena crouched next to it; beyond that, a tangle of buildings, playing fields, and parking lots sprawled north and east across several acres of precious Ann Arbor real estate. On the other side of Main Street, lighted windows glimmered along residential streets.

The lights they were following were still there. Three of them, in a vaguely triangular formation. Not blinking but steady. Funny, Zoe thought, they don't look any closer now than they did from South U. Maybe they were higher?

"They're over by Crisler." Zoe pointed again.

"Maybe it's a flying saucer that thinks it's found a friend." Jenna giggled, and Zoe joined in. The low, round dome of Crisler looked like a set from "Close Encounters."

"Well, it's some sort of flying object, and right now it's definitely unidentified." As she spoke the words, Zoe felt the beginning of a small bubble of excitement. "Hey, you think we're really in on a sighting?"

"Of what? Little green men?" Jenna snorted with laughter.

"No, of course not." Zoe wasn't sure what she meant, exactly. Except, a Sighting would be a Story, capital S on both words, and so far this summer she hadn't found anything at all worth writing about.

"Go on in through the parking lot," she told Jenna. "Around behind Crisler."

"Okay." Jenna steered past a big blue University bus and came to a stop. The dome of Crisler Arena was to their left; the dark wall of the stadium loomed up in front of them. "Now what?"

"Damn. The parking lot's too bright." Zoe threw open the car door and scrambled out. She continued to watch the lights—had they moved?—while at the same time registering the presence of four or five other people. They must have just gotten off the commuter bus, she deduced with one corner of her mind. But the lights captured most of her attention.

One thing—here, they were even brighter. Too bright to even consider that they might be stars, unless a whole cluster was going supernova all at once. So bright, in fact, that they almost blurred together. The closer she got, the harder it seemed to focus on them.

"Damn," she repeated. "I wish I had a camera."

"I have one," Jenna said unexpectedly.

"Yeah? Where? Can I use it?"

"It's in the glove compartment; I was taking some pictures in the cemetery yesterday. Hang on." Jenna turned back to the car and returned with a small 35-millimeter camera. "Self-focusing, with a coupled strobe. You just look through the viewfinder and push that button."

"Great. Thanks." Zoe took the camera and aimed it upward until she had the triangle of lights in the viewfinder. She clicked off a couple of shots.

The lights moved suddenly. One moment they seemed to be floating over a corner of the stadium; then, abruptly, they were directly overhead. Zoe heard a babble of voices, and turned to see a small knot of people staring upward.

"Must be something military," a young guy in torn blue jeans was saying.

"Not necessarily," a balding man in a heat-rumpled business suit contradicted. "There's plenty of aerospace research going on in Ann Arbor." Zoe recognized him as Gerald Cochrane, an assistant dean in LSA.

"Big difference," the young guy said gloomily. "The space program was taken over by the military during the Bush era."

"What nonsense." The short, stocky woman with short-clipped gray hair looked familiar. Zoe racked her brain for a minute before identifying her as Ann Carrick, political science department. "NASA is still . . ."

"You know perfectly well NASA is nothing but a military front," a girl in a black tank top interrupted.

"It's always impressive to see how well undergraduates can draw conclusions without the bother of actual data to confuse them," the older woman replied.

"Oh, and I suppose your definition of 'data' is whatever the government tells you," the young guy retorted. "I'll bet you . . ."

The triangle of lights overhead blazed, seemed to expand. Zoe jumped backward involuntarily, and as if in sympathy, the arc lights that studded the parking lot flickered, dimmed, and then blazed in their turn before finally going totally black. Blinded, she squeezed her eyes shut instinctively, but not before the image of the lights imprinted itself on her retinas. She blinked quickly two or three times, trying to clear her vision, before risking a sidelong glance upward once more.

The triangle of lights was gone.

"Holy shit," she whispered to herself in the inky darkness. "What was . . ."

"Jesus, did you see that?"

The babble of voices stopped abruptly as the arc lights came back on without fanfare. A circle of faces, white under the harsh glare, gaped in stunned amazement. Wow, Zoe thought. And wow again.

"You people all right?" A tall, skinny man in the uniform of University security raced toward them from a low building on the west side of the parking lot. The huddled group stared at him, stared at each other. A couple of them shook their heads, not in response to his question but experimentally, as though testing their state of consciousness.

Zoe was the one who spoke first. "Do you know what that was?" she asked.

"Me? No." The security guard shook his head. "I thought the lights had blown." He peered up at one of the light poles, frowned, scratched his head. "They're back on now, though." He looked puzzled.

"Where were you?" Zoe reached to pull notebook and pen from her backpack before realizing she'd left it in the Thunderbird. She swore silently. She didn't want to give him time to think up an explanation; she wanted his first impressions.

"Me?" The guard answered question with question. "Over in the Security Building. Why?" His nameplate read Joseph DiMarco; Zoe filed the name in her memory, praying that she'd remember everything without taking notes.

"Did you see the three lights that were hovering over the stadium?" she asked him.

"What lights? When? There isn't supposed to be nothing over the stadium." The guard looked at her suspiciously.

He was obviously hopeless. Zoe turned her attention to the person most likely to theorize. "Professor Carrick?" She fought her journalistic conscience for a moment, then identified herself. "I'm Zoe Kaplan, from the *Michigan Daily*. Do you have any idea what just happened?"

"Not a clue." Carrick shook her head. "Not even an hypothesis."

"Has to be military," the young guy in the torn jeans reiterated.

"Professor Cochrane?" Zoe turned to the assistant dean. "Is it military or government, do you think?"

"Good Lord, how would I know?" He ran a hand through untidy hair, looking annoyed. "More likely a plant department malfunction, I should think."

"Well that might explain the lights in the parking lot, but not the lights over the stadium." Zoe waited, but the tactic didn't work. Cochrane merely shrugged. "Sorry."

He turned and headed toward a small line of cars at the edge of the parking lot; a few of the others began to do the same. Carrick was already gone.

"Did you report this?" Zoe asked the security guard.

"Not yet." He turned slowly, a full 360 degrees, then shook his head. "Don't see nothing *to* report," he announced. "You kids better get yourselves back home. I don't want no more trouble, okay?"

"But—" Zoe stopped. What was the point? "Thanks anyway, Mr. DiMarco. Ready to go, Jenna?"

"Better believe I am." Jenna still looked pale, although it could have been the lighting.

"Okay, let's roll. Would you drop me at the *Daily?* And can I hang on to your camera until morning?"

"No problem. Think you got anything?"

"Damned if I know." Zoe threw herself into the passenger seat. "I'm dying to find out myself."

• • • • • • •

Every window in the huge city room was flung wide, but there was no breeze outside to do any good. Zoe looked around the room, saw nobody, and trotted down the back stairs. She gasped with relief when she entered the air-conditioned production room.

"So this is why you agreed to be summer editor," she accused Gabriel Marcus.

"Yep, rank hath its privileges." He swiveled from the computer screen and grinned at her. "Come by to get out of the heat?"

"No. I've got something."

"I thought the sports page was done." Zoe, in the absence of anyone else who'd wanted it, was summer sports editor, a job that carried a small stipend and virtually no responsibility. The summer *Daily* was a once-a-week tabloid, with a single sports page drawn almost exclusively from wire services. She'd already thanked the journalism gods that this was Tuesday night, with publication the next day.

"It is," she said. "This isn't about sports."

"Oh?" He shook his head dubiously. "Unless it's really major, it'll have to wait. The pages are already locked; I was just about to send it to press."

"If it waits, it's dead."

"Okay, what've you got?"

"It's—" Zoe stopped. What did she have, exactly? "—a sighting, I guess you'd call it."

"A what?"

"Lights. There were these weird lights, hovering over the stadium." Even as she said it, Zoe realized how feeble it sounded. "Well, they were. Weird, I mean," she added defensively. "And then they sort of blazed up and disappeared. And all the lights in the parking lot went out."

Gabriel cocked his head and stared at her. "You're not pulling a Morton Oliver on me, are you?"

"Dammit, Gabriel, you know me better than that." Nothing could have stung Zoe more.

Morton Oliver had been a sophomore beat reporter covering the University libraries back in the early eighties, on the day that the head of the grad library received an unmarked package. It was wrapped in brown paper and plastered with far too many stamps, and the librarian took one look at it and yelled for security. Security yelled for the cops. The cops opened the package, found a clockwork device nestled in wood shavings, and yelled for the feds.

Morton Oliver picked up the story and ran with it. For days his byline was featured on the front page; for days he was the Man on the Spot, covering the biggest story of the year. By the time the feds declared the package a non-explosive hoax rather than the work of the Unabomber, Morton Oliver was semi-famous around campus.

Zoe wasn't sure when or how the *Daily* editors found out that Morton Oliver himself had sent the package—it was long enough ago that everyone who'd been there was now gone, but not quite long enough to have passed into folklore. Oliver had never been arrested, or even questioned, as far as she knew. But his byline never appeared in the *Daily* again, and his name had become a kind of shibboleth, a synonym for journalistic sleaze.

"Sorry; lousy joke," Gabriel said. "Did anyone else see these lights?"

"Yes." Zoe felt on firmer ground. "There was a whole group of people there, including Gerald Cochrane and Ann Carrick, from political science."

"Quotes from them?"

"Enough to validate the sighting. Nothing substantive. Oh, and by the way." She dug into her bookbag and brought out Jenna's camera. "I *may* have photographs."

"Really." Gabriel's eyebrows rose as he reached for the camera.

"I said 'may'," Zoe warned him. "I'm not much of a photographer, and the conditions were pretty bad. Is there anyone around who can develop the film?"

"Probably. Let me go see." He disappeared for a while, and Zoe chewed anxiously on a fingernail until he returned. "Barney McCormack was in the computer room. He said he'd do it."

"Good." Zoe sighed with relief. "So how much do I get?"

"Depends on what you've got." Gabriel thought for a minute. "First thing, you'd better check with the police and find out if they got any calls about it."

"Right." Zoe crossed to an empty desk, sat down, and dialed. When the police dispatcher answered, she said: "Hi, this is Zoe Kaplan, *Michigan Daily*. I just wanted to get a late update on the total number of calls about the UFO." She pronounced the three letters with amusement in her voice. "Have you got a final tally handy? Oh, good. Thanks." She wrote "107" on the pad on front of her and directed a thumbs-up sign at Gabriel. "One more thing," she said into the receiver. "Can you patch me over to—I think Brad Weinmann is in charge of this one, isn't he?" She scribbled again on her pad. "Oh, that's right, sorry, it is Wes Kramer, isn't it? Could you put me through? Thanks."

She'd never heard of Detective Wesley Kramer, but when

he came on the line, sounding harried, she made her voice as friendly as possible.

"Hi, Detective Kramer. Zoe Kaplan, *Michigan Daily*. Sorry to bother you—I've only got a couple of questions and then I'll get out of your hair. I assume the military spokespeople said they didn't know anything about it?" She made it one long, verbal run-on sentence.

"That's correct." The voice on the other end of the phone was abrupt and cautious.

"Yeah, that's what I figured." Zoe kept it light. "And no joy from the National Weather Service, either?"

"They've said there were no weather balloons in the area," Kramer replied.

"Right. Any ideas what it was?"

"Not at this time," Kramer said, speaking formally. "We're still investigating."

"Sure, I understand. Thanks for your time." She hung up the phone and turned to Gabriel.

"The usual. No military exercises, no weather balloons, they're investigating, et cetera, et cetera." She gnawed her lower lip. "I really should go down there and check out the actual reports."

"You don't have time." Gabriel jerked his head toward the clock on the wall. "You can describe the actual event yourself, after all, and you've got reliable witnesses to back you up. There are other things that are more important."

"What've you got in mind?"

"Well, for one thing, you said the lights in the parking lot went out," Gabriel pointed out. "You ought to check with the Plant Department."

She nodded and dialed, but got only a recorded message directing emergency calls to University Security, and she already knew she wouldn't get anything useful from them.

"Nobody home." She turned to the computer. "Guess I

better go with what I've got." She stared at the screen, gnawing her lower lip. "Wish I could give it more sex appeal."

"Ed Stempel." Gabriel snapped his fingers.

"Who?"

"Professor Thomas Edison Stempel, history department. The University's resident expert on UFOs."

"Resident expert on *what?*"

"You mean you don't know about Ed Stempel?" Gabriel leaned back in his chair, grinning widely. "Ed Stempel teaches a course called 'History of Spirituality,' and another called 'History of Historicity,' which is basically anti-history. Or at least anti-historians. He's one of the anti-Dominant Paradigm people."

"Oh, shit." Zoe groaned. "And what's his idea of the New Paradigm? Little green men controlling American society?"

"Well, it's hard to say." Gabriel steepled his fingers. "He talks in such ultra-scientific jargon that sometimes it's hard to tell. Basically, he insists that the hegemony of the Dominant Paradigm has made it impossible to seriously study what he calls 'alternative science,' including the possibility of alien visitation, and that therefore we have no data on which to make an informed judgment. What he wants is for the University to establish a UFO research center."

"Oh sure, that'll happen." Zoe snickered. "Like, the U is really going to spend money on something like that."

"He's not asking for money." Gabriel shook his head. "He says he can raise the money from outside sources, and he means it. There's a lot of UFO money out there."

"Are they seriously considering it?"

"Not as far as I know. From what I've heard, the history department would give its front teeth to get rid of him, but of course he's got tenure. Besides," Gabriel made a face, "his classes are pretty popular."

"That figures." Zoe reached for the faculty directory.

"Well, he sounds like he'll be worth a couple of good quotes, anyway." She dialed the number, and when a male voice answered, said: "Professor Stempel?"

"This is Professor Stempel." The voice was low and beautifully modulated, an actor's voice—or that of a great lecturer. Probably one reason his classes were so popular, Zoe thought.

"Professor Stempel, this is Zoe Kaplan, from the *Michigan Daily*. Have you heard about the sighting tonight?"

"Yes, in fact I have." He sounded amused. "Several people have already called me about it."

"Do you believe it was a UFO?" she asked.

"Of course it was." He chuckled. "It was clearly a flying object, and so far it remains unidentified. Therefore, it was a UFO."

"Yes, sure." Zoe laughed weakly. "But do you think there's a chance it was a—some sort of flying saucer?"

"Not unless someone has attached a motor to a piece of crockery," he said. "Now, I assume what you're really asking, young lady, is whether I believe it was an alien craft of some sort. Is that right?"

"Yes, I—yes." Somehow he was making her feel like *she* was the goofy one. It wasn't a feeling she enjoyed. "Do you think that's what it was?"

"Now how could I possibly know that? First of all, I did not personally see the object. Second, even if I had, there would be no way to make such a determination without further investigation."

"But you do think it's possible?" she pressed.

"I think a number of things are *possible*, including the existence of a reporter who asked intelligent questions. Unfortunately, in the absence of scientifically valid proof, I withhold judgment."

"You referred to 'further investigation'." Zoe gritted her

teeth and plowed ahead. "Are you planning to investigate this particular sighting?"

"Not an entirely silly question." She could almost hear Stempel nod his head in approval. "Since it occurred more or less on my doorstep, as it were, I will probably at least consider it. But you should know that night sightings are fairly common, and far less interesting than other manifestations."

"What sort of manifestations?"

"Physical evidence is always preferred, of course. Evidence of an actual landing, for instance—something like traces on the ground, or low-level radiation. Even a photograph would be of some help, although they are far too easy to falsify."

"What about the lights in the parking lot going out? Does that qualify as physical evidence?" She didn't mention the photographs she'd taken. Let the bastard see them in the *Daily*.

"The lights going out?" Stempel was suddenly alert. "I wasn't told about that. Are you sure?"

"Oh, I'm sure," Zoe said loftily. "At the moment that the . . . object blazed up and disappeared, all the arc lights right under it blacked out."

"You were there?"

"That's right."

"I see. That does make it somewhat more meaningful." Stempel's voice had returned to its original smug tone, but Zoe thought she heard an undercurrent of interest.

"So you are going to investigate?"

"Probably so," he said. "Probably so. Now, if you have no more questions . . . ?"

"Not at the moment, but would it be all right if I got back to you tomorrow?" She would have preferred to throttle him, but she also smelled an ongoing story.

"Yes, you may. Depending," he added, "on the accuracy of the story you write tonight."

"Okay." She fought the urge to slam the receiver in his ear. "Thank you, Professor Stempel." She replaced the receiver gently and turned to Gabriel. "I may have something going here," she told him. "I'm going to stick with this guy, for a couple of days anyway. And then," she announced, "I'm pretty sure I'm going to kill him."